PENGUIN BOOKS
JAVASCOTIA

Benjamin Obler is originally from St Paul, Minnesota but has also spent time in Glasgow, where he studied creative writing. He now lives and writes in Minneapolis. *Javascotia* is his first novel.

D1440195

Javascotia

BENJAMIN OBLER

PENGUIN BOOKS

PENGUIN BOOKS

Published by the Penguin Group
Penguin Books Ltd, 80 Strand, London WC2R ORL, England
Penguin Group (USA) Inc., 375 Hudson Street, New York, New York 10014, USA
Penguin Group (Canada), 90 Eglinton Avenue East, Suite 700, Toronto, Ontario, Canada M4P 2Y3
(a division of Pearson Penguin Canada Inc.)
Penguin Ireland, 25 St Stephen's Green, Dublin 2, Ireland (a division of Penguin Books Ltd)
Penguin Group (Australia), 250 Camberwell Road,
Camberwell, Victoria 3124, Australia (a division of Pearson Australia Group Pty Ltd)
Penguin Books India Pvt Ltd, 11 Community Centre,
Panchsheel Park, New Delhi – 110 017, India
Penguin Group (NZ), 67 Apollo Drive, Rosedale, North Shore 0632, New Zealand
(a division of Pearson New Zealand Ltd)
Penguin Books (South Africa) (Pty) Ltd, 24 Sturdee Avenue,
Rosebank, Johannesburg 2196, South Africa

Penguin Books Ltd, Registered Offices: 80 Strand, London WC2R ORL, England

www.penguin.com

First published by Hamish Hamilton 2009
Published in Penguin Books 2010
1

Copyright © Benjamin Obler, 2009
All rights reserved

The moral right of the author has been asserted

Printed in England by Clays Ltd, St Ives plc

ISBN: 978-0-141-03832-2

www.greenpenguin.co.uk

Mixed Sources
Product group from well-managed
forests and other controlled sources
www.fsc.org Cert no. SA-COC-1592
© 1996 Forest Stewardship Council
FSC

Penguin Books is committed to a sustainable future
for our business, our readers and our planet.
The book in your hands is made from paper
certified by the Forest Stewardship Council.

For Amelia

Contents

were the filaments of desolation, reminders of loss, the oppressive shadow of a new day.

New days at that time meaning twelve, maybe sixteen, hours of depression, an unringing phone, the catcalls of afternoon talk-show audiences filling my apartment like the bleats of hungry chickadees, a kind of penitential soundtrack drowning out undesirable notions – the terror of answering to those who expected more from me, answering for my sins, my lust, my greed, my sloth; brain-voices scrounging for excuses, clamoring for answers, concocting reasons I was skeptical of myself. Sure, occasionally the phone rang. *What are you gonna do, Melvin?* Friends who wanted to help but could only do so much. On these days, a cup of java was the only hope for a decent start. And the whole sad spectacle carried on through evening when, my neighbors returning from work in their shiny new VW Jettas, I would have breakfast, toast and a fried egg, and into the sweet closure of obligation when night fell and the offices were shut – too late to call on that ad – all accompanied by half-pot after half-pot, the supply of clean mugs exhausted and started again from the top, like a pathetic four-man batting lineup, on through jitters and dehydration, bloating, gas and unspeakable sessions on the toilet, a burger put down, a carton of milk chugged, laying a fresh tarp of high pH on which to pour more of my acidic, diuretic friend, coffee. Past that last landmark, midnight, when all clock hands reach up to the sky like a prayer, when I'd let the worrying stop, safe from the harassment of friends wanting to help, when the logic of loneliness had expired. If no one calls after midnight, you can blame the late hour. Night was when the offenses committed against my family were less apparent, when the unsightliness of my choices and actions was draped in the merciful blanket of dark, punctuated by stars. Black in the sky and black in my cup.

But Glasgow was nothing like this. And I not yet nothing, but *less* like the *I* I was then. So in the airy dining room with its paneled walls, fancy molding, regal carpet, and gold chandelier – all so British! – when I happily replaced a demure white ceramic tea cup with a rim into the matching saucer, having gulped its contents of paltry and tepid yet welcome coffee before it had even cooled, the skein of jet-lag on my skin; having completed this familiar act of consumption and having thought only of the wholesome satisfaction I found in the anticipation of work, I laughed. Aloud. It was glee. Uncanny glee. At that moment, my own situation astounded me to the point of hilarity. But it wouldn't be funny to others, and in an unusually adroit reflex, I disguised the outburst by transitioning straight into a call for the check. I raised my hand – forgetting this was not grade school – and called 'Ma'am!' I cleared my throat. 'Miss!' My server came, thankfully showing no evidence she had heard my guffaw, her eyes reflecting what I already sensed was a particularly British reservation and patience, and I presented the Plunkett Research Corporation Citibank Visa card. (I wasn't about to sweat my first corporate expense, though I did note that this 'wee brekkie', as I'd learn to call it, with its hot tomatoes and black sausages, ran near to thirty bucks after conversion.) When I signed, she said, 'Cheers.' It was a bit early for a drink, I thought, so I replied thank you and sauntered with elation through the revolving door and out onto Sauchiehall Street.

A man of sincerity is less interested in defending the truth than in stating it clearly, for he thinks that if the truth be clearly seen it can very well take care of itself.

– Thomas Merton, *No Man is an Island*

1   A Great Hunger

I have a great hunger for coffee.

Already I had done some work, informally, a portion of it, at the hotel, where I had a cup of coffee with breakfast. Breakfast was a slightly unpalatable surreal medley of fried meats, grains and vegetables arranged decorously on a plate, which I tapped with my fingernail to see if it had been fried too. My appetite and attention were devoted to the coffee, though. Foremost, it was watery, as if the grounds had been sponge-bathed, rather than thoroughly doused, soaked or steeped. And that was on the presumption that this cup had in fact been made from grounds – the flavor was stale, dangerously close to the artificiality of rehydrated freeze-dried crystals. I hate artifice, but I hadn't brought my notebook down, so didn't jot anything. This was a kind of rehearsal for the habits of my work. Even as practice, it was strangely satisfying to feel the encroachment of order, the anticipation of beginning a work-day, of daylight resuming its traditional role of dictator. But I tried not to get ahead of myself, something I often did. Carson himself had insisted I take the first day or two to recover from jet-lag, get acclimatized, buy maps, find an apartment. Or 'flat', as of course they call it here. The prospect was quite appealing – a strange concept: me, Melvin Podgorski, waking at seven, showering (showering!), dressing in creased slacks and punching in to work.

Well, almost punching in. With my new job, I didn't have a time clock, per se. It was more of an honor system. They could hardly monitor me from Chicago, four thousand miles across the western hemisphere. My weekly reports would show if I'd been keeping up – the dress code and schedule were really psychological policies. Carson expected the same level of professionalism in his field agents as the folks at headquarters. Punctuality, manners, civility – all the regular corporate blandness. Yet when I spoke with

Klang, who was to be stationed in London, before our departure, he seemed confused at my mention of borrowing money from my parents just to buy khakis and shirts. He didn't seem to know what I was talking about, not only why I was short on funds, but why I was overhauling a wardrobe for this non-office job, as if Klang hadn't been given the same set of guidelines for his London stint. Had Carson only given *me* these orders? Only given me this speech about representing the company, about presenting myself, looking professional? Did Carson have reason to suspect me of falling out of line, of taking advantage and slacking off, such that he'd deliver me a special sermon?

In a word, yes. He had every reason to suspect I would be a complete fuck-up. For starters, my résumé had a year-long gap of unemployment, going back to the previous fall, when I'd quit Nexis Corporation, the only reputable company I'd been with. On top of that, the position was only remotely related to market research: I'd been doing data entry and customer support. Just beef up your qualifications, people told me. Everyone does it. Well, I tried that, but on the barren meadow of my career, my beefed-up items looked bloated, elephantine. Even I couldn't believe the things I'd made up. In the end, I stood on the truth, listing even a job driving forklift in a warehouse. My references were spotty. There was James, the fast-talking innovator who'd hired me at Nexis, and subsequently had nothing to do with me. And there was Greg Esposito, a cohort from the Wynton High *Gazette*, the high-school newspaper where I'd been staff photog. But I hadn't heard from Greg in a while and had to list his last-known number, which whenever I called rang and rang, dead as dead can be. My own contact info was no better – different addresses on my cover letter and driver's license, which kind of worried me, since the HR manager, in the pre-interview, said she'd be running a routine background check. (A vehicle violation in Arizona came to mind, though it may have been waived.) Everything about me was rag-tag. The suit I wore to the interview, resurrected from confirmation and high-school graduation, bespoke an outworn past life. My newly acquired spare tire strained over the waistline. Blue-grey sacks sagged beneath my eyes. It was yet another instance where the primary struggle reveals itself as an unburying. And how I abhorred it. Unburying from surface realities, from the horrible truth of visual impressions, tearing through the shroud of statistics and factoids to say, Look! Here's me, get to know me, give me a chance! I can do this job! I'm the man!

Well, I had pulled it off somehow. Despite not expecting to be hired on my qualifications, now here I was in the Glasgow Hilton putting breakfast on the tab of Plunkett Research Corporation of Elgin, IL. I had a corporate Visa issued in my name, with a $10,000 credit line. It was to be tightly monitored, I was told, and excepting initial set-up expenses, for use only in extreme emergencies. I was enjoying the security of a six-month contract on overseas assignment in a field in which I had zero experience, with possibility of renewal or reassignment on completion and subject to review. I was looking down the throat of not only a full-fledged, above-the-board, upstanding professional life but the possibility of promotion, none of which would have been possible, say, a year prior. Melvin Podgorski, dubious divorcee, coffee connoisseur, slurping slacker, rudderless rogue – draft dodger if the call comes. I to whom the very thought of a set alarm clock is as ludicrous and inconceivable as bedding down beside a bomb with a lit fuse, was now facing the end of afternoon mornings (my cherished oxymoron), the solitude, listlessness, money-borrowing, scrounging, loafing, tennis shoes, ripped jeans, shaving weekly to save the blades. On this precipice and admiring the view.

I was proud, but I wouldn't say I was puzzled. I couldn't be. No one should be shocked to feel a craving for the end of their depravity. It was only when I finished my cup of coffee and caught my mind thinking in Plunkett Research Corporation terms, of flavor, quality, price, service, ratings sheets (form 27G, plenteous copies of which filled my briefcase), when it struck me – the vast gulf between my past associations and my present circumstances. That is, the incredible number of mugs of black coffee I had brewed in careful measurements in the shoddy faux-woodgrain kitchen of my bachelor's apartment, how many rings of last dregs I had stared into, cupped my hands around on lonely afternoons. How many I had savored, flipping through photo albums with feigned nostalgia and biting confliction, both my black and white prints and vacation snapshots (Arizona, as mentioned). How many I had slurped over the classifieds, deciphering their esoteric abbreviations meant to alienate those not in the know. The hypocrisy of them, supposed to be tools of convenience, springboards to bargains and futures, but in actuality serving only the initiated. All promise secreted away with code. What madness! For apartments, BR (bedroom), N/S (non-smoker), CLG FN (ceiling fan); for cars, HI MI (high mileage), PS PW (power steering, power windows), BO (best offer); for personals, SWPF (single white – what? Protestant? pregnant? preposterous? – female) for friendship and POSS LTR (possible long-term romance). All of which I needed: a new, association-free pad; a vehicle in which to traverse the pedestrian-unfriendly avenues of Hargrove and greater Chicago (my Honda had departed along with my ex-wife, Margaret); a job; and a fucking lay. Though, to be honest, this last I wasn't that keen on extending myself for. And none of these I could afford on the slender budget of my self-worth. None of these I could muster the will to earn.

These were my remembrances of that American elixir, that bitter pick-me-up, the true breakfast of champions. And they were sour. In the black grounds, in the smell of roasted beans, in the violently crepitant, manic whir of the grinder, in the sight of the stray bean on the countertop, its little oval mound and symmetrical folds cruelly resembling a vagina, in the cooling of the tap and the ritualistic measuring of water along the even-numbered scale of 2–12, in the fingering of a cluster of #4 recycled paper filters (cheaper), trying to thumb off, as you do with paper plates, the perfect thickness of just one, in the volcanic *POOF* of the first douse of water onto the heated coils, in the tired waiting, the shuffling of bare feet on dusty tile floor, hands in pajama-pants pockets, in the pupil adjustment of curtain opening, in the mirror avoidance of morning. In the entire ritual, especially in the accumulation of black syrupy drips and the spread of the scent around the room,

2 Snapshots

I had my camera with me. I was under orders from my family to send photos, and figured I should get some taken right away, because by the time I got them developed and mailed people would be wondering whether I was alive or dead. My Aunt Jane had told me, based on corresponding with a London friend, that the Royal Mail was notoriously slow, saying it took two or three weeks for a letter to 'cross the pond'.

Generally, I am not a nostalgic person. Among the boxes I had hauled to my parents' suburban garage in Wynton, Illinois, for storage, only one little Xerox-paper box contained mementos. Trinkets, hockey-team patches (we won state when I was a freshman on the bench), Margaret's garter from our senior prom, old notes passed in class, postcards, a form letter of congratulations from President Carter for winning a spelling bee. A minimal quantity of photos. I'm not big on memorializing or marking occasions in this manner; it cheapens them. Snapshots are just that, snapshots, when what is really needed to know a thing is a study. Perhaps my marriage suffered under this creed: I committed little of our courtship to film, even less of our connubial adventure.

But to be clear, that's not to say I'm not a photo-taker. I'm no expert, but I dabble. I got my first manual SLR at sixteen, and learned print-making as an unofficial apprentice to the editor of the high-school paper. Later it was my shots of the wrestler's pin, my careful framing of a proud Principal Mullroy beside his '25 Years of Service' plaque, which graced its front pages. Free periods were spent in the library poring over books on Paul Evans and Margaret Burke-White, and the *Time-Life* annuals, of course. I was the photographer for the *Gazette* all through the prison sentence known as High School. Then, as a senior, licensed to drive, Margaret and I would go downtown, and I'd shoot black and whites of the Sears and J. Hancock towers, the river, and men in Greek Town carving lamb off the spit, the aisles of imported almonds, dried pineapple rings and shapely olive-oil bottles. It annoyed Margaret that I'd expose a $4 roll on strangers and inanimate foodstuffs but had no interest in posing her by landmarks and the Fendi purses she cooed at in the shop windows along Michigan Avenue. Glitz and photo-album stuff rubbed me the wrong way. So fake, so staged. Like a half-truth. I didn't want to do to Margaret what family snapshots had done to Mr and Mrs Podgorski: always capturing the forcedness of Mr P's smiles, the disappointment in my mom, yet her determined cheer. How full were our family albums with birthday-party shots in which Mother's chagrin played on her visage, the guests' appreciation for the cakes and streamers and activities falling far short of her investment.

Those trips downtown. Me shooting, she shopping. Expectations of coupledom's rewards. Narrow expectations. One time we fought – about restaurants and parking and walking, ostensibly, though this was only a glaze over the real substance. I remember realizing that what Margaret wanted was to go through the motions of this day – young lovers downtown – in some prescribed way, with all the set scenes like birthday-party props. Maybe she had in mind Matthew Broderick and his girlfriend in *Ferris Bueller's Day Off*, which was a hit around that time. But I wasn't zany and adventurous or clever or doting, and she grew upset. She didn't like my inattention. When I questioned her motives and said this wasn't like her, she had to argue against her own nature to remain right. I made the mistake of pointing this out, and the rest was ugly.

My photographic attentions were always outwardly directed, to capture and claim something about the world, not myself or the dysfunction of the Podgorski clan. Snapshots were snapshots, but photography was selfless observation, sanctioned theft. In Chicago that day, my lens had been trained on a toothless guy hawking chains and watches out of his coat. Had the lens been directed inward, I would have emerged from the darkroom with evidence of the ways Margaret and I, not even married yet, were already taking on marriage's ugliest aspects. Pasted-on happiness, the get-it-over-with grin. And that was something I wasn't ready to see yet, though I would in time.

Besides all that, in Glasgow I did not regard myself as a tourist. Tourists tour. They do not work where they travel. I didn't want to look like one, and I didn't want to be one, now that I had reached, finally, at long last, this blessed UK outpost. I wanted to get some shots, put the camera away, and blend in. I wanted to reclaim some independence, and forget that I had lived with my parents.

Yes, I had performed that death-defying feat, the stuff of twenty-something nightmares across America, the scourge of adult life: I moved back into my parents' house. I returned to 8460 Meadow Prairie Lane, the yellow rambler, one-car garage and backyard with chainlink fence, lawn dotted with patches of dead-brown turf where the family cocker spaniel, Mitzy, laid her *merde* bombs. Plunkett had hired me in early July, and there was a month and a half wait before I departed, time to put in notice on my apartment (goodbye faux-grain panels and good riddance), pay the final phone, electric and gas bills. Time to get my ducks in a row, as my father would say.

To sleep on your old single bed, toes hanging off the end, revisiting the same frame creaks, poky springs and musty smells that accompanied your sweetest nights, when – wearing Pac-Man pajamas – you awaited the sandman thinking of nothing more worrisome than cartoons and a new baseball glove. The same streetlight shadows and furniture shapes that you beheld as a pubertic teen, your shinbones aching with growth, strange visions of Leah Anderson undressing atop a desk in algebra class. And of course there are the uncontrollable, gratifying and shameful nocturnal ejaculations. All of it – that room, those closet doors, the wallpaper now looking horribly tasteless, the diamond-shaped light fixture, the carpet beaten down by footsteps – it gives you the same feeling you get walking the halls of your old junior high. The lockers are short and narrow. You're puzzled that the combination dials are below waist height when you recall having prudently shielded yours with your chest. The ceiling lingers mere inches above your head. You are certain that it has all been reduced, not you enlarged, the whole building put through a shrink cycle, in size and importance.

This is the feeling you get in your folks' old house. And despite the obscure unreality of it, I'd recommend it. It's like a demented theme park. It's a free drug trip, an altered state without the illicit connotations. A sojourn into the past can do a person some good. If nothing else, it'll really get your ass in gear.

Of course, there are qualifications. The experience would probably not be beneficial for someone whose family home is their own personal hell. My stay at *L'Hôtel de* Podgorski provided some valuable perspective, but I'm speaking here as a person who was not beaten, sexually abused, whose parents were, to the best of my understanding, happily – though certainly not always blissfully – married. A person who didn't cry himself to sleep, pillows held tight over the ears, muffling screams of anger and smacks of fist on face. I didn't shiver under a threadbare blanket, didn't share a cot with four siblings – none, in fact. Didn't grow dizzy in my slumber from the fumes of dope smoke, didn't keep a bat under my pillow with which to greet likely bandits. My lullabies were not gunshots or ghetto blasters, or trailer-park traffic or hippie commune campfire anti-guerrilla-warfare acoustic sing-alongs. I wasn't strangled with rosary beads or whipped into penitence, I didn't go to bed with fingers bleeding from fretting the neck of grandpa's violin under forced practice, in search of some war-torn retribution. Sleep for me was not a release from the exhaustion of chopping wood or scrubbing floors. I had no evil stepmother, no Sister Wendy Rulerwhacker, no one called 'Mom's boyfriend' or 'Dad's girlfriend', no imprisoned half-sibling. The door of 8460 Meadow Prairie Lane was not rapped upon by repo men, social workers, sheriffs, or the ATF. And, likewise, there was no Jeeves the Butler, no Spanish maid, no befriended 5th Avenue doorman in topcoat. Which is all to say that my upbringing was entirely MOTR – middle of the road. Midwestern, nuclear. If my childhood was a color, it would be gray.

During my August layover I found nothing traumatic on a

clinical level, no deeply painful memories, no flashbacks of blocked-out, repressed molestations and the like. It was a stay at the house of the past, the place where I grew up; there was some fondness lurking around and a lot of dust settled. Much more than you'd expect to fall during a less-than-two-year absence. While there, I felt some resentment, some regret, and a lot to be thankful for. There were a few nooks where I stood, particular spots, like some kind of temporal vacuum in a sci-fi movie, where the organization of the walls, the furniture, and the fall of light through a window awakened something distantly unsettling, where it seemed my former self had made a departure or suffered an adolescent infliction – my ghost still there, waiting for a bandage, a kiss, and a pat on the head. But what can you do but wander the house and place yourself in an archway or at a vantage point where the view is more picturesque? Indeed, the nicest moments of my stay were of this nature, spent with my mother, looking across the backyard at a copse of Norway pine and maples at sunset, which we could agree was beautiful and right, the house itself and all it stood for out of our focus, our periphery, and perhaps our realm of understanding.

So, speaking as a person who needed to save money to go abroad, I'd recommend it. As I strolled down Sauchiehall Street, my Pentax slung over my shoulder, now a good distance from Meadow Prairie Lane, I reflected on that and afforded myself some much-needed confidence that my game plan was on target. It was a step back that had led to two forward. Fruitful. I had driven into the city and attended training sessions at Plunkett Research, met Klang there, and four or five others who were headed to other posts outside the UK – around the globe, in fact. I had looked over briefs from Carson about my duties, filled out my W4, checked my belongings against a list provided by Plunkett of recommended things to bring, about culture shock and how my American hair drier would blow sky high if plugged into the 240v wall socket of my future Scottish flat. I had even bought a marketing textbook from a secondhand store and sat on the back patio in the Illinois August heat (nursing glasses of iced cold-press French Roast) skimming the numbing, clinical language, looking for basic concepts and terms which Carson had doled out in his instructions so I could convey – nod knowingly – some glimmer of comprehension. I was diligent and responsible. I prepared, though not without interruption. In our neighborhood my reappearance had been noticed (reversing in and out of the driveway in Mr P.'s Buick), and the neighborly word had spread. Mrs Brown approached from the proximity of her backyard, where her shrubs were in sudden need of pruning. She was a placid woman who wore knitted sweaters and an Illinois pompadour, perky of spirit despite her saggy eyes laden with Kool Menthol toxins. She said she had heard I was going overseas, to Scotland. Well, Lo and Behold! She had been there herself many years ago.

'My maiden name is MacDougall,' she had said, leaning on the chainlink fence, Mitzy, enfeebled by age, unenthusiastically sniffing her feet, where once she would have yapped and leapt with a spaniel's insatiability and probably hurtled into Mrs Brown's arms. 'Ed and I went to the Highlands and saw the old family castle, what's left of it. I looked up my ancestry and made a family tree. My great-grandfather came over to Cape Breton – that's in Canada – in the 1930s. So we went and visited Oban, where he came from. It's a beautiful country. So green, and all the villages so quaint.' It seemed like Mrs Brown had been longing to tell someone this for years, yearning in all her heart for a person in Wynton to pass into her range, bringing relevance to her memories. I sat in a lawn chair, my thighs and back itching with sweat, blocking the sun's glare with my hand. I drained my drink and swished the ice around, held the cool glass against my forehead, waiting for a kind moment to retreat indoors.

'You must go to Urquhart Castle,' she said. 'It's just lovely. And stay in a B&B. The *Scotch* are such dear people. And take lots of pictures. You'll wish you had when you get back.'

'Yes, I've heard it's very scenic,' I told her, standing up. 'But I'll be working in Glasgow. I don't know how much traveling I'll be able to do. Probably not much. I expect to be extremely busy.'

'Fair bit of rain, though,' she announced, her voice shifting into a light brogue, as if a natural consequence of her reminiscence.

'Yes, I've heard that too.' It's hard to be short with an elderly lady steeped in nostalgia while your dog appears to be navigating an angle in the chainlink through which she can piss on her slippers.

And more reports came in just like Mrs Brown's. Wouldn't you know it, everyone had a bridge partner, co-worker, dentist, neighbor or drycleaner who had dipped their toes in bonnie, bonnie Loch Lomond! Suddenly all my aunts and uncles were Rick Steeves, though they got a few things wrong. *Edinburgh Castle is fantastic. Pet the sheep in Skye for me. Are you going to eat haggis? Send me some haggis. You must try the haggis. Whatever you do, don't eat the haggis, it's cooked in:* (insert here all the misconceptions and old wives' tales) *a sheep's butt, a goat's stomach, a pig's carcass. It's made from brains and snouts. No, it's offal, which is the hooves and organs ground up.* Equally ill-informed stereotypes were thrown about in regards to whiskey, bagpipes, kilts and what is or isn't worn under them.

Now, mind you, all these reports had to be taken with a grain of salt, because they arrived through the network of familial communication, which is bound by a tradition of deceit. It's a Podgorski heirloom. You see, my parents' siblings, my aunts and uncles and their families, are spread about the Midwest – Illinois, Wisconsin, Indiana, Iowa. There's one stray in California. Reports of well-being are shared every few months, passed from state to state and then along intrastate lines. And the thing is, these communications are notoriously biased, one-sided, padded as a Bellevue cell. My mother – Mrs P., as I usually call her – since she retired from teaching elementary school five years ago, has more time and brain space to devote to the family gossip. This per-missible white lying, you find it anywhere. It's this sort of thing, your standard all-American parental bragging. And then the petty mudslinging follows, the slide into surreptitious supposition. 'Oh,' Mrs P. would say, 'Aunt Lizzy says David's studying hard. I sure hope his grades aren't slipping. I mean, do you think he's a good student? He doesn't seem all that bright to me.' From there it is not a far stretch for her to surmise that drugs or ADD is involved. However, I don't doubt that the same thing happens on the other end when reports of me leave Wynton. But it's all done out of love and concern, so I accept it. It is the *modus operandi* for the Podgorskis, spread as they are around these central plains and corn-fields, connected by tenuous phone lines, safe to interpret behind the distance of the US postal service and the infrequent, at most annual, holiday road trips.

My father, for his part, is less malicious. He's a different animal, takes his jabs at himself, privately. He doesn't take part in the slandering, and tries to tame Mom's gossipy imagination with gentle scolding. 'Rose, really,' I can hear him say, in his kindliest voice. Occasionally, though, he cannot deny the likelihood of my mother's assumptions.

'Richard, come on,' my mother will say. 'Your brother Mark has been through treatment. You think Alex wouldn't try a reefer or whatever his friends are passing around? Like father, like son.'

'Well, no, Mark hasn't always set the best example,' he'd concede.

Mr P., as I call him, tempers his obvious malice. He's not crazy about his family, but he's resigned to them. He seems to regard them with his scientist's forbearance, like he would at work study-ing the results of a trial, hoping for one defining success. This idea has stuck with me; it remains at the center of my understanding of this man who taught me how to swing a bat, carried me on his shoulders, read me my first books, but who otherwise is an enigma. I once thought I'd go to film school, and conceived of a screenplay based on him. In it, the protagonist is a scientist, like Mr P. All day, he tweaks chemicals recipes for delicate but durable plastics. He binds and blends otherwise benign substances into helpful applica-tions. He creates non-toxic adhesives, long-lasting but noncorrosive polymers. We see him at the lab in his white coat, amid beakers, Petri dishes, proton microscopes: ordered, controlled, the master of cause and effect, predicting outcomes, controlling small fates. Every ingredient added and subtracted can be measured, traced, quantified, reproduced. When he hangs up his coat, however, leaves the building and drives home, this applicability of his pure reason disintegrates. In his personal life, his family life, he cannot make connections. The arbitrariness of emotions agitates him. Rattled, he lashes out with small cruelties, further confirming his belief in the heart's capriciousness. He's oblivious to the effects of his actions, can't understand why his kids and wife are repelled by him, though they are no different than particles charged with his insensitivity and bristly bearing. The next morning, he eagerly returns to the chemical company, to his insular lab, soothed again among the cold, tractable implements.

All this is to say that the system of Podgorksi linkage is far from ideal. But if it's anything, it's consistent and time-honored, and it went into full swing with my Scotland adventure upcoming. When I was hired by Plunkett Research Corporation, Mrs P. launched a full-scale briefing. In fact, she began the media blitz the night Mr P. came home from 3M with the printed flier he'd obtained through some colleague or other avenue – the flier that advertised Plunkett Research's job fair and their need for market research consultants. How vindicated I felt! Worthless classifieds! All their cryptic, in-the-know acronyms had gotten me nowhere. The position that would prove fruitful for me totally circumvented the classifieds: I checked, there was no public listing for these Plunkett positions. That only confirmed the old trope: *It's all who you know*. Then Mrs P. issued a second round of press releases when Carson scheduled my interview, as if my being hired were a foregone conclusion, a sure thing, a dead lock. I guess a mother's hope knows no bounds. She called Uncle Bill, wrote her sister Elizabeth, my Aunt Lizzy, telling them of the serendipity of it all, how the job has to do with coffee, and I'm a big coffee drinker. A godsend, she called it. Our prayers have been answered.

When letters and calls came back in response, Mrs P. dropped her church fundraiser envelope-stuffing or her baking – even with me and my appetite out of the house, she continued, as if by command of some unalterable wiring, to bake cakes and pies that were never all eaten. She would scurry to find me in the house, wherever I was, planning the arrangement of my luggage (should I pack any short-sleeve shirts, any shorts?) or boning up on my job on the back patio, and she'd share these nuggets on haggis and kilts and castles.

She didn't always know what they were talking about. She had never even heard of Glasgow, and even had to ask, to double check, when Carson awarded me my placement: 'Scotland? That's in the north of England, isn't it?' I could visualize the cogs cranking there, her brain trying to sift through, trying to reach a disused folder containing geography's faded shapes. Let's face it, there really hasn't been that much else to bring Scotland to the forefront of the average American's mind, has there? There was Lockerbie, but all that did, from this remote viewpoint, was create a distorted clash of nations: green Scotland and sandy Libya. The aftermath on the ground, roofless homes, a crane lifting a shattered fuselage, men in police-neon jackets. Footage of the square-jawed Gaddafi deny-ing involvement. In places like Wynton you heard, 'Are you safe on an airliner? Tune in at ten to find out.' There was the occasional half page in a national magazine on Silicon Glen. The juxtaposition of Midlothian and the microchip. I myself had little more to go on when all these questions and comments came in from relatives, but their presumptuousness annoyed me. One factor was common to them all: they each addressed my upcoming venture as if it were a sight-seeing tour. Which it was not. It bothered me, made me even more impatient and dismissive of the input of these rarely seen blood relatives, more than I would normally be. Mainly because they had missed the point. No one said, *Congratulations*. No one said, *Way to go, sounds like Mel's got a real future there. That's great*. No. Nor did anyone pick up on the altruism of my cause. These were people – *the* people, in fact, *the* very demographic – who fre-quented drive-thru coffee huts, who bought lattes, double half-cafs, who had, in recent years, propelled the success of franchise coffee chains – Burback's, most notably. Plunkett would not tell me which particular megaglomerate it had contracted me for, because my data might then be biased, might subliminally, subconsciously, or even deliberately lean toward favorable results *for* them, in some hope that it would yield Plunkett and thus myself more money, I guess. ('It's the principle of the double blind,' Dad explained. Oh, right.) But what I knew was, this was a company that had peddled coffee with such success and had so infiltrated American cities, downtowns and strip malls alike, that it was considering expanding into the British market. Clearly, it was one of the big ones that you see in every town big enough to support a cinema, the place that Aunt Jenny gave a buck sixty to every morning on her way to her Milwaukee office and would miss dearly if she were ever deprived of the luxury. The one all the Podgorskis raced to, in Ames, in Indianapolis, in Springfield, and surely out there in San Mateo – raced to without a second thought whenever they needed a boost, a hangover helper, a travel mugful, a Sunday-newspaper companion. And so here I was employing myself in the pursuit of information that would assess the beverage-consumption tendencies, the spending habits and tastes of the Brits, to see if the UK would be a suitable place for this facility. Let's face it, I would be researching, largely, the prospect of profitability, but there was also the question of bettering whatever society I might find in Britain by the addition of a more affordable (this was contestable), higher-quality, quickly served coffee.

Did, then, my relatives ever mention any of these aspects of my future exploits? Like hell they did. They were fixated on the petty. Maybe it could be excused, since this was pre-information age. But it wasn't the Dark Ages. They possessed that Midwestern tendency to mock that which is not understood, reinforced by a culture of stars and stripes car accessorizing and bumptiously patriotic T-shirt slogans. Had I been going into space to study how cancerous tumors grow in zero gravity, they would have said, *Hey, I heard the moon's made of green cheese, bring me back a chunk.* Had I been embarking on a tour of the ocean floors in search of clues of primitive life that would give humankind a greater understanding of itself – would have placed the whole Podgorksi clan on the chain of all the universe's life forms – they would have joked, *Oh, are you going in a yellow submarine? Keep an eye out for the Octopus's garden in the shade.*

This is what you get in an America of spoon-fed impressions.

Snapshots. At my parents' that August, CNN ran play-by-play of OJ fleeing in his white Bronco, asserting the truth through repetition, bestowing the 'event' with the importance of airtime – circular logic and circling helicopters. Innocent until proven guilty was thrown out the window, like so many ill-fitting gloves. Likewise, every account of Scotland available to the masses was that of a heather-strewn paradise and misty moors populated by buxom lasses in ripped bodices. To learn otherwise required effort; a world of comfortable impressions, and cozy denials, was more accessible. CNN never went off the air, so why get up or change the channel?

And so, on Sauchiehall Street, on my first day at work, strolling through what could be considered my office, the effect was twofold. On the one hand, my briefcase of 27G forms was a matter of personal pride to me, but the work was also a private pursuit, an undertaking driven by my unique appreciation of it. I could, and would, take it all the more seriously if no one else was going to. And, on the other, I was a little bitter. With the exception of my mother, who is unconditionally proud of and hopeful for me, the Podgorski family could not shed their impression of me as a deadbeat loser, and apparently were not willing to believe I could handle real responsibility or contribute something meaningful to society, even a foreign one. They thought I was on paid vacation, had been visited by the angel of cushy jobs, been hit with Plunkett's pity stick. And so they wanted tourist photos. They wanted snapshots of pipers and kilts, plowmen and pipe smokers and Highland cattle, hill and dale, glen and firth. Well, I decided, while shoving and dodging my way through the crowded cobblestone mall (not strip mall, but pedestrian mall), working my way to what on my map looked like the heart of downtown, the so-called City Centre, I wouldn't give them the satisfaction.

3 Reportage

I snapped photos of buildings. Buildings with boarded-up windows like patched eyes. Buildings with SPACE TO LET signs, £72 per sq. ft. Gothic or Edwardian or Victorian or completely modern tenement flats – whatever they were. Not exactly picture-postcard stuff, but I felt justified. What else could I photograph? This was all there was. Buildings nestling against each other, inches apart, four or five stories high. Stores – 'shops' they call them – on ground floor, friezes of angels and gargoyles supporting balustrades and balconies above. Intriguing, but the conditions weren't good: every street was cast in shadow; the sun only crept in at the occasional intersection or square. But this was reportage. This was my first impression, and it would be theirs, my relatives who insisted on postcards and images from abroad.

I made my way around town, repeatedly forgetting the traffic's directionally inverted tides, keeping a dim register of the sequence of reversed lefts and rights I would need to get back to the Hilton. Scores of people were out, more than seemed appropriate at 11 a.m. on a weekday. Why was everyone out? Shouldn't they be working? Unless it was lunchtime or the day of a Bulls Championship parade, Chicago's Michigan Avenue would not be this clogged with pedestrians, shoppers, amblers, even kids. But something about the infrastructure seemed different. Districts were less defined. I found dance clubs within blocks of elementary – *primary* – schools. There were hospitals and pubs, plush, multistoried department stores and the job centre, a bus station and Burger King. Retail and heavy industry, restaurants and pubs. Shopping and pubs. In fact, pubs were the recurrent element. They were everywhere. Hundreds of them. The Rat and Parrot. The King's Arms. The Hogshead. The Wig and Pen. I photographed some of the clever ones, their signs and mascots and window decorations, catching also the drinkers in the windows, people leaning over beers, pints with their distinctive bulging glasses, at brunchtime.

I was on my way up to Bath Street, which I had read in a *Let's Go Britain* was the most polluted intersection in the UK, looking for a few more shots before I found a place to try a cup of coffee and make my first report, when a streak of white caught my eye. On a building halfway up the hilly block, a sign flapped high above. On the street, a small crowd gathered. I stepped out of the flow of pedestrian traffic, shielded my eyes from the sun, which now lasered through a celestial crevice at the horizon end of this street, and looked up. A banner read, 'NO M77.' I made out the silhouette of a person on the roof, a man, breeze-blown hair backlit, face cast in shadow. This would make as stark a subject as any: it was some kind of protest, though what M77 was, I had no idea. Maybe it was one of these European test-market birth-control devices, like RU-486. I negotiated a better angle for the photograph, so I wouldn't be shooting directly into the sun. More people had stopped on this side of the street now, opposite the building, watching. Still others were oblivious and trundled along in annoyance, tripping past those like myself who congested the sidewalk. Protruding from the exterior wall by the bluish glass doors of the building where the fifteen or twenty people, mostly young, it seemed, were gathered, was a company logo. WIMPY, in stark block letters. Was this the fast-food burger-chain headquarters? Maybe M77 was a chemical they were putting in the meat that yielded mutant babies in rats. In a nearby restaurant doorway, a man and woman spoke.

'He's a daft one, eh?'

'Aye, he'd best mind himself up there. If he falls, that's our lunch hour buggered. Whole street'll be jammed up wi' folk.'

The man put a hand in the pocket of his tomato-stained apron and dragged on a cigarette. 'All for a bloody road, mind you.'

Aware of the presumptuousness of the act, I took my camera out and snapped a shot of the man on the rooftop and his banner. He sat up there, legs dangling over the sides, raising his clenched fist high, a sign of defiance or victory. He shouted down to the crowd, but I couldn't make it out, due to his accent and the grumbling, exhaust-chuffing buses passing and the pedestrian-crossing indicator beeping every half a minute. I had a few exposures remaining on my roll and shamelessly tried to get both the man and the crowd in the frame, using the portrait length of the viewfinder. Trying to capture the synergy between them, I crouched and maneuvered – maybe people would think I was a newspaper photographer. I aimed through bystanders' legs and waited for passing cars to clear. It was with the zoom lens that I noticed a second person on the building. A girl, one story up, perched on an overhang, clinging nervously to a sandstone bust of some figurehead, awkwardly angling her torso streetwards, trying to display the message on her T-shirt: LABOUR LAND THIEVES. I aimed my photographic crosshairs on her, her jeans, boots and hair, all black, nearly camouflaging her in the building's shadow. She was young, her face alabaster, her body thin and fragile up there, like a bird on a narrow branch. I changed my camera settings to manual, trying for a longer shutter speed – more time to pick up what little light reflected off her. If she moved, she would blur. She looked down, nodding in approval with the assembly below, who goaded her on, nodding so as not to let go of her tenuous fingerhold. I zoomed in, framed her, steadied, held and snapped.

This would flummox Mr and Mrs P., my aunts and uncles: a strange girl hanging like a bat from a building, dressed in defiant words, a righteous sneer on her face. What could be more antithetical to their visions of rolling landscapes and highland lasses? My mother, eager to convince her kin of her boy's success, would make copies, pass them around. I wanted to annotate these photographic reports in the accompanying letter, to strengthen their ugly facticity. I needed to know what was going on.

I looked for someone on my side of the street to ask, someone affable, someone comfortably detached who could give me the plain facts. Just then a commotion began to stir outside the WIMPY doors. I discerned a voice from the assembly.

'Right! A coupla minutes! Everyone get yer signs, okay? Okay? Let's give it laldy.' 'Laldy'? Perhaps he had said 'loudly'. They were going to make some noise. Around me, people began to disperse, and the two restaurant staffers retreated inside. It seemed things were breaking up. I crossed to where the action was, in the hope of overhearing something. I thought I would ask someone what they were fighting for or against. I'd read a whole page-sized text box in *Let's Go* about slang in Scotland. Maybe a laldy was a break. They were taking a break. But no. Placards were up in the air now, reading 'NO M77' and 'HANDS OFF POLLOK PARK'. So much for contraception or hamburgers. The red light at the intersection held traffic in front of the building; one driver shouted, 'Fuckin' right!' out his window, and received a roar of solidarity from the protesters. I looked to other cars to gauge reactions, maybe get an unprofessional consensus, all too aware of my layman's under-standing of probability, margins of error, and bell curves. A few men in suits looked stoic and unimpressed behind tightly sealed Mercedes windows.

Then the eruption came. Voices went up. I turned on my heels. The protesters closed in like pigs to a trough on the WIMPY doors, one of which I could see open through the small forest of cardboard signs stapled to sticks. The group encircled uniformly, as if the open door created a vacuum. A chant began arrhythmically and fell into order: 'NO EM SEVEN SEVEN! NO EM SEVEN SEVEN!' I was left behind the crowd, seeing only backs, and stepped up onto a low ledge to spy a man's dapperly parted hair moving like the eye of a hurricane. He was trying to get out of the building, the shoulders of his gray suit jacket showing in glimpses, the same with his face, which was small-featured, clean-shaven, annoyed and patient, and he maintained a corporate silence as he baby-stepped along, his enemies clearing a path for him, not touch-ing him, not roughing him up or striking him as they might have wanted to do as payment for whatever atrocity his company was doing to this M77, this Pollok Park. He endured the shouting faces, probably having halitosis huffed up his nose, and the inevitable spittle flying at him, dotting his cheeks. The further he reached – ten, fifteen yards now – away from the door, the more protesters broke off like debris from a comet, from the moving cell of which he was the nucleus, and drifted back, exchanging congratulatory smiles and high fives. Only three of four stuck by him, Mr Gray Suit, beyond the perimeter of the WIMPY building. Once clear, the man picked up speed, strode along, surely with some relief, throwing the last few off. Only one man – in tattered cords, obligatorily long-haired – side-stepped all the way to the intersection, the pedestrian crossing, belting out a few last 'NO EM SEVEN SEVEN's before jogging back to the group, where it had reassembled at the door, some lighting cigarettes, some tying shoes like a pre-game athlete in the locker room, some looking skyward to their rooftop cohort, giving him a wave, as if in conference with an instructive god.

I felt a little precarious, though the assembly hardly noticed me, their minds all collectively intent on delivering their message to the next bird to spring from the WIMPY cage. It wasn't going to be a violent scene and I was in no fear of getting trampled there on my short ledge to the side of the entrance. But if something were to happen that would bring the attention of the law – bobbies! I remembered the term from *Let's Go* – I might be implicated. I figured, too, that I was probably welcome in a way, if my presence gave the impression of adding to their numbers. The protesters obviously wanted to be noticed, and the larger the group the more of a fuss they could make. But I wasn't about to ask anyone, say, 'Excuse me, kind socially conscientious person, but what exactly is M77 and what is Wimpy and what has it done?' I was content to know it was something to do with land and a park. I could mail a somewhat informed report home accompanying the photos.

I wanted to stay and shoot the group in action when the next executive came out for his or her lunch, but I also wanted a cup of coffee. My caffeine barometer had dipped dangerously low and, though my days of swilling potfuls in isolation and misery were behind me, my body was still accustomed to more of a jolt, in the morning especially, than what I had received from the hotel's dainty tea cup of dishwater. That dosage just wasn't cutting it, and I was, after all, still jet-lagged. It was noon or so, but really 6 a.m. to me. And, further, it was my goal to try a place today, scout out a café here in downtown, maybe somewhere that specialized if I saw any – an espresso hut, a Turkish smokehouse, one of those Italian bistros. Whatever they had here. I'd be getting a jump on my work. Before 5 p.m. Chicago time I would have to call Carson, just to say I made it, to check in with him; I wanted badly to impress him by being ahead of the game, on the ball, right into the flow of it. Don't worry about ol' Mel, already on the trail, like a blood-hound, sniffing leads, punching the clock. Researching markets like nobody's business!

No – I would go. I rewound the film with the pop-up crank. I dug in my pockets for an empty canister to put it in. And then the voices rose up again, the NO EM SEVEN SEVEN chant sputtering into unison. It was a woman this time, with a head of curly red hair – ginger hair, as they call it. She was set upon, just as the man had been, and the cluster drifted around her. But I heard something different in the protest chant, something that registered as shrill and dangerous. A voice came from outside the group, fearsome and divergent from the message. It was from above and behind – a scream. I spun: above me the pale-faced T-shirt girl was slipping, spilling down the wall, but holding on. Her weight was on her torso as she slid off the overhang on which I had seen her standing previously. Her right leg swinging and flailing below her, looking for a foothold, her hands gripping at anything, the lip above her, but there was nothing on which she could anchor her weight. She let out another scream and then, 'Help! Hullo?', seemingly directed at me. I scaled the low ledge to the wall below her.

'Yes! Yes!' I shouted at her, my arms helplessly raised towards her.

'Ah cannay hold!'

'There's a lip below your right foot! About six more inches! It's narrow, but you can –'

I couldn't explain anything fast enough: her boot was out-stretched, toe pointing groundwards, revealing a Doc Martens diamond-shaped tread – well worn. Her body was sliding off, but she wasn't going to land the foothold. Even if she did, unless she were a gymnast or a ballerina of incomparable balance she wouldn't stay up on it, not with one toe, but pitch outwards off the face.

'Wait! No!'

Her shriek was truly birdlike – fearful, primal.

'Left! Left!' I yelled, trying to direct her foot. She was sliding faster.

'Where?'

There was a decorative kind of waterfall of curved stone that formed a ramp which she must have scaled to get up. I leapt onto this, threw my weight up, grabbed at a higher ledge with one hand, reached her ankle with the other, and tried to guide it to safety.

It didn't work. She came down on me, I planted a lucky foot behind me, solidly back on the first low ledge, took the weight of her backside into my chest, thankfully not much, an image flashing, wordlessly saying, Does she have hollow bones?, a spark of relief passing through me that, however we hit the ground, she wouldn't crush my ribcage, yet knowing that the one solid plant was not enough, no matter how light she was, our weights top-heavy with gravity's momentum.

On my way down, I caught a glimpse of the pavement approaching through a veil of this girl's straight black hair, which was wafting like a wind-blown curtain into my open mouth as I shouted an anticipatory 'Grraaahh!' My weight toppled over my good foot – it was good no more. She twisted in mid-air, yelling, 'Fuck!' I heard the sole of her boot meet the concrete with a slap. We dropped to the pavement like a bag of Christmas toys.

From years of experience, jungle gyms, tree limbs, contact sports – basically from growing up a boy – I knew I was unhurt. My back was wet somehow, but I was fine and able to ask instantly of her, 'Are you okay?'

She swore and thanked me alternately – 'Oh, fuck,' – giving herself a dazed once-over and settling on her ankle as the part most in need of comfort, holding it in her hands and wincing. 'Oh, cheers fer catchin' me. Shite!'

'I don't know that I really *caught* you,' I said, out of honesty more than chivalric modesty. 'I just kind of got in your way. Is it your ankle? Does it hurt?'

'Aye, it's fairly buggered.'

'What? Broken?'

'No, Ah dohn think so.' She wiped her hands, dusted them on her jeans. 'Wha' abou' you, eh?'

'I'm fine. Somehow.' I laughed. 'I'm all wet, I don't know what from.'

She pointed to the sidewalk, a paving stone with a loose corner protruding above the rest, latent rainwater underneath. 'Musta been thah.'

I stood up, tested the stone with my toe, wobbled it. 'God, that's lucky.' I laughed again. The water had dampened my impact. 'Can you stand up?' I offered her my hands; she took them and raised herself, cringing and hobbling.

'Bugger!'

'Okay, okay. Don't stand on it. Here.' I draped her arm over my shoulder and led her to the low ledge, sat her down. 'You need to have that looked at. I don't know, it could be broken. Maybe fractured.'

'Och, Ah'll be fine,' she said.

'You should at least get an X-ray . . .'

The assembly continued. 'NO EM SEVEN SEVEN! NO EM SEVEN SEVEN!'

She straightened her clothes. Blood dotted her shirt amid the writing LABOUR LAND THIEVES. She lifted it, revealing grazes, scratches, one main L-shaped abrasion carved out of her sunless skin which reached to her sternum and vanished beneath the underwire of her bra. She seemed unfazed both at exposing her flesh to me and at the pain. 'From that fuckin ledge up there,' she said.

My instinct was to touch it, as if it were my own, some reflex towards intimacy, probably a habit from kissing Margaret's wounds, a cut finger while chopping vegetables, a stubbed toe.

Margaret had always presented her owies (her word) to me for a kiss, on terms of true belief, retaining all the innocence of a child. I raised my hand towards this girl's tender stomach, winced myself, as if sharing the pain. 'Ooo,' I groaned. 'Ah. Right. Well.' I stopped and held my palm there as if to say, *Sympathy, kindness and healing flow forth from me to this stranger whose flesh is revealed unto me now before mine eyes.* 'That's gotta sting,' was all I could offer.

She put her shirt down. Flustered – smooth, feminine belly has always suggested to me what lies southward – I muttered something about bacitracin and infection.

'Thanks a lot for catchin me. Ah'd'a been fucked if you hadnay been there. Probably bashed my head and cracked it wide open. Cheers.'

'No problem. Glad to help.'

'Really, Ah owe ya one.'

'What happened up there? I take it you were on your way down?'

'Aye, Ah was comin' down, like. Ah was gonnay join the others there at the door.'

All the while 'the others' kept on with their campaign, ushering WIMPY employees, whose occupations and misdeeds I still didn't know the specifics of, from the front door, down to the end of the street. They railed at them, got in their faces, pumped their placards in a gesture like I used to make along the Illinois highways to get the truckers to blast the horn. Since this girl had done her impression of Newton's apple on me, they had escorted two or three others, oblivious of their wounded sister-in-protest. What with their own noise and racket-making, the chaos of their cause, I understood why they hadn't heard the screams, but still I wondered why no one had come to her aid – surely someone could see now, she was down, hurt?

'Some friends you got there,' I said, trying not to sound too judgmental. 'Not one of them seeing if you're all right.'

'Aye – what're they like?'

'Not too thoughtful, I guess.'

'Wha'?' She looked at me, a funny smile on her face. 'No, thah's just a wee sayin'. *What're they like?* Dinnae ken?'

'Sorry, you lost me. I'm new here. Maybe they *are* thoughtful – I don't know them.'

'Never mind, Nirvana. I dohn know 'em either, the gits.'

'No?' She moved her ankle around a little, turned and studied it.

'Naw, they're Friends of the Earth folk. They've goh a camp at the park as well. Ah juz goh roped along by . . . well, by one of 'em.'

She gave me an embarrassed, I-don't-want-to-say-any-more look, the look of someone facing up to a mistake.

'I see,' I said, though I didn't. Asking what more she didn't want to say – that seemed untimely.

Abruptly, she stood up, as if struck by some resolve, favoring the hurt foot, grimacing, saying, 'Ri', well, thanks a loh. Yer a champion. Ah'd better join up here. They're callin' for tenders today and it's expected to pass. It's now or never, he says. And you're probably away to Helensburgh, so see ya round.' She took a few steps, cringing under every movement, biting her lip, making it towards the door.

'Wait! Who's calling who tender? Who says it's now or never? *What's* now or never?'

'Eh?' She turned.

'What I mean is – what's your name?'

'Nicole.'

'Nicole – great. I'm Mel. Pleased to meet you. Listen, Nicole, you shouldn't walk on that. You could make it worse. I don't even know who Helen Burrow is, I don't have anything to do with her. I'm not a reporter or anything – just a tourist, kind of. The camera's just for kicks. I'm not on either side. Here, sit down. Let's see if it's swollen.' I tried to keep desperation out of my voice but sensed I hadn't succeeded.

She did sit down again, collapsing back onto the ledge. 'Helensburgh,' she said with a laugh. 'It's a place, noh a person.' She pronounced this *pair-son*. 'Are ye noh away to the Burrell Collection or somethin'?'

'You're not making any sense. It's the pain. Let's just see if it's swollen.'

'Course it's swollen. It's throbbin' like a bugger. Every pulse is like a knife in there.'

I crouched down at her outstretched foot. 'Then let's get this boot off, take the pressure off.'

I touched her foot; she pulled it away. 'Ah! Fuck! Leave it! Thanks for the help, Mel, but Ah can manage on muh own. We've goh a protest tay do. It's Ruaridh, this is the big one ... This is the big one,' she repeated, and broke into a throaty, slang-infused tirade I couldn't quite follow, her voice growing teary, tired, anguished. She gestured vaguely upwards for reasons I didn't understand, talking about it being now or never, we've got to stop this thing, stand up for something, set a precedent if Scotland ever wants to stand on its own two feet. Her eyes ranged away from mine, darted though I tried to meet them.

'The council votes tomorrow,' she said. 'He's been waitin' fer this. He keeps sayin' after the vote, like, we'll know. Then we'll have more time the'gether.' Her voice grew wet and guttural. A tear streamed down one cheek. 'It was Ruaridh's idea tay climb up it. He's always got tay be the most radical one. And now my fuckin' foot! If it's broke, Oh, Ah'll fuckin' kill him! Ah dohn have any money to get tay hospital, my mum cannay find out Ah've been here, part ay this.'

'Whoah, whoah, whoah. Hold on.'

'Serves me ri'. Ah should juz mind muh books.'

'It's okay.' The male circuitry be damned sometimes: I put my hand on Nicole's thigh, not even her thigh, closer to her knee, as a comforting gesture, purely to appease her hysterics, to offer my condolence, get her to calm down so she could make a clear-headed decision that getting her ankle looked at was more important than protesting against WIMPY right now – and through all this good intention my brain still received a jolt of sexual impulse, a twinge of electricity that I thought might betray me when there was nothing intentional to betray. I let go, sat on the ledge beside her again until her gasps abated.

Nicole mopped at tears with her shirt-front and drew a black contrail slashing from her cheek to her ear in evidently not-so-permanent marker.

'Bloody Woolworth's Biro,' she said.

Would it comfort her to learn Mr P.'s company had probably made that very ink, through rigorous sub-particle tweaking, the slap-dashing of dyes, isopropyl alcohol, a pinch of hydrocolloid, an iota of xantham gum?

I said she needed to have her foot seen to and forget about everything else. She wasn't listening, rather berating herself for 'greetin' like a wean' ('cryin' like a baby,' I'd learn some time later). I asked if she had a doctor, a family clinic or something around. I said I'd go with her. But Nicole insisted I'd done enough, though I was willing to do a lot more for her. All I'd done so far, I said, was literally get in her way. I didn't want to leave her; I was sure she'd get up and walk, maybe even rejoin the protest.

'What about this *Roo-ree* person?' I asked.

'Eh?'

'*Roar-ee? Roor-ree?*' I contorted my mouth, trying to repeat the name as I'd heard it. My tongue twisted around: I nearly sprained it.

'Aye, Ruaridh,' she flipped with ease. *Rurr-ee.*

'Where's he? Can he take you?'

She paused, looked down at the street between her feet. The crowd's chant erupted again, that stalled thing kicking back to life. She pointed up, looked me in the eyes and, over the uproar, said, 'Tha's him up on the fuckin' roof!'

4   *The Infirmary*

I hailed a cab from in front of WIMPY, helped Nicole in, and we sped off, leaving the sense of urgent disagreement of the protest. 'The Royal Infirmary,' Nicole said to the driver, leaning forward towards the partition. Sitting back, she told me she was skint, broke. Don't worry, I said, I can pay, no problem. Well, there was one slight problem. Arriving at the emergency-room doors after zipping for a few miles down confusing streets, having long forgotten my mental map of the route I had walked, I realized what I was too distracted by Nicole's injured presence to notice before: I had no cash. No local currency. No pounds sterling. I had $24 US in my wallet, which did every bit of good as a ruble or drachma. Embarrassed, I asked the driver to wait while I served as human crutch to get Nicole into the lobby and propped against the reception desk to begin the paperwork. Then I ran back out to the cab, asked the driver could he take me to an ATM. But the acronym for Automated Teller Machine was not a part of his vernacular. Once the man finally surmised that if he was going to get paid he needed to get me to a *cash point*, we were off, navigating the network of inroads back off the hospital grounds and into town again. The driver threw over his shoulder through the glass partition tokens of diplomacy in the form of friendly questions. *What part of the States do ye come from? What brings you here then? How you find the weather?* Finally, the fare on the meter reaching £17.40, the cab pulled up beside a Clydesdale Bank. I used the Plunkett Research Corporation Citibank Visa to take out £100, an extraction I was a little nervous about – emergencies only – but had no alternative to at this point. It would be noticed by Carson's secretary, Melissa, and brought to his attention. But it would be okay, I told myself, I would just have to explain. *You see, I was photographing a riot to send to my ungrateful, stereotyping family when a cherubic pseudo-renegade lost her grip on a Victorian bust-frieze. She had a hysterical lapse, but I took her to the hospital and the cabby didn't know what an ATM was, but it's okay now. I'm sure you'll understand, I'm not abusing my privileges before I've even started one iota of proper work, well, it's just that, Mr Carson, I think I have a crush on her, which is something I cannot say has happened since my wife . . . left me.*

Or something like that.

A glowing report of the driver's vacation to Disneyland – his *holiday*, he called it – got us back to the infirmary, and I gave him £30 and told him sorry for the trouble. 'Nay bother,' he said. 'Welcome to Sco'land.' The nurse at reception, who looked as if she hadn't slept in three days, told me Miss Marston was being treated and I was welcome to wait for her, leaving me to finger through home-decor magazines and whisper, by way of sampling, using a variety of inflections and emphases, her full name, *Nicole Marston, Nicole Marston, Nicole Marston* to myself as if rolling a candy around on my tongue.

Expecting Nicole's treatment to consist of having x-rays taken, developed, examined and possibly a cast or splint molded and thus to be waiting for at least an hour or two, I made myself at home and fended off impatience's onset. I read about matching colors and fabrics in lounges – what I call living rooms – and tried to ignore the man slouching in the chair opposite me, who stunk of body odor and the inside of a port cask. I sat for a while studying my shoe, holding my hand over my face as if in grief or despair or overwhelming anxiety, when really it was to deflect the drifting stench of booze breath. Finally I stood up and paced to the other end of the lobby, where I spotted a pump-top thermos and stack of Styrofoam cups.

Coffee!

I am well-versed in the art of making public coffee palatable. I've worked in a Chicago high-rise, I've worked in a lowly warehouse. The struggle is to produce a passable beverage using the basest elements: woody, flaky bulk grounds, pre-shredded, freeze-dried, having not a drop of the lustrous oils that coat recently roasted premium beans. The industrial makers in offices – brutish machines – always impart a tinny flavor. The carafes have a patina of permanent char. The water input, coffee's lifeblood, is typically the main in a kitchenette that somehow is always backed by a men's room – the tap's stream inauspiciously weakens at the sound of a flush. Even the filters are questionable, a case of forty gross caked in dust dating to the Carter administration. Given all that, the best bet is to make it yourself and drink it fresh. Absent this, who knows how long the pot has been heating on the element, and if you have to mask a burnt tinge with chalky milk powders and the artificial sweeteners that the health Nazis have used to replace all the sugar, then you're in coffee no man's land, beyond repair.

Knowing this, I cautiously filled the cup from the pump – a worryingly tan fluid came out. I reclaimed my seat, steam rising from my hand, and eyed the magazines for another article to read. But when I sipped, what hit my tongue was not coffee at all. It was tea. I did a spit-take, à la Johnny Carson, half in the cup, half on the table and magazines. My mouth was instantly coated with hideous tannic residuals. My drunk, half-conscious wait-mate opened his eyes, grumbled and shifted. Using the cuff of my shirt, I dabbed the magazine covers, now bubbling with moisture. The receptionist sat with her head propped on one hand, barely keeping it from meeting the desktop. I searched the pockets of my coat – one of these extortionately priced Thinsulate jobs with compartments for carbines, Swiss Army knives, and bear repellent – for a stick of gum, a mint, anything, and the Velcro rips apparently reached the synapses of the drunk like fingernails on a blackboard. He slurred curses.

That's when she appeared.

'Nicole!' I jumped to my feet.

'Mel, wha' you doin' here?' she said. 'Ah thought you'd have fucked off.'

'No, no, no!' She smiled at me – touched, pleased.

Nicole was younger than me, I was sure of that. How much younger, I couldn't yet say. Her skin was taut with that freshness that I seemed to recall vanishing from my own features in the weeks after my twenty-first birthday, when my demeanor had sunk into something approaching a permanent frown, as if the warranty on my facial elasticity had expired. But that benchmark may not be a good measure, because at that time I had been married just over a year, things with Margaret had hit the rocks, and the situation weighed on me. At any rate, I put Nicole at nineteen, which was fine, perfectly legal, just a few years' gap, not unbridgeable. Looking at her now, her smile, the brightness in her face, struck me like a thump to the chest. She carried a remarkable imperturbability even as she leaned on a pair of crutches, her foot wrapped in bandages. Crucially, though, it was not a banal, cloying, arbitrary smile but rather stemmed from an inward flow of positivity that had already rounded naiveté's corner, left it in the dust.

All her earlier hysteria was gone, soothed by the caring sterility of the hospital. Tied to the handle of one crutch was a plastic bag bearing the shape of a size six or so boot, hanging limply like a lunch sack secured by a mother as a measure of loss prevention. Catching me looking at her foot, Nicole spoke, through a grin tempered with apology.

'Ah've sprained it,' she said, handing me a photocopied sheet with an illustration of the ankle bones. In red pen was scrawled 'Grade 2, partial tear', and the typeset words 'TALOFIBULAR LIGAMENT' in the diagram were circled. 'Ah'm tay rest it fer a fortnight, keep the thing elevated. And Ah'm noh to puh weight on it.' This meant using the crutches, she said, when she walked, if she had to at all. She was distinctly unhappy about that, the hindrance to her mobility, yet she concluded with an accepting shrug, saying, 'Och, well. It'll be all ri' in a wee while. Let's get out of here.'

On her one real leg and two false ones, Nicole reached the automatic doors, in the undignified gait, such as it is, of the crutch user. But she was not self-conscious. In fact, once outside, she peered over the parked cars, instinctively scouting for a bus shelter, not the least cowed or helpless, then set towards it in something nearing a stride, pronouncing, 'Ah've only got enough for the bus, but once we're in town Ah'll get a tenner out the cash point and get ya back for the taxi, 'kay?' She powered along on the aluminum crutches, her determination emanating like pheromones. 'Ah take the 10A up Kelvin Way, but Ah could do a transfer and see ya off at yer hotel. So's you don't end up in Govanhill, like.'

'Would that be bad?'

'Unless you fancy a knifin' before bedtime.'

'Govanhill: noted. I'll stay away from there. No, but listen, we can take a cab. You don't have to ride around town on a bus in your condition.'

'Naw, it's nay bother. You've already spent a mint gettin' me here. Ah'll noh have you blowin' all yer dosh.'

'Nicole, I don't mind. I want to.'

She stopped. I stepped around in front of her, and we faced each other. 'Are ya sure?' she asked.

'I insist.'

'That would be grand,' she sighed. 'That would suit me down to the ground.'

The street lamps cast pyramids of orange light down on the evening roads; we passed under them, reflections blinking in our cab windows. The shopfronts had their shutters and cages drawn, awnings unlit and tucked up accordion-style, like brows over retail glass eyes. The streets were mostly empty. A cool breeze ruffled in the driver's open window – the scent of hot oil, the flutter of air pressure. The peaceful resolve of the city seemed to leave bare my anxiety, which I was certain Nicole could detect, though she made no indication – sneering in jest as she gingerly lifted her wrapped foot off the bouncing floor. I clutched the camera case in my lap, and fidgeted with the strap clip.

The driver's eyes glinted in the rear-view, and the road rolled up under us. 'Wha's all this on yer shirt then, love?'

'Aw, it's nothin'. Just havin' a laugh.'

'You in that carry-on over at the park?'

'Och – someone put me up to it. Nevermind, Nirvana.'

'Eh?'

'Nevermind, but.'

'Aye.'

The driver said no more – not looking to start a mano a mano with his fare. I beheld Nicole's nonchalance, and let it reach me, breathed it in, the faint scent of lilac coming off her hair. I set the camera case beside me. Silence prevailed for a few more of the West End's long blocks. Nicole smiled at me at one point and, while a lovely sight, it brought the return of my worry that she would be suspicious of my aggressive charity. Something popped into my head and, unfortunately, it came out before I realized it might seem forward or suggestive.

'Today was kind of like a date.'

'Sorry?' Nicole said, with her 'flipped' R's, somewhere between *solly* and *soddy*. She turned towards me.

'I mean, we sat together, traveled around together, spent money, waited. All the things you do on a date.'

'Aye, ri',' she laughed.

'Not that it was a date!'

'No, Ah know,' she said, seeming to understand my non-implication. 'Listen, Ah owe you a jar. Ah hope muh foot's behher before you go.'

'Before I go where?' I said.

'Home. The States. When's yer holiday up?'

'My vacation? Oh, no. I'm not on vacation. I *live* here.'

'Oh, brill. You at Uni then?'

'Uni?'

'University,' she said. 'College.'

'College – of course. I must sound like a broken record, always asking what you're saying. No, actually, I work here.'

'And living in a hotel? Tha's swish!' The driver zipped off the main road at a Y intersection, bringing us into a residential area of narrow, sinuous streets. With every tipping turn, Nicole unabashedly put her hand out and braced on my shoulder.

'Well, for the time being. I've got to find an apartment.'

'Mmm. Wha' a hassle. Ah hate moving house. Most flats are rubbish. Well, it's grand you'll be around. Ah'll buy you a jar at Curler's then?'

'Curler's?'

'Aye, if ye haven't been, you must go. They've got good prices on drinks and brilliant music as well. And specials on voddie lemonades. We'll go on a Tuesday, when the band plays. When is that – what's today?'

'Thursday.'

'God, Ah'm supposed to sit on my arse for a fortnight?' she said. She gestured despairingly at her foot. In a moment, she leaned up to the partition. 'It's just at the end, number twelve.' Then to me again, 'Ri', thah's me away. Tuesday, though, that's five days, counting today, like. Ah can go down to the pub. There's no harm in that, is there? It's noh like Ah'll go out clubbing or anything. As long as Ah just keep my foot up. Do you noh think?'

'There's no hurry. I mean, we can wait until you're healed.' Play it cool, Mel. Only fools rush in.

'Nah, it'll be good. Ah can just sit there like a cripple with you bringin' me drinks all night. It'll be brilliant,' she laughed. 'Ah'm only jokin'.'

The cab swung in along the curb – or *kerb*, as it's spelled here. She dug in her pocket, pulled out some change. 'Here, that's two pound eighty, it's all Ah've got.'

'Don't worry about it. Get yourself some aspirin or an ice pack.'

'Are ya sure?'

'Absolutely. And I'm sure I'll need your number if we're going to get together.'

Back in the monotonous order of my hotel room, accented by my scattered belongings, my stay too transitory to warrant their arrangement, I called Carson. It was still midday in Chicago. He sounded surprised. He was in his succinct and dismissive mood, which from my experience is one of his two moods: the other is choppy and brusque. I was grateful to him for hiring me – he had had a strong pool of candidates, he said, very strong – but he was not an agreeable man. Looking at him, he seemed warm, jovial, walking down the hall smiling in contemplation of his many duties, or leaning back in his office chair, on the phone, relaxed, as you approached his fishbowl office. He had a rubicund face and a horseshoe of silver hair like a moat around his gleaming cranial mound. He wore charcoal suits. But this avuncular neutral look belied his icy temperament. When interacting with the other trainees during sessions he'd organized, of overhead projections, policy hand-outs and procedure packets, he was attentive, open, accommodating in answering their questions, while with me he was terse, ungenerous, even dismissive. I felt as if he expected from me something extra – or nothing at all. Catching him at an unscheduled moment was no better; a quick request or signature on a form was met with downright rudeness – like now, when I began to speak of the flight and the weather, and he butted in.

'Fine, Podgorski. Take the weekend to get your roots down and get cracking on Monday. You've got the starter materials, the 27Gs and whatnot. And you've got Klang's number in London. He'll make initial contact with any prospective vendors or co-clients. Call him with any concerns, all right? And, of course, turn in your paperwork to him.'

'Yes, fine, sir. One thing, though. I had to use the credit card for cash already.' I waited for him to respond, to say something, but was met with silence, which unnerved me. I paced the room, grabbing something to fidget with: my ex-wife's Katsina doll, a quasi-authentic Hopi trinket from our vacation together. My mother must have stuffed it in my suitcase; I'd found it unpacking. She was more foolishly sentimental than I when it came to such things. I tossed it in the air and caught it as I continued with the stoic Carson: 'I was – well, as soon as I got here I just got so excited I started looking around the cafés and everything. And, the darndest thing, I forgot to go to a bank right away and cash the stipend check. So I had no other choice. I took out £100 from the cash point, that's like $168. But I'll pay that back out of my first check.'

'Very good, very good,' quipped Carson, like a dad receiving another of his kid's 2-D crayon renditions of yellow-rayed sun and squiggle-grass hill. 'Melissa, at reception, takes care of all that. Send her your receipts.'

'Yes, of course. And I'll open a bank account tomorrow.'

But I didn't open an account in the morning, though I tried to, first thing. At Clydesdale Bank, they wanted a permanent address, which I didn't have. The hotel's could not be used temporarily until I got an apartment – a flat. They needed some proof of residence, such as a gas bill. Nor would they convert and cash my Plunkett check from dollars. That had to be deposited and mailed back to Chicago for clearance, then the funds would be 'redeemable'. 'And that,' the man told me, in a tone evidently universal to bank tellers of all nations – one of cold, insincere apology – 'takes seven to ten banking days.' By which he meant business days, I gathered. Equally perfunctory was his head-tilting sympathy to my predicament when I reiterated it to him.

'Do you mean to tell me I can't cash a check without an account, and I can't open an account without an address, when I can't get an address without some money?'

'For security reasons, Mr Podgorski, we are unable to –'

'Fine!' I swept up my papers and stormed out. In the queue, heads turned, eyes gawking politely. 'What are you looking at?' I barked.

I had not yet had my coffee.

That was all the progress I made towards establishing myself as a Glaswegian until Monday. The rest of the day was a wash-out. I bought a *Herald*, whittling into my cash supply, took it up to my hotel room and made calls on apartment ads, which were called neither apartments nor ads. Rather, most of the listings were bedsits – in American English, *studios* or *efficiencies* – and the section of the paper was headed *adverts*. Regardless, I didn't speak to a single soul, got either no answers or machines, and a few mobile numbers which when called were dead or mobile voicemails. Frustrated, I futilely stewed the rest of the day, lying on the bed watching TV and picking through a plate of room-service fish, chips, and peas.

In the evening, a few calls were returned. When the first one came in, patched through from the front desk, I grappled with my shoes and coat while the man told me about the place, thinking I could be out of the hotel yet tonight, I would just go see the place and, if it was okay, I'd put money down somehow and take it.

What money, I didn't know, maybe I could show the landlord the Plunkett's stipend, tell him my story, and he'd let it slide, take my word for it until Monday, hold some collateral or something.

'It's a one-bedroom flat,' he said. 'Security entrance, en suite shower, cooker, fridge, microwave, electric panel heating . . .'

'Yes, yes. Okay.' I rushed him through, grappling with my high-school French for a memory of the term *en suite*.

'The rent is £425 per month, council tax not included. That can be paid in cash, of course, as well as cheque. Or we can do a direct-debit scheme.'

'Fine, fine. Where is it, please?'

'It's near the Sainsbury's on Dumbarton. You know where thah is?'

'Sure.' I didn't, but I had my map. 'Can I take a look at it, please?'

'Aye. Do you wanny come round for a chat, say, on Mondee?'

'Monday?'

'Aye. Or we could do, let's see . . . Thursdee.'

I nearly dropped the phone. A chat? On Monday? If I'd wanted a chat I'd have called one of these 0891 numbers I'd seen stickers for in phone booths, the UK's equivalent to America's 976 numbers. Lonely ladies were waiting to speak to me – how did they know where I'd gone? And as for Monday, Monday was no good if I was going out on Tuesday with Nicole and wanted a place to be moved into by then, have cleaned up, unpacked into, a place we could perhaps come back to after Curler's.

Whether this sluggish pace was stereotypical British formality, where everything was done 'properly', I couldn't say. Or whether it was Scottish lackadaisicality, something rustic and vaguely spiritual, having to do with the mystics of simplicity, that ethereal appeal you find in Celtic jewelry and song. Or whether this was Glasgow talking, some post-industrial whiplash that had ingrained a hopelessness so deep that there was no point in rushing to disappointment.

Saturday I spent in front of the tube watching sports I didn't realize were played professionally. Lawn bowling, an indoor tournament live from the Kelvingrove SECC (whatever that was – Scotland's Entertainment Complex and . . . Community Center? I had plenty of time to wonder), where barrel-chested, dog-jowled men in white pants and pastel polos rolled balls down a lane with dire seriousness. The spectators in the packed grandstand oohed and ahhed as every bowl crept at a turtle's pace towards the others, slowly arced, and at last tipped onto its flattened side. I was reluctantly captivated. It was like a visually administered sedative. When the announcer said *We've goh an exciting match here, folks*, I laughed aloud.

I was alone, watching TV, drinking coffee, but at least I was laughing.

Darts followed, a barroom game legitimized, ennobled by broadcast. This was a game I had played in the unfinished basements of my grade-school friends' houses, the prime objective being simply to hit the board – and even that was a loose guideline, given the destructive appeal of stabbing one in the plywood wall. Here, an emcee in a tuxedo called the scores down from 501 to zero with fatalistic wonder, as if announcing the distance of an approaching comet. The telecast had production values that shamed the Super Bowl. There was a decorated platform, colored lights, sponsors, technicians, cameramen, a producer making split screens and star wipes – the board, a player's concentrated face, a rapt crowd. For darts! It was surreal.

Bad movies came on at night just like they do at home and probably anywhere else, and I laid propped against headboard and pillows atop the bedcovers, in jeans and bare feet, half listening to the actors reciting lines, half waiting for an inkling of sleepiness to arrive that would bring the moment when I could close my eyes and pull Sunday – and thus Monday – a little closer. At eleven I finally sipped down part of the Famous Grouse and Schweppes from the mini bar, and by midnight I was asleep. But at three, a nightmare awakened me. It was a variation on a recurrent dream, in which I stood at the side of an endless desert road, dusty and wind-blown, prickly cacti, sagebrush and open sky all around me. I stood alone, no one for miles. My ex, Margaret, was there in spirit, entreating me to go home but herself unreachable. This time, though, something was fundamentally different, and when I sat up and tried to grasp it, the thread snapped. It reeled in like a tape measure with whiplike ferocity and coiled into secrecy, leaving me only the silent, still reality of the hotel room. I sat a moment, taking deep breaths, then heard laughter and singing from the street below. I went to the window.

From the tenth story I couldn't see to the pavement, but voices rose up, drunken singing, accented by the *clop*, *clops* of high heels on pavement, echoing up the tall buildings, the waltzy song falling in and out of unison.

> *Oh, flower of Scotland . . .*
> *when will we see . . .*
> *your likes again?*

Back in bed, I fretted over what I would tell Nicole about Margaret and how I would tell it to her – and I must have exhausted all scenarios, or the scenarios exhausted me.

5 *The First Report*

I secured the flat on Monday, though the landlord was late and dallied around the rooms pointing out every light switch and giving me a full course in the nuances of the radiators, how to heat the bricks inside overnight and let the heat out during the day. Mr McScobie, pinching a cigarette between two nut-brown fingers, heard me out, the story of my financial woes, and surprisingly took some sympathy with the monetary black hole I was in at the moment.

'It's a bih out of order,' he said, 'but okee.' He agreed to accept £200 as a deposit that day, with the first month's rent to be paid by the end of the week. So after a walk back to the bank and a long wait in line, I got the £200 on a cash advance off the Citibank, met him again at 'half two', after he'd had his lunch, and got the keys. Then I took the tube back to the Hilton and took a taxi back to the flat, dragging my suitcases and bags in the rain. By then my work time was seriously encroached upon. Well, it was shot in the foot, to be honest. But determined not to undermine my credibility and start any bad habits, after hanging my clothes in the wardrobe and folding my socks in the drawers and dumping my shaving kit on the tub ledge, I walked down the lane to Byres Road, the West End strip, wolfed down a kebab from the nearest cart and set out for a few coffee stops with a folder of 27Gs. It was here, close to home, on this long, wide avenue, a street with an off-campus feel, without an ivy-strewn wall in sight, that I entered my first Glasgow coffee-house and found that nothing was as I expected.

I had thought my day-to-day work would largely be a matter of comparisons. I had thought there would be an existing coffee-house chain, an establishment which would serve as the rule of thumb by which to measure up the competition – or the prospective competition anyway – for Plunkett's unnamed client. A place where I would go in and observe, take notes, blend into the crowd and assess the basic structures of the market. What kind of hours did they keep? How much seating space was there? What style for decor? Were beverage emporiums in Scotland pitched on themes, slogans, mascots and corporate logos à la Caribou, the American franchise, who had somehow linked their product with the image of an antlered woodland animal frozen in mid-leap? Or was irreverence in fashion? Were there any precedents, companies or individuals who had set up shop and gone under? Anyone whose mistakes could be learned from? Of course, the main thing was prices – what were they charging for a small house blend, or a Kenya AA, Colombian or Hazelnut? What about cup sizes? Eight-, twelve-, sixteen-, twenty-ounce? Probably no manager would hand out quotes on the price of a 20lb. bag of unroasted beans including British tariffs and VAT. For those, I would have to hit the library for some almanac of economic indicators, hunt some supply distributors, an import/export company or whatever, do a little leg work. Then from that I could make a per-unit price index, calculate margins. That part I understood, that some of the nuts and bolts would have to be gathered elsewhere, and I was prepared to do it. I took the position grateful and willing to face the challenge. Yet I thought certain key factors could be gathered in the shop. The proof is in the pudding, as Mr P. would say. The culture of the place, the rituals, traditions, ambiance, attitude. On this point I felt the most confident in my ability, for it was something I had come to understand and even value in my years as an American consumer, and had recognized when I saw it in print, raised to the level of importance by being in bold, in the Plunkett briefing materials: **The Retail Environment**. You can have top-of-the-line goods, cut-throat prices, and demand up the wazzoo, but you'll never turn a profit if the buying process is not easy, and pleasant, pleasant, pleasant.

These were some of the basics I had intended to quantify: what is typical to the region, to Glasgow. I would wait in the same pre-work-rush line, be treated with the same level of customer service – that golden American hallmark – hold the same material cup (what do they use here, Styrofoam? wax paper? cardboard? plastic?), fiddle with the same lids, sugar packets, milk, cream, half and half dispensers, napkins, stir sticks, and sit at the same tables (clean? unclean? sturdy? requiring alteration by stuffing napkins or a folded-up section of newspaper under the short leg?). These were the fundamentals I was prepared to scout as part of the initial rounds, which I thought would make a foundation for my reports, yield something immediately recognizable once I plugged my findings into the business-term translator, something like, *Demand here is higher than the supply. Average wait time is six minutes. Lattes and cappuccinos are popular among the business classes, but novelty beverages comprise less than 5% of sales. Early projections suggest a viable market for X and Z, but not Y. Service is faster/slower. Product is served hotter/colder. Product is more/less flavorful than that of, say, Burback's, for example.*

These were the preconceptions I started with. What I found was that there was no basis for comparison. My imagined rule-of-thumb establishment did not exist and my whole proposed plan of attack was thrown seriously out of whack.

I found a little place called La Scala a block up from Dumbarton, around the corner on Byres Road. Close to home. It stank of fried foods, a smell that wafted in from the neighboring fish and chip shop, relentless, overpowering, rendering fruitless any attempt to savor the aroma of the beans. That should be an integral part of the coffee experience – the nose – as much as it is with wine, but here it wasn't even an option. The sandwich board outside had advertised tea and coffee, fresh filled rolls and snacks. What I found was a deli case displaying a few strange sandwiches: cheese and pickle, chicken tiki (looked like urine-soaked chicken), and bacon and mango chutney. A few pastries, mince pies, one browning pine-apple tart. These were not too unlike the snacks you expect to find in a café, but their visual unappealingness was amplified by the dense stench of boiling oil – and beer: that odor was always in the air throughout the West End. There were Twinings tea boxes on the counter, a tin of Cadbury's hot chocolate on the shelf and sodas in the cooler. Finally, I spotted in the lower corner of the menu board, as if an afterthought, as if a reluctant inclusion, listings for coffee. Small 85p, Large £1.30.

'Do you have different roasts?' I asked.

Behind the counter was a young boy of seventeen or so in student clothes, hair gelled in a dozen different directions, a silver stud in his eyebrow. 'Roasts of wha'?' he said, rocking slightly to the beat of the in-house techno.

'For coffee.'

'It's just regular.'

'Just regular?'

'Ri'.'

'I'll have a large coffee then.'

'Whi'e or black?'

'Sorry?' I'd already learned that using the flippy R's removed the barrier between myself and the Scots, though I did it only mildly. It was effortless, natural even. Such affable people, you couldn't help wanting to liken yourself to them.

'D'you wannit whi'e or black?'

'White.'

White coffee, it turned out, taking the last open seat and eagerly taking a sip, is coffee infused with steamed milk. *Tons* of steamed milk. I put the ratio at 65/35, milk with the win. Finding the coffee flavor under the froth was like getting a rabbit out of a cage. Most pronounced on the tongue was the tinge of sourness you get from hot 'cow juice', Margaret's term for milk. The weak extraction was evident too in the caffeine effects. A decent *cuppa* should get all the gears cranking. By the last swallow of a satisfying brew I should feel compelled in some way I hadn't been before. Compelled to move, perhaps, as in a domestic situation to scrub dishes or load laundry. If at work, my fingers ought to itch to type, click, file and phone. In a hangover scenario, suicidal urges should be minimized, perhaps even a glimmer of encouragement arriving, if only the welcome nudge towards a bowel movement. And if the drink is not physically revitalizing, it would qualify to put the mind into a whir of the sort involved in serious thinking, problem solving, or introspection. If not inciting action perhaps escalating the synaptic tachometer to a speed that keeps pace with the snappy dialogue of a Woody Allen classic, or stirring enough mental wind to sail Coppola's narrative great lake, *Apocalypse Now*. What I was getting from this sample was steamed milk and virtually no jolt factor. As far as brain machinery was concerned, resuscitation, cognitive fuel, this La Scala cup was akin to a single crank on a dusty, cobwebbed Victrola.

I crunched some numbers for the stat sheet. The serving I estimated to be about ten ounces. It was a sizable mug, neither a Hilton tea cup, nor the two-fister common at home. But the mix being half milk, there honestly was no more than five ounces of coffee in the cup. Now, an average cup of American coffee might fall around $1, not Manhattan ultrahip high-octane Versace stuff but not Texas truck-stop sludge either. And the smallest cup you could expect to find anywhere in America, where bigger is better, would be twelve ounces easily. That's about 9 cents an ounce. Now, I had five ounces here for £1.30 – in dollars, $2.21, the pound holding somewhere between 1.68 and 1.71. So $2.21 for five ounces of coffee is, on a per-ounce basis, – scribble on a napkin – over *five times* as much as in the States. Line 9 on La Scala's 27G got a rating of 1 on the 1-to-5 scale for 'Product Value', the scale that ran

POOR   OKAY   GOOD   VERY GOOD   EXCELLENT.

The remainder of the form I completed scathingly and with regret, since I was obliged to be honest. La Scala seemed to be a local favorite. All the seating was taken – about a dozen people, including a few standing at a chest-high counter. Lots of book bags and cigarettes, blue smoke filling the globes of the track lighting. I rated Cleanliness and Ambiance more favorably, though they lost a few notches under Service, due to the boy who hadn't explained or amended my question about roasts, and who now had a line, a *queue*, four people deep backed up as he poured water on one tea bag at a time and rang them up with the muddled caution of the stoned under scrutiny.

I chose the next place as randomly as I could, and tried to impersonate a less deliberate customer, someone just casually looking for a coffee. I attempted to wipe clean my mental slate of expectations. But I knew also, trotting along Byres Road that night past the empty newsagents', the pubs with Dickens-era woodwork and the closed florists', vegetable stands and fishmongers' – iced flounders gazing dead-eyed out of the window – that I would be trying them all eventually. Enough time to size up coffee culture in this city: it was almost too good to be true.

Before calling it a night I stopped into virtually the only place open that wasn't a bar serving just drinks or a restaurant serving sit-down meals to night owls. I had had a pleasant amble, from one end of Byres Road to the other. I saw the night-lit dome of the greenhouse in the Botanic Gardens, then turned around. Down the hill I sauntered. In the southern sky, the four-pronged university tower reached into view above chimneyed roofs. Near the Hillhead tube stop I spotted Curler's, Nicole's pub, pleased to gather from the sign showing a gaggle of men sliding those handled orbs across ice as they do in the Olympics that it was not, as I'd envisioned, an effeminate hair-salon-themed bar. Curling, of course. Winter's answer to lawn bowling. Countless other pubs populated Byres Road; I passed them by. At the bottom of the hill I read a plaque on some old stone arches framing iron gates. It was the former entrance to the Western Infirmary, from the days when it was a teaching hospital. On the final stretch before Byres ended at a T, the cranes of the Clydeside shipbuilders were visible in silhouette on the horizon like skeletal necks of Brontosauri. There I found a place called The Living Room. I entered, as if on a wind, buoyed by hope. The interior impressed me: wrought iron and light oak carved roundly into wave-like forms; an ornate candelabra on the wall imitated a peacock's massive plume, holding waterfalls of white candlewax and flickering flames on curved arms. Low leather couches; spacious, moody; the sounds of Hammond organ riffs, baritone sax and feathered cymbals softly from a discreet source. Wood floors, black ceilings – opium-den stuff, fantastic ambiance. There were two rooms, one with a small bar in the corner having the tasteful simplicity of only two draught taps and a dozen upside-down magnums mirrored behind; the other serving non-alcoholic beverages; single smokes for sale, 5p out of a jar; almond/cherry biscotti – all the usual stuff. On the chalkboard were offered Light, Medium and Dark roasts and I spotted a machine with an auto grinder attachment on top, real beans inside, the glass funnel slick with oils. Iced coffee and cappuccinos too. Glee stirred in my sternum. My mouth watered. I ordered a large dark, anticipated the offer of white or black and got none – a public carton of semi-skimmed and diner-style sugar shaker by the register. The people in there were friendly, some folks I sat near said hello and moved coats, carried on their conversation unchecked. I clutched my pint glass of coffee – an excellent quantity – just to warm my hands. With great anticipation and hope I raised it to my lips.

The verdict: weak. It was definitely from a quality bean, an Arabica, finely ground, but too watery. Way too watery. A fraction of the desired intensity. The maker was being chintzy. The proportions were grossly undershot.

6 Curler's

Tuesday night I waited outside Curler's, as we had arranged by phone. Nicole approached from the underground station, making steady time on her crutches. I walked towards her. 'Still wrapped?' I said. 'How's it doing?' She said it was okay but a bruise had appeared under the skin, now at the yellow-purple stage. 'Looks mingin',' she said.

Inside the pub, we bypassed the ground floor, where horse racing played on a corner-mounted TV and pensioners in bonnets did pull-tabs among the putrefactive tang of cigar smoke. We took a booth upstairs. Nicole took off her coat, revealing a sleeveless sky-blue dress. One, I was flabbergasted. I told her she looked great, and she thanked me, her alabaster face flushing. Two, I was put at ease for having worn a button-down shirt and my wingtips. I tucked her chair under her and nearly tripped over my own feet getting to the nearby coat rack.

There was a bar across the room that I made a trip to, and lots of other people – I think a band's equipment was laid out on a small stage. I can't say I took much notice.

Over a jar of Tennents 70 Shilling and a vodka lemonade, she told me that she was a student at the Glasgow School of Art, in her second year, and that was where she had met Ruaridh, the guy on the roof, the unofficial godfather of the Scottish sect of EarthFirst!, a US-born environmental group with branches growing in Europe. Over the years, Ruaridh had campaigned around campus, vigilantly rounding up troops, hiring transit vans and driving around the country to protests, chaining himself to trees and cranes and bulldozers and encouraging others to do so as well.

'He's made himself known, thah's fer sure. Was on TV and in the papers and all for the Twyford Down protest. Tha' was the M3 motorway. Tha's the only one that actually got stopped. Och, he's no Robin Hood buh – comes from Bearsden, folks are minted. He's goh a flat on Sauchiehall Street and everythin'. He's been at Uni five years now. No matter. His da'll foot the bill for another year of courses. The school's noh about to chuck him out. His grants have run out, so they're fillin' their coffers, ri' enough.'

His dad, Nicole explained, was the director of a bank in Edinburgh and held the *Daily Mirror*'s ranking of fifty-fifth richest person in the UK. This gave him a comprehension of big money, its power and sway, that the average tree-hugger lacked. At Oxleas Wood a few years back, Ruaridh had brought such large crowds outside the City Chambers that the cost of security during the period of contract negotiation had reached £2 million, which the councils refused to pay, so the first bidder pulled out. That put construction back a few months and alerted everyone that these grassroots groups were not all the disorganized, savvy-less whiners that the media and Tories made them out to be. It got them on the front pages and got other groups believing their fights could be worth the time and effort. It even got them thinking they might get the result they hoped for: affecting change.

When the World Wildlife Fund for Nature backed the anti-M77 demonstrations, the issue took on larger than local proportions. Ruaridh's recruitment numbers soared, with even more first-timers. These included Nicole, who, until then, had been resistant to his recruiting tactics. Brandishing a megaphone outside the doors of the Mackintosh building, the center of the GSA campus, Ruaridh had attacked the artistic credibility of his fellow students, denouncing them by name as weak and bourgeois. Ruaridh and Nicole had had a few courses together, life drawing and sculpture, but he had always put her off with his posh clothes and long hair. They had mingled at various shows, at the campus pub and at parties, but always from across the gulf separating their social and artistic cliques. Finally, they were assigned as partners for a design project, required to spend time together outside the studio.

'He's a good artist, ri' enough,' Nicole added. 'Just a wee bit angry to get an exhibition. Misanthropic. The galleries tend to go for the accessible, life-affirming stuff. Anyway, we were workin' at

his flat one ni', and when we finished stopped off for a pint. Well
. . . we had a snog, nothin' serious like.'

'A snog?' I asked.

'Aye. Do you no' say that?'

'Whatever it is, no.'

'Just means kissin' and stuff. You know. But *noh* a shag.'

'I see.'

Nicole blushed. 'What do you call it?'

'Making out. Necking. Well, I guess "necking" is a little dated.
Getting busy. Very immature terms,' I said, trying to distance
myself from my own imagination, which pictured Nicole in a
passionate embrace.

'Never mind – Ah was pissed, havin' a laugh. But, you know,
things went along for a wee while. He was away a loh, buh there'd
be weeks we were together, happy. Stayin' in, makin' curries,
watchin' videos with a couple bottles of wine.'

'You mean watching *a couple videos* with *a* bottle of wine?'

'Wha'? No. Anyway, he can be dead sweet, he can. Och, Ah
dohn know. Ah think – Ah mean, Ah *thought* he should juz concentrate on his art, get his degree sorted. Buh he wouldnay have it
from me. Then the M77 thing turned up, like.'

I was impressed with Nicole's forthrightness. There was none
of the secrecy and duplicity that had plagued and often outright
blocked lines of communication with people in my life – namely,
the Podgorskis. She was open, honest and seemed mature for her
age. She was so frank, I was made squeamish, both frightened and
captivated by her candor. When I looked at her, I thought of my
aunts and uncles and their half-hearted well-wishing, their family
letters, so rife with gloss. To engage Nicole's stare was to refute
my family's assessment of me as a tourist – a stranger headed to a
strange land, a bumbler on the way to his next bumble. I mean,
look how competent she was, and I had her trust already. Her
kindheartedness was a crutch to my ego – like her crutches leaning
against the table, whose foam handles I occasionally pressed my
finger into, fidgeting. I enjoyed how she enjoyed herself, most
importantly how she could admit her shortcomings and laughed at

them over a drink. Several drinks, in fact, which I made trips to the bar for, running a tab on the Citibank, as I was again cashless, having maxed the advance limit on the Plunkett CBV on the flat deposit.

The pub filled up, and the band Nicole had mentioned came on later, the JazzWegians, horn players in tartan vests and bowties, a portly woman crooning standards like 'Down by the Riverside' and flinging her feather boa in the faces of the men seated stage-side. Nicole rolled her own cigarettes from a tin of Old Holborn and smoked unselfconsciously, relighting when her talk left one ignored and extinguished. We were in our own little corner of oblivion. The server came around and collected our empties, swapped ashtrays. We didn't miss a beat, though, locked in conversation, leaning into each other, sometimes too close to focus, directing mouths near ears and conversing on a direct and private auditory plane that ducked the amplifiers' blares and trumpets' toots. We were huddled in, and my knee often touched her outstretched leg, which was propped on a chair; I would rest mine against hers under the table, our eyes unflinching, acknowledging the contact by a winkless wink that said, *Okay, cool.* A mere flicker that, judging from my pulse, was like a 200z espresso-hypodermic straight in the vein.

The M77 thing that had led to Nicole falling on me had started back in 1939, when a wealthy Scottish landowner, Sir John Maxwell, had given to the people of Glasgow a large piece of undeveloped land on the south side of the city on the condition that it remain so – undeveloped. It was only a half-dozen square miles or so of grass and woods, but such a thing was rare then in the congestion of post-industrial Glasgow, and even rarer now as urban sprawl gobbled up the Clyde Valley. Pollok Park was named after the nearby district of Pollokshields – nothing to do with the splashy painter – and remained a refuge of greenery in the city throughout the twentieth century. Among its frequenters were birdwatchers (sparrowhawks were the big ornithological treat), deer-spotters, horticulturists and pram-pushers. It acquired gravel paths, then paved walkways, then jungle gyms and swings, statues and fountains. Strathclyde District put money into it over the years when residents complained that it was falling into disuse. As high-rise tenements – *council flats* – went up, it became even more precious. 'It is noh central,' Nicole told me, 'like London's Hyde Park. There's noh even a tube stop nearby. It's a short ride on the train towards Ayr – tha's why some folk call the M77 the Ayr Road Route. Still, motorways in the fifties were built around the park. The agreement was kept.'

She leaned back, sucked a vodka-lemonade dry, and dragged on her fag as if in satisfied reflection of this. Then she fell forward again, her bare arms in front of her. 'There was a proposal in '65,' she continued, 'to upgrade the roads to Bridgeton, Shawfield, Polmadie. It was booted. "Cannay do it. The Maxwell agreement." It was all for naught, tho', cuz then somethin' changed. The father died, and one of the daughters, Mary, I think it was, gave the house and the estate to the city of Glasgow. That was the late sixties. Within twenty years, they cashed in, sellin' the land to Strathclyde Region. The first thin' they did was to get a waiver from the National Trust, permission to build on it like, no problem. On it, through, over, under, however they fancied. 1988, Ah think it was, they puh in their first plans.'

The band slowed things down with a bluesy rendition of 'Amazing Grace'. Nicole explained that there was a long spell of public debate, speculation about cost and the usual party lines about where transport monies should be spent. Politics played a part as well – a re-election or an under-the-table handshake with a contractor. 'People were outraged; all these groups formed. Star Alliance, Scottish Wildlife Trust, Friends of the Earth Scotland, Glasgow for People. And with the pressure they put on, Glasgow District Council gave the roadworks the slam,' she explained. 'The reason on record was tha' the expansion wasnay needed, though they mighta thought it wasnay quite *ri'* in some way. Even the worst of that lot has a conscience.'

I must have glanced away or fidgeted or otherwise seemed disinterested. 'Ah'm sorry,' she said, 'I'm bletherin'.' She was very much attuned to slight gestures, the meanings in brief silences.

Margaret had acted like she could read minds, often saying she knew something was wrong or insisting that I was mad even when I wasn't. Presumptive women made me wary, but Nicole was right: I was uneasy, distracted. I had a bad association with that old funeral hymn 'Amazing Grace'.

'Wha' about you, Mel? You a political person?'

'Not really. I mean, as much as I'm an underwater basket-weaver when I'm weaving baskets underwater.'

She laughed. 'Wha' are you on abou'?'

'Famous American expression. Never heard it? It's right up there with *The only thing we have to beer is beer itself*. No, I don't know. I suffer from spells of irreverence. And irrelevance. It's like Tourette's, only nonsense instead of swearwords.'

Nicole cocked a skeptical eyebrow at me while upturning the last of a drink.

'Seriously, though. It's oddly comforting to hear there're the same sort of problems here that we have at home. Alaska, for example. It's protected, for the most part, but if the right people can turn over the right legislation, they'll have it tapped for oil faster than you can say *Exxon Valdez*. So what compelled this daughter to give away the family legacy, this estate?'

'Spite, some say. A family rift. Maybe the domineering father.'

'Uh-huh. And if the M77 has the go-ahead, why the protest last week? Just to put a thorn in someone's side? Running up someone's security bill?'

'Aye.'

'But I didn't see any security.'

'That's down to Ruaridh's brilliant leadership.' Another inverted Briticism. An American onus is *up to you*, in the UK it's *down*. 'See, Wimpy is a construction company, one of them that are submitting tenders on the project.'

'Sorry, *tenders*? That's not in my travel book.'

'Tenders. Proposals. Bids. See, when the roadworks was okayed Ruaridh was down at City Chambers with Friends of the Earth and some other folk. The councils were gonny allow some people in to join the dialogue – a totally superficial number, noh enough to swing any votes buh. This tosser got intay the chamber room, ontay the floor and started shoutin' and raisin' a kerfuffle. Threw all their chances of representation out the winday. Conservatives jumped on that one, sayin', "This deviant posed a threat of violence." Said he might've flung shite around, might've had a bomb. They blew it all out of proportion. Nothin' new there. Ri' enough, next day all the papers say' – Nicole made a line in the air with a C-shaped hand, the universal gesture for headline – '"Bomb Threat Over M77".'

I shook my head disbelievingly, my mouth being occupied with the draining of a pint glass.

'Mind you, the nutter actually wasnay Ruaridh this time, buh an Aussie bloke taggin' along with Star Alliance. No affiliation. Some loose marble. Doesnay matter though. Since then, Ruaridh's recruits have dried up. Cannay get anyone tay come along, 'cept them diehards who wannay bomb parliament anyway. You start talkin' about bombs, and the SNP nationalists come outtay the woodwork.'

The band had resumed with upbeat Dixieland, which, by the way, was quite authentic. Eyes closed, I never would have pegged them for a Scottish band. But they were ruthlessly loud, with bleating clarinet and splashing cymbals. By now, Nicole was nearly shouting straight into my ear, and I had to pull back to meet her gunmetal-grey eyes, had to angle my ear to her mouth while I drank. Now she sat up and back a moment, repositioning her foot, checking on it, just touching it for habitual reassurance, like you would a jacket you'd folded onto your seat in a dark theater. I asked her was it all right; and she said never better. She tucked her fine black hair behind her ears, stabbed at the lemon wedge in her drink with the straw and leaned towards me again.

'Sorry, I'm bletherin' like mad. To answer yer question – so last week Wimpy looked to be the highest bidder. £52 million. Friends of the Earth put out a statement sayin' they had nothin' tay do with this nutter at the City Chambers and would still fight the M77 by non-violent means. Direct action, they call it.'

'Direct action? What's that mean?'

'Well, the idear was tay raise a fuss at the builders. Kill-the-messenger-type thing. Only they planted a false lead in *The Independent*, saying Wimpy Construction of Blythswood Street had the bid.'

'How was that a false lead? Another company won it?'

'No, Blythswood Street are the offices for the home-building division. Where we were was –'

'Bath Street.'

'Aye, Bath Street! Well done. See, yer at home already. No, buh it was the wrong site, like. All the while we were carryin' on, the Road Works division in town, on *Buchanan* Street, was draftin' up a proposal in peace and quiet.'

'Holy shit.'

Nicole upturned her drink. I did the same.

'They didn't know?' I continued. 'Ruaridh didn't know?'

'Noh a clue.'

'How'd you find that out?'

'Ruaridh told me. Ah talked to him over the weekend. Wimpy sent a cheeky letter to Friends of the Earth.'

'Hm.' I leaned back.

'He phoned me. He was phonin' me all weekend.'

'I see.'

'He's put off, ri' enough. Ah did bugger off our date, after all.'

'You had a date with him?' The walls of the bar, the other tables and their occupants, the bandstand and the feather-boa-flinging songstress: their forms all bent and curved as in a fisheye lens. The aperture of my attention shrunk; my depth of field retreated, my perspective warped by this information.

'Aye, the Wimpy thing. Tha' was his idear of a date. Wimpy was supposed to be some kind of reconnection, a coming together. We hadn't seen each other much, cuz Ah was always doin' muh art or workin' at The Corn Exchange. He wahned me tay protest more. He was always doin' my head in for eatin' sausage suppers and wearin' a leather belt. Fuck's sake, we were gonny get a flat the'gether. It was mad.'

I was fiddling with Nicole's cigarette lighter and, though I was listening closely, I only just drifted off a moment, feeling stung, not sure what to make of her involvement with this guy. Had the frankness that so drew me backfired in my face? Nicole was terribly kind, with not a drop of guile, seemingly incapable of manipulation. I thought it was a product of her Scottishness – but at this moment it pointed me back to Margaret. Margaret had been kind. So kind. So sweet once. But what? Had that changed, or had I? Maybe only my perception had changed – of her, of myself? It was soupy. That instant I wished I knew. Without knowing, how could I begrudge Nicole her continued involvement with Ruaridh? I had no right to let it hurt me; I hadn't said a word about Margaret. It was a subject that would have to come up later if not sooner, though even the thought made my blood vessels constrict.

I was not leaning forward now, and must have looked a little glazed to Nicole.

'Ah probably seem like a nutter to you,' she said. 'Last week Ah was climbin' roofs for this bloke and cryin' muh eyes out to people Ah'd juz met. You, Ah mean. Buh Ah had a good think sittin' round with ma foot up. And ma roomies Sophie and Deb stayed up fer a chat and a bevvie – they totally agree. He's a nice bloke, ri' enough, buh he's noh worth it. He was tryin' tay make me intay somethin' Ah'm noh. Look wha' ha'ened – he wants tay test how Ah feel fer him by takin' me to this big protest and Ah fuckin' bugger my foot, and it's noh even the ri' buildin'! Ah mean, that says it all. It's just noh meant tay be. There's other fish in the sea.'

'Other fish in the sea?' I repeated, contemplatively. The sportscaster, pushing the mike back under the victor's chin. *Can you expand on that?*

'Aye, and the sea,' she said, 'is a big place.' She looked me squarely in the eye, unwavering. I felt enveloped by a sea. I swelled like a sea. Melting with delight (and lager), I nearly emptied the sea in my bladder.

'Indeed,' I managed to say. 'Seventy-five percent of the world is ocean.'

'So it is,' she answered. We understood each other, and she shifted gears, while shifting in her seat, picking up her Holburn and a Rizla paper. 'Ah ought to ha' read my horoscope is wha' Ah shoulday done.'

'Oh? You think that would've helped?'

'Ah'll bet there was somethin' abou' it. Ah should look at an old paper at the library. Wha' was it? Thursday last? Ah'll bet there was.'

'Like what? "Family problem comes into focus. An old friend teaches a valuable lesson. And, by the way, if you're trying to keep a romance alive by protesting a highway construction, don't bother, because Mercury is descending and you'll sprain your ankle and fall on this American guy – though he could be cool to hang out with, so it's your call"?'

She laughed, pursed her lips coyly at me.

'Nicole, I hate to break it to you, but they're usually not that specific.'

'No, seriously buh, mine are dead on.'

'They're so general, there's bound to be some truth in 'em.'

'No, Mel, it's true! This one time when my folks were gettin' divorced, it was spot on! Ah was at this totally fucked stage, tryin' to decide who tay live with, my mum or da.'

'Living with mom and dad? I wouldn't know about that. What did it say?'

'I don't remember now. Tha' was ages ago, buh it made clear ma mum was never gonny change.'

'Uh-huh,' I joked, patronizingly.

'No, really, and it's noh been the only time. Never mind, Nirvana. Mind refillin' this?'

'Not at all.' I tended nature's call and got us fresh drinks, which at this point required navigating through what I thought was a fairly large crowd in the main room for a Tuesday night, even trickier given the impaired state of my motor skills.

'So, wha' do ye do, Mel?' was the question Nicole put to me with marked unselfishness when I returned to our booth. The barman had been to the table and taken away the empties and cleaned the ashtray, a newly rolled smoke was in Nicole's fingers, and her slim lips shone with a fresh coat of gloss. It would have seemed apt if a bell had rung and a woman in heels had strode by holding a ROUND 2 sign. Nicole had spilled her guts, and now I had to spill mine.

'What do *I* do?' I repeated, a sarcastically grandiose stall.

'Aye, wha' this job like?'

What could I do but give her the whole nine yards, as my dad would say, he being a fan of colloquialisms. I told her about Plunkett hiring me for a special project of market research. How they had a client in the beverage industry who was prospecting, feeling out the UK, maybe setting up shop. How they'd started with me, their man in Glasgow, and Klang down in London. How it is my job for the next ten weeks to frequent various and sundry establishments and analyze my findings in terms of profit margins, product placement, brand loyalty and so on. There was a lapse in my monologue as I grappled for recollection of some textbook terms, but I was able to smooth it over by taking a casual drink at an opportune moment, and went on to say that so far I found the work very rewarding, if not all that rigorous.

'Lemme get this sorted,' Nicole countered, with narrowed eyes. 'Yer gettin' paid tay go round drinkin' coffees all day?'

'It's not that simple –'

'You bastard!' she laughed.

'What?'

'You said you *worked* here.'

'I *do*, Nicole.'

'That's noh a proper job. Tha's pure Mickey Mouse shite!'

'What about you? Painting pictures is hardly what I call slave labor.'

'Fuck off,' she laughed. 'First off, it's sculpture I do mostly. Mixed media. Second, Ah'm a barmaid as well, and it's bloody naff. Wha' a thankless job! Listen buh, Ah'm only havin' you on. It sounds dead hard, like.'

'To be honest, it's not so tough. But it is work I believe in. It might even be my calling.'

She asked what part of the States I came from; I dispelled her belief that the mob ran Chicago.

'What else has it got, Chicago? Isn't that where they make loads of steel?'

'That's Pittsburgh.'

'Ri'. The Bulls, though, they're Chicago. Ah've seen that on the telly and hats and stuff. Chicago Bulls.'

'Michael Jordan.'

'Sure, we get him over here. See, Ah'm noh totally ignorant.'

'I never said you were.'

As the band came back from a set break, launching into 'Smoke Gets in Your Eyes', she told me she'd always wanted to see the States, had a friend who did an exchange over in Boston for a wee while. And her half-brother had taken his bairns to Florida, which led to me asking what 'bairns' meant, learning it meant kids, apologizing for always asking what she was saying and to repeat herself, her saying no, it was okay, sympathizing, saying it must be hard sussing out the accent, me adding not to mention the vocabulary, her admitting the Scots talked fast in the first place and noting that the Glasgow accent is particularly broad, as everyone knows, me saying yes, of course, it's just not something they prepare you for, or that I never really thought of. Nicole appeased me, saying, don't worry, you'll get used to it – this leading to conversation about what part of Scotland she was from, me learning she was from the east coast, several places in fact, that her family had started out in a place called Berwick-Upon-Tweed, then Kilmarnock, as her dad got moved about for his work as a lorry driver, and then in Fife, north of Edinburgh, with her dad since the divorce, and now Glasgow for the last three years since she'd been at Uni, which she was eager to finish up this next year because she had a massive overdraft, which had to be clarified as being the equivalent of a bank loan, without the terms of a bank loan, more like a credit line attached to her savings account, me expressing surprise that banks would do that.

'Loads of folk have overdrafts,' Nicole said. 'Especially students.'

I remarked that in that sense things were the same all over –

leading to her asking what I had done for college, if anything, me entering a long story, prefaced with the fact that it was a long story and giving her the opportunity to decide on hearing it now if she wanted, a polite offer never intended to be taken up, but also providing a moment to get us more drinks, which were depleted, Nicole then insisting that she get them, saying I had bought enough, and saying she had to go to the loo anyhow, a Briticism I knew for once, and which made sense, because she had had about four or five tall V&Ls now. She hobbled as gracefully as could be expected, as I saw it, giving me a cheerful smile on her departure that shot like a laser through the bedlam of the place, the band, romping out 'Sweet Georgia Brown' now, the punters clapping, whooping, stomping feet. I leaned back and admired as she moved across the room on her crutches, eyeing even as little as a shoulder as she folded into the crowd, though certainly it wasn't her shoulder I had studied at first.

From the proximity of the corner booth, I endeavored to take a well-oiled mental break from the frame of mind I had been in since my arrival in Glasgow, being as I was preoccupied with getting a head start on my 27Gs and impressing Carson and deflating the preconceptions of the Podgorski clan, whose members all but said *Bon voyage* while snickering under their breath, which was to say that I suspected whatever blessings they had bestowed on me and my fortunes were with reservations to say the least. And as I sat bolt upright, at my sitting tallest, inflated with pride, I felt a sensation strange and distantly remembered – then knew I was being watched. I turned and caught two guys standing by the entrance, looking at me, then looking away. They were holding their pints and coats, being neither in view of the band nor included in any conversation, looking forlorn at their lack of female companionship. It was an undeniable fact that not a single girl in the place was giving them the time of day. I figured then that the strange sensation was related to posture, this pose I had struck in the corner seat, which must have been outwardly confident and *cool*, having, as I did, the choicest booth, and being attended in company by one sultry, sharp-faced, long-haired art student in a clingy dress, who these two clowns had obviously just witnessed departing my table, while she had just emphasized to me in no uncertain terms her intentions to swim in the sea, my sea. She was a woman who, though slightly injured, remained still unquestionably the tastiest dish in Curler's, and in fact whose presence here in her hindered state could have been seen as a testament to a determination to spend time with me, despite setbacks. The pleasure, the satisfaction, should have been small, should have been familiar but, due to drought, instead quenched like a deluge. It was with egotistical pride that I allowed myself to ponder how, in light of my previous circumstances, things were reaching an *intriguing* level, as those who use understatement as a wink-wink, nudge-nudge kind of chauvinist boasting would say, and that all the other jammed intersections of my psyche were clearing up too. Green lights shone on Wounded Avenue, Heartbreak Street, Failure Boulevard, Disappointment Expressway, the distinctly non-American ambiance and people about me illuminating the simple and obvious fact that my troubles were 3,500 miles behind me. No reason was in sight to perpetuate this image and act the part of grief zombie over Margaret: this truth was abundantly clear in a glimpse of my surroundings, as unlikely as it was for me to have a lucid thought, being saturated with so much lager.

And drowned as I was in the overflow of good feeling, sensing the exorcism of my ghosts (however petty they were, they were ghosts nonetheless); all the images from my marriage that had haunted me as the tell-tale scenes of downfall with Margaret shrank, whereas before they were vast projections of cineplex magnitude. Flavors of foods eaten the night of a rancorous argument. Certain effects of wan evening light that were imprinted with sadness. The ailment of helplessness that takes hold when your lifelong love is determined to self-destruct. These perceptions, prior to now certainties, seemed to dislodge themselves from that capsule of intangible ooze that is a person's identity, shrivel into pods and spiral across the chamber of my mind, making room for

Nicole – all of it having a dizzying effect, my mouth drying, me draining my pint – and making me want to speak of it.

Nicole emerged from the area of Curler's where the Ladies was, and people tucked in their chairs ahead of her – drawing many eyes – as she made her way back to me. And my eyes followed her, too, as she slashed a hobbling path to the bar. I was blind with clarity: the thing was to open myself up to Nicole, to include her on my fresh start by demonstrating an emotional inclusiveness, a gesture of respect, unlike the whitewashing which described Margaret and I as 'having problems', the victims of chance and circumstance, as accidents having happened, and which couched my directionlessness in the terms 'occupational transitioning'. I wanted to tell her everything. I would leave nothing out, not the problems that plagued our marriage, and not my faults either. Each word would propel me further into a new mode of existence whose means of attaining had never been more obvious. Unexpected, yes, but happening here, in a place I couldn't have foreseen, and I felt unconquerable and so was led to conclude that a brilliant idea was to roll a smoke from Nicole's kit, which I did, poorly and sloppily, but successfully enough to smoke, and which went straight to my head, so that when Nicole appeared table-side, propping the crutches behind her chair, and the barman set down more drinks, which he had obviously carried for her, I put it out in dregs of lager, where it was extinguished with a *pssss!*

'For you, Mel,' she said, taking a seat. She slid towards me a short glass of amber liquid. 'For literally savin' my arse.'

'I'd like to do more than save it,' I muttered into my pint.

'Wha'?'

'I said, "I'd like to know what is it?"'

'A twenty-four-year-old Glenmorangie. *Uisge Beatha.*'

'*Ishky bah?*'

'Tha's Gaelic for whiskey. The water of life. Welcome to Glasgow.'

I raised my glass and smelled the drink: butter and wood and dark spices. I was pretty sure I wasn't seeing double yet, but a second glass passed under my nose. It was attached to Nicole's hand. She'd hooked her elbow inside mine, and brought herself near.

'Cheers, ma dears!' she hollered.

'Cheers!'

Down the hatch.

7   A Certain Amount of Prettifying or The Universal Tones of Commerce

The neighborhood where I secured a flat, on a street called Hyndland Circle, was called Partick. I had lived there two weeks before realizing it was not *Patrick*, as in Irish saint. I walked the streets self-conscious, mindful that a handful of locals might recognize me as that American chap who had asked where Patrickhill Road was. The area was dense and busy – with buses, narrow streets jammed with traffic, and narrow sidewalks so snug up against the shop entrances you couldn't even read the names on the awnings. Shopping became an art of guesswork and acting. Looking for a pharmacy – 'chemist', as they say – or electronics store, before I became acclimatized to the neighborhood, I would crane my neck or sometimes yank out a map or directions I had written down, the result being that I bumped into a lot of prams, people, litter bins – as I learned to call them, rather than 'garbage cans'. Nothing like a first impression, as Mr P. always said. The West End must have embraced me, if it embraced me at all, as the clumsy oaf that I am. Eventually, I'd simply dash confidently into an unfamiliar shop and, if I didn't see what I needed or wanted to buy – an important distinction – I'd check my wristwatch and slap my forehead and hit the pavement again. One exception was a corner shop at Lawrie Street, where I bought cigarettes and got on nodding terms with the Pakistani clerk. Perhaps because he was a foreigner too, I was unabashed in asking him where to find nine-volt batteries and blades to fit my razor. Provisions that were provisional.

Piecemeal efforts. That's what it took to get things done. And in this way, I finally equipped my new flat with a toaster, shampoo, light bulbs, all those accoutrements you take for granted that, at home, can be stashed in the trunk of your car in a single trip to the local strip mall. It would be some time, however, before I'd catch on that people in shops talking about carrying their *messages* home, did not mean communiqués. 'Messages', don't ask me why, were grocery bags.

The flat was decent enough. It wasn't flashy, but my needs didn't encompass flashy. One bedroom, bathroom, kitchen, and a small living room – correction: 'lounge'. The carpet had seen better days, and the fixtures were perhaps not the latest designs, but it was freshly painted and the furniture wasn't broken. It was furnished, and I got to know the furnishings, for better or for worse.

The kitchen cupboards revealed an assortment of mismatched cookware, remnants from households that had come and gone, such as an electric kettle with a mineral-caked coil like a fuzzy caterpillar at the bottom, bowls bearing faded floral prints, lids to once-present pots. The flat could not be accused of being cheerful, through no fault of its own. When there was daylight – which was not often, it seemed, so far – none reached inside, as the windows were flanked by a tenement house. Water bugs greeted me in the tub many mornings, having emerged from the drain, where I sent them returning. Most enervating, though, was a discovery I made in the bedroom, where a bare mattress was provided on a foldable frame.

I lifted the dingy pad, wanting to size up the support and quality of slumber I might receive on the contraption. I anticipated retiring here many nights, belly sloshing with Glasgow's coffee. A bit of comfort would be needed. Instead, I got a shock: a large bloodstain was revealed on the underside, kidney-shaped – that is, the kidney of an adult Indian elephant. It was huge. A plum-colored, dried black ring thick with a deathly residue. Its crusty rim reminded me of the dirty foam that laps at a lake's edge. My mouth watered, not in a hungry way.

Reflexively, I dropped the mattress and retreated. Right out of the room. I sat on the edge of the tub, looking across the hall into the bedroom at this befouled piece of furniture – wondering would the landlord replace the mattress if asked? Should I demand he replace it? Would he be as good as his word, or say that I had signed, agreed to lease the flat as seen, warts and all? I tried to imagine what could cause bleeding of that nature. It boiled down to two things, one natural, cyclic, foreseeable, the other thoroughly opposite – instantaneous, unforeseen, most unnatural. What had happened here? Hadn't I read in one of my guidebooks that this was a nice part of town? Blood-tinged images from beyond this city flashed across my mind, pulled right down off the shelf of memory not bound by the oceans and continents, images zipping into view faster than any digital archive.

Shaken, I took my coat and billfold, and left the flat without even locking it. At a shop nearby I grabbed a set of bed linens and a mattress pad – then a second for good measure; okay, a third too. Protective layers between the indignity, the hideousness, and myself. Determination to make a good impression on Nicole drove me. I would not have *my* house befouled. I shimmied through the crowded Debenham's aisles towards the checkout, arms piled high, and was struck by my first wave of homesickness.

That is, I took it to be a kind of homesickness, though it resembled regular sickness, a hotness in the gut. Why? – I backtracked and saw that it was the idea of what my mother would do that had compelled me to rise and dash out of the flat on this mission, this solution. Undeniably, I had acquired her make-do spirit, which entailed a certain amount of prettifying. That was all fine; I was nostalgic for her influence, fond of her memory. But the hotness in the gut struck again as I remembered that I had first thought of my *own* way to deal with the bloodstain, one that was head-on, one that would hold Mr McScobie accountable, one that would address the chilling stain out in the open. That had been my first instinct, my own. But I had rejected it, stuffed it in the out box as fast as it hit the in box. I had opted for covering up. To the extent that I recognized this, the searing sensation could literally be called homesickness. A sickness *from* home.

A tall, broad-shouldered American loaded down with a household's worth of bedclothes, I maneuvred to the checkout, saying, 'Pardon. Beg your pardon.' The effectiveness of this phrase over its American counterpart, the brash, self-centered 'Excuse me,' I had learned to employ. It was not simply a matter of following custom;

I preferred its sound to that of Ex-*cuse* me, so much like *Accuse*, so heavy on *Me*.

I made a mental note to get in touch with my mom, and that appeased the churning in my stomach that threatened to rise into a throat-lump. I would send off a letter or stay up late some night, mindful of the Greenwich-to-Central disparity, and reach her by phone in sated after-dinner ease. This intention lessened my guilt, and I allowed myself to be lulled by the pleasant beeps and blips of the barcode scanner, the universal tones of commerce. Cash-register bells have no accent, no dialect, no jargon. I was pondering, *What if Nicole's bare flesh were to meet these very sheets, the ones I'm holding in my hands right now? Her black hair fanning out . . .* when the lad said, 'Two hundred forty pounds, twenty pence.'

In my haste, I hadn't looked at the price tags. I was no expert – Margaret had always handled matters such as this, she loved to shop – but I was certain a few sheets and pads could be had at home for a fraction of the sum in dollars.

'Holy shit,' I blurted – then a gasp and a snicker, neither my own. A look towards the queue behind me revealed a young girl beaming upwards at me, orange soda exaggerating the corners of her smirk like Nicholson's Joker. The legs and coat beside her were obviously her mother's and, with embarrassment, I followed them upwards to find a scowling matronly face.

'Sorry,' I said. 'I'm very sorry.'

Fearing my personal account couldn't handle the charge at the moment (being a permanent resident now, I had managed to open one with the aide of the same terse teller who'd first refused me), I handed over the Plunkett Citibank. The lad eyeballed the plastic, the logo foreign to him, then tugged it through the channel timidly, as if it might explode in his hand. The swirling post-swipe moments: when digits tunnel into untold tubes and soar over street-strung wires, beam and bounce to unknown corners of space, blip into databanks, bringing back acceptance.

The clerk started handling the packages of sheets, pillowcases, mattress pad, mattress pad, mattress pad. 'Shall I double up the carriers?' he asked, in a broad Glaswegian accent.

'Sorry?'

'Shalla doubleup thay cadday-urz?'

Blank stare.

'Shalla doubleup thay cadday-urz?'

Blood, undoubtedly serving a purpose at the furthest reaches of my appendages, dropped all plans and made a course to my face. I looked in the clerk's brown eyes, desperate for a clue, a lifeline. Mercifully, the orange-soda girl blurted out, 'Do ya want two bags, mister?'

There was no desk, so I piled my Plunkett-logo-embossed binders, marketing textbooks and highlighters on the coffee table in the lounge. It was no bigger than a checker board, but it was just sufficient for filling out my timesheets and the paperwork, other than the evaluation forms, which were completed on site.

And that's what I did for the week following Curler's: I canvassed the immediate neighborhood of Partick with penitential verve – kickback from a night of debauchery. I wore my slacks and my loafers; I peppered my bookbag expertly with Plunkett pens and business cards, snugger than a PFC's footlocker. Several cafés were located on the bustling stretch of Dumbarton Road just at the bottom of the hill sloping off Hyndland Circle. Perhaps they weren't so much cafés as I think of a café, more like deli counters specializing in peculiar breeds of sandwich, with menus incidentally, almost begrudgingly, offering coffee. To sight a grouphead, with its nozzles and tanks, was a rare find. Had I asked for a barista, the reply might have come, 'Aye, alongside the stairs, where else?' From tables and booths, I spied production of coffees using press pots and standard twelve-cup household makers. 'In the realm of connoisseur,' I wrote in the Notes field of my 27Gs for these Partick establishments, 'we are dealing with nothing more than vending machines. The only difference is the coin slot has a pulse. The product is generic and uninspired. There is certainly no personal touch. There exists an astounding obliviousness to coffee traditions, not to mention brewing methods. Adding to that, no consideration is paid to flavor, freshness, aroma or presentation.

A scanty form of coffee is made and handed over the counter and the money collected. Hard to imagine specialty drinks going over in the absence of the fundamentals.'

If I was harsh, it was out of necessity. I had to be blunt and to the point, because my concentration suffered. I was thinking about Nicole, battling to stay focused. One thing I knew was that bold statements like these, while damning the quality of the coffee, would be perceived by Carson as stringent work. He would think of me as a straight shooter, a term he had used in my interview and often in training. I would gain favor that might leverage his sympathies for me when he got wind of my expenses, which were preying on my mind again now that'd I'd spent another wad of sterling on bedding and personal effects. This worry I fought off with reminders that a few weeks would pass before the Visa statements would cycle through Melissa for signature. For now, these keen assessments shot brass tacks – more playing into Carson's terminology. But I wondered, Did it bode well for Plunkett's client that these Scots had no taste for quality coffees and other upscale drinks? Would that mean the market was ripe for planting, or hopelessly infertile? A curious question, though I didn't need to concern myself with the answer. My assignment was only to evaluate the predicament, a fact which became more torturous the more outlets I frequented.

Not one cup of joe I met in the West End met my standards for head-clearing, jolt, and inspiration factors, though a half-dozen weak ones will put a certain itch in you. Yet I was relegated to the role of observer – I couldn't offer pointers, I couldn't make demands, I couldn't influence the counter help or the wait staff into bringing me anything other than their usual fare, no matter how uninspired it was. The potency of liquid comfort I had known at home in my previous anxieties – nerves jingled into shimmering preoccupation by acidic, tart, opal-black coffee – was nowhere to be had. Worse, not only was my sole recourse merely to witness the making of thin cappuccinos with tap water and Sanka, it was my job to record it, document it. It was like being forced to watch snuff films – they were murdering these beans.

On top of this stress were the differences of culture. I sat at these cafés and sampled and, once I'd done my forms, thought about such things – a welcome distraction from the fetid coffee. A backlog of nuances had pooled by now, one that would be adequate conversation for the Podgorskis at home. The pound coins so heavy in the pockets. At home, the silver dollars had never taken off, the Kennedy coin a relic that got tossed in junk drawers, left to mingle with pencil sharpeners and paper clips, the Susan B. Anthony a flop. The persistent rain – okay, not a cultural phenomenon but, nevertheless, stepping out of one's native climate is a shock. No autumn colors, no dry air, no southbound geese overhead, no hardening ground, no wind-wafted odors of burning leaves, that lovely earthy harbinger smell no one's ever had the good sense to put in a candle or incense stick. The lilting inflection of speech, so infectious my thoughts now bore this cadence. All kinds of notions normally stated to myself, rather blandly it seemed, were now posed as reverberating self-questions. Toasting bread, picking a pair of socks, anything. *Shall I wear these? Canny find the jam? Is it not nice?* The Cadbury's and Fantas and Walker's and all these unfamiliar brands. The way phones rang: two short *brrrs*, a silence. The *KNEE-ner* of ambulance sirens. The list went on and on, grew daily. In fact, the things I noticed during my very first days and outings – the dense hedgerows everywhere, for example – were second nature now, and I forgot they were new. I had to remind myself that it was still a detail that Uncle Bill or Aunt Liz might find interesting, something I could use to fill in the picture that it was different here and remind them that this task was no walk in the park.

Only the urge stayed away. I didn't want to speak to any Americans. Or family.

And then there was Nicole Marston. She, I did want to speak to. But I didn't know how, with what *aspect*, because I didn't know what had happened after the whiskey had flowed. It was pure mystery to me. I had gotten too drunk. Blitzed. Bongo-ed. Blootered.

*

The morning after Curler's, I woke on the couch, a cold rain splashing me. Several prolonged moments of hazy fright elapsed before the *mise en étrange* became the mise en scène. I stared at the molding of the high Victorian archway between the lounge and kitchen. Nothing registered: all I knew was that this architecture didn't belong to 8460 Meadow Prairie Lane or to the Wright Street apartment where I'd lived with Margaret. Then it crystallized. I recognized my environs. It was my flat. In Glasgow. Where I was now. Where I *lived* now. (That was a relief.) Where I drank too much last night. (That was not.)

With Nicole. 'Oh, fuck . . .' I closed my eyes on the molding.

Rainwater pricked my face, until I mustered the coordination to sit up, reach, and pull down the sash. The sill was soaked, and two Rizla roll-ups floated in the pooled rain.

When it comes to hangovers, the gesture of grabbing one's head of course does nothing, but I sat there palming my cranium anyway, not really believing I could massage the pain away, rather mostly assuring myself that everything was intact and accounted for. It was like feeling with your tongue a tooth that's been drilled and filled. You want to size it up before you go chewing something. In this case, chewing was thinking, operating. I noticed my temples only stung and pulsed when I breathed, and I thought of that old joke – *Does it hurt? Only when I do this, Doc. Well, then don't do that.* Though it was tempting not to, I figured I'd better breathe on.

My mouth was cakey. My eyes felt like they'd had ash flung in them. My reflexes were sludgy, even reactions from thought to thought. I looked a long time at the coffee table, distracted by the sounds of cars splashing outside and the hoots and screams of playing children, while considering what I saw. There was an orange and silver beverage can and a wad of grease-dappled brown packing paper. Stumbling up the road to the chippie with Nicole: I remembered that. With trepidation, I prodded at recollections of what else we'd done, hoping I hadn't confessed something to her about Margaret or gushed about how glad I was to have met her. I remembered having the sense all night long of wanting to tell her that every time she said something I found it either outrageously true, a keen observation, an unfortunately un-common perspective, hilarious or endearingly sweet. I didn't know which would have been worse to recall having done – spouting stories of my failed marriage or being the overbearing, needy drunk. Not knowing what had transpired compounded my nausea. My consolation was I couldn't say yet which sort of idiot I'd been, a walking-wounded idiot or a just a garden-variety soft touch.

With agony, I concentrated. The bartenders yelling 'Finish up, please! Finish yer drinks!' and the tragic spectacle of a roomful of Scots parting with their last pints. Crossing Byres Road near the tube stop, against the light, in a swarm of people – students, pensioners, the musicians who'd played – all mindful of Nicole's crutches, saying things, even just 'Poor dear' and 'Want a piggy-back, love?' Peering in the cabinet at Loretto's, Nic – I'd started calling her this at times – identifying this and that crusty fried thing, both of us leaning on her crutches. 'Fish supper, sausage supper, mince pie.' Me leaning over the countertop – perhaps, more accurately, slung over it – watching the man in the apron and hat plunge items into the fryer, the heavenly smell of grease every-where. Speaking with the man, but he only smirking and muttering to his buddy in Italian, keeping his eyes on his work, keeping up with demand. A raucous queue behind us. Fumbling with my wallet, Nicole insisting she pay. Me holding the hot packages so Nic could walk, then her dousing everything in vinegar at the station and pocketing a bottle of HP brown sauce on the way out.

We walked to the Botanic Gardens and sat on a bench just inside the gate. She got out the brown sauce and we both got serious with our chips, plucking them, steaming, out of the paper trays in our laps. I was asking about brown sauce. What was it? Why brown? Nic threatened me not to slag it, not to bad-mouth it, 'cause it was her *fave. Brilliant.* She insisted I try it, and fed me a chip drenched in it. I could hear her saying, 'Do you noh think it's nice?' in her lilting way, which I was probably hooked on. I remem-bered the sight of the stuff but not the taste: it looked separated like vinaigrette and road mud. I was quite content with the novelty on my plate, salt and vinegar. I suppose I talked about how we didn't have that in the States. There were flowerbeds and bonsai trees and rose bushes around us. Nearby was a white-domed conservatory. Other people passed by, laughing, smoking, saying, 'Mind the crutch,' to one another and stepping around where it lay poking into the path. We finished our food, down to the last bit. Cans of lager and a half-pint of Dewar's were produced from Nicole's pockets. We moved onto another bench, in a darker area, away from the street lamps and shishing tires and grumbling trucks. Laughing. Stumbling. Bigger trees. Night-dark alcoves. Another park bench. Another dram.

That was it. Lights out.

I sat up and leaned forward, picking up the orange and silver can. My head nearly imploded. By my account, every synapse was on strike, with a team of untrained scabs standing in. One and exactly one task could be performed at a time; sitting up *and* grabbing produced critical overload. I turned the can sideways, *then* read it: IRN-BRU. There was a silver figure of a man, arms akimbo, encircled in a hoop as if performing acrobatics. He was reminiscent of Da Vinci's Vitruvian Man, only angular, futuristic and compelled to accelerate. The can was still ice-cold, as was the entire flat, owing to the open window.

Nicole bought this for me, I figured, not remembering with any certainty. But the sound of the words 'iron brew' was familiar, like I had said them myself. I hoped to God I hadn't bored her, or worse, offended her, with tourist talk – why the name, is it made of iron? Why brown sauce? Why vinegar? Why this, why that? *Why the fuck are you here, Yankee xenophobe?*

I opened the can and drank. The fizz was initially dry and tinny, like sucking on a penny. Then lush orange followed, but not exactly orange, somewhat in the realm of bubblegum. Salty and remotely pink. Tangy but not tart. Sweet but not cloying. Upon the first swallow I realized how dehydrated I was, and drank again, chugging this time. I pounded half the can, then sat back as my head lightened. I belched with satisfaction, as if the bubbles had bonded to noxious elements in my gut and escorted them out. The bubbles felt good on my teeth, too, seeming to corrode the fur away. I filled my mouth and swished, looking again to the printed can. Just playing, I read aloud the text that edged the top rim: 'Made in Scotland from Girders'. It came out in my voice, with Nicole's accent, something roughly like 'Made en Sco'land frem Gardars'. With a tilt of the head, I downed the rest. If I could have, I would have transfused my blood with the stuff.

The IRN-BRU gave me the strength to get up, shower and hit the bricks – to downtown, that is, which was the territory I wanted to start researching. I hadn't completely covered the West End, not by a long shot, but I could pick off local joints piecemeal in my comings and goings. But along with the will to rise – enabling me to ingest a small handful of acetaminophen – the IRN-BRU also gave me the clarity of mind to realize I may have botched a good thing with Nicole. I really didn't know what had happened in the park or after. Had we snogged? More? In the shower, the equipment didn't look used, didn't feel used. But there definitely had been a call to arms, shall we say. Chambers had been loaded, hammers cocked. This proved nothing, though. In this regimen, the troops stand on the slightest order, whether battle or drill. In actuality, I was relieved to find no evidence she'd stayed the night or of me disrobing; I didn't want things to transpire cheaply with Nic. Not knowing what impression I had made on Nicole left me feeling unresolved, and the hangover obviously contributed a great deal of fogginess. Whatever had been started the night before I finished on my own in the shower, as an act of closure. It was Nature's reset button, expelling all misgivings, generating a clarifying rush of blood to the head. Yesterday's residue I kicked down the hatch, the way of the waterbugs.

The day was gloomy, cold and extremely windy. A block beyond Hyndland Circle, trudging against whipping gales, I knew I was underdressed. Yet the chill that penetrated my fall jacket and Oxford refreshed me with its keenness. For a dulled mind, a serious Scottish wind wasn't a bad thing, and I pressed on, determined to reach City Centre. (No one here used the word *downtown*.) I inured myself against the cold and against dread – dread that if I'd spilled my guts, I might have put Nicole off. Of course, there was the possibility that she had listened thoughtfully to me spinning the standard Podgorski legends, down to the falsest detail. Whatever the case, I was desperate to unearth a proper cup of something strong and black – a palliative to treat uncertainty. City Centre had to have a *proper* black coffee, it just had to. I'd picked that up from Nicole. It was a Scottishism. A proper meal, a proper shag, a proper job. A thing done rightly. Worthy of respect. Legitimate. Anyway, it was a matter of faith now. If I hadn't believed I could obtain a solid java, I never would have left the flat, only stumbled to my bloodstained bed, encased in layers and sanitary now – or at least appearing so. Then, instead of facing frigid winds, I'd be curled up with some footie or darts or Poirot on the telly – whatever was showing on any of the nation's four broadcast channels.

I stopped in at the shop on Lawrie Street, the one with the Pakistani clerk. I asked for ten Silk Cut, and today the clerk, who usually said, 'Hello, how are you?' eyed me with suspicion from the moment I walked in, like he had never seen me before. He made change coldly, saying only 'Ta,' quickly averting his eyes from mine, and standing there behind the racks of sweets and tabloids, looking away. I don't know why that should bother me, but it did. For some reason it weakened my will to fight my pulsing temples, amplifying my hangover all the way down to the tube station, where I plunked in my 50p coin and took my ticket and swiped it through the turnstile. Down the orange tile stairs and, just as I reached the landing, the train roared up, pushing a hot gust in front of it, screeching murderously to a stop, and I walked straight into the opening doors of the car without breaking my stride. And though it was absurd, this sequence cheered me and made the misery of my hangover seem to add depth to my world, I don't know why. I guess these things were all I had and, in the grim reality of a dreary Glasgow morning, three thousand miles from a former life, they came through as portents, disheartening then propitious. I was at the whim of the city: the previous night it had blessed me for a while, gifting me with Nicole's company. But then maybe the night had betrayed me. Or I had betrayed myself. I didn't know – and I just had to go along for the ride. And for now, my ride was on time.

One of the documents Carson had compiled for my and Klang's use was an itinerary, a loose schedule of goals. Seated in the tube, I perused it again, cued by the slowing tempo of clacks to look up and observe the station signs as they whizzed past on the tiled walls. Hillhead. Kelvinbridge. St George's Cross. Six stops total to the bustle of town. Certain reports were due fortnightly and, consulting the table, I saw that I would need to fax Klang in London today. All that was required was for me to provide a vague plan, a lax framework for my duties. A simple thing. I put my papers away and observed the train car. Apparently, shopping was on tap for most of the locals; the train filled after two stops, and by Kelvinbridge was standing room only, with dozens left stranded on the platform to await the next train. My bag hugged to my lap, I compacted myself as best I could. There was nothing to see but people's legs. Even the ads, what they called *adverts* here (one clumsy Briticism I'd never adopt), were obscured by the crowd. I gazed unfocused at kneecaps and shoes, all jostling in unison. I tried to anticipate the work I would do in town, but one thing became certain: I wouldn't get much work finished wondering about Nicole. By the time we reached St Enoch's, I vowed, I would decide whether or not to phone her.

A decision was nowhere near when I'd counted the sixth screeching of brakes, the sixth reunion of my shoulder and my seat-mate's. The struggle to depart the car was tedious and slow, while shoppers on the platform inched forward, frantic to enter and get home with their goods. When I emerged in the wan gray light of Argyle Street, I lit a Silk Cut and decided, No, I couldn't call her. If she called and was her normal lighthearted, sweet self, I could take that as a sign that I hadn't made a royal douche bag of myself. If she called and was aloof, perhaps indefinite, then I had blabbed something, but not enough to completely drive her off. If she told me to fuck off or didn't call – no explanation needed. In the meantime, there was work, which was more than I had had when I lost Margaret and was alone with my putative wretchedness – or so the story went.

8 *Calling Home*

The Silk Cut was not the right thing for the day ahead. Unfortunately, I reached the butt before being fully sure. You never know, sometimes it clicks over. I guess I don't always make the best choices for myself. I desperately wanted to get a small batch finished representing City Centre to include in my fax to Klang. The Silk Cut, though, made my chest heavy with fatigue and clouded my head, graying out what little clarity I'd found in the decision not to phone Nicole. I leaned against the wall, my energy sapped, toxins coursing. I'd seen Silk Cut ads, with their central motif, a curtain of billowing purple silk, representing smoothness. They were far from it. They tasted like one part tobacco, three parts additives. As much as I hated to be the Ugly American pointing this out, hated to hear it even in my own mind, Marlboros weren't the same here. It was a plain fact – much stronger, even the Lights. These companies were smart: they assumed nothing and catered to international tastes, just like Plunkett's client hoped to do. It seemed obvious now the more I thought about it: their client had to be *the* major American chain, the one people cited as an emblem of retail's ubiquity, the apotheosis of franchising outside of the burger milieu, the one people joked about being on every corner. Then again, what did I know? America was a big place. Maybe there was a coffee chain on the East Coast I knew nothing of. Maybe Plunkett's client was a broader entity, a bakery or food service, looking to specialize. Ultimately, though, it would remain unknown to me – for my own good.

Propped against the wall outside the tube stop, I was like a floating branch snagged on the shore of a stream. People of every stripe flowed past, and I watched unmindfully, content with inertia. Buchanan Street thrummed, car horns bleating, bus brakes pealing, the blind-man's-crossing signal chirping – all muted through the gauze of my epic hangover. Oh well, as for the smoke, I thought perhaps I could get ahold of Dan from the warehouse, have him ship over a carton or two. They'd probably get hung up in customs, though. I could always try the other brands. Roll-ups seemed popular, and you could get them in any newsagent's along with the papers and the wee filters that looked like pencil erasers. It's just not the same, though, asking for a sack of loose-leaf Borkum-Riff. There was enough strangeness across the sales counter already – the alien packaging: gold B&H, mahogany Dun-hill, regal blue and white Parliament. Not a dromedary in sight, no phallic-snouted Joe Camel. Parliament, though – that one puzzled me. Imagine an American brand called Congress. *Bum me a Congress.* Or *Here, light up a Senate.* Senate wouldn't be a bad name for a brand. Sharp, concise, authoritative.

It made me think of Rick Gedes, the project manager at Plunkett's who had led some training seminars. Rick wouldn't shut up about *branding.* Talk about latching on to an industry buzz-word – I think this guy had it tattooed on his knuckles, he was so hardcore. You didn't just market a product that turned out to be either utile or useless, tasty or revolting, a seller or a dud. You branded. Rick had a degree that conferred his branding capabilities. Well, I had just done in twenty seconds what took him four years, and my cognitive state was not exactly at its peak. Senate: there's your brand. Springs off the tongue like a flung dagger. *Pump four and a pack of Senate Milds,* I thought – then knew at once, by the sight of a woman glaring sharply at me, that I hadn't just thought this bit of dialogue but spoken it. Her brown eyes darted with bewilderment. Reflexively, I scowled back. Then distance severed our connection as she turned away, her look concluding: *American nutter.*

I shoved off from my brick shore, carved a path up to Mitchell Street, Gordon Street, St Vincent Place. It doesn't take long to tire of being the out-of-towner in a crowd, so my map remained in my bookbag. Wind danced around the urban corridor, dank with rain either recently ended or impending. The exhaust of buses and cabs and cars – it was stirred but never flushed, never swept away.

The residue of Glasgow was always on. Soon my eyes itched again. The ribbon of a trumpeter's tune curled about, sinewy amid chugging and clatter; at the next corner the trumpeter materialized, an upturned fedora at his feet receiving coins and notes. Oily fumes tumbled from chippies and pubs and doorways – one labeled Drury Close, which I read at first as close, as in near, until I recalled that Dickensian term for *alley*, which I probably hadn't heard since reading *Oliver Twist* in high school.

The paper vendors smoked as I waited for a walking man, and kids who should have been in school smoked, standing half my height, and bums with cans of McEwan's poking out of their pockets, asking *Spare some change?* – they smoked. Eventually I lit another Silk Cut, going with the flow and, despite aggravating my hangover earlier, it *was* smoother now. It was practically a health hazard not to smoke. At least you knew what you were getting.

Along a cobblestone esplanade that cut back from broad Buchanan Street I found a picturesque bistro. 'Endive', read the sign in elegant ironwork. Stucco and ivy. All that was missing was Mediterranean air and the sun. Two smartly dressed women emerged as I approached, carrying bags from upscale shops, one ridiculously wearing sunglasses. It was a cut above the egg-and-beans breakfast counters I'd been eating at in the West End. And lucky I found it when I did: as I was being seated, my body hit empty. In a cold sweat, I ordered, to a waitress with hazy features, the first thing I could read on the menu that I figured could be kept down. This was no day for logging triumphs of culinary adventure. There'd be other times for blood sausage and all the rest.

'I'll have the bacon and brie baguette. And a coffee.'

'Cheers,' said the lady, taking my menu, needing no specifics about the coffee. Which was fine by me, because my investigative engine was sputtering. The IRN-BRU boost had fizzled, and to sip ice water steadily required clenching the glass with two hands.

Wearily, I looked around. There was a poster of endive with the Latin name in italics and a picture of the plant, a bulb that looked like an ear of corn. God's sense of humor: what the pigs slopped on back in Illinois was indistinguishable from this supposed haughtiness.

Even impaired, every unoccupied moment, my mind returned to Nicole. I had to make an effort to break this hangover and get my wits. I spotted a newspaper on the bar across the room. On approach, the bartender turned eagerly towards me, ready to whip up a bloody mary or screwdriver. Not a chance, pal. I've never had the constitution for the hair of the dog. I grabbed the paper, asking permission with an inquisitive pause mid-lift. Ever since the carrier-bag incident, I'd been terrified of a Scot saying something utterly elementary only to have it bounce off me, unregistered, like a soccer ball off my forehead. Embarrassing vignettes played in my mind. *Shine yer shoes, mister?* Derrrr? I'm American! *Got the time?* Pardon me while drool oozes from my slack jaw and my stare pierces an unfathomable void.

Silence could be a nightmare when it was your own and not your choice. Silence could fuck you, turn you inside out. But I already knew that.

The return to the table across the room was a flight, my head the cockpit of the beer-battered vessel below. I flopped heavily in my chair, intending to relax amid the pages of newsprint until the grub arrived to restore my strength.

LENGTHY ROAD BATTLE HOTTING UP

Once I'd grasped that *hotting* was some Brit form of *heating*, the light went on. The M77. 'Holy shit.'

'Pardon?' The waitress stood nearby, wiping a table. 'Och, sorry,' she said, as if recognizing me as an acquaintance from long ago, 'Yer coffee. Just a wee moment.'

Dazed, I skimmed on.

> Ruaridh Gilmour ... resistance builds against a
> new motorway ... the battle over the Ayr Road
> Route, a £50 million, seven-mile extension to the
> M77 south of Glasgow, which would cut across

the city's treasured parkland Pollok Park, which
was given to the people of Glasgow before the
Second World War and is close to many council
estates.

... Contract tenders are due in by the end of
September and work could begin by the new year.

The article continued with details of councils in talks and European Union laws and community activism. *Cont'd A5.* I thumbed through the broadsheet, folded it open and, boom, there was Ruaridh. Nicole's Ruaridh. The rooftop megaphone yodeler.

At first I was intimidated. This guy was high profile, a public figure. He had clout: he could easily woo Nicole back – if it really was *back*. Had she even finished with him? Okay, so the guy is a bit extreme in his views, at least he's good-intentioned. And now he's something of a celebrity. How could I compete with that? I studied the picture closer and, shallowly, I was relieved. He was ... well, not handsome. Ruaridh was a right ugly fucker.

He was shown standing beneath a banner strung between two massive tree trunks. POLLOK FREE STATE. Black paint on bedsheets – so this was not a well-funded endeavor. He wore boots, cargo pants, and an Aztec patterned poncho that reminded me of something my mother would have made me wear in the seventies. He had a thick build, and he stood proudly, chin tilted up, almost too much, like you see in Senior portraits, where it looks contrived. His arms were folded across his chest – an affectation of defiance – and one hand held a small booklet. Covering his boyish face was a scraggly, uneven beard, which though not thick obscured his jawline with unflattering shapelessness. He had flat cheekbones and a shallow brow, so his eyes had nowhere to recede into. Puffy eyelids featured prominently, their sleepiness contradicting the tales of confrontation and ruthlessness. Wind at the moment of exposure lifted a few strands of hippie hair off his back, but his coif at the front was unmistakably gentrified, public school – by which they mean here private school – with a long-trained, obedient side part that cast him in the likeness of John

Cleese or Stephen Fry. This evidence of his gentility Ruaridh had neglected to obscure.

In his eyes, his countenance, perhaps not balance, but depth, and it was this complexity which allowed for paradox: his using militancy in the pursuit of peace. His activism marring the cityscape with slogans and rallies, yet aiming to preserve a sanctuary within it – Pollok Park. His inflicting indefinite turmoil on Glasgow in hopes of securing an oasis of permanent respite. Ruffling legislators to bring comfort to the legislated. Driven by egalitarian duty, his tactics were troublesome but admirable. I felt guilty for glorying in his hideousness.

I read the caption:

> Likely the first citizen of Pollok Free State, Ruaridh
> Gilmour clutches his self-authored passport which
> absolves holders from allegiance to the British
> Crown and pledges to defend the free state against
> destruction of wildlife, pollution, and a 'car
> owning elite'.

The article described people who, like Gilmour, had set up camp and were living at the protest site, the Pollok Free State, round the clock. There were as many as fifty, and that figure tripled on weekends. Nicole hadn't mentioned he was living in the park now. Groups she had named were mentioned, though: EarthFirst!, Glasgow for People, and more. The chairman of a roads committee was quoted: 'It's not clear how representative these protesters are, but they are winning the propaganda war at present. I'm eating and sleeping the Ayr Road Route.' This was a classically Scottish quote, a fine example of their sloppy tongues. Scots were open, personable, and imprecise. Phrases like 'eating and sleeping the Ayr Road Route' took getting used to – and with each one I encountered, in media, in Nicole, in coffeehouse staff, I felt a few dozen miles farther from home, farther from the linear precision of Mr P.'s ducks in a row, and closer to myself.

The camp was made out to seem peaceful, if dirty and rudimentary, with Ruaridh all but named as the ringleader. These were not benign tree-huggers, the report made clear, though it did seem to be a jab, and I couldn't help but snicker when Ruaridh was described as 'a jobless art student'. But he had a following, and the campers' methods didn't stop at hugging trees. A brief history of 'monkeywrenching' was given, a tactic of damaging builders' equipment and delaying progress which had been practiced at other UK road projects such as the M1 outside of London. Spikes in trees. The inexplicable slashed tire on the morning of scheduled razing.

> 'We will step up our action,' Mr Gilmour said, 'for as long as possible. As soon as the contractors are announced, we will disrupt their project, adding millions to their costs with the aim that participation isn't economical for them.'

The article ended in the characteristically sensational British tabloid manner, despite this being a major mainstream newspaper, musing on how far, to what extremes, this direct action might go. The suggestion was that, with the resistance intensifying, the battle could escalate exponentially, stopping at nothing. I tended to hear things in accents now, and could imagine the emphasis on the first syllable of *direct*, opposite of American. '*Di*-rect action,' I thought. Or I had *thought* I had thought. I must have spoken it instead – must have been itching to speak.

'Sorry? Direct wha'?' The waitress at my elbow inquired.

'Oh, God! You scared me.'

'Sorry!' she exclaimed, placing an apologetic hand on my arm. Here I was chatting to myself like a lunatic, hungover, being a pain-in-the-ass, and she was apologizing to me. It was an unmistakably East-of-the-pond phenomenon. I imagined a Denny's waitress at home barking an ultimatum: *Listen, mister, go sleep it off if you can't get a grip. I'm trying to do my job.* Abashed, I folded the paper and cleared a space for the sandwich and coffee.

I thanked her profusely and ate, not caring that the side salad described on the menu turned out to be a small pile of corn, cucumbers and shredded lettuce, *sans* dressing, *sans* flavor, *sans* purpose. Many pond-crossers of both stripes will argue to the death on the merits of bacon rashers versus American bacon and so-called Canadian bacon. At this moment, I didn't care one mote. It was meaty and salty and heavenly. The coffee was actually not bad, but probably I would have settled for anything at that point. I didn't do a 27G. I hadn't studied the coffee, I had studied Ruaridh, so this was a personal visit, off the clock. I paid up and left, brazenly tucking the *Herald* under my arm. I figured I could do no worse.

Rain fell in sheets; the streets were abandoned.

I had no sampling of City Centre for my fax to Klang, but so be it. With more effort and trouble than I care to recall, I located a public fax machine and sent off a sizeable stack to him at a number in London – everything I had done thus far. As for how I managed, let's just say, in City Centre Glasgow there are copy shops with coin-operated fax machines; there are shops with fax machines that take phone cards, but these shops don't sell phone cards; there are shops that sell phone cards but for cash only; and there are places that take plastic but are closed. Then there's the hole in the wall I happened upon just short of gouging my eyes out in frustration. While the clerk rang up sweets and fags for teens dodging the rain, I tried Klang's number. No luck. When he had a moment the clerk assisted me with the dialing codes. Go figure – drop the zero. Then why is it there? Yer man – any guy you're dealing with or speaking of is *yer man* – didn't care to speculate, and his facial scar and chipped tooth persuaded me not to press the issue. The illumination, on the machine, of the word *Transmitting* was to my eyes a miracle rivaling in splendor Lourdes and Fatima combined, which was apt because the baud rate seemed to hail from the time of Joseph and Mary. While ninety would have been standard at home, this felt like about five. The bill, when it came time to pay up, would come to over twenty quid. In the meantime, I wanted to step out for a Silk Cut.

'I'll just be outside, if that's all right,' I said to the clerk, flashing him my packet of ten and walking away from the machine.

'Nay bother,' he said. 'I'll just see that it finishes.'

The shop door closed behind me. The streets were bare, rain slobbering into every nook. I leaned against the plate glass, shielded by an awning, and lit up. I took a heavy drag, and heard a replay in my mind of the man intoning *Ull juz see thaddit feneshes*. I said – intentionally aloud this time and with satisfaction – 'He'll just see that it finishes,' and blew all the lovely toxins up to the purple Glasgow sky.

I had put it off since my arrival because, frankly, it didn't seem as interesting as my present reality but, finally, I telephoned my folks. I'd swept all week through Partick and the West End, towards City Centre, sampling coffees, working fourteen-hour days, filling every line, corner and margin of 27Gs, sometimes spilling onto the back, hitting about six places a day, and one in the evening, where I'd linger longer, chat with locals, read the papers, following the M77 dust-up from a distance. One night, fatigue caught up with me, and I took a nap after dinner, during which the phone rang, a ring that I sensed, even from the depths of a nap-coma, to be a call from my parents. When I got up, revived by an IRN-BRU, I figured I could delay the inevitable no more.

Overseas calls. One instant you have a lifeless tone in your ear, alone in a rented flat in a strange city. Ten seconds later, you're in contact with the opposite side of the globe and the people who've been with you since you arrived, placenta-covered and gasping, into this glorious world. There doesn't seem to be any accounting for it; it's precisely the type of thing that's always been inconceivable to me. You can look it up in the encyclopedia, read the particulars, the terminology – no matter. *Conversion of audible waveforms to electrical impulse, network of wires, satellite uplink*. Abstractions like these never stick with me; I have no use for them. Margaret once admired that in me, that I had no ambition to know everything or nurture my masculine, mechanical aptitude. She, too, was content to leave plumbing to the plumber, car repairs to the mechanic. She studied dance, I studied photography, and we agreed that mundanities occupied valuable cognitive real estate that elbowed out your dreams if you let them. Mr P., seeing that Margaret encouraged this domestic laziness, resented her for it.

Why would the sound of *brrrrrrrrrr* three thousand miles away teach me this at this moment?

Brrrrrrrrr. Brrrrrrrrr.

I sang a vocal warm-up scale, up and back down – *do, mi, sol, do, sol, mi, do* – to loosen the knot out of my throat. That was a trick I used in my desperate times, the months of making calls, looking for work. You could make yourself sound more confident, more pleasant, more affable than you really were.

Brrrrrrr. Brrrrrrr. The ring I heard in the earpiece was the British one, two short chirps and a short pause. Of course, at Meadow Prairie Lane, I knew a brassy bell clanged, as it always had. Somewhere along the line was a misrepresentation, a transmutation of what was actually taking place.

'You sound so far away,' my mother said.

'I *am* far away, Mom.'

'Aren't the phones good over there?'

So it had begun.

'They're good, Mom. This is an industrialized nation. There are four thousand miles to cover, you know.'

'Is it that far?' The statistic had been cited before, probably one of the first things covered, back in early summer.

'Indeed.' I had to recognize that, just as Margaret and I had not prioritized home ownership with its attached repairs and upgrades, DIY, trivialities of domesticity, so had it always been my mother's way to apply her energies to empathy, health concerns and the mastery of the broader matriarchal catalog. Mileage and hemispheres and other talk we'd covered had not imprinted. I was her baby, and I was far away.

I caught her up on my work, the weather, the layout of the city, for what it mattered.

'Do you have a car?'

'No, I don't have a car. I walk everywhere. Public transport is quite popular and widespread.'

'Public transport? What's that?' my mother asked. She was not ignorant; it was a language issue.

'Public *transportation*. Buses, subways, trains.'

'Oh, right. What did you call it?'

'Just what they call it here – never mind, Nirvana. I walk everywhere now. It's a nice change. You should be glad, I'm getting a lot of exercise.' Naturally, she'd never approved of my smoking, but that was not a lifestyle choice so much as a symptom of inertia.

'That's good. Do you wear a coat?'

The conversation was strained, owing I suppose to the irrefutable fact that, while staying at home over the summer, I hadn't been shy about my eagerness to get the hell out of Dodge and Mrs P.'s easy perception that I'd made the call mainly out of obligation. I said yes, I wear a coat, and told her not to worry.

'Well, here, your father wants to get on the line.'

I heard Mr P. in the background saying he would go downstairs.

'He's going downstairs,' Mother related.

Mr P. joined the line with warm greetings and, after stumbling over the synchronization a few times – there was a slight delay, a blank second on the line between utterances – I caught him up on many of the same things I'd covered with Mom. The unspoken element between all fathers and sons – of the father watching hopefully for his life's failures to be avenged in his son's – had been dimly registered between us. It was obvious I was not cut out for science or chemistry. Nevertheless, he had spoken of many of the Scottish inventors, Baird and Watt and Dunlop, and my suspicion was that, though he had accepted I would not be walking in his career footsteps, Mr P. hoped the spirit and tradition of Scotland's innovators would somehow infest me. This eagerness was apparent over the phone now that I was gone from his house, the urgency of long-distance rates pressed upon us. At home in the same room, he tended to putz with things when we talked, and I'd often scan the newspaper or needlessly clean a camera lens during a conversation. Now – not an option.

He sounded weary and unsure, but he delivered a certain level of optimism my way. I steered to topics he could appreciate and, to my relief, that kept us clear of Nicole and the M77.

'There's a huge museum of transportation near my flat, Dad,' I said.

'Really?' he asked excitedly. I mean, excitedly for him, which is a few beats per minute over seventy.

I told him of that, and the university being the epicenter of the West End, which lent an academic air to my whole endeavor, by proximity. I talked about the industry nearby, the shipyards in sight from certain hills, and how there's always debate in the papers over management of the Clyde Firth, other waterways and their resources. My knowledge was secondhand, but it pleased him that I took note of things and remembered them, seemingly for his sake. He repaid my attention by asking about the music and the pubs, which I supposed he believed were closer to my young heart. With that, we seemed to fulfill an obligation, survived unscathed. I yawned, and the unintentional cue was immediately seized upon with an offer to let me go. After a repeat lesson for Mother on the time difference, she hung up her end.

'Well,' Mr P. said, the line ours alone, 'Carson says everything's going fine for you, so I guess we won't worry.'

'Carson? You talked to him?'

'Hmm? Yeah, he called the house about, ah, your W-4 or something. I think they had the wrong social security number for you. I forget what it was. You mother took the call.'

'Wait, I'm confused. So Mom talked to him?'

'Yes, your mother spoke with Carson.'

'And what was the matter?'

'They had your address wrong in their – you know, their computer system. Or your social. One of the two. Like I said, I don't recall. It wasn't important.'

'That's odd. I received my paychecks all right during training. They were mailed to the house. And I distinctly remember my social being listed correctly on the stub.'

'Maybe it was your married status – had you down as married. Nothing major, I'm sure. Anyway, he mentioned that he was receiving your work through Mr Klang, and that everything was copacetic.'

Copacetic? I'd never known my father to use that word. *On the up and up, right as rain, snug as a bug in a rug* – these were more his style. 'Maybe I should contact him, make sure everything's all right.'

'No, no, it's fine. Bob said he got everything he needs. It's getting late, I better let you go. Take care. Work hard, enjoy yourself.'

I put on a jacket and went out to the front steps of the building, where I sat and smoked.

There was no rain this night, and the wind was warm. The stone steps were cool, though, through denim. Moss on the pillars was bright green even in the half-dark. I had read that in December sunset would come at four in the afternoon and at summer solstice the sky would remain light to midnight. Now, the neighborhood was dark but for a street lamp casting an orange pall on the hedgerows and Vauxhalls and Citroëns. I sat still and let my focus dissipate until what came into prominence was Hyndland Circle's hilly slope contrasting with the flats across the road, their upright stance in accord with gravity, on the axis that aligned to the heavens and the earth's core. I let everything blur, and the sky above appeared as a level lid, a mushroom cap on the stem of the world. It bulged with airy beingness, and I sensed how far north I was on the globe, saw the sky's immensity in a fragment. The vastness of the Atlantic, too, the sea between myself and Mr and Mrs Podgorski, surged in my awareness.

I looked again at the moss on the pillar, the brickwork. Patches like these, and lichens, grew on every open inch of exposed stone in this city and on the lee side of tree trunks. In the absence of soil, these prehistoric weeds had adapted and flourished. There was a persistence to creation that forced it up out of even the direst conditions.

My chest filled with dense heat, like mercury. I flung the Silk Cut and pressed my fingertips into my eyes, containing what threatened to burble out. Not for Margaret, not because she was out of my life – I was okay with that. I'd been okay for some time. And not for myself – I wasn't that vain or self-pitying. And not for Nicole, because she had nothing to do with that piece of flatland, that wafer of Illinois plains sprawled under this same sky that reached here. But for the Podgorskis all over the Midwestern US, Aunt Liz and Uncle Peter, their kids, my cousins, and their good-hearted blindness, the sad compulsion in them that wanted Scotland to be one big heather-covered paradise for me. *For me.* Dick and Rose's boy tramping across hill and dale to the strains of *Auld Lang Syne* huffing from a bagpipe's guts. Disconsolate Mel traipsing away from his misfortunes. Because they thought this was the only way to react to misfortune. Never mind his misdeeds – Podgorskis didn't commit those.

I sat numbed, but enlightened, feeling that perhaps now I could call Nicole. But I'd only begun to consider it when a figure emerged from behind the hedgerow, unlatched the gate and walked up the front garden. It was a man, with broad shoulders, in heavy clothes. He headed towards me, a backpack over one shoulder, a briefcase in the opposite hand.

9 *Klang Arrives*

'Just the man I'm looking for,' said the voice.

'Klang?'

'I thought I might find you here.'

'Holy shit, Klang, what are you doing here?' I got up and shook his hand. He stood now in the light cast from the single bulb over the front door to my flat. He wore a beige mackintosh – *trenchcoat*, we'd say at home – hanging open, over a double-breasted suit coat.

'Just checking up on my charge. Surprised?'

'Well, yessir. Geez, lucky I was out here. What if I'd have been out?'

'Oh, I would have hunted you down.'

'Hunted me down?' Was this about the expense reports, which I'd fudged a little – cab rides to hospitals and bedding? Or the faxes I'd sent that day, the second batch? A shockwave ripped through me. The reports weren't good enough; I was getting fired. The first batch, I imagined, had been atrocious; Carson had said to wait it out and see if I improved; now, the second bunch completed, the verdict was in.

Attempting speech, I sputtered air.

'I'm kidding!' he said, his mouth as straight as the lines on a 27G. 'And since when do you call me sir?'

'Oh, hey, sorry, Klang. "*Sir?*" Did I say that? Just habit. You know me. Professional at all times. Minding my manners. Representing Plunkett to the highest degree.'

'Mm-hmm. Are you going to invite me in then, Mr Manners?' He handed me the backpack and followed me up the stairs.

Inside, I took his overcoat and urged him to sit down, make himself at home. 'It's nice to hear an American voice,' I said. This wasn't pandering – it *was* nice. It was orientating, like a recognizable blip on my cultural radar. At first, anyway. However, Klang would make himself at home, he'd stay two nights, and the more he spoke, the more the connotations of home rankled me. I felt like I was being chased by my past. His business lingo reminded me of James, my boss from Nexis, and the flat accent of Chicago's news anchors, teachers, parents – authority figures of all kinds. Everything here, whether Scottish or English or Irish or Welsh, was spoken with such inflection, feeling, tenderness, reverence for the simplistic. It was soft-edged. The American dialect was sharp, like a finger in the ribs. Klang evidently was immune to the infectious UK lilt; his vowels blared with nasal brightness, redolent of his Milwaukee roots.

I asked if I could get him anything to drink.

'Actually, I brought *you* something,' he said, remaining standing, scanning around my flat at the IRN-BRU cans and Debenham's bedsheets packaging I'd never managed to throw out.

'Oh?'

He set the briefcase on the tiny table and sat down before it. One eye on me, he thumbed the dials of the combination lock. Two snaps sounded, and the lid popped open.

'You *are* a coffee lover, aren't you, Podgorski?'

'Don't you have to be in this line of work?' Whenever possible, I tried to cozy up to Klang, elucidate some kinship between us. It rarely worked.

'No, actually.' Another strike. 'You think shoe salesmen like the smell of feet? Don't get me wrong, I like a cup of coffee in the morning as much as the next guy. But any other time, gimme a cold Budweiser. But what're ya gonna do? Right now I'm paid to care about coffee, so I care about coffee. Anyway, we're not talking about me, we're talking about you. Judging from your reports, you're quite the enthusiast, and you're like a fish out of water up here. So . . .' Up until now, he'd kept his hands hidden behind the lid of his open briefcase. Now he stood, smiled broadly and extended a shiny black package in a shape I knew all too well.

'Hey!' I exclaimed, stepping forward and receiving the offering.

'There's a place in my neighborhood that roasts beans. One of a few I've found.'

'Tanzanian Peaberry,' I read off the label. 'Twelve ounces. Ground. The White Swan Café.' There was a London address, devoid of numbers, chockfull of Knights, Bishops and Bridges. I held the bag under my nose and drew breath. A tangy, nutty pungency broke through. 'Thanks a lot, Klang. I can't find anything like this around here.'

'You can have a cup of something a bit more authentic after a long day of dishwater, as you call it.'

'I'll make some right now. You want some? I don't have any beer.'

'Sure, why not.' A smile of obvious, sly pleasure arched across his face, pushing his chubby cheekbones up. 'When in Rome, right?'

While I put on the electric kettle and prepped the French press, Klang yelled from the lounge, asking about the IRN-BRU.

'Oh, that's just a local soda they have here. Kind of funny stuff, actually. Lots of iron in it, I guess. I think it's for hangovers.' Once the grounds were steeping, I joined him; he stood on one side of the room with his hands behind his back, looking out the window at an angle. His suit coat was laid over the back of a chair.

'You should have let me know you were coming,' I said, snatching up some trash that was lying around – wrappers from HobNobs, a heavenly oatmeal biscuit I'd discovered and now gorged on most evenings while trying not to think about Nicole. There were a lot of new staples to my diet. Eggs and beans and toast for breakfast. Fish, chips and peas for dinner. HobNobs at all other hours – they were great with morning coffee too. It's amazing how your appetite increases when you're not depressed and you're walking everywhere. I don't know how many miles I put on in an average day. Maybe ten. The waistline flab that'd jiggled and pressed under my Plunkett interview suit was down to a single pinchable inch.

'It was a last-minute decision,' Klang acknowledged, turning from the window. 'When I got your fax –'

'Yeah, did they both come through all right? I sent them in.'

'I got them,' Klang said. 'Thirty fucking pages or something!

Amazing.' He seemed to be loosening up a bit. I thought he might even swerve into his joking manner at any time, as I'd seen him do with Carson during training back home.

'Sorry about that. It took forever to send them all,' I called, drifting, hands full, to the trash bin. 'The technology here, sometimes it can't be trusted.'

'Pod,' he said, annoyed. 'I got them, don't worry.' Ah, yes, *Pod*. I had forgotten about this nickname he had given me, in the grand American tradition of labeling and categorizing. In some social circles, it's as if you don't even exist until you've been crowned Boner or Mad Max or Killer. Here, I'd yet to hear mention of one, not even an allusion, and I'd been watching TV, reading the paper, following the M77 protest. It's not like I was cut off from society. *Pod* was an unwelcome blast from the past, but I didn't protest.

Klang sat down on the couch and lit up. While I threw the bedsheet wrappers in the closet, he explained that when he got the second batch of forms, a week's worth of work, he immediately looked through them. They piqued his interest. They were very detailed, very thorough. And the contents were quite intriguing. And of course there were a lot of them. He was impressed.

'I'm listening,' I said, as I drifted to the kitchen, my eyes on him, to plunge the coffee. Once around the corner, I silently mouthed 'Yes!' and pumped my fist.

'I haven't read them all yet –' Klang continued, louder now, 'they're pretty long – or entered scores in the database – but a pattern emerged.'

'A pattern! Obviously!' I yelled, showing my serious face around the doorframe.

Disappointing product, weak service, poor quality, no real tradition: this was the kind of information that needed to be wrapped into the end package for which the client was paying a tidy premium. A picture was emerging of how their bread and butter would be received, and Klang wanted to see for himself just how much of a blank slate of a market Glasgow was. He wanted to hear it straight from the horse's mouth – the horse being me.

'The phone rates being what they are,' Klang said, 'I figured I could buy a train ticket for the same price, talk about things in person. So here I am.'

'Here you are!' I called, in a congenial, unfazed tone, as I leaned with all my weight on the plunger. I'd put a lot of grounds in the cafetière; I wanted it dark.

'Actually, I thought I'd be here sooner,' he said, appearing in the doorway to the kitchen, as the plunger finally reached bottom. 'I caught the BritRail out of Euston at three-thirty.' Three-thirty: this was dissonant to my ear, unrefined; a surprising inversion, given that only recently 'half-three' had sounded so queer. 'I guess I underestimated how close Scotland is. Thought it'd be like going from Chicago to Madison. But there must have been fifty stops. Took forever.'

'You're not in Kansas anymore,' I said, handing him a mug of steaming black brew, purple and pink oil streaks on its surface.

'Thanks,' he said. I took my own and we moved to the lounge and sat.

'Cheers,' I said, raising my mug to Klang.

'Mm-mmm,' he answered.

Talking, I was reminded of what I had observed in Klang while enduring the Plunkett's training with him: that his predominant quality was ambiguity. He was enigmatic. His personality wavered and dodged, from calm patience to biting opportunism. He had a wrestler's build, with bulging shoulders, tree-trunk thighs, and those semispherical glutes that protrude, shelf-like. He could come at you low and have you on your back in a second, yet he didn't seem capable of a tangle or scrap. I had heard him tolerate a lot of bullshit from Plunkett staff, standing around bantering on cigarette breaks, nodding in agreement with obvious fabrications, laughing at jokes that were nothing but rationalizations, excuses, petty gripes. Maybe he had found it easier not to make waves, since we were due to hop a plane in a matter of weeks, leaving Chicago far behind. But his obsequiousness persisted, mixed unsystematically with his own brand of Midwestern bluster and knowingness. Despite his lumberjack's legs, his tidy heft, at certain moments I felt I could wave my hand and pass it through him as if through a flame.

At one moment so stout, jocular. Then, seemingly when I expressed or even implied warmth towards him, vaporous and shrewd. Occasionally he inquired of me with what seemed like genuine deference. But just as often, he dealt me jarring adamancy. Suddenly he became bluntly closed-minded to my ideas. Every exchange demonstrated a new, often contradictory, blend of traits.

For example, one morning Plunkett's held a group exercise in Grant Park. It was a team-building seminar led by some third-party consulting honcho versed in corporate dynamics. It was summer, a day of role-playing activities was built around a much-hyped picnic and, as further enticement to attend, casual dress was allowed. Klang showed up in cargo shorts and a jersey from one of those T-shirt stores where you can get custom lettering for your softball team. His had that homemade look. It read, 'The Young Columbo's, U.W., 1992,' in the splotched serif type of an old Corona. The back bore a halftone picture of Peter Falk in a trench-coat and fedora, head tilted, squinting. Quoted above him: '*Oh . . . and just one more thing?*'

'Young Columbo's?' I asked Klang.

'Founder,' he said coolly, 'and President.' Klang kept his eyes on the action and spoke out of the side of his mouth. We were standing in a circle around a lady falling backwards blindfolded so she could get caught by her co-worker. It was a trust exercise, and we were supposed to be watching and learning from it.

'What is it?' I asked. We were outdoors, traffic hummed nearby, birds sang in the trees. No one was too enthralled with the banal demonstration. I made no attempt to conceal that we were conversing.

'Just a group I started,' Klang said.

'What for?'

He looked at me now, sizing up my curiosity. 'Criminal Justice majors, if you must know.'

'Ohhh,' I said. 'So that's what your degree's in?'

'In the end, no.' He looked at his shoes and shifted his weight around. 'I switched to MBA. But I declared it for a while, and we needed some representation on campus.'

The consultant was going around the circle, giving everyone a chance to fall backwards and get caught.

'What'd you do, get together and solve crimes?' I asked.

'A couple wannabe cops and sleuths and me, once a week, we'd have a few pitchers and talk shop.'

'Hmm. So how come you dropped Criminal Justice?'

'You know what a beat cop makes his first year?'

Then we were pulled into the center of the circle. Klang had to catch me and, afterwards, I caught him, my hands hooked under his flared, meaty lats.

Why had someone who'd once planned to make a career out of getting to the bottom of things flip-flopped, and now never quibbled or confronted, in fact should have been awarded a black belt in kowtowing?

And then to go along with this crusader aspect, Klang had his playful side. He could be wickedly funny. I'd sometimes refer to our UK assignment as a 'mission', as if it had a James Bond-like mystique, and he'd play along, talking about needing a 'Q' figure to build him gadgets – disguised American items he could smuggle abroad so he wouldn't have to go without. Cigarettes, for example. (He was a voracious smoker, and the cost was nearly double abroad, thanks to Value-Added Tax.) About the copious planning meetings, about being groped by the company doctor as part of the physical, about the filling out of waivers, insurance forms, next-of-kin decrees, and so on, he always had a biting quip. Coming from a household of such staunch literality and polite rigor, this acidity cracked me up. Maybe that's why I was so attentive to him – I was quite eager for his next wisecrack or sarcastic jab. From the start, there was a tacit acknowledgement between us of my clinginess to him. That was okay with me. I was living at my parents', recovering from the loss of my wife. Klang took the edge off; he'd have me in stitches before long, riffing impressions of people, or harping on the idiocy of the OJ coverage. He was a compelling guy. He drew you in. You wanted to know him.

Seeing him again now at my Glasgow flat – and definitely by the end of my stay in Scotland – I realized this could never happen. I could never really know him. Because the closer you got to him, the more frequent became his divergent one-liners and gruff rants, delivered from within a cloud of cigarette smoke, rebuffing your approach. He had many endearing, enviable qualities that invited emulation. You wanted to be like him. Yet the self-deprecating edge to his humor clued you in: *he* didn't want to be like him.

Saturday morning, we set out for a walk, to give Klang an idea of Glasgow. He wanted to trek to the north and reach the rim of hills that could be seen at the end of certain streets in the West End. I had another direction in mind.

We trudged through Byres Road's bustle, past the tube station, where Klang had trouble making out the sales pitch of the homeless magazine seller, which sounded like *Beg Eschew!* but was in fact *Big Issue.* I took us through a quaint cobblestone lane, past the pub Jinty McGinty's and a small cinema – the sign listing American films that'd been released what seemed like years ago. Climbing up University Avenue, it was sunny and clear, as it often is in the morning, with that blinding morning precision that erases discord. At the university gate, we looked at the coat of arms, its smattering of symbology, arcane to modern eyes, representing the school's origins. Staggeringly, the 'established' date for the university was 1451, three hundred years before America, with its over-large sense of self, gained its cherished independence. I was about to express my awe when Klang spoke.

'Into fish, I see. That's good. Omega-3 fatty acids. High protein, low fat.' He took another look at the university crest before walking away. 'And the olive branch – healthy too.'

We entered a set of heavy doors and passed through a cool, musty corridor. A second set of doors led into an open-air cloister of stone pillars flayed at the tops like exultant arms into a network of continuous arches. The sweet, resinous scent of incense came from the nearby chapel, familiar to my nose. Sunny quadrangles flanked two sides, their lawns carpeted with fallen sycamore and crab-apple leaves – gold, orange and rose. My voice echoing, I told Klang we were now under the tower he'd seen and asked about. He nodded dimly. On the opposite end of the cloister, a propped-open door showed a view like something out of science fiction, a window into another dimension: under a fire-code exit sign only treetops, rooftops and cargo cranes on the horizon. Walking towards it, the mundane colors of asphalt and yellow parking-stall stripes came into view. Reality returned. We stepped out of the sheltering cloister into the small lot and crossed to benches at the edge of a steep hill. Klang placed his small daypack at his feet, and I set my camera atop it rather than on the eternally wet ground. We sat and took in the vista.

I identified what I could in the landscape below: the Museum of Transport, the Kelvingrove Museum, Dumbarton Road, Park Circus. A gaggle of crows swooped down from behind us, alit on a tree nearby and cawed cacophonously.

'So how are you *doing*, Mel?' Klang said after a while. This was a continuation of the previous evening's discussion, over Tanzanian Peaberry, in which he asked about my education, my work history, my qualifications, the experience of interviewing with Carson. Now we were up to the present – the result of all that came before.

'It's an adjustment,' I said, 'don't get me wrong. But it's not like it's the third world.'

'I meant with the divorce,' Klang said.

'Oh, the divorce.'

'It was only a few months before you started training, right?' Klang said. 'So not that long at all. It must feel like yesterday.'

'Well, no, not a few months. The papers were done in the spring. But we'd been apart since last August. So over a year.'

'I see. Even so.'

The birds continued, in anxious, logic-less rhythms, their caws deflecting off the building behind us to disorienting effect. Klang lit a cigarette. A minute later, as they do, one grackle took flight, and the rest followed, shuffling noisily to the east. I dug out my Silk Cuts and lit up. We had drunk more Tanzanian Peaberry that morning, two carafes brewed bitter as tar. Well, mainly, I had drank them, remembering what good coffee tasted like.

'The divorce is fine. Thanks for asking. But it's fine. It's what I wanted.'

'Maybe. But then to move to another country alone. That's two significant changes in a short period, Mel.' His tone verged on condescension.

I cast a diversionary bait of faux philosophizing. 'Alone? What is alone? Are we ever really alone?' Klang had never been so persistently personal with me; usually a wave of earnestness was countered by a high tide of aloofness. I thought perhaps he was driving at something to do with my work. Carson, I was aware, had bestowed him with some degree of managerial status over me, and I accepted that, because Klang was a more competent businessman and shmoozer. We had built a friendship, but was his concern for my well-being or Plunkett's?

'What is this about?' I said, looking at him.

'It's not *about* anything, Mel. I just want to see you succeed in your work.' Klang picked up his pack and handed me my camera so he could get inside. He took out two cans of IRN-BRU, the healing qualities of which I had told him about. 'Isn't this the stuff? I popped out while you were in the shower this morning.'

'Ya sneaky bastard,' I said, momentarily trying on a Scottish accent.

We drank IRN-BRU and smoked, and took guesses at the distance to the rim of green-grey hills at some reach beyond the city proper. Airplanes floated down silently in the distance, angling in from Icelandic stopovers. Activating the self-timer, I propped the camera on a ledge, directed Klang into the frame, then joined him. I took two exposures, an extra in case of blinking. You never know quite how things will line up when you take these shots.

'Send copies to me down in London,' Klang said. 'I'll include one with our next packet to Carson. Come on, let's walk, while we're young.'

'I know somewhere we can go,' I said. 'But it's a ways from here.'

'Fine. You can tell me about this ex of yours. Is there a trail or something? I mean, this place isn't all city, is it?'

'Not yet it's not.'

Despite rumors of the scandalous things that took place in it, I'd cut through Kelvingrove Park many times coming and going from Partick to the cafés in Kelvingrove. I knew its sinuous paths and tree-hidden entrances. Klang and I barreled down the grassy incline from the bench overlook to the paved paths. My plan was to walk us to the edge of my familiarity, Central Station, and take a train from there. On the eastern edge of the park, by a fountain where chickadees and sparrows bathed, a gap in the spiked-iron fence ushered us from black tarmac to beige sidewalk. We waited at the light at Clairmont Street.

'I've got a picture of her,' I said, producing my wallet and digging it out.

The photo was from our wedding day, a side-lit portrait of Margaret's sharp, feminine features, one shoulder forward, chin over it, toward the camera. Her brown hair was done in splendid cascading ringlets for the occasion. Her cheekbones were prominent and proud, lips glossy with the erotic promise of matrimony. The jewels around her neck – something borrowed – glimmered, but like all the high features that caught the light, the gleam was muted by soft-filter. Stillness and peace fill her eyes, which I suppose explains why I cherished this likeness, many of my Margaret memories being of turmoil, tumult. Margaret had questioned the competency of Greg, the friend I'd hired to take the photographs. He didn't have the best equipment. The lighting gear, for example, had looked crude during the sitting, the stands rickety, bulbs garish and industrial. But his work turned out well, and the effect in this shot was flattering, even exquisite. An impressive achievement: Margaret appeared serene.

Klang was in the unenviable position of being obliged to compliment. 'Oh, wow,' he offered, neutrally. 'Very nice.' As if admiring a car I'd shown him. I didn't design it; I didn't build it. I'd simply paid for the privilege of driving it.

'Yeah, thanks. She was a looker. I mean, *is*. She still is even though we're not together.'

The crosswalk beeped and we stepped out, Klang at my right but looking around me for oncoming traffic.

'Traffic comes from the other direction, there, Chief.'

'Of course,' he retorted. 'I must have been distracted by the picture of the hot lady who dumped you.'

'*Touché!*' I elbowed him in the ribs to let him know I could take a joke, which evoked a relieved grin. 'But she didn't dump me. It was mutual.'

'Right, right,' he said. There was that slippery, squinty duplicity on his face, the one I'd seen when he was with the exec-wannabes at Plunkett training. For them he'd turn his chameleon skin a shade of MBA, but then splitting up after a smoke break, Klang was Klang again. Competitive, surly, misanthropic. 'Mutual.'

I pointed Klang in the direction of an angling lane that cut over to Argyle Street, which led into town. Soon we'd reach Charing Cross, a junction of motorways with exits ramps for City Centre that rose to street level, while continuing traffic zoomed into a tunnel beneath. We passed lane after lane of row houses with narrow painted doors slitted with gold mail slots like tight-lipped mouths; bay windows; and concrete steps worn into a welcoming sag by centuries of footsteps. Bikes chained to trees, their seats taken indoors, promised an uncomfortable getaway for would-be thieves. Kebab shops had empty cooking-oil drums on the sidewalk for pickup. We puzzled at the window of a video rental shop, where Indian film posters hung, brown-skinned versions, strange to our eyes, of *Gone With the Wind*-like melodramas, the chiffon and bodices and Stetson hats replaced with saris, nose studs and bindis. Cats snaked around in the alleys, wetted, cowering, near Indian grocers' where curry and sandalwood odors seeped from the open doors. Then a pub called the Uisge Beatha, Gaelic for whiskey – as Nicole had toasted me – showing booths and pints and the iconic gold-on-black harp of the Guinness poster. Glasgow.

Further along, buildings were obscured by high labyrinths of scaffolding, levels of piping and rickety planks that made the stone edifices accessible to repairmen. Patches of stone showed through, soot-black in places and the bumpy maroon of clean sandstone in others. This was a common sight around Glasgow, the erasure of its industrial past. The shedding, via sandblaster, of its dirt-poor skin. Banners declared 'Glasgow's Miles Better' accompanied by a toothy cartoon imp. This was an overture, I derived from newspapers picked up in cafés, to the panel that, every year, unbeknownst to millions of Americans like me, elected a European City of Culture. The comparative 'better' was a veiled reference to Edinburgh: gleaming, historic and wealthy but, as traveler's tropes go, less friendly and more anglicized. Some felt Scotland's capital was its least Scottish city.

At street level, these renovation sites were fenced in by hastily erected plywood walls, which became slabbed with posters for clubs, DJs, raves and *drinks* specials (again, the plurals here, where one studied *maths*). A slew of names whizzed by: Cat in the Hat Club, Queen Margaret Union. Then something caught my eye. I stopped in my tracks, saying, 'Holy shit.'

Klang walked on, but I stayed anchored to the pavement. When he noticed me, he backtracked. 'What is it?'

Atop the posters were five-foot-high spraypainted characters in the evidently universal scrawl of the graffiti artist. Angular with defiant energy, yet stylistic, controlled.

NO M77

'Nom seven seven?' Klang pronounced.

'No em seventy-seven,' I corrected. 'As in, "We don't need no em seventy-seven." It's a motorway.'

'Motorway?' he said. 'Don't give me that. You've been here under a month. You sound like a BBC news anchor.'

'Presenter,' I said, just to irk him. 'Over here, they're called *television presenters*.'

'Jesus Christ.'

In this seclusion, at this remove, all we had was each other. 'When in Rome,' I concluded.

I unzipped the camera case. 'What are you doing?' Klang said.

'Getting a shot of this.'

'Don't waste film on that,' he barked. 'Christ, come to London. There's graffiti on every corner. So what?'

'I collect graffiti,' I lied. Ironically, Klang's haphazard kidding was the perfect ruse to use against him. He so often drifted into obscure jest, riffing on ideas, leaving you wondering whether he was serious, doing it in return was only fair. 'You know, urban scenes. Murals and whatnot.' I felt my pupils contract – that hyperkinetic response of the body when concealing truth. The lyin' eyes of country song. Klang glared suspiciously, sucking his cigarette to the quick. He appeared to believe me for approximately half a second. A nanosecond, my father might venture, always ready with a technical term.

'Well, hurry up, then.'

I snapped a few quickly. I crouched, to be level with the message, but there was no clever composition I could conjure of this flat panel, no toying with the f-stop to achieve dramatic contrast. It was a plain subject – but not that plain to me.

'I'm done.' I capped the lens, zipped the case. 'Let's go.'

We soon reached the cobblestone section of Sauchiehall Street, where motor traffic ends, condemned left or right by a row of indubitably British posts, thick with black paint, rings of regal gold on their tops. Here traffic bottlenecked and retail sprouted like weeds. Each stride notched up the stimuli dial: guitar buskers, thumping bass spilling out of clothes shops, eight-foot-high book covers in Waterstone's window displays (a misguidedly literal play on *epic*), neon cotton tops over window mannequins' erect nipples, the newsman's gruff shouts.

'What is he saying?' Klang asked, just as he had about the *Big Issue*, about the man at the corner stand and his pirate-esque pitch, "Erald 'n Evenin' Toyemmmmzzz!'

'*Herald and Evening Times*,' I iterated clearly.

At a crosswalk a crowd waited, no one even flinching to move against the red man. In Chicago, some self-important suit was always willing to press his luck. Brellies were up, though no rain fell. Force of habit, I supposed. Lorries and BMWs poured through the intersection in a seemingly never-ending stream, their drivers steering past in what I still thought of as the passenger seat.

'Come on,' Klang said, 'let's take a side street or something.' I agreed, and he cut to his right, through the pedestrian clutter, saying, 'Excuse me, excuse me.' I followed in his wake, uttering Pardons and Sorrys. We cleared the mob and climbed an open sidewalk up a short hill to the next corner. There I guided him left, in the direction of Central Station – and spotted the oxide-green copper plates mounted on the building (there were no signposts here) reading Bath Street. Déjà vu tickled me. Sure enough, further down the block were the glass doors of Wimpy's Bath Street offices, the red-herring offices. Now the sidewalk was empty of ruffians. A glance roofwards confirmed the building to be no longer under siege.

In my head, I had replayed all manner of moments featuring Nicole. I had thought of her while trying to fall asleep, when working, taking scrupulous notes on unpalatable coffee, on the tube around town. Wastefully, I had worn my memories thin; now they were recollections not of her but of the last time I'd put the needle of thought to memory's groove. The notches were wearing thin, the audio fuzzy. Dim crackles remained. Her hair wisping into my mouth as we tumbled off the Wimpy building, her derrière crashing into my chest. Her embarrassed deliriousness, trying to deny she needed medical attention. Her emergence, heightened by my negative connotations of hospital waiting rooms, as a vision of vitality, from the Royal Infirmary's dismal dungeons. Our legs touching beneath the table at Curler's, her clinging dress and matching blue eyes.

'Earth to Mel. Come in, Mel,' Klang said.

'What?'

'What's that billboard about?' Klang said. 'It's very odd.'

I looked where he pointed, on the side of a building at the next block. It was a massive sign, cartoonishly drawn. On it a red-headed woman with a lunatic's perfect-toothed smile, her head emerging from a cracked egg. Teetering kid's book lettering arced above her: *Goosey, Goosey Glasgow! A Cracker of a Panto!*

'A cracker of a panto? I don't what the hell that means,' I said, dejected by my ruminations. This listless reply was all I could muster; I couldn't tell Klang what I'd really been thinking about. The last thing I wanted was for him to know about Nicole. He might realize the cab fares and business lunches I'd expensed on the Plunkett Visa were not entirely germane to our client's objectives. Massive piss-ups weren't exactly professional either. I imagined introducing them – Nicole, Klang; Klang, Nicole – and she breaking in with *Thanks loads fer the taxi tay hospital. Cheers, m'dears!* Or worse, *I cannay believe how blootered ya goh. Yer head musta been ringin'!* I'd be back in Wynton in no time.

We slipped into Central Station via the Gordon Street side doors. The air was cool and sound bounced between the cavernous roof and marble floor. Some platforms were empty, some were dominated by the one-eyed face of a hulking locomotive, sunlight behind it from where the tracks let out onto the world. We crossed the bustling floor, weaving between travelers dragging wheeled luggage and overburdened backpackers, past the tables heaped with dried fruit and nuts for sale, through clusters of waiting smokers. Fat pigeons with their ever-bobbing heads scrounged at fag ends, blithely scurrying from feet that could crush them. The immense signboard, with its flickering graph of letters and numbers, lorded over a crowd lingering in tired bunches. British train travel – it was half timetable, half crap shoot. But the results were all there, an atmospheric soup: the sadness of parting, the drudgery of business travel and the thrill of newness, new lives begun in new cities.

10 *History, Legend, Romance*

We found the ticket counter in an enclosed room at the front of the station.

'So how did you and Margaret meet?' Klang asked.

On the walk, we'd managed to skip Klang's suggestion that I fill him in on my ex, having been occupied with the pleasant weather and Glasgow's sights. Now there were no distractions. We sat in a corner, in adjacent chairs, as two ticket counters serviced the roomful of punters – at least twenty had been waiting already when we arrived – and I told him the story of 'Up All Night', a song that'd brought Margaret and me together. Told it not in so many words. Not in these exact words. But something like them. The difference – if anyone's keeping track – between what Klang heard and what really happened is one of depth only, not accuracy.

I first laid eyes on Margaret in Monsieur Drummond's French II class during my junior year at Wynton High. In the spring semester she and I were assigned, along with a third student, to work together on a project in French. A five-minute presentation. Poetry recital, a scene from a play, a faux newscast – whatever the group wanted so long, *bien sûr*, as it was *en français*. '*En français, classe!*' Monsieur Drummond entreated whenever a student blurted something in gaudy English. '*En français!*'

At the announcement of the project groups, my pulse raced to hear Zoë, Margaret's French name, read in succession with mine, Marc. All year I'd noticed her from rows away and enjoyed her exuberant use of the language. She had been flirtatious, if at times sharp, with me in our comings and goings; there was a tacit excitement between us, I felt, as we arranged our desks in a cluster. The other student assigned to our group was Philippe, real name Justin Johns, a rancorous but timid kid with a wardrobe culled from the army-surplus store on Lincoln Avenue. He was harmless though. At assemblies and pep rallies, the most mainstream of school events, he dashed from podium to soundboard, adjusting microphones and cables. And he was a mainstay of the Quiz Bowl team; ask him something trivial about a war, and his edifice of toughness crumbled.

In brainstorming ideas, Margaret remembered a pop song with French in it, and suggested we might sing it. From her backpack she produced a tape, The Distended's *Into the Midst*; a cassette player was borrowed from Monsieur, and we had a listen. The melody was simple and catchy. The chord progressions were elementary, bouncing across one interval, then the same a step down. Once the chorus began repeating and we got the idea, she stopped the tape. 'Well? *Qu'est-ce que vous pensez?*' she said. Then, the verb *chanter* eluding her, she asked, '*Voulez-vous* sing-ay *cette chanson?*' She was a ruthless practitioner of Franglais, Monsieur's term for the bastardization of his beloved language. She would say things like '*Je ne* remember *pas*' and '*Je* teach-ay *au studio de danse.*' This infuriated Monsieur but tickled me. It was absurd yet sensible. It really didn't jar my ear – the meaning came through. Margaret would laugh at odd marriages of the known and unknown that slipped from her mouth; and Monsieur's playful anger, his spit-flinging corrections, only brought her closer to paroxysms. '*Non, non, non, Zoë! Pas de* "teach-ay"*!*' She laughed now, at her Franglais verb 'sing-ay', and I succumbed to the infection of her glee. Her beet-red face lit up, and mine warmed with affection.

'You guys are weird,' Justin muttered, grabbing the cassette player.

No one had any better ideas for the project. 'Well, I perform in front of people all the time,' Margaret said. 'This is the easiest thing for me to do. We can take turns on the verses and sing the chorus together.'

'That's cool,' Justin said, and I agreed, so it was settled.

For the next two weeks, at the final ten minutes of every French period we'd grind desks across the floor to huddle, plan, prepare. '*Le vrai travail,*' Monsieur Drummond instructed, was to be done outside of class. '*Il faut préparer pour le projet après l'école, classe! Vous comprenez?*'

'*Oui, je comprends, Monsieur!*' Margaret called out loudly. 'After school!'

'*Très bien, Zoë.*'

We each memorized the lyrics on our own and, once the verses had been divvied up and our outfits decided on (black jeans, white shirts), there was little to do at the end of French hour. Justin carved and doodled on his book covers while Margaret and I talked. She told me about her figure skating – traveling to places like Gary and Ann Arbor for competitions. She'd been skating since she was six; the cabinet at home was full of trophies. The skating had no affiliation with the school, though, so her classmates knew nothing of her accomplishments. When she placed at regionals and nationals, only a mention was printed in the paper, buried behind features on the football and basketball teams. The daughter of an unmarried and separated couple, she had moved across states a few times and wasn't well known in this town. It wasn't a family name with roots in the community. That kind of comfort had dried up at the age of eight, when her parents split and she and her mom relocated to Indianapolis. Winters, she was on the cross-country ski team, another sport that got little recognition, being ill fit for spectators, lacking the brutality of contact sports, having no buzzers or scoreboard, no measurable quarters or periods. Just nature and man, strapped to a rudimentary pair of slats. It's a race against time, she said. It's a test of stamina. People think it's physical, but it's mental. No trophies in that, though. Good exercise, but she got bored out there on the course and lost focus.

Finally, there was dance, her true passion.

'I bet you have a pile of ribbons and trophies in that too,' I said.

'Hey, when you got it, you got it,' she sassed with a blush. I liked this attitude of hers, so take-charge and antithetical to my parents' apologetics, my dad's dour aphorisms like *A man's gotta do what a man's gotta do.* 'Dance is what keeps me sane,' she said. She had lost plenty – her father when he left, her neighborhood friends, schools, familiarity, safety – but she always had dance. That was just her.

Nothing to lose in it. That seemed to be her approach to competition too. She had nothing to lose in trying. Now, that lesson under her belt, she taught – whole roomfuls of kids at a school called Culkin.

When it came time to synchronize our routine, the Podgorski house was chosen for its proximity to school. Margaret and I met after seventh period and walked there together, this time talking about my school subjects, how I was doing all right in trigonometry, but how I detested science, my father's field. Maybe that was a just a teenage thing, I speculated, rebelling against my parents. But I was pretty sure I wouldn't be following in my dad's career footsteps. My lowest grades were in biology and chemistry. I had no knack for abstractions. Diagrams of bonding molecules, neutrons and protons, mitochondria – lifeless pencil sketches of the unseen. Having never witnessed these sub-cellular doodads and the behaviors they were purported to have, I wasn't even convinced they existed.

In my parents' entryway, Margaret's vitality and boisterousness, I saw, assaulted Mr and Mrs P.'s formal reserve. 'Great to meet you, Mel's parents!' Margaret said, but they only nodded and uttered hello. 'Hey!' she said with a gasp, 'You guys should be the audience for our rehearsal!' But Mr and Mrs P. were neither flattered nor interested.

'Oh, you'll probably want to practice first,' Mr P. dryly stated, 'and get it perfect.'

'Yes, we don't even speak French,' Mrs P. said with a shrug.

It was not that my folks were humorless, only that for them conviviality was earned through small talk and cordial interchanges, not through forceful assertion. A lab-dweller and a retired teacher, they did not have social circles in which they practiced banter and civil debate. Breaking the ice was difficult, melting it sometimes impossible. Mr P. was not very much like anyone he knew outside the office, and his tack in conversation was to draw others to the common ground of current events or suburban civics. The problem was he rarely moved past this stage. You could only float out so many generalities until things hovered awkwardly or died. He had been known to explore a subject's opposing sides – asphalt driveways versus concrete, say – without anyone else contributing. At least Mrs P. made efforts toward polite fascination with any topic. Yet so much as an utterance of negativity sent her reeling into a mystification at how things worked – technology, teen fashions, social norms. At the sign of any contest, she became all bewildered exhaustion.

Justin hadn't arrived yet, but Mr P. ushered us to the downstairs rec room, where he wanted us to practice, leaving himself the solitude of the living room and his newspaper. 'Mel, give me a hand with this table,' he said. 'We'll move it to make more space.'

'Obviously,' I said quietly in Margaret's direction, rolling my eyes.

Removing the rug, Mr P. continued, 'I don't know if you're preparing choreography or if it's just the words but, regardless, now you'll have room to move around.'

'Yeah, thanks, Dad. We're all set then. We'll try to keep it down.'

'Mel knows how to operate the cassette player, so I guess you have everything you need.' My father believed this sort of sober fastidiousness comforted people, though it just made me ill at ease. I'd been listening to this all my life. His instructions were so ridiculously banal! They insulted the intelligence. He gave people no credit for common sense, much less preference or their own capabilities – that struck a nerve.

'Sorry,' I said to Margaret when Mr P. finally retreated upstairs. 'He's a chemist. Slightly anal-retentive.'

'Oh, he's sweet,' Margaret chimed, placing her hand on the back of mine. 'He means well.'

That Margaret could separate my father's kind intentions from the bungled, near-crippling rationality of their expression impressed me.

'I guess so. But it gets tiring.'

'Yeah?'

'Yeah, like there's this running joke in the family,' I explained. 'This one time, he was making drinks for company – I don't know what, probably a margarita, they always make those. And he hands my Aunt Jane her glass and says,' – here, I adopted Mr P.'s stolid baritone – 'Jane, I provided you a straw there. I didn't know if you'd want one. Don't feel obligated to use if you prefer not to.' Margaret laughed. 'My aunts and my mom and me were cracking up, trying to hide it, you know. He gets all huffy and pouty when you criticize him. So now we'll all say, like, "Uncle Bill, I'm passing you the gravy now, but don't feel obligated to pour it on your turkey." My dad has no clue we're making fun of him. He thinks this is how everyone should talk.'

Justin, the bright recluse, arrived in his army pants. I tried to include him in conversation but struggled to divert my attention from Margaret. He was a good sport and desensitized to our flirt-ations in his presence. We began practicing, at first stumbling over pronunciations, behind the beat, our vocal chords cold. Justin was skittish and timid, but game. We both followed Margaret's lead in affecting a stage presence, standing tall, gesturing with our hands despite our fears of effeminacy. We both wanted to impress her and win her praise. As we had planned, I took the first verse.

> Au volant de ma voiture je te voyais partout
> Tu venais vers moi dans mon miroir
> Tu es passée tout près
> Et puis plus rien tu as disparu.

Margaret took the second, her voice louder, projecting better than mine had. At the chorus, I was at first embarrassed by the intimacy of my voice blending with hers. Justin's I didn't mind – there was nothing intimate in it. In subsequent run-throughs, I ignored his voice altogether and savored uniting with Margaret. We all sang:

> Je suis resté debout toute la nuit
> En pensant à toi
> Je ne peux pas dormir sans toi
> Que faire, je n'en sais rien.

The third verse was Justin's, and he sang flatly, not always in tune. Clearly, it was the low point of our performance, but with luck it would be forgotten after the bridge, chorus, solo and final two choruses, for which Margaret instructed us to 'really let it rip'. Being a dance teacher, she was practiced in the art of instruction by gesture, doling out nods, smiles, swooping movements of the hands to signal increased energy. She delivered all manner of nuanced directives to Justin and me, without missing a lyric herself. Spurred by her didactic zeal, I upped my efforts. So did Justin. Margaret possessed both assurance in the song's structure and a familiarity with the concept of routine – the idea that meaning did not have to be invented, only the words produced, with feeling, yes, but more importantly in the prescribed order, until the song ended. From her confidence I borrowed heavily to alleviate my panic, the bone-deep chill that came when I thought of performing before the two classes. (The two sections of French II would serve as audience to these projects.) What I really wanted to do, though, was let the music recede from my consciousness and just watch her – her shapely hips, bright eyes, pert breasts, the coy smile that flashed between phrases. The obligation to practice annoyed me; yet without it, she wouldn't even have been there.

I sang on, take after take.

Behind the sensory shield of the music's volume, a kind of fantasy took shape in which I was a performer and a talent too – an artist/partner to Zoë's dancer/teacher. Suddenly M. Drummond and his pedagogical fervor, his furious love for French, made sense. I thought of him – his barrel chest, scraggly beard and popping enunciations; the deep passion in his eyes that roared up like flames when he led the class. He put on comical airs to engage us students, but what he did was profoundly serious. The reason he bore the repetitive drudgery of Bonjours and Je m'appelle Pierres with crop after crop of first-years was because he had vowed to honor the transformative effect French had had on him when he first spoke it. This was a very noble thing. His reason for being. Not to be taken lightly. A language, like art, was an exotic vine on which you could swing over the jungle of the mundane. More terrestrially, the sequence of shapes used in *J'ai été vers le haut de toute la nuit* satisfied the mouth, and the melancholy stepdown in pitch at the chorus's end – I don't know what to do – pleased the heart. It was a sensation I'd never dreamt of encountering under the roof of 8460 Meadow Prairie Lane.

Even Mrs P.'s brief intrusion, bringing in a tray of iced tea and walking out, quietly impressed, with a lift of her eyebrows, did not break my trance. In the third run-through – 'We have to get it perfect,' Margaret insisted – I was loose and spirited. The words came without thought, and I was able to concentrate on Margaret's suggestions to add singerly emphases, like the occasional vibrato and the all-important cutoff consonants.

It was in the final run-through, when Mr P. passed through the room wearing yardwork clothes and heading out the patio door, that I became self-conscious and screwed up. Singing my solo verse, I stumbled over the lyrics, needing to skip a line to get back on track. I blushed and grinned apologetically, first at Margaret, then Justin. Justin, his emotive exertion bared, could see what was happening between Margaret and me, and understood me correctly to be transfixed by an effortlessness and purity in her which I could never match. But the revealing effect of the performance acted on him too: he looked absurdly scrawny in his army garb, the shaved hair above his ears a laughable imitation of a Marine's.

Margaret wasn't fazed by Mr P. passing through. Accustomed to displaying herself, she stood proudly before us both as if prepared to vouch for us boys to an interrogating panel.

The song never really closed; the debonair protagonist just faded into silence, repeating:

> Up all night . . .
> Up all night . . .
> Up all night . . .

Sufficiently practiced, we sat and drank the iced teas, talking about Monsieur and the class. He was a weird guy but pretty cool for a teacher, we agreed. Justin said he had started German but found it too hard – the last of his hardened façade gone. He asked Margaret and me if we thought we'd get an 'A' on the project; acting on the implicitly shared feeling between us, we turned to each other with deferential smiles, and said we figured so.

When Margaret asked for a bathroom, I escorted her rather than sending her unshielded into my parents' upstairs domain. I walked ahead and filled the silence that might invite Mrs P. to interject a conversational mundanity. 'This is the living room,' I joked, passing through the living room – obviously that's what it was. Margaret's brash laugh sounded behind me. 'Entryway, front door, window,' I narrated flatly, pointing to each. Passing the kitchen, the chopping of vegetables and a talk-radio program could be heard; Mrs P. was absorbed in both. 'My mom,' I whispered. Entering the hall, Margaret's shoulder brushed mine.

'Extra bedroom –' Panic struck too late. I pointed into the first open door, and the sight of its embarrassing contents was before us. I tried to reach for the door handle, but Margaret leaned in to inspect the somber, curious room, and the swishing of her hair past my face ruled out any chance of me moving an inch.

'What is it?' she asked.

Only once we were married would I explain its origins: a segment of pew and kneeler salvaged from St Wenceslas, the Near West Side Czech church of my grandmother's youth. The church suffered a fire in the twenties, mercifully only an echo of the Great Chicago Fire, but was razed nonetheless. Pews that had escaped immolation were unbolted from the floor and offered to congregants as keepsakes, as if hours spent in supplication had earned them partial ownership. Grandma took one, and when she died Mrs P. claimed the relic, meeting no protest from her brothers. It'd been at 8460 ever since, a glaring anachronism, looking like the railing of an old sailing ship.

When I was a boy and equal to the pew's height, I would sit on the kneeling pad, walk it like a tightrope, clutch the rail and lean back as if riding a sailboard. But I hadn't been on it since.

There was a spring-wound latch above the hymnal holder that I used to fiddle with, pressing with all my might, until my fingers slipped and it slapped on the wood. I had assumed this device to be related to some sacramental rite, like the church's other hardware – chalices, incense urns, offertory plates. Its tight grip seemed to correspond with the hold God was said, in mass, to have over us, the power from which we pled for relief with weekly petitioning phrases such as 'Lord have mercy'; 'Christ have mercy'; and with comportments of the body like kneeling, bowed heads, and crossing ourselves. Not until my teens did I understand that this was a clip for holding coats, hats, gloves.

'That – uh . . .' I stammered.

'Is this your mom's craft room?' Margaret asked into the dimness. Relieved, I looked at the room, considering this interpretive error. The blinds were drawn down, the slats open, allowing in light as if the prayer station were a plant, a living organism. Lit votives on a small table beside the pew showed the Virgin Mary and the Christ Child flickering from within. Only Mrs P. knew whether these icons were sacrificial in nature, for dramatic effect, or if they amplified prayer delivery. This room was not discussed.

'It's my mom's prayer station,' I told Margaret. My tone was like you would use in the company of a mental patient – just play along, don't ask questions, and this will all be over with momentarily. Only, oddly, I felt like the deranged one.

'Ohhhhh,' Margaret whispered back, a world of unfathomable acceptance in it. She paused, taking in the room, during which I dreaded my chances with her were ruined. She laughed at herself quietly and put her hand on my forearm consolingly. 'I'm sorry. I thought it was, like, a drafting table or a loom.' She stepped back and looked at me, smiling, as if everything were completely normal.

Emboldened by her sympathy, I touched the small of her back and guided her to the end of the hall.

'Here's what we're looking for,' I said, letting her off at the john.

Soon I escorted both guests to the front door. Mr P. was gone, the lawnmower in the backyard murmuring his whereabouts. Justin scurried out of the house, issuing a curt 'See ya in class.'

Margaret and I exchanged prolonged reflections on our prepared-ness for the performance, until eventually I held the door and stood watching as she walked to her Mazda, parked under the sheltering boughs of Meadow Prairie Lane's aged oaks.

Mrs P.'s voice broke my reverie. 'That song sounds fun. What do the words mean?'

'Oh, just a silly torch song,' I lied. 'I can't sleep at night, thinking about you. Stuff like that.' Some parts were in fact a lot racier, but I couldn't bring myself to say 'sweating bodies' or 'can't sleep without you near'. Even more – I couldn't turn from the sight of Margaret drifting away.

At last I stepped back inside.

'Oh, my Lord!' Mrs P. exclaimed. 'Look at you!' She wore a dish towel over her shoulder and was twisting her rings back on, taken from the apron pocket.

'What?'

She grabbed me by the shoulders and squared me up to her. 'Your eyes – you're as giddy as a schoolboy.'

I couldn't repress a smile.

'Her?'

'What?'

'That laugh!'

'What's wrong with her laugh?'

'I don't know. Let's ask the neighbors.'

'At least she laughs. It's not a crime, in case you haven't heard. I know it's not a *practical* response.' This was a jab at one of Mr Podgorski's hallmarks. Practicality, reason: he brandished these against Mrs P.'s swerving, diluted passions. When she spoke of vacations, recreation, purchases, he stymied her with the all-trumping practical. 'We'll have to consider how that factors into the *equation*,' he would say. I knew the whole theme was a sore spot for Mrs P. It got to where she doused her own fires before he could. She expected little.

'Be nice,' she scolded. 'She's very pretty. I'm sure she's a sweet girl.' This meant her assets were not immediately apparent. She was not delicate, not angelic, which should be a girl's most obvious charm. Margaret was flashy, vibrant. She didn't glow and she wasn't demure; she had a bright gleam and declared. 'Did you ask her out?' Mrs P. continued quickly, trying to gloss over the implied snub and make me believe she really trusted my judgment.

Klang asked a few questions and made a few remarks throughout my story. He had a friend like Justin, nerdy and militant, and he wondered if we got an 'A' on our project after all. But for the most part he listened politely. When our number was called, I said, 'I'll take care of this,' and headed to the ticket window, waving away his cash offering.

I used the Plunkett Visa, though I had no intention of trying to convince Klang of the pertinence of the outing to our clients' endgame. It was only twenty quid or so, but it was the principle of the thing. Telling Klang the intimate details of my first love and now ex-wife, the emotion of reliving it, had been taxing. I felt I deserved a reward. I chose a company-paid trip to Pollok Park.

I found Klang at a John Menzies' magazine rack across the station. He bought a *Loaded* magazine, a near-naked girl on the cover. 'These are great,' Klang said. 'It's all about laddism.'

'Laddism,' I repeated, without interest.

Crossing to platform twelve, he added some free brochures from the *i* kiosk to his reading library.

We had a smoke, then boarded, only to find other passengers puffing away. We had kept it outdoors out of habit – American laws, state-specific Clean Indoor Acts. None of that to contend with here.

We sat on opposite sides of a booth, facing each other. A family across the aisle unpacked sandwiches, crisps and Lucozades. Klang took out the brochures and chose one to begin with. 'Highlands and Isles,' he said, reading from the decorative, stylized cover. From my upside-down perspective, I saw the ornate drop-case S of the opening paragraph. *'Scotland has everything you could ask of a holiday destination,'* Klang read, leaning forward, arms tucked in his lap under the table. *'Romance and misty mountains, friendly* people, inspiring scenery, superb food and drink, a fascinating culture and history, great wild outdoors and a vast range of things to see and do.' I saw each photo in the inverse: blue peaks topped by a purple heather sky. Klang flipped the page. Highland dancers' tartans defied gravity. The mouth of a Highland Cattle, or 'hairy coo', appeared perversely human, as if not only its image had been inverted but also its animalistic qualities.

The family across the aisle ate silently.

'So that was the beginning really,' I said after a minute of silence – silence that seemed obscurely to bridge Klang's reading to my story.

'The beginning?'

'That was how we met, essentially. With the song.'

'Margaret,' he said, leaning back, away from the glossy brochure. 'So you lasted, what, two years? I know you told me once, but I'm trying to piece this together.'

'Just over a year.'

'Wow, you guys married young.'

'Nineteen, both of us.'

'How'd it end?'

'End? Don't you want to know about the middle?'

'The middles are usually the same, I find.'

The train rocked a hair, the brakes releasing. Then the tiles of the Central Station wall, a pattern that filled the windows across the aisle, slid leftwards. A BritRail employee, in his neon-green vest, glided past in a still posture. We were rolling.

Once out of the station, I watched the network of rust-brown tracks multiply and angle away. The ticket-taker came by with his silver card-punch.

'I don't suppose you'll ever marry,' I said. 'That's in your best interest.'

'Why's that?' Klang closed the brochure, and moved the one below it to the top of the stack. *Planning Your Holiday*.

'Isn't that what you were driving at this morning?'

'What?'

'At the university. That my business acumen is lacking, due to my recent divorce, estrangement from family. You don't have any of that baggage. You've got your MBA, this position.'

'Pod, man, I never said anything of the sort.'

'No, but . . .' I thought Klang would fill something in here, but he merely held his assured demeanor. He seemed to teeter with some discomfort between his roles as compatriot and professional superior. Because Carson had made him accountable for my work too, his ass was on the line – twice. Which was apt, given his meaty wrestler's buttocks.

'Then what was that about unhealthy habits and stuff?'

'Those aren't my words. You're being paranoid.'

'Whatever you said!' I leaned in and whispered, 'Whatever you said.'

'Okay, yes,' Klang confessed. 'I was saying that, you know, you should watch yourself. Your reports are very detailed, almost obsessive. I wondered if you're not overworking yourself. Give yourself a break – there's a lot of factors at work. Culture shock. Work stress. Maybe you're a little stung from the divorce, you want to prove yourself. But you can't overdo it. You look a little pale, to be honest. I'm just saying, make sure you're eating right, getting some exercise and fresh air.'

'I don't know if you noticed, but Glasgow is not exactly Club Med.'

Klang said nothing.

'You don't know what you're talking about.' I threw a glance at the family across the aisle. They were tidying up their areas of wax paper and banana peels. 'Okay, the fact is, yeah, splitting up is no fun. But that's behind me now. I did my atonement. I paid my dues. Now I'm here. And . . .'

Klang waited. Eyes locked on me, he licked his thumb and flipped open the next brochure. I swallowed, then lost the stare-down and turned to the window. Outside: the backs of tenements, narrow grass yards – they called them *gardens*, never mind whether anything was growing in them or not. I'd seen four concrete paving stones called a garden. There was a guy on BBC2 always twittering on about how to make use of your garden, no less arrogantly than Rick Gedes, the Plunkett's branding guru. The show had this corny premise where they painted fences, planted hostas and installed water features while one spouse was away visiting friends or shopping. It took place down in England mostly, and the yards, though not huge, were sizable – you could do something with them. Here, the gardens were slim, claustrophobic closets of hanging wash, footballs, and rubbish bins. (Laundry, soccer balls, and trash cans.)

'I'm just trying to rebuild my life,' I said, turning back to Klang. Something had to be said, though this wasn't quite it. 'I thought I was doing a good job.'

Klang held me in his gaze for a long while with a look approaching sympathy, which for him was like coveting an object, an indulgent treasure, through department-store glass. He couldn't touch it, he could only imagine trying it on. After a minute, he turned to the glossy copy and read aloud again. '*Majestic glens and mirror-like lochs form the perfect backdrop to picturesque towns, isolated crofts, towering castles and pagoda-topped distilleries.*'

I leaned my head against the window and put one leg on the seat. 'To be honest,' I said, 'the divorce was fairly painless. By that time, the worst was over. The proceedings were just a formality.'

'*Pagoda-topped distilleries?*' Klang mused. 'As in Chinese gazebo-type thing? Sorry – yeah? Fairly painless?' This lightness was his offer of a peace accord, a resumption of negotiations.

'I loved her. I *did* love her. Very much.'

Klang jumped in at the pause with, 'But?'

'There's no but.'

'Come on. You were headed to a *but*.'

The rails sank down between bramble-laden banks taller than the cars themselves, casting our booth in shadow. My reflection appeared in the darkened glass, hedges and poles and rubbish blurring through it. I focused on the outside. Carrier bags, tangled and rained on, zipped by, white flecks nestled deep in brush.

Klang returned his attention to the brochure. To me, his intermittent reading wasn't rude or inattentive. Actually, I appreciated his detachment. It was healthy, a coldness that bolstered.

Remembering what I was remembering put a lump in my throat, and Klang's evenness steadied my own stirring emotions, which were not sadness, loss, so much as resentment.

The traveling foursome across the aisle were near enough for their conversation to be heard, but they didn't seem to be aware of a word we said. They took no notice of our accents or my frequent glances at them. A brown-haired boy of about ten silently tolerated his father's instructions. The dynamic stirred me. If I had had the nerve, I would have taken out my camera. But they weren't actually oblivious, just polite. We are socialized to respect people's privacy even when it overlaps our own. A shutter's invasive click would not go unnoticed.

'*A startling variety of wildlife,*' Klang read, with the dreamy gravitas of documentary narrator, '*makes its home in the sea-lochs and glens where an unbroken thread of human history reaches back into the mist of time.*' He looked up and met my eyes. 'Holy mixed metaphor, Batman.'

I sniffed out a laugh but was uncheered. I took out my cigarettes and lit one. I didn't like to smoke in this enclosed space with children around, but the natives seemed unfazed. I found an empty soda bottle in the trash cubby under the window and unscrewed the cap to ash in. The bottle was IRN-BRU, which of course made me think of Nicole.

The father of the dining family directed his charges in clean-up. 'Here, Ah'll take tha'.' He crumpled things and stuffed them into a Safeway bag, which then was zipped into an outer compartment of a backpack.

'Paul, d'ye want yer headset?'

'Aye.'

The daughter evidently did not need to be asked how she'd like to occupy herself during the journey. 'Yer book, Anna,' father said – *book* rhyming with *fluke*.

I watched them askance but intently. The civility and discipline of the family unit was heartwarming – the affectionate obedience of the children. Though I had no desire to be a father myself – a matter that had been a point of contention with Margaret, for sure, and one that had met its resolve – the way some people parented at home in America riled me. Getting a haircut or picking up a pizza in Wynton over the summer, countless times I'd been stuck in line near some pugnacious little shit whose parent endured three seconds of the child's gripes then collapsed like a tent in a squall. *Here, have your toy. Go ahead and stand on the furniture. Sure, eat all the candy you want. Yeah, tear the pages of the magazine while you're at it.* I'd seen discipline, and that wasn't it.

Margaret was amazing with children. When she taught at Culkin School of Dance, I'd stood and watched her in action many nights for the overlap between my arrival to pick her up and her finishing class. Leaning on the barre, hands in pockets, I'd silently admire. She towered over the tikes, but treated them as equals. Their bony legs didn't even fill their stretch-cotton tights, whereas Margaret was full and curvaceous in her own dance gear, her muscular femininity doubly alluring packaged with her stern but affectionate authority. Her voice filled the room, and she met each student's eye, moving from one to the next, keeping them on task, juggling their attentions as a magician attends to spinning plates. All her simple vanities dispersed in this role. Her overdone clutter of wrist bangles and flashy clothes were put away in a locker; her attention-getting sass, a habit born of ingratiating herself, again and again, to new peers in new schools, was not needed here. Here she could win affection with authenticity and discipline. When she taught, she wore her hair brushed straight and forgotten in a neat ponytail, not the sticky sculpted array she usually kept it in.

This point revealed something to me, an interpretation. She could be herself with the third-graders because she identified with them so closely, more so than she identified with me. Telling the children what to do – telling them kindly, constructively, where to put their bodies and how, when to be still and when to move – was like telling herself in the manner she wished she'd been directed at that age. Guided and cared for. Instead, she'd been bullied around by circumstance and her parents' inconstancy. Staying with her mom in Warrenville, with her dad weekends in Indiana.

Sleeping now here, now there, one weekend then the next. Friends left behind. Bumped around on a sea of new bus routes, new desks, new classmates whom she had to woo through subservience to their cliques, their games, their jokes and neighborhoods and Nikes and Jordaches and all the rest of the American flim-flam. And finally, when she was older, capable of some self-government, her mother, when Margaret needed her most, going out night after night with an ever-changing cast of men. Abandoned again.

Margaret had always been resistant to my ideas, my concepts of how we should be as man and wife, but it was late in our short marriage when I pieced this theory together. When fights began breaking out over the most inane things, there was no connection in her mind between her childhood and our disagreements. She wanted her way, and that was that. So did I, of course, and that felt to her like yet another outside force asserting its cold will. She had meant marriage to be her last compromise.

All this seemed so long ago.

'History, legend, romance, and the great outdoors,' Klang spoke again, 'combine seamlessly here to guarantee visitors a warm Highland welcome and a truly memorable holiday.'

The train had gathered speed and now pulsed into our seats.

Cl-clack. Cl-clack. Cl-clack. Cl-clack.

The beverage cart came by and Klang treated us eagerly to large coffees – he had a bit of fiendishness in him after all. 'Cheers,' he said, receiving his steaming foam cup, here called polystyrene. We gulped heedless of its heat, nodding with satisfaction, even though its flavor was a prosaic tinge of tannin, like sucking on a penny. Anything would do: the slew of memories recalled had left me foggy and vertiginous. I needed clarity, grounding.

'You know,' I said, after a bit. 'I don't think I'll ever forget the words to my verse.'

'Verse?' Klang said.

'J'ai passé la nuit à penser à vous. Je ne peux pas dormir sans vous.' It amazed me that my mouth and throat remembered how to form these sounds.

'Oh, that song.'

I rattled off the rest. It was all a memorized sequence, like my father's parlor trick of reciting pi's decimals to a few dozen places.

'How's that translate?'

'Oh, like, *I've been up all night thinking about you, I can't sleep without you.*' These lyrics had always been veiled in their Frenchness. In English, they sounded absurd, melodramatic. I started laughing – a light laugh at first, pushing breath out my nose. Klang watched me, perplexed and apprehensive, as if gauging, Are you laughing at what I think you're laughing at? His disturbed look made my laughter grow, and I slumped in the seat. Klang began giggling too, out of contagion, and cautiously steadied the sloshing coffee in his hand. The family looked our way now. The boy, entombed in his sonic sepulcher by large earphones, smirked at me. Just then the train's *clacks* slowed.

Klang, giggling and red-faced, motioned for me to follow him as he slid out of the booth. I grabbed my camera, Klang hoisted his pack. We pressed the lighted button, passed through the chuffing doors and waited between the cars. We sucked in deep, calming breaths and wiped our watering eyes. Against the heave of the slowing car, we braced ourselves on the wall, while a signpost coasted past reading POLLOKSHAWS ROAD.

11 *Pollok Free State*

We got off the train and walked. The weather was gray, raining lightly. It was mid-afternoon, but nightfall encroached. Across the street from the station was Pollok Park: a sprawling lawn with gravel, on the horizon distance-dimmed steeples and chimneys. And in the tree line, a glimmer of crisp white. Wavy like cloth, clean as a sheet, dotted through the foliage by bold black lettering. Ruaridh's banner.

'Hey!' I exclaimed, turning sharply on Klang. 'Right here, right here, right here.'

'Hmmm?' I'd caught Klang lighting one of the last American smokes.

'This is what we want – c'mere.' I guided Klang to the exterior wall of a nearby building, over to a map mounted in a weather-proof case. At the top, the wide Clyde snaked left to right in logical blue, descending slightly as it inched inland. A green mass (what else?) stood for Pollok Park, severed into county-like sections by dotted lines which the key indicated were *Walking Paths* and by a blue rivulet named *White Cart Water*. This vein-like fissure took a straight course, excepting a violent dip midway in its journey and an equally abrupt resumption eastward, drawing a symmetrical U. Scattered over the emerald expanse were rectangular structures named *Rugby Football Club, Sherbrooke Riding School, Cowglen Golf Course, South Lodge, Maxwell House, Playing Fields*, and *Cricket Ground*. A red X marked our location at the *Welcome Centre*.

'They've got a Maxwell House here,' I said. 'Good to the last drop.'

Klang smirked and nodded mid-drag. He stepped away from the wall, dropped the butt, and toed it out. I read the names of the roads framing the park. Langside Avenue to the east, Barrhead Road to the south, Dumbreck Road to the north. On the map they were narrow, yellow and winding, as spotless and innocent as the path to Oz. Along the western edge of the parkland slithered a heartier breed of snake, its back doubled by red stripes. Dual carriageway. Motorway. Heart racing, I traced the winding tail towards City Centre until meeting a unique label I hadn't noticed before. The now familiar characters M77, which had, since their first appearance on Nicole's shirt, become an emblem of yearning, were preceded by the cautionary words *Proposed Site of*. I drew back, pondering. In the corner of the map read 'copyright © 1994 Wimpy Construction PLC.' Then, under this bright sheet, I noticed a second layer of paper, one of faded orange. The old overlaid by the new.

'This was a great idea,' Klang said, already at the curb. He seemed excited to find himself removed from the density of London's urbania – eager. 'Let's check out the park.'

'How about a picture first!' I said, walking to him.

'A picture? What of?'

'Me and you. Right here.'

Klang acquiesced but added, 'Make it snappy.' I putzed with the camera, balancing it on an uneven stone ledge, crouching behind it while aiming the viewfinder and finally tenting a map over it to fend off the sparsely spattering rain. The last touch was to peel off a lens wipe, silken and fine, with which to dab the single raindrop beaded on the glass eye. A Glasgow rain even at its fullest was never as vigorous as those I was accustomed to. Glasgow rain had no capacity for torrent, like those downpours hurled upon the plains of suburban Illinois, issuing from the massive thunderheads that barreled together when weather systems collided over the heartland. The massive rumbling – a vying for airspace, a power struggle, with swooping pressures and scurrying wildlife – was magnificent. High pressure and low pressure colliding. Scotland, however, lacks the expanses that yield such heavenly drama. It has near-constant piddle, but never the thumb-sized drops that awed me as a kid, with their angry thwaps as they divebombed on angled winds against roofs, reaching under eaves. Never Scottish hail, never Scottish sleet. Wind, yes. On all coasts. But I would never see Scottish lightning or hear a Scottish thunderclap, its echo bespeaking vastness. No, in Glasgow, clouds blow in from the North Sea, and their underbellies are slit gently open by mountaintops. Rain drops on the Clyde Valley, where Glasgow sprawls, for days, in staggering abundance, but without violence. The citizenry is dulled by its ubiquity. They have little cause to be smilier than Edinburghers.

I scurried out from behind the camera and threw an arm over Klang's shoulder. With a sneeze of light, the colors of this razor-thin moment were encoded in the inverse language of silver-halide and photons.

'Come on, let's go,' Klang implored, as I repacked the Pentax in its case. Waiting to cross the road, I unfurled my hood from its system of self-enclosure. A dozen yards into the park, though, I put it down again, not liking my hearing obscured. Also, the precipitation was directionless, a pervasive mist that could not be shielded. I allowed Klang to drive the path of our walk, but I was hesitant doing so. If he should notice it, I couldn't refuse to venture near the banner, whose glimmering whiteness in my periphery pestered me like a hovering mosquito. I left it to fate, and fate now drew Klang's curiosity toward a two-story estate house that sat, like a lion on its haunches, on a rise to the south. Maxwell House. Between us and the manor was a footbridge that spanned a narrow gulch containing the divergent rivulet known as White Cart Water.

'So,' Klang said, with a grand, resumptive sweep, 'How did your folks take your getting divorced? Were they supportive? Disappointed? Hopefully, they understood it was for the best.'

'They understood, in a way.' We exchanged a glance that acknowledged we would leave it at that.

We matched strides now – long strides, refreshed after the sit-down of the train ride. We moved over thick and tangled grass, swampy in places, sunken. The sky spilled above us like cold porridge, unsightly. We kept our heads down, intent on the pungent earth; no towering buildings drew our focus upwards. Our American boots swinging in and out of view created a unity of purpose, an echo of consciousness declaring its forward impetus. There swelled around us something tender and encompassing. It seemed linked to our foreignness, and equally to our displacement and movement. Apart from wondering if we didn't look like Laurel and Hardy or Kramden and Norton, with my height and his paunchiness, I was selfless, unencumbered, a sensation that had accumulated since we set out from the West End. Always I had been able to focus on Klang or on our pace. As I stepped, I saw Klang step. As my nerves were numbed with nicotine, I saw Klang draw on a Camel. As I puzzled over unfamiliar language on a road sign – and dozens of other places – I saw Klang's head turn, deciphering in tandem. On the train, I had watched him drink coffee; now my tongue was coated with stale residuals. Here in the misty park, he blinked away droplets snagged on his eyelashes, just as I felt accrued moisture, overburdened by its own weight, streak down my forehead. This bond was solid and trustworthy, like family. Hell, better than family.

'Another cup of coffee would hit the spot,' I mumbled.

'Yeah, it's so wet, the cold goes right through you. Your parents big coffee drinkers?' There was something conspiratorial in his posing of this question.

'That's enough, there, Sigmund.'

'No, I didn't mean –'

'No?' I paused. 'Anyway, it's not something I got from them. Mom is a tea fanatic. Once in a while she'll have coffee in a restaurant. Then the next day, she'll complain, "It kept me up all night." Dad never touches the stuff. He winces at the smell, puzzles at my obsession. He's too sober for caffeine. Entirely too sober.'

'What, is he in AA or something?'

'No, nothing like that. All I know is, he's pretty even-keeled, doesn't drink coffee or soda or anything. He's one of those corn-fed dads you see at a steakhouse ordering chilled milk.'

With a laugh, Klang gestured for me to go first onto the bridge, which we had reached now. It was wooden, painted gray, with tar paper nailed to the footboards for traction – and not quite wide enough for two to cross side by side. Hollow clomps replaced the mucky squishing that had sounded the tempo of our gait across the green. Over the water, the air smelled brackish and mossy. We stopped halfway across, leaned on the railing, and looked down: a shallow, barely moving stream, skirted by tall grass. A single lilypad dotted the otherwise blank tabletop reflecting the unremarkable sky.

'But to answer the question,' Klang prompted, his question like tiptoeing.

'I just said they don't touch the stuff.'

'The other question. Did it cause a big rift in the Podgorski clan, your divorce?'

'My mother never liked Margaret,' I said, turning to Klang. 'That's something I've come to terms with. But I also realize she would have found fault in anyone I married.'

'Was she *happy* you guys split up?'

'Conflicted, I think. She put in a lot of hours at her prayer station around that time.'

'Excuse me?'

'You heard right. Prayer station.'

'Like a shrine?'

'Like a shrine. Minus the production values.'

'Wow, that's old school.' Klang was silent for a while. I watched the surface of the stream, trying, as in a mental carnival game, to anticipate the appearance of the next tiny ring. 'God forbid,' Klang said at last. 'If I got married and had a son, then he got divorced, I'd be jealous.'

I snorted an uncertain laugh.

'I mean, I raise this kid for eighteen years or more. He grows up, he gets married, toughs it out a few years, then calls it quits. "I've been married twenty years! I'm ready to pack it in too! You think you've had enough?"'

'There's more to it than *having enough*.'

'I wouldn't know.' Klang spat – a frothy glob that he let drop. It plopped on the water and idled there. I looked away. Two people and a dog approached from the direction of the Welcome Centre, and an older couple milled around the entrance of the Maxwell House. 'What about your dad?'

I continued across the bridge, and Klang followed. On the opposite side stood a plaque.

'My dad?' I sighed, noticing a patio with tables and umbrellas at the side of the house. Possibly a café in the former mansion. 'Do you suppose they charge admission to this place?'

'Hang on – what's this?' Klang said. I turned and followed him, cutting across the lawn – vibrant green and trim now – to the edge of a prim gravel path that snaked the grounds. The plaque had raised bronze lettering, tarnished brown, set in a crumbly plaster base. Klang read aloud, still piqued by tourism's learning opportunities, which had incited him, on the train, to voice the brochures' contents.

'*This magnificent countryside park with its superb walled gardens and woodland walks was once part of the Old Pollok estate and was the ancestral home of the Maxwell Family for seven centuries.*'

'Fascinating. Let's go inside,' I said. 'I think I smell coffee.'

'*The park has been the site of three castles. The first a wooden structure dating back to 1160 which was located on the banks of the White Cart Water. The second was a fortified tower with a mant* – I mean a moat – *and drawbridge and was built around 1270 on high ground where the woodland garden is now located. Around 1500 it was replaced by a new castle named Nether Pollok Castle, situated on the banks of the river where the Old Stable Courtyard now stands. This castle was destroyed by fire in 1882 and the area was cleared and the stable courtyard built. Pollok House was built in 1752 and this became the family's main residence.*'

'Okay, Inspector,' I said. 'This is all very interesting . . .'

Ignoring me, Klang shifted his weight in the crunching gravel, took a deep breath and continued at the top of a second column. His voice rattled and scraped but bent to his determination to narrate the entire plaque – either as diversion or instruction. '*Pollok House is regarded by many to be an example of one of Glasgow's most elegant family homes. It was built by successive generations of the Maxwell family, who are known to have lived at Pollok since 1269.* Damn, 1269. *It is believed that this fine example of a country house is the fourth residence of the Maxwell family to be built here since its establishment in the thirteenth century.'*

Klang cleared his throat. Looking up from the rows of lettering, he surveyed the house and the grounds with a set mouth, as if imagining this parcel of land all those centuries ago. Then he read on, quickly now. *'The park was created by the owner of Pollok Estate, Sir John Stirling Maxwell (1866–1956), who was a founder-member of the National Trust for Scotland. He realised the importance of maintaining green areas within cities and gave the people of Glasgow access to part of his estate from 1911. A conservation pact with the NTS was made in 1939 in which they together agreed to maintain the land as open space in perpetuity.'* Here Klang raised his chin, punctuating and evoking the regal spirit of the precise legalese of the ending words: *in perpetuity.* But with the opening phrase of the next line, he sank to a grave aspect. *'After his death, his daughter, Mrs Anne Maxwell Macdonald, gave Pollok House, a substantial proportion of the estate and her father's art collection to the Glasgow Corporation. This gift of land eventually allowed the Glasgow city fathers to erect a building to hold the Burrell Collection.'*

'What they don't mention,' I said, 'is that this ultimately allowed the city to sell a portion of the park to Strathclyde Regional Council for the M77, breaking the original agreement.'

'Really? What do you know about it?'

'Well, it's got nothing to do with me. It's all over the newspapers. I work in coffee shops, you know – I can't help reading newspapers.'

We breezed through the Maxwell House, looking at the oil portraits of the family, the oriental vases, the Belgian wall tapestries. The rooms were laid out as if the whole clan might show up the next day, the long dining-room table decked with gleaming silver and fresh unlit candles in the holders. There was a hairbrush on the matron's vanity and rimless spectacles laid faux-casually on the desk in the library. Enjoying the sad yet tantalizing air of ghostly occupancy, I was eager to experience the emptiness of the house's many rooms. Klang lolled behind me, and several times I urged him on until, finally, on the second floor, we entered a cavernous drawing room. Two Louis XIV chairs and a side table topped by a stack of books sat angled toward twin French doors offering a view over the back garden, which was now the grounds of the park. I stood at the doors and looked out and, just as I made sense of a messy spectacle in a treetop, Klang shuffled up next to me, asking, 'Hey, what's all that?'

He pointed to the grove of trees, which contained, high in its boughs, a crow's nest of sorts, edged by a railing of square panes of glass. (Ruaridh would later imply, by sarcastically thanking Wimpy for the generous donation, that these pre-framed windows had been nicked from a building site.) A man's head – not bearded – peered out over the railing, in conversation with a group on the ground, where among the trunks we could make out only vague commotion and clutter. There seemed to be a clearing on the other side; one strip of tarp-like green could be seen. What couldn't be missed was the white banner among the branches.

Exactly how I answered Klang escapes me. Frozen with nerves, I must have stalled, because before I knew it, Klang said, 'I've had enough of this place, let's go check it out,' and I was on his heels, out the door of the drawing room, down the marble stairs and crossing the yard.

'This might not be such a good idea!' I called, jogging to keep up with Klang's stride. He must have been imagining himself in a Columbo trenchcoat, its tails flapping behind him like the tail of a comet called Justice.

'Why's that?'

'This city has a bit of a reputation, you know.' I got alongside him. 'Come on, slow down. You got any cigarettes left?'

I got him to stop and light me up. Huffing out the first plume, I looked at him intently. 'These protesters don't kid around, you know. They put spikes in trees. They chain themselves to equipment. I read one quote, the ringleader was talking about, "It's a shame the tires on the bulldozers spontaneously deflated the morning the clearing was slated to start." If they carry knives, they might carry guns – who knows?'

'Please, Pod. Don't make me laugh,' he scoffed, pushing smoke out his mouth's side hatch. 'A bunch of British tree-huggers. They're probably drunk and stoned, singing "Kumbaya". It's getting late, let's go.'

It was true, the gray daylight was nearly sapped, sponged up into the unending cloud blanket. He sped on and I followed, watching the towering treehouse grow larger. The platform was about five feet wide, and it circled the tree 360 degrees at a height of about twenty feet. Holding it up were the tree's lowest boughs – strong boughs, thick boughs – and a network of two-by-four supports emanating from the trunk like an umbrella's arms. From a distance, the whole thing looked like a budding flower, its glass petals reflecting the diffuse light one after the other, as we approached.

Klang tried to lead us straight through to the people, but after a few strides we were mired by snarled undergrowth. 'Hang on, hang on,' he said, reversing course and skirting the thicket to the north. Vague voices from the campers faded as we rounded the copse and came into a clearing – a suddenly very clear clearing. A wide swath of ground had been shaved of all trees and turf and smoothed, obviously, by machine. The grade was perfect, the exposed soil flattened and tamped, industrial-size tire marks showing only at the edges where the machines had come and gone before painting themselves out of this corner. The only blight on the pristine tract was a message laid out in stones: NO M77.

'Here we go,' Klang said, seeing our path was clear to reach the encampment. Facing us now, and in clear view, was the banner. The banner from the newspaper article. The banner proclaiming this an independent nation: POLLOK FREE STATE. Down the trunk from the crow's nest hung another, this one vertical and cut from sheets. It bore a clenched fist, bolts of power rising from it; NO MOTORWAY read vertically, the hand-scrawled block letters stacked like totems; IN POLLOK PARK concluded as a horizontal footer. Sagging wet and heavy from another tree was the Scottish flag, a white X on a blue background. As we approached, the half-dozen people sitting on crates and log benches watched us and chatted amongst themselves. Behind them were four or five tents set back under the tree canopy, and also a desultory arrangement of stuff: bikes, chicken wire, tarps draped over piles, toolboxes and shovels, a hardshell suitcase. One of the sitting men, crouched in a hooded jacket, clutched a tambourine-like drum – later I'd learn it was a *bodhran*, a Celtic folk instrument. As we arrived, this man stood and set the drum down.

'We've given enough interviews for tahdee,' he said to Klang, who I'd let drift in front of me. It was Ruaridh. The beard, the puffy eyes, the poncho, all recognized from the *Herald* profile.

'Interviews?' said Klang.

'Aren'tja a cuppla journos?' He nodded towards my chest, where my camera hung.

'Reporters?' I said, stepping forward. My throat was tight; I cleared it. 'No, no. Nothing like that.'

'Och, Americans? Wha', come to join up?'

'Well –'

'Ri' enough. Come one, come all. We've goh Aussies, some folk up from London.' With a hooked thumb, he indicated over his shoulder to a cluster of people twenty yards beyond the tents at the other end of the clearing. The uniformly bold primary colors of their anoraks and rucksacks pressing though dusk's sheen broadcast a stronger sense of cohesion than did the ragtag cluster nearer us. I could hear an acoustic guitar – maybe Klang was right about these people – and a timely burst of men's laughter and yelling bounced through the copse to our ears. 'Aye, jolly lot,' Ruaridh confirmed. 'Never mind the Sco'ish flag, tha's William's. He built the treehouse, so Ah've allowed it. This is Pollok Free State, and it's not abou' nationhood. It's abou' sovereignty from tyrants, from a car-owning elite.' So he was repeating himself: this last phrase he'd already used in the *Herald* interview. I was relieved to know he was not limitlessly articulate. His wheedling ways came off him like a stench. You could tell he saw the world as black and white. Justice, injustice. Calling them out was his occupation – he had dubbed it a duty. He was probably on drugs.

'So who're you with?' Ruaridh said. 'EarthFirst? Greenpeace? We've not heard a thin' fra the likesa those gits.'

'We represent Plunkett Research,' Klang explained. 'We're here on business.'

'Ah've no haird of them,' Ruaridh puzzled, and moved right into unabashed tirade. 'You know wha' they're doin' here? This park –'

The people sitting behind Ruaridh, in rain jackets, gloves and hats, paid no attention to us. I shifted my weight and stole glances at them around Ruaridh, but didn't recognize anyone. A girl was saying to one of the guys that Oasis were playing Glastonbury this year. The guy pushed his toe in the ashes of the dead fire. A blond-haired boy stirred indistinctly, his movements concentrated but stuttering, tripped up by camping's unassailable restraint: there was nothing *to do*.

Then it happened. Nicole appeared.

She came out one of the far tents, her crutches giving her away, though I felt I would have recognized her without them. Her ink-black hair, her lovely gentle demeanor, her narrow hips and tapering legs – well, except for one, which was still wrapped. She zipped the door behind her and crutch-walked towards us, looking at the ground, saturnine and sluggish. I was sure the drumming in my chest would reach her ears, but she made no indication.

Not until sitting with the others did she look over; then our eyes met and she scrambled up at once, shouting my name. 'Mel!'

Ruaridh stopped ('... weans nearby wi' asthma –') and spun around.

'Wha're you doin' here?' She planted the crutches and catapulted over the campfire's remains. The sitters yanked their toes in.

I returned her hello. A scowl immediately formed on Ruaridh's pasty face. 'Eh?' he squawked.

'Pod?' Klang asked, turning to me.

'We're visiting,' I said to Nicole. 'Touring. We were in the park. Out on a walk, really. Well, talking. We checked out the Maxwell H–'

'Who's this, then?' Ruaridh fired at Nicole.

'Yeah, Mel, who's your friend?' Klang hissed.

'I *told* you,' Nicole said to Ruaridh, in a biting, accusing voice I'd never heard before. 'Mel's the guy who took me to hospital when you couldnay be bothered.'

'This is the bloke?' To my dismay, he was relieved, as if I posed no threat. He could've had the decency to consider me a viable competitor.

'*Aye.*'

'Mel, what's going on?' Klang pressed me in a low voice.

'Och,' huffed Ruaridh. 'Ya never said he was American, like.'

'Wha's the difference?' Nicole said. 'Sorry.' She looked to Klang and me now. 'Welcome, welcome! Come on and sit. Cup of tea?'

'I could take a load off,' Klang said, stepping forward.

I smiled uneasily at Nicole, with forced dispassion. As she invited us to sit, her eyes met mine; they shimmered with some kind of secret exigency yet skittered away, slick with indecision.

'Aye, any friend of Nicole's is a friend of mine,' Ruaridh said, full of strained jollity. He proffered a smile my way, obscured by the fading light and his thick beard.

'I don't know, we should really get some dinner,' I said. 'It's getting dark, it's a ways back –'

'Bugger tha'!' said Nicole, practically shouting. 'We've loads of sannies. Come on, have a wee sit-down. You must be knackered.'

At Ruaridh's insistence, the blond-haired boy brought another crate and a tree stump and put them around the fire. Then he fetched firewood from under the rain tarp, tented the logs and set to work lighting kindling under them. The back of his leather jacket faced me, showing a design of interweaving, serpentine lines. The motif's self-ensnarled symmetry evoked that of the Pisces fish. 'Alba' topped it, in Celtic script. Ruaridh introduced him. He was Lewis, and he came from the Isle of Lewis – No joke, Ruaridh added. He was a first-year at Glasgow School of Art and a good man, as well. The others were introduced too. The woman was Emma and, except for the snakes of dreadlocked hair that slithered from her hood, she looked to me all of fifteen. 'Hi-ya,' she uttered in a yielding voice, slouched over with abstracted boredom.

'Emma's Mark's lass,' Ruaridh explained. Emma's face twisted into puzzlement at this summation. On the end of the bench, the boy who'd drawn in the ash with his boot, was Mark. His deep, nasal voice issued a hello. Mark did sculpture, Ruaridh said, and had been at the Free State from day one. 'He'll be the first I raise a jar to when we stop this thin'.'

On Klang's lap, Nicole plopped a loaf of Sainsbury's bread and a packet of ham slices. To me she gave a block of Orkney cheddar and a dirty hunting knife – but not before glancing to Ruaridh. Seeing his eyes on her, she kept hers from mine, except when adding, 'There's crisps as well.' And in that moment, glinting with the growing fire, her eyes flashed something not of crisps but fearful and tentative. As Klang and I assembled sandwiches, Nicole hooked a kettle over the popping fire. I watched her furtively. There was a cast-iron contraption straight out of the Middle Ages, perfectly preserved and perfectly functional; she operated it with innate deftness, despite having to grasp the two crutches in one hand, keep her weight off her bad ankle, and lean over the fire.

'Oy, Mark!' Ruaridh barked from the camping chair he'd enthroned himself in opposite Klang and me. 'Give a hand, eh? She's gonnay tip and bloody immolate hersel'!'

'Sorry,' Mark said, getting up. 'Here, give uz tha'.'

'Away wi' ya. Ah'm noh daft.' Hands back on her crutches, Nicole directed Mark back towards his seat with a nudge of her head.

'Just mind when it's ready and do the pouring, will ya?' Ruaridh snapped at Mark. 'So!' He turned to Klang and me. 'Plunkett Research? Wha's tha' then?'

Oh, God, I thought.

'Aw, it's brilliant,' Nicole interjected, sitting again. Ruaridh set on her with acid eyes. 'I mean, it's quite interestin'.' She was seated now on mine and Klang's left, the crow's nest and banners backdropping her. Scuffles and woody thumps sounded from the arboreal abode, but no one paid any attention to them, so I tried to ignore them as well, though they did distract me for some time as

I squinted up in the light-flickered branches, through the rising smoke, for signs of life until Klang began speaking.

He explained that we were field agents for a market-research firm based out of Chicago. We were on assignment for a corporate client, a very large corporate client with deep pockets. He was quite cool about it, and made the horrendous error, I thought, of expecting Ruaridh to be impressed. 'Basically, there's a very popular coffee chain in the United States. I can't say who. I can't even confirm that I know. But let's just say, you've heard of it. That's who we work for.' My head hanging, I noshed the sandwich I'd made, savoring the dry tang of the cheese.

'Maybe you havenay nohiced,' Ruaridh said. 'Buh we're noh exactly rollin' in dough here. We dohn pop over to America for coffees anytime we fancy.'

'With any luck, you won't have to. Depending on what we find, you might have them here. Maybe in fiscal '97, all things considered.'

'Luck?' Ruaridh gasped. 'Are you mad? Wha' would be lucky abou' tha'?'

Profuse apologies were on the tip of my tongue, but Klang was undeterred. 'Maybe not Glasgow. We don't know that yet. I work out of London, and the outlook is favorable.'

'London can have it, as far as Ah'm concerned.' Ruaridh said. 'As far as *all* of us are concerned – ri'?' He looked around to his protégés.

'Ah know wha' you're on abou',' confirmed Lewis, who crouched by the fire as it crackled to life. He was somewhat reluctant, far less aggressive in tone. He didn't seem personally aggrieved, merely showing himself to be informed. 'Ah've a cousin works in America. Must be Burback's. They've goh 'em everywhere. Cappuccinos and espressos and all tha'. Bloody dear, so Ah'm told. Buh it's true, we've no use for 'em here.'

'Aye, well said, Lewis,' Ruaridh encouraged. 'Does it look like posh coffee is gonny fix Glasgow's troubles? There's no jobs to be had. We've got 17 percen' on the dole. The streets arenay safe. There's more and more council flats but no money to pay rent.

What little we do have goes to Westminster. Our representation is crap. Our parliament was ta'en away three hundred years ago. Now our ain folk've turned tail on us and voted to sell off our ancestral lands. Why? So's wealthy suburbanites can drive into the city quicker and do their jobs. The city they dohn dare live in themselves for fear of their lives. That's why they live out here and beyond – Eastwood, Newton Mearns. Naturally, they vote in favor of demolishing parkland to get themselves home safer and quicker. This is a Tory stronghold, ya know. John Douglas holds the safest Conservative seat in the whole of Sco'land. A majority of some twelve thousand votes.'

'Aye, and the weather's crap,' Emma added flatly.

Everyone laughed.

'The cheek,' Ruaridh scolded with a smirk. Just asserting his dominance; he'd chuckled too.

Just then water roiled from the kettle and sizzled into the fire. 'I'll get the mugs,' Nicole said, lurching forward.

'Stay where you are, lass,' Mark said. He crossed into the shadows behind Ruaridh, beyond the firelight's reach.

As Ruaridh had spoken, I'd watched the dancing tongues of fire, chin down, my hands in my lap. The sky was black now, and I could only see what was lit by the fire. Daring to gaze at Nicole, to venture a read, was a risk I couldn't take, with Ruaridh squared off across the ring from me, keeping us both under inspection. What I did glimpse, within the bounds of courteous looks people afford each other, was her tensely set mouth, nothing like the gleeful mouth of which I had eroded memories – on a park bench and across the Curler's table. Also her blue-gray eyes, normally guileless and in-breathing, were now hawk's eyes, slitted, wary and cunning.

'I'm sorry,' Klang said, chewing the last of his sandwich, 'but I'm still not clear – Mel, how do you know these guys?'

I told Klang what'd happened, that'd I'd been out in search of somewhere to work when I stumbled on a demonstration. How, needing photos for relatives at home, I'd begun snapping pictures. For Ruaridh's sake, I downplayed the nature of 'work', not specifying that 'looking for somewhere to work' meant a café, to drink coffee, so I could score it against the gold standard, in our client's eyes, of American coffee. The whole idea of assessing how well people are served, of whether good Styrofoam is used, not to mention the fair-trade issue, rainforest destruction – I thought he'd leap across the fire and strangle us. Mark had returned with mugs and a box of Tetley's and had poured tea for everyone. As I talked, he handed around the steaming tea cups. Walker's crisps packets, too, were distributed, by Nicole. Before I could finish, the hot tea had been gulped down and the crisp packets upturned – then cans of lager were handed out, and cigarettes lit. Having opened beer and now puffing on a roll-up, Ruaridh was, as the Scots say, fightin' fit.

'Pathetic existence,' he said. 'Searchin' out foreign cities for global expansion. How do you two sleep nights?' Ruaridh asked.

This was like a kick in the stomach. I just wanted to grab Nicole's hand and run away with her. Run away – or hobble, as the case may be. We could live in the empty Maxwell House. We'd turn the parlors and halls into darkrooms and work studios. When we weren't making art, we'd sit in the chairs overlooking the back-yard, sipping coffee to our hearts' content. Thankfully, Klang stepped in. He seemed to enjoy this type of thing.

'Oh, we sleep fine,' Klang asserted confidently. 'Like babies.'

'Is tha' so?'

'Why wouldn't we? Wait – don't tell me. Because we work for a corporation, and they sell products and use resources and make money and build buildings?'

'All hierarchical organizations are inherently evil,' Ruaridh asserted.

'That's ludicrous,' Klang laughed.

'It's just their jobs, Ruaridh,' Nicole offered, softly. Lewis, Mark and Emma were quiet but for the occasional belch and bumming cigarettes off whichever of them was holding, the phrase for which was not bum a smoke but *crash a fag*.

'*Just* their jobs?' Ruaridh spat. 'Aye, and the M77 is *just* a wee road.' His glare said Nicole was not to question his infallible convictions. Turning to Klang and me, he continued, 'How much does the CEO of Burback's make? Millions, no doubt. And the farmers? The shippers? The counter help? Pennies on the pound, Ah reckon. Why should that be so – the folk doin' all the labor livin' hand to mouth?'

'So you're a socialist,' Klang stated with his trademark side-blown smoke.

'I'm a radical, first and foremost,' Ruaridh said.

'Hmm,' Klang pondered, drinking from his McEwan's. 'I thought you were an art student.'

'Wha'?' Ruaridh said. His dopey eyes, though no wider, registered affront, alarm.

Nicole snickered, which gave me hope.

''A jobless art student.' That's what I read in the *Herald* at Mel's place.' Klang turned to me. 'You were in the shower, Mel. I needed something to read.'

I shrugged.

'That thin',' Ruaridh laughed with a wave of his hand. 'Rubbish.'

'I didn't read it closely. Christ, I didn't expect I'd be meeting you. Perhaps Mel did, though. Or maybe you already had,' he said, turning to me.

I opened my mouth –

'You've goh some nerve,' Ruaridh said, not with ire only. In his round, mouthy delivery, in which words like *nerve* and *person* shared the vowel sound of *care* and *dare*, admiration bubbled. We were the monopolists he opposed, yet we had some status. A coy, challenged grin took over his face. He sat back and studied Klang over the flames. He'd put his hood up at some point, and he looked like a basement-dwelling wannabe Jedi knight trying to read the mind of his adversary. 'Lewis, the fire's getting low,' he grumbled, too British, too educated to be menacing, though he tried to make up for this by not looking at Lewis when issuing the order, as if his servitude were a given. 'We bring you in like a stranger outtay the cold, we feed you –' he continued to Klang.

'The wood's ri' behind you!' Lewis said, mustering courage a moment.

Klang overrode the drama with his demurral, 'Listen, I'm just giving you shit.' Lewis stayed seated.

'Givin' me shit?' Ruaridh puzzled.

'Takin' the piss,' Nicole translated.

'Yeah, takin' the piss,' Klang said, remembering.

He must have came across that one in London. Funny how many Briticisms were opposite. Giving you shit, taking the piss. Both are poking fun, but one adds, the other subtracts. One's solid, one's liquid. In America when you urinate, you *take* a piss. The Brits *have* a slash. Of course, when a Yank is pissed, he's angry. When a Brit is pissed, he's having a blast, a ball. No wonder they set sail for Plymouth Rock.

'No, seriously,' Klang said, 'I appreciate your concern. You know, the size of some corporations, globalization – it's a tough one. We can't let 'em just grow unchecked. But this particular one is pretty harmless. At the same time, that's what Burback's, if it *is* Burback's, wants me to think. I understand PR. They want me to associate their name with relaxing times and pleasant flavors. Likewise, with the *Herald*. They have their own interests. Are they a conservative paper? Maybe they want to undermine your credibility. Maybe they're in the contractor's pocket. Maybe they're in the pocket of this conservative councilman who's got a lock on this district. Regardless, if you wanna know what I think about this protest you're doing, I'll tell you. I don't know the whole story, I only know what Mel has told me and a few details from the newspaper. But looking at what you've got here, it's not going to amount to anything.'

'Yer fuckin' wrong, mate!' Ruaridh blasted, with a jab of his cig-clutching fingers.

'Ruaridh!' Nicole reprimanded.

'No, lemme finish,' Klang said. 'Look at it. The land's sold. The title is signed, sealed and delivered. The contract was just awarded to this Wimpy outfit. They've already started chopping down some trees, right?'

'They goh only nine, thanks tay uzz. Took 'em two days, van-loads of polis, cranes –'

'But it's started?'

'Aye, tree-felling's begun. Ah've juz said as much!'

'Well, the way I see it, you can protest all you want, this road is getting built.'

'Yer out of order, ma'e!'

'How am I wrong?' Klang squawked, his voice rising to a righteous fever pitch, matching Ruaridh's. 'Power stays with power. It's primarily inert. It's rooted, that's the nature of it. Maybe it seems like it's constantly in flux, changing hands, falling to the deserving. But it's a rare thing. History books are just the turning points: empire's crumpling, battles lost, dynasties falling. Sure, it happens, but in these condensed histories it appears more regular than it is. In between are centuries, *grueling* centuries, of the biggest and strongest, the ruthless, greedy, privileged and monied, with their boots on the throats of the little guys. Don't get me wrong, I admire what you're doing. And I'm glad for it. Citizens can't just roll over and let the fat cats run everything. But, you know, looking at your numbers here, and what's already gone down, the outlook is not favorable.'

'Bloody defeatist.' Ruaridh punctuated his comeback with the *pfft* of another lager top. Emma, on my right, yawned. Nicole shifted, eyeing her foot. Klang raised his chin, giving Ruaridh his due attention. 'Exac'ly wha' they want. Juz go away. Let 'em get on wi' it, no questions asked, cheers and ta. Buh tha's noh uz. Noh the Sco'ish way. Sco'land deserves behher. We can stay out here months on end if we have tay. Och, most folk tire of it, the inconvenience, the cold, the weh. "Oh, I cannay be bothered. What's this tay do wi' me?" Problem there is, tha's puttin' yer own interests firs'. If Ah do tha, Ah'm no behher than the enemy. See wha' Ah mean? Cuz tha's wha' they're doin'. Motorists cannay be bothered tay drive an extra *six* minutes. Did you know tha', Mr Klang? Mel? Tha's wha's at stake here. Six minutes is all they stand to gain, rather than usin' the existin' Barrhead Road. Tay them tha's worth more than a thousand acres of parkland, wi' 850 trees, home tay deer and fox and pheasant, untold numbers of creatures who've every ri' tay be here.'

'Disgustin',' Lewis said. He'd been occupying himself with bending and twisting branches in his lap and now had a small pile at his feet, all green – I don't know how he expected them to burn.

'When you put it like that . . .' I said, trying at least to acknowledge the sentiment, that the motives for expansion were selfish and short-sighted.

'Aye,' Nicole added, sadly.

'That's an interesting stat,' Klang mused. 'I imagine it's been used on both sides. At least it could be.'

'How's tha'?' Emma asked, furthering the conversational awakening on my right.

'Well, six minutes doesn't sound like much. Makes the project sound indulgent and wasteful. But how many people will shave those minutes, how many times a day? There's probably thousands of commuters, maybe tens of thousands counting both ways, east and west.'

'It's a north/south route,' Ruaridh said.

'Okay, either way – could easily add up to weeks' worth of driving time each day. Gallons of gas saved, pollutants not emitted. X barrels of oil. Surely that strikes a chord with you guys.'

'We've heard these arguments,' Ruaridh said. 'Strathclyde Regional are quick to remind us wha' a service they're doin' the environment. Yet despite this, the fact is they've noh done the proper studies required by the European Union. An' they freely admih this! They've openly said so in the city chambers, *The Guardian* and *Observer* have both reported it, yet nothin's been done! They're allowed tay do wha'ever they like, so long as they themsel's vohed in favor of it! They dohn gi'e a fuck wha' the people wahn!'

'Bah, don't get discouraged,' Klang exclaimed, just as I elbowed him, intending to tap my wristwatch in his view. Momentarily, he eyed me as if I were a gnat, then faced Ruaridh, Nicole and the other, quieter three as he spoke. 'Politics are the same all over. People think they're untouchable. But listen, even if the road is built, that doesn't mean you've failed. What you do will serve a purpose. You have to define success on your own terms. You have to allow yourself some success even when – *especially when* – by conventional terms, you've failed. You might be powerless to stop this,' Klang gestured into the dark towards the cleared dirt strip, 'but you're not powerless. And you let them know that. Self-assessment is one thing we miss out on in the corporate world. In our work – and, Mel, this is off the record – there's one measure of success, and we either reach it or we go down in the record books as having dropped the ball.'

'Wha' d'you mean?' said Nicole.

'If we don't report back that the UK is destined to be the frontier of our client's next expansion, this whole project goes down in the books as a big fat L in the win/loss column.'

'Buh are you noh paid to report the facts?' Nicole asked. 'Mel, that's how you put it. You're meant to be objective, and just say whether their coffees would sell here.'

'Yes, but there's an implication in this business,' Klang said, before I could answer. 'They *want* to expand. They *want* to grow. That's why they hired us. They have money to burn and share-holders to answer to. Shareholders loathe stagnancy. The writing between the lines in a contract like this is that we find the client a place where the results are favorable, and give them the green light. Because a green light is an endorsement of their product. A green light overseas is an endorsement of its universal value. Really, with a brand as big as this, it's a judgment on their whole corporate identity. So we research in the field, and the higher-ups at home, in Chicago, do the interpreting and forecasting. Sure, we guarantee them impartiality, we're legally sworn to it, but as far as Plunkett's is concerned, the client must move into the UK market. Part of the handshake is that if they do and it's profitable, Plunkett's gets a bonus.'

'Millions, I reckon,' Ruaridh intoned, bitter and omnipotent.

'Hmm,' Klang hummed, not disagreeing but conceding nothing.

'How do you know all this?' I said.

'This is the way the world works, Mel. Plus I made a few friends in training.'

'Money makes more money,' Ruaridh added, beginning an

account of Wimpy and their many European divisions. How they –
he, as founder of Pollok Free State, and the members of EarthFirst!
– have put out literature, naming these divisions and calling
for boycotts. Don't buy Wimpy homes, don't build with Wimpy
materials. They're Fascists.

Smoke from Lewis's green twigs, which he'd set on the fire one
by one, stung my eyes. Tears flooded my eyes, my nose ran. I was
tipsy, too, and tipsy and tired are often one and the same with me.
That's why I like coffee. When the senses blur, it's tantamount
to sleep. You're vulnerable. Vulnerable to your own errors in
judgment. I found myself thinking about this as Ruaridh spoke, and
I set my beer down on the ground. I looked around, wondering
if they had a press pot amongst the camping gear. But I saw no
cookware and listened in patches to the ramblings of the regal
renegade.

Excited by his excoriating brand of politics, his hands busy with
roll-ups and lager cans, his mind attentive to the curves of his own
logic, Ruaridh lorded over Nicole less and less. I'd been looking to
her throughout the night, and continued to do so, less hesitantly.
Occasionally, she turned my way, but only for moments at a
time. Her eyes would meet mine, gleam with a kind of repressed
urgency, elemental like the fire they reflected, then fall away, as if
casually, as if I were just another object on whom her attention had
haphazardly fallen, on par with the stones around the fire, the
ancient kettle-holder. I'd be left with the offering of her orangely lit
profile – the line cut, the visual equivalent of a dial tone. Still her
lips were tight with worry, her Scottish pallor evocative less of
tanless clarity than the stricken colorlessness of fright. Eventually,
I'd let my gaze fall away too, passing over the thigh I'd clutched,
the foot I'd debooted from its puffy pain.

Ruaridh was talking about the model homes Wimpy had
opened in the suburbs, up in Bearsden and Lenzie. They were, by
definition, as a matter of purpose, open to the public. A lovely
destination for a daywalk. (Ruaridh himself didn't own a car.) A
few times now, Ruaridh'd taken groups to them on the weekends,
when they were staffed by a single sales rep, typically a woman.

Och, the look on her face when we walk in! he boasted. Here, Emma and Lewis laughed in agreement, and Emma commandeered the storytelling. Aye, it was brilliant, she said. She'd gone along twice now. They'd clomped around in muddy boots, asking daft questions, lightin' fags, refusing to leave. One of them'd put his feet up on the settee, another would have a shite in the loo, another'd phone Dublin or Edinburgh – the silly git would be gobsmacked. Regular folk'd come round to see the house, and turn on their heels. Clearly, Emma preferred these subversive histrionics over rhetoric. In the end, she said, the polis would be called, and they'd be ushered out. Aye, we were just leavin', they'd say. Lovely place. I quite fancy it. Bit small though, they'd laugh.

'No sales that day,' Ruaridh assured us. These grinding tactics were aimed at one consequence, making it not worth Wimpy's while to bid on contracts that tore up parkland. If not this time, then the next.

'Class,' Mark said – a synonym for *brilliant* – capping the feeling on these endeavors.

At this conclusion, I got up to find a bush. Mark said he needed a slash as well, and we walked, stiff-kneed, into the speckled dark, chilly out of the fire's reach. Upon my return, Klang went too. The coming and going brought the uncertainty of transition. What would they do all night? What was etiquette for visiting in their makeshift home these people who had denounced society's structures and strictures, including time? Into this vacancy, Nicole offered a suggestion, one that acknowledged mine and Klang's imminent departure. 'Ah was jus' sayin' to Ruaridh he should write you'se up passports tay the Free State.'

'Aye,' Ruaridh answered, perfectly neutral. I didn't imagine he'd be thrilled with the idea. But then again, anything that added numbers to his cause would probably suit him. Getting up from his chair, he said exactly that. 'We need all the support we can geh. Pollok Free State accepts all punters. Coupla American businessmen backin' us doesnay look so bad, eh?' This was directed at Nicole and the others, as if the strength of his convictions had recruited even the most unlikely converts. Nicole answered Aye, brightly, eagerly. In fact, this was the most cheerful show of support she'd made all evening. It was as if she were greasing the path that led Ruaridh to the passports. 'Course, donations are welcome too if you cannay be put out,' Ruaridh jabbed, as he walked away, headed where the tents and supplies lay under protective tarps, headed into the shadows.

'You'se two are welcome back any time,' Nicole said.

'I appreciate that,' Klang said. 'But I have to get back to London. I guess you could say London's Calling.'

There was laughter from my right.

'Crackin',' Lewis said.

'Spot on,' said Emma.

'Aye, ri',' Nicole said. 'Well, whoever can make it then. We'd be pleased to have you.'

12   Whistler's Mother or
The Douglas Pickaxe Incident

The coffee at Whistler's Mother was striking but problematic. I don't know how I'd overlooked the place. It was right there on Byres, off the corner of University Avenue, next to the Royal Bank of Scotland. I guess I had thought it held furniture or art supplies, with its reproduction of the famously glum matriarch's profile. Or maybe because I usually walk on the opposite side coming from the tube, headed to Havelock Street, where I turn to get to my flat, I'd not looked closely. But not Monday.

Monday, I was out the door at 8 a.m. sharp, nothing on my mind but filling out the 27Gs in my bookbag. My only intention, my only hope, was to do the job Mr Carson had so generously hired me to do. Then I passed Whistler's Mother – sure enough, students hunched over egg plates, big mugs of froth at their elbows. I made like a Xerox and copied. Corner booth, fried brekkie and a large black.

Klang'd left. Gone back to London on the train. I'd seen him to Central Station Sunday afternoon, after a dreadful time trying to entertain ourselves for four hours. Thank God we slept in after the late return from the Free State, or it would've been eight. Outside, everything had been dull silver and dripping, the wind blowing, streams gushing along curbs. We kicked around the idea of going to a movie, but couldn't muster interest. A walk was out of the question. You can't walk around Glasgow on a day like that – you get soaked to the bone even sporting a bona fide rain jacket like mine. The gales press it tight against your chest and the rain sloughs onto your thighs. In minutes, your jeans are three times their dry weight, your cuffs dragging in puddles. Except for a jaunt to the corner shop, we stayed in. Even the television programming reinforced Britain's dreary caricature of itself, with a channel of cricket, one of football, a gardening show and a documentary on Singapore's economy.

We drank too much Tanzanian Peaberry, smoked too many cigarettes and played the little radio I'd bought, enduring the pop froth of Kylie Minogue and Zig & Zag, holding out for Blur and Oasis, Britain's closest heirs to The Who and The Stones. At this point, my and Klang's shared like of these bands and their hooky anthems seemed about all we had in common, apart from our employer and the photocopied passports to the PFS we each held. Klang perused *Loaded* while I read the *Observer* cover to cover, including a feature on Glasgow's bid for European City of Culture. There was no coverage of the M77, not in this Sunday edition, anyway. Neither did Klang and I really speak of it, aside from him saying, at the train platform, that I was to keep him apprised of the developments, that he hoped the best for my friends, and that I was to stay out of trouble.

Now the only trouble was that I may have found what I'd been looking for but couldn't stomach it – the coffee at Whistler's, that is. It was just about the real deal, nearly authentic. It was served quickly, the price was fair, but it wasn't sitting right with me. Despite the stout aroma, thick consistency and full flavor, with hints of berry and a subtle tannic aftertaste like red wine, my guts protested in warbles. Pangs pierced my kidneys. The bitterness was too much. My mouth was Saharan, my tongue expanding, searching my palate for moisture, a cleaner finish. I asked for ice water and in the 27G wrote:

Glasgow shops and attractions draw customers and tourists with their Scottish themes, décor and wares. From stained-glass windows borrowing on Charles Mackintosh's design elements, to the flag in the bank logo, to the kilted pipers on the pub sign, all things Scottish are hung out to entice punters. Whistler's Mother counts among them, its name a reference to the famous work by Scotland's famed painter. This little West End luncheonette goes nearly unnoticed behind its amateurish reproduction of the slouching matron facing sideways with her rocker and bonnet.

Unfortunately, when it comes to coffee, this quaintness doesn't jive. The Scottish character is bold – a 'coarse tink brute'. And indeed coffee should be pungent and revitalizing, not dainty and easy like tea. But the boldness in this blend is forced, unnatural. The coffee is not twee, that adjective that Scotsmen fear, it is punchy. It does anything but blend in and play nice. But it's not acclimated, not integrated. It's trying hard to be a diamond in the rough but is coming out only rough. It's as if some kitchen-mad Dr Hyde has formulated a private tonic to the profuse rain, perhaps to the previous evening's indulgence. This stuff on the morning after, though, would be a waking nightmare. We'd all be dangerous Jekylls. The drink is too big for its britches. Its capacity is strained. The question is, Is this true of only Whistler's Mother – or Glasgow, or Scotland? Perhaps fine coffee is outside the Scottish collective interest. Perhaps it's too antithetical to its national character.

Though admirably vigorous, this coffee badly needs a context. W.M. is another in a line of Scottish-themed shops, but there is no continuum of quality on which its coffee can fall, fit, thrive. Glasgow has a tradition of the former but not the latter – there's no pride in it.

I hit a handful of other cafés that day, following my whims somewhat. I retraced the path through Kelvingrove that Klang and I had taken and happened upon a small deli, Rumi's, serving döner kebabs. Not the type of place you would expect to serve outstanding coffee, and it lived up to that expectation. There were puddles outside browner than what I was brought by the unsmiling man in the turban emerging from the back room. Countertop kettle and Nescafé – the instant stuff – was my guess. The taste was a mouse, trampled by the olfactory elephant barreling around the shop: spiced lamb turning on a spit, flanked by a glowing coil. Any decent coffee should have scared it off, but not this pipsqueak brew. If the deli's name was a tribute to its founder's wife – a hunch of mine – she may have been honored by the cuisine, but the coffee defamed her.

From there, another one-room, one-name joint, this one drawing me, by a sandwich-board invitation, down a crumbling alley beside the Kelvin river. Called Jen's, it was staffed solely by its

namesake, an optimistic baker in her thirties, cheek-floured, hair
frizzing out from under a chef's cap in heat-blown curls. She had
banked, obviously, on the neighboring bookshop generating foot
traffic. It was a rare-book shop, however, its window crowded
with yellowed, jacketless tomes of obscure works. Equally obscure
was Jen's coffee. Also aimless, deficient, heartbreaking. And what
a jack job! £1.65 for about twelve ounces. While her beaming smile
endeared me to her; while I admired her pluck and was flattered
on this grim Monday to have my Americanness inquired of, these
things were only so useful – as useful as the broken umbrellas
you see abandoned on Glasgow's sidewalks. Poor woman, she was
pleased – chuffed, the Scots say – to have me lingering. Little did
she know I was tallying up a numerical score that would put her in
Glasgow's lowest tenth percentile.

To my surprise, even as I knew empirically that these coffees
suffered greatly, even as I thought of the bounty of home, with its
competing chains and independents in the cities and suburbs alike –
thought of the American ease of travel, people on the go, how for
a buck fifty in change scrounged out of your car you can pull
up and in a minute or two have enough caffeine and flavor to carry
you three, four hours, well into lunchtime and beyond – I didn't
entirely mind. My criticism felt less personal, more a professional
obligation. Yes, finding worthy Glasgow coffee was laborious,
nearly impossible. I slogged over the hilly streets in the rain and
cold, pockets heavy with pounds sterling, their weightiness reminding me of their added value in dollars. Yet they ran out
quickly. Taking the tube to other areas, such as Cowcaddens and
Maryhill, only added time and token money to the pursuit. The
breadth of difference between this and the American experience
staggered my patience at times. What a disparity. Still, I drank what
I was given. Though not *true* coffee, it went down. These flounder-
ing beverages held me alert and fortified just long enough to reach
the next site. In a way, their subdued tenor matched my lessening
fervor, my growing sympathy with the decaffeinated world. I was
becoming awake enough.

The rest of the week was much the same. Coffees of wildly

fluctuating character, made by unorthodox means. Pressure-blasted through an espresso maker, yet the wrong grind, or stale. Scalding yet impotent. Tea-like, woody like gin. More freeze-dried and reanimated. One actually tasted of broccoli. Another cup bore something noirish and acidic, not rounded, its aroma like the bituminous scent of pitch as you drive through a construction zone on a summer day. I flunked that one.

I topped my days with visits to local attractions. Having set out precisely at eight each day, I finished at half four, pulling the cord on my internal afternoon whistle. From the last café, I picked up supper and caught the tube to wherever I'd be killing the evening. Doing this kept me from going back to my flat and watching crap shows like *Home and Away* and *Neighbours* – evening soaps imported from Australia. Time for brooding on Nicole was burned up. In the Necropolis, I smoked a cigarette on the base of the reformer John Knox's statue, looking down on the winding path I'd climbed to reach it. Tower blocks and houses sat tiered on hills to the east under low-hanging clouds. I ambled among rows of headstones and monuments, reading of MacDonalds and Pattisons, Douglases and Stewarts – alive and dead in centuries past.

Glasgow Cathedral chilled me. It's an active church and an open tourist destination. Spurned by a sense of intruding, I sought out secluded corners, passing through the nave's grandeur, past the stained-glass depictions of saints and tradesmen, into the chilly St Mungo's tomb below the pulpit. There history overwhelmed me. Floor-laid plaques described institutional overthrows; monuments honored the Scots guard; and a royal pew was roped off for a colonel who'd carried the King's colors in Egypt in 1801, as if he might again attend mass. The context of these objects of tribute seemed beyond me. Their meaning was ethereal, like incense's silky pungency, which lingered everywhere, its source hidden. I slipped into the Blackadder Aisle, another ten steps down, like a church sub-basement. This worship room, with its holy white pillars and a cloth-draped altar, felt eerily important, like a post-apocalyptic bunker in an imaginary world. I was a foreigner here.

The forward-thinking inclusivity of St Mungo's Museum, visited the day after, with its mission of promoting understanding and respect between world faiths, made for a less somber tube ride back to the West End. I felt I had on my shoulders not the weight of a nation's oppression and rebirth but the guardian spirits of Shivas and Buddhas and cherubs alike.

Wednesday was the Mackintosh House in the Hunterian Museum, a showcase of the Scotsman's furniture, elongated and rose-embedded, reminiscent of Lloyd-Wright houses at home. Masculine rectangles blended with subtle Art Nouveau curves. The proportions were small, of a more frugal era; I felt I was walking through a dollhouse. The dressing-room mirror beheaded me. The carpet, walls and furniture of the master bedroom were all egg-white; words stitched into a blanket dressing the four-poster bed echoed this austerity:

GOD KNOWS AND

WHAT HE KNOWS

IS WELL AND BEST

THE DARKNESS

HIDETH NOT FROM

HIM BUT GLOWS

CLEAR AS THE

MORNING OR THE

EVENING ROSE

OF EAST OR WEST

Shops were still open when I left the GU campus that housed the Hunterian, the architect's rose-strewn aesthetic and words sheltering my spirits from the night's rainy gloom. On familiar Byres Road, only a glance in a bright shop window wrested my attention from my puddle-dodging feet. It was Woolworth's, and I suddenly remembered the roll of film I'd dropped off there. 'Holy shit,' I said, looking in the store's rain-streaked windows. I'd forgotten all about the pictures. Somewhere in that fluorescent interior were prints of Nicole on the ledge of the Bath Street

Wimpy building and whatever else I'd shot that day. They'd probably been ready since the week before, but with Klang's visit I'd forgotten. Receiving them from the clerk at the photo counter, I fought the urge to peek at the results, the released time capsule of three short weeks ago. I added a packet of air-mail envelopes and a book of stamps to my purchase. The Royal Mail packaging, with its queenly motifs of red and yellow, pleased me; it suggested some primacy befitting a nation of stature.

My flat was cold. With a mug of steaming tea, I pulled the checkerboard table next to the fireplace – not a real fireplace but a hearth that enclosed a sterling-swallowing electric heater impersonating a fireplace. There, under the glazed eyes of Margaret's old Katsina doll leaning on the mantle, I filled the page with my sharp longhand, honed on 27Gs. *Dear Mom and Dad*, I wrote.

I'd cut back since Klang'd left but now lit a smoke.

Hello and how are you? Everything here's going well. I've met a great girl. Her name's Nicole, and she's an art student. She's from a town in the east of Scotland, Dunfermline. She's a few years younger, but we aren't really serious, so don't worry. Actually, things are kind of up in the air. She has other interests and a life here so it's not like we're dating often. But it's great to know someone here. She's very conscientious – I met her at a protest. That's her in the pictures – these are from a demonstration against the expansion of a motorway (highway). I was just shooting around, like I used to do in Greek Town and Grandma's old Czech neighborhoods.

Work is good. Klang was up from London. You'll remember, he went through training with me. He seemed impressed with my output and results. The coffee is pretty terrible, but whether or not a Burback's-type franchise would go over here, I don't have a guess. That's all there is to say about that. As you know, client relations are handled by Carson. I just my file my reports. Did you get things sorted with him, by the way? (Briticism, that: sorted.) Has he called again about my SSN or address?

Life is different. The city is big, crowded and rainy. Darkness

comes early. Would like to see the Highlands and Isles, or even Loch
Ness, like Mrs Brown recommended, but no time. Out of space!
Love, Mel

I'd ordered doubles of the prints so included with the letter one of them all: the Rat and Parrot, random buildings, Nicole on the ledge, the tussle around the Wimpy doors. This required a photo mailer, which I bought first thing Thursday morning. Finally, sealed up and weighed and slathered with a quadrant of Elizabeth II's profile, I sent the package off.

For work, I pushed out a ways, west on Dumbarton Road away from the city to Jordanhill. Coffee-wise, it was more of the same. I took my lunch in Victoria Park, watching swans on a pond, kids stumbling from seesaw to swings to merry-go-round, like they do anywhere else, I guess. I got into an area called Whiteinch. I may have been a turn or two away from stumbling into the wrong loading dock – it looked like the kind of place where guys in mob flicks get taken in the trunk of a car.

By the time I got home each night, I was beat, my legs throbbing, thirsty for nothing but sleep. I'd bought an *answer phone*, as they call it, just in case Nicole decided to reach me, but the display never read anything but zero. Before bed, I'd check the papers for news of the Free State.

Tory MPs had their knickers in a twist because children from a Corkerhill school had been let out by a green-minded headmaster. Let out to 'greet' the workers, he said with typical Scottish cheek. The next stage of tree-felling encroached. A photo showed two Wimpy execs clutching rolled-up scrolls, hard hats on their heads. 'Hands off Pollok Park!' the children had chanted at them. Eastwood MP John Douglas complained that this slogan must have been taught to the weans by radicals. 'It's a shameful abuse of innocent minds,' he said. 'Isn't truancy enough of a problem?'

The headmaster countered that environmental studies and ecology had been on the curriculum for several years now. 'Not all learning happens in the classroom.'

Then there was the Criminal Justice and Public Order Act,

passed in September, but making its purpose known now. The act made preventing a lawful party from carrying out a lawful act illegal. Police 'stop and searches', raves and squatting were named in the legislation, and slipped in with these were mass protests. Wimpy was a lawful party, and building the M77 a lawful act. The bill had been drafted in the aftermath of the M11 protest in England, but it read to me like it'd been slapped on the Scottish books in response to the escalating tensions at Pollok Free State. Indeed, in response to the establishment of the Pollok Free State. A member of Glasgow for the People was arrested and detained.

Another day, children were let out again. This time, they brandished placards against police in cherry pickers trying to roust demonstrators from the upper limbs of oaks and from the fortified tree platforms. God bless 'em, the scamps managed to immobilize a hydraulic digger, swarming onto it like ants on a log. Without this piece of equipment, the trees that had taken hours to depopulate couldn't be uprooted – they couldn't be cut down because of extensive spiking. (If a chainsaw met an embedded nail, the chain could snap and fatally lash its operator.) Thus stymied, operations shut down for the day. Ruaridh's boast of direct action's effectiveness and panning of a 'roads-obsessed' government were quoted widely.

At night I lay on my ultra-padded bed, the dried bloodstain I'd found under the mattress when I first moved in all but forgotten. Buzzing with the day's coffee, I thought of the Free State across the city. Ruaridh, Nicole, Emma, Mark, Lewis from Lewis. The invisible man who stirred in the tree. The Europeans (continental) and Aussies at the other campfire, with their primary-colored unity and gay laughter. And now schoolchildren.

Schoolchildren! I was flabbergasted.

When Catholic primary schools in the West End let out, the side-walks teemed with rucksack-laden girls in tartan skirts and crested jumpers – *sweaters*, that is. Cardigans. Clutches of red-headed Scotch-Irish and thick-pigtailed Pakistanis, the tall flanked by the short, swarming through the underground turnstile like bees into a hive. They looked so young, outside the corner shop opening chocolate bars, streaming in and out of the bus shelter, alighting and dispersing on double-deckers that came and went. They *were* young, but I guess not insensate. Not afraid. Not voiceless.

I stirred in my bed. No one sang outside my window.

The bill was pretty steep. All told, over four hundred quid. Oh, well. I wasn't about to wake up in a park on the other side of Glasgow naked to the open air. I couldn't rely on mooched tea bags for my waker-upper after a kip on cold ground. Thankfully, the Plunkett Research Citibank Visa had a hefty credit line. I'd just have to be sure to reach Melissa, Carson's secretary, before the expenses were presented for sign-off on – reach her and come up with something. I'd worry about that later.

No family sat across the aisle this time. The train car was empty and quiet.

Ever-watchful, Ruaridh spotted me approaching and stepped forward, as he'd done last time. 'Ah had a feelin' you'd return,' he said, shaking my hand. I took it for the generous assessment of character it could have been, not the self-congratulation it looked like in his beady black eyes.

'Gonna put a stamp in this?' I said, holding up my PFS passport.

'Come on, there's a spot you can pitch. Lewis, gi'e Mel a hand, eh.'

'Och, coffee man,' Lewis said, turning from some task involving tools, rope and hardware.

'Hey, Lewis,' I said.

He set an axe against a makeshift table and removed a pair of work gloves. 'I'll take that.'

'I got it.'

'New gear?' he said, as we followed well behind the frenetic Ruaridh into the camp.

'Yeah, yeah.'

'Nicole isn't here,' he said, conspiratorially.

'No?' I didn't know if she was or not. I tried to play this casual – no small task when your heart scrapes the bottom of your stomach.

'Away for supplies?' I said, as if asking after the weather.

'No, away home I think.'

'Too bad . . .' I said, which could have meant *too bad for the cause* or *too bad for her.*

Lewis gave me a stare that seemed to answer something for him. 'Aye, right,' he said knowingly. 'Here, give me the small one.' He pulled the daypack off my shoulder.

Ruaridh stomped around a sodden grassy patch near the others, feeling it out. He wore the same striped poncho with the hood up, and his boots were brown with mud. 'Mind those,' he said, kicking a few knotty roots. I swung the weighty kit off my back and stretched my shoulders. I didn't want to be shown up by him, but when he asked, 'Need a hand?' I swallowed my pride and confessed that I did. I hadn't put up a tent since I was a boy.

He and Lewis had me up in ten minutes. I unpacked and offered to make coffee.

'That'd be grand,' Ruaridh said. 'Cheers.'

When I set the plastic press pot and hand-crank bean grinder outside the tent, he picked them up and laughed. 'Marks and Sparks. Swish.' He turned the crank. 'Can I put a John Douglas' knob in here?'

'I'm pretty sure that voids the warranty,' I said, climbing out of the tent.

He laughed. Pointing to my Pentax, he said, 'Wha's that fer? This is no Loch Lomond.'

'It's what I do,' I said. 'This is my vacation in a way.'

'Crap holiday,' he said. He probably thought I meant my stay at the Free State, when really I meant my whole assignment abroad.

Having shopped the previous evening after work, I'd set out early that morning, catching the tube from Partick at eight and the first train out of Central at 8.50. The sun was still on the rise as I cleared the pit of ash and rubbish and built a fire. Emma and Mark emerged with bed-head and creased faces; they muttered hellos and huddled on stump-seats against the morning cold.

'There'll be coffee in a few minutes,' I said.

'Lovely,' Emma said.

'Cheers,' said Mark.

With coffee, we had fire-roasted toast made in an iron clamping device that could be turned on either side, tins of Heinz baked beans, and cheese. Lewis opted for tea, Tetley's with milk. The only sound, apart from forks meeting plates, was the babble of the Euro-protestors heading from their tents to the open green, in shorts, jerseys and sports socks.

Didn't they intermingle? I asked. Wasn't this one cause?

Mark said they all got on swell – class blokes – they'd just staked out over there from the start. When Wimpy came round and some evenings over 'hash and cans', the two groups were as united as they'd ever be.

'Right, let's get to work,' Ruaridh said, scarfing his last bite. He set his plate beside Emma. 'Would you, love?'

'Aye, nay bother,' she said, seeming to find it easier to comply with Ruaridh's narrow conception of her utility.

'Cheers.'

The rope and lumber and hardware were for Lewis's brainchild, a network of connections to be made between the treehouses so people could move from one to the other without touching ground. I climbed into the first treehouse – the original one with glass windows, near the banners and the campfire. Rungs nailed into the trunk brought me to the top by the clenched fist with its beams of power. I peeked in the enclosed area around the center: a mussed sleeping bag, some food wrappers, a flashlight – or *torch* – and books. The guy who'd been sleeping here was away, Ruaridh had said. They'd had a bit of a row. A row like a *cow*. A fight, that is. Now he was away, tending to his regular life. Ruaridh wasn't sure when he'd be back. The nook was awash in the silence of its forty-foot height, a height which felt more treacherous and removed than it looked from the ground.

I could see the Maxwell House in the distance. On an impromptu soccer pitch, the members of the other camp jogged about, planets whose shifting orbits responded to a bouncing, checkered sun. Beyond them was the footbridge, the grassy expanse Klang and I had crossed, and Barrhead Road, the road that wasn't good enough. In the other direction, the cleared dirt strip and the arrangement of stones reading NO M77, whose lines had thickened. The message was upside down to me, directed at the dormant diggers.

I lay on my stomach, reached around to the underside of the floor and screwed in a weighty U-hook. From below, Lewis directed me on the placement. It took some doing, lacking leverage, needing two hands, and hanging off the edge. 'Brilliant,' Lewis called up when I finished. He and Ruaridh worked out whether to cut each section of rope or run a continuous line. I went down and back up, clipped a pulley to the hook with a carbiner, threaded the rope through the pulley. Ruaridh took the other end up the other tree. That way we didn't risk cutting too short before tie-off. Then I went to Ruaridh with the cordless drill.

Whereas my treehouse, as I thought of it now, was in an old oak, the second was in a younger elm. It had no center enclosure or windows, just some boards forming a creaky platform.

'Is this gonna hold?' I asked Ruaridh.

He lay on his stomach, awaiting the tools, eager to install the hardware as he'd seen me do it. 'Och, aye. We had four of uz up here once. And two them were havin' it off.' He grabbed the drill and practically dove over the edge.

'Holy shit!' I yelled, grabbing his legs.

'Cheers!' he shouted.

His ankles twitched in my hands as they tried to counterbalance. 'I gotcha, I gotcha,' I said. 'Ya nutter.'

'Eh?'

'I gotcha!'

He took a long time getting one screw in and afterwards swung up, his hood flipped up, face beet red. 'Bloody hell,' he said. He pushed the hood back and rubbed his chest, where the edge of the floor had been digging in. 'Listen,' he said. 'Be warned. Certain days, the polis have been comin' round wi' video cameras, askin' folk their names and where they're from. They wohn do it in sight of me, cuz Ah've given it laldy. Buh if they geh to ya, answer "Ray Vaughn".' He spelled it. '*Rave on*, see? The lasses say Teresa Green.

And yer from the Pollok Free State, nowhere else. Noh American. Noh Scotland. They're aimin' to hold people on CJA charges. They juz havnay sorted out wha' they can trump up yet. So yer name's noh Mel –'

'Podgorski.'

'Podgorski. Wha' is it?'

'Ray Vaughn.'

'And where're ya from?'

'The Pollok Free State.'

'Aye, and Bob's yer uncle,' he said, swinging back over the edge.

Back on the ground, we lit cigarettes and looked up at the rope strung over the tents like a power line. 'Well, then?' Lewis said. 'Who'll try it?'

'Yer idear, ma'e,' Ruaridh said.

'Mel?' Lewis offered.

I pictured myself in the Royal Infirmary, bandaged from head to toe, phoning Carson to ask for Plunkett's insurance-policy number. 'I don't think so.'

Lewis said he'd have a go, and we decided Ruaridh and I should be on either end. I went up in the deluxe treehouse, and Ruaridh the other. Lewis was in position and testing the line when we heard a car. A blue BMW pulled up on the clearing near the campfire. Lewis signaled to Ruaridh. We all watched as three men got out.

They strode up to the site, and one of them, a gray-haired man in a suit – they were all in suits – jumped up and tore down the 'Hands Off Pollok Park' banner.

'What the fuck?' Lewis said.

'Oy!' Ruaridh yelled. He started descending the elm. Lewis went down our oak first. I followed. Scrambling down the ladder, I heard Emma screaming, 'Stupid git! Fucking ponce!' When I hit ground, she and Mark were circling behind the men as they sauntered towards Ruaridh, who was coming across the clearing.

'What's all this then?' the gray-haired man asked. The other two men flanked him, one muscly and shaven-headed, the other a sadistic-looking beanpole with shaggy hair. 'A tightrope for your circus?'

'Wha' you doin'!' Ruaridh roared, coming towards them. 'Tha's personal property you've juz destroyed!'

'Oh, you've respect for property now?' the man answered, familiarly.

'Yer makin' a big mistake, Douglas!' Ruaridh reached him now and faced off against the man.

Douglas. John Douglas, Eastwood MP. The safest conservative seat in Scotland.

I followed Lewis, who cautiously stepped around near Ruaridh. We faced the three men, who formed a line, Douglas at the center. 'I don't make mistakes, lad,' Douglas said. 'It's you's made the mistake. You cannay build on these lands.' He gestured to the rope in the air. 'This isnay your bloody playground.'

'He's fuckin' pulled down this banner,' Mark said. He stood behind the men and off to the side, the evidence, like a crumpled bridal train, in hand.

'Aye, we'll have you on charges for tha',' Ruaridh said.

'You'll do no such thing,' Douglas glibly answered. 'There's plenty of offenses here. Davy, use the car phone – make the call.'

'Aye,' the pock-faced goon answered with a pleased snarl. He left Douglas's side, staring down Mark as he passed.

A shouting match ensued, with Douglas calling Ruaridh a 'self-appointed guardian of the public' and reminding him of the democratic process, that the city council had approved the roads building. Ruaridh countered that the M77 wasn't in the people's interest and, furthermore, the elected representatives were crooks. Had they followed EU guidelines? Had they done an environmental-impact study? Were the trees and animals asked to vote? (Douglas and the bulky henchman laughed at this.) Voices were raised – others adding in, too, Emma saying Douglas's car should be ticketed, Lewis badgering him on tree-felling progress and it having been slowed by arboreal occupiers and 'a load of weans'.

'You've no business!' Douglas bellowed. 'Yer wastin' yer time! You wannay go home and get proper jobs, all of ya!'

I was just slipping over towards the fire, where I'd left my stuff, when the footballers rounded the corner of the copse at a jog. A few of them puzzled at the out-of-place luxury sedan and switched to a sprint. I picked up my camera as they reached Douglas, who spun around, startled.

'And you lot!' he yelled. 'Coming into my district! This is noh yer concern!'

They were a dapper group, fit, with spiky gelled hair, strong calves, lots of five-o'-clock shadows and stylish specs. They wore jerseys colored with team and sponsor logos – Arsenal, Real Madrid, Carling lager, the Swedish flag. A ropey-armed one in a yellow jersey with Fosters patches led the pack; he got nose to nose with Douglas. A brash Australian voice blasted out. 'We don't discriminate, mate! The earth's the fackin' earth!' Fragments of his clangy Australian broke through the din: the park's off limits – swindlers – mindless expansion needing to be held in check.

Douglas puffed up his chest and yelled over him, 'Aw, go back where ya came from!' In a moment, neither of them was intelligible. Their faces reddened, spittle flew. I began snapping pictures.

'Shuh up! Let him speak!' Emma yelled at Douglas. She and Mark pressed in behind the footballers. Ruaridh, who'd been displaced by the Australian, edged alongside him to remain in confrontation with the councilman. Lewis hugged Ruaridh's back, though he looked scared to death. The meaty goon clung shoulder to shoulder with Douglas and put his arm between his charge and the Australian, but Douglas began to drift backwards, seemingly blown by the force of the Australian's wind. The whole clump was like a galaxy drifting and collapsing.

I shuffled around the perimeter, shooting.

Then something snapped – like a table leg giving out under this vitriolic feast. I don't know what, I didn't see it. A space opened at the cluster's center, and Douglas and Ruaridh were down – the charcoal suit and the striped poncho out of sight. A collective uproar sounded, and everyone stepped back. Only Douglas arose – a pickax in hand. He assumed a defensive stance, the ax raised. Ruaridh was on his back in the mud. He screamed, 'Fuckin' pratt!'

The bodyguard looked surprised, like a bulldog who'd been kicked. The grotty one appeared near me, returned from the car, taking in the developments but not looking too keen on stepping into the fray.

'Back off, you goblins!' spat Douglas.

As Lewis helped Ruaridh up, the campers sputtered aghast. 'Yer mental!' 'Fuck's sake!' 'Take it easy!'

I didn't use the viewfinder. I just snapped and wound, snapped and wound.

Douglas must have heard the shutter – he turned to me, mad-eyed, his pudgy, old-drinker's face red as a beet. 'Eh? Who's taking photos?' he said. His eyes met mine through the clump. 'I was provoked! Put that down! I was provoked! You saw it!' Now he appealed to his sworn enemies. 'You're all witnesses! That wee troll came at me!'

He put his pleading look back on me; everyone turned towards me now.

Ruaridh said, 'Tha's a load of shite! You shoved me! You'll be arrested on assault!'

'Bollocks!' Then the quick-thinking politician changed his tune. He set the ax-head on the ground but kept a grip on the handle. 'Good, good, you've got evidence,' he said. 'This was self-defense. Just give us the film. The police will sort the evidence.'

'Fuck tha', Douglas!' Ruaridh yelled, shoving through the footballers to reach me.

'Yeah, over our dead bodies,' the Aussie said. 'That's his film.'

'Don't be ridiculous. It's public record. Phil, seize the camera.'

'I don't think so, mate,' Fosters said, stepping forward on a line between the bald man, Phil and me. 'Lads,' he summoned over his shoulder. Sweden and Arsenal and the rest squared up behind Fosters. Phil pursed his lips in unhappy consideration and remained stock-still.

'Hang onto that, Mel,' Ruaridh said in a low voice, standing beside me now. 'Stay put.' He put his hand on my shoulder. To everyone, he bellowed, 'He'll juz destroy it! Tha's all his kind knows tay do, destroy thin's! Yer the menace, Douglas. You wan-nay be put away, where you belong. Maybe they will do, now that you've assaulted me.' He lifted his poncho and shirt, baring his doughy white chest for all to see. 'There's the mark. He sent me six feet backwards! The papers will have a field day! Mel, did you get him shovin' me?'

'I don't know,' I said. 'I was just shooting blind like always.'

'Americans too?' Douglas said. 'That's out of order, Gilmour. All of you – this is a local matter. It's no concern of Greenpeace or any other –'

A violent *thunk* silenced him – everyone turned. A police van drove straight up the curb, bounced past the BMW and stopped just short of us. The side door slid open, and officers poured out – six of them, four in chest protectors and Plexi-masked helmets, two in ordinary white and neon jackets. The shouting resumed. The officers shimmied between the two factions, the shaggy henchman resuming a place beside Douglas; Mark and Emma and Ruaridh clinging tight opposite them; the cluster of bare legs in soccer shorts shuffling towards the edge of the tent-grounds. I stayed where I was, which happened to be behind the cops now. Everyone was yelling about what'd happened, about the ax and the banner and Ruaridh flying backwards and the demonstrators being a menace to public order and setting upon Douglas. When this gave no sign of letting up, I edged around the police van towards the oak holding the deluxe treehouse, reaching it un-noticed. Luckily, the rungs were nailed to the opposite side; I mounted them without a sound and out of sight. Halfway up, I peeked around the wide trunk and caught Lewis's eye. He winked at me, then shifted his attention back to the melee. Reaching the top, I softly put one knee on the platform, then another. Without making a peep, I crawled into the enclosure. It was dim and silent. Slowly, I laid back on the sleeping bag, cradling the Pentax on my chest.

I took a deep breath and let it out, lightly, lightly.

Should I rewind the film, get it out, get it safe from exposure, get it stashed? How many had I taken anyway? The window said: 22. I decided not to make a sound, not even the soft grinding of the camera. I let it sit on my chest, staring at the bumpy black plastic of the housing and shiny metal of the hot shoe and lens ring. I tried to sort the voices below. Emma, Ruaridh. An officer. You're coming in, he was saying. And you're coming. We'll take reports at Barlinnie. Wha' about Douglas! Ruaridh squawked. Assault with a deadly weapon! Aye, Lewis and Mark said. We saw it happen. We saw it happen. Don't worry, Mr Douglas will be questioned as well, the officer said. Then my heart leapt. Where's the American? I heard Douglas say. I want that camera. But the officer was trying to end the bickering and hurry things along. Douglas was informed he'd have to ride in the van. He protested this, of course. He had his car here, he hadn't done anything, he wasn't going to flee, this was his bloody district! It was for his own safety, the officer said. Police protocol. He didn't want to be seen receiving special treatment, did he? This sent the demonstrators in fits of sarcasm. After that was calmed, Douglas asked again about the American, the journo.

'Right, what's this about an American?' the officer said.

'There's no Americans with us,' Lewis said. 'Is there, lads?'

Aye, no. Aye, no.

'I'm from Melbourne,' Fosters boasted.

'Arsenal, mate!' an English voice said.

'We're fra Glasgow!' Emma chimed. Mark and Ruaridh echoed this.

'Cuffs?!' Douglas bellowed, evidently having been clamped into a pair. 'That's out of order! I've done nothing wrong! I'm not a criminal!'

'It's for your own safety, Mr Douglas. They'll have them on too. I won't have you lot in the same van with your mitts free.'

Mark and Fosters said cheekily that they could be trusted with free hands. Enough, enough, the officer said, and the sliding door grated. Then a slam muting all voices. The gearbox clicked, the engine whirred. Earthy squishes of fading volume reached my ears. Shortly, the silence of the tree returned.

I slept.

I slept and dreamt of running through O'Hare's terminals, late for a flight to Glasgow for which I had no ticket, no boarding pass, no itinerary or gate number. I was helpless and panicked. When I heard Nicole's voice, it was at first a sound amid Chicago's travel chaos. Thankfully, my dream-mind was alert to its richer tonality, and slapped me awake. I scrambled groggily out of the treehouse. A foreshortened Nicole, the crown of her black-haired head bared to me, moved among the tents, peering in, calling my name, 'Mel? Mel?'

'Do you have a passport, miss?' I called down.

She jumped around. 'Oh, God! You gave me a fright!' she said. 'Hi-ya!'

'Good morning,' I said.

'Wha' ya doon'?'

'Um . . . Havin' a wee lie-down.'

'Aye, ri'.' She laughed.

I inhaled deeply and stretched. 'Coffee?'

'Sounds lovely.'

She was off the crutches and showed me the stretchy cloth brace under boots borrowed from her roomie Deb, who was a size larger. She fetched a new jug of drinking water from under the supply tarp; I'd never seen her long strides and brisk, bouncy walk that suspended her hair in the air a half-second between each step.

'How's it feel?' I asked.

'Yeah, feels good. Cheers. Thank fuck, the crutches were a hassle,' she said with a smile.

She put the kettle on the ironwork contraption and swung the arm over. I stuffed wads of newsprint under the kindling and lit it. After minding it a bit, I sat down and counted scoops of grounds into the presspot. When I was done, I set it down.

She wore jeans and a brown suede jacket over a blue sweater, and sat with legs extended and crossed at the ankle, 'praying' hands pressed between her thighs for warmth and in timid self-containment. She smiled hesitantly at me for a minute, then said, 'Mel, Ah'm sorry.'

'Sorry? You don't have anything to be sorry for.'

'Naw, Ah do, buh.'

'Not in my mind. Think there's any milk around here?' I stood, motioning to the supply area. 'Do you take milk? I don't.'

'Black's fine. Listen, sit down though.'

'Nicole, you don't have to explain anything.'

'Aye, buh I *wahn* to.'

'Okay,' I said. 'But wait until the coffee is ready, I don't want my heart to give out,' I joked, meaning only that I had a weak pulse, not that I expected heartbreak. She looked like she took that the wrong way, but I didn't have the presence of mind to clarify. I crouched at the fire and propped the logs up to raise the flame. I adjusted the chain two links to lower the kettle.

'Ah heard you goh a photo of Douglas goin' mad?' she said – a mixture of factual acknowledgment and incredulity at the MP's violent act.

'Well, I may have. How did you know?'

'Ruaridh phoned me. Mel, tha's why Ah came down. Tha's wha' Ah wannay explain.'

'All right, then.'

'He told me wha' ha'ened today. He phoned from Barlinnie, the jail. He's bein' held on obstructing legal acts under the CJA laws. He's got the dosh for bail, buh he won't agree to the terms for release. They're sayin' he's to stay off Pollok Park grounds permanently. He's mental – he's in fuckin' prison, and he's over the moon because of wha' Douglas has done. Mark and Emma signed the agreements, and Mark was to go straight to the *Herald* offices. This is Ruaridh's plan. And he used his one phone call on me, Mel. Why? Noh because he loves me – because he wants to *use* me. First thing out his mouth is askin' me to come down here – aye, *telling* me to come down and get yer film. "Do wha'ever's necessary," he says.'

NESS-ess-ree.

She paused and blushed.

'Oh!' I said, catching on. I blushed too. 'Well, there's the tent or the treehouse ...' I joked, raising my eyebrows.

'Mel!' She smacked my shoulder with the back of her hand.

'Sorry.' I got up and filled the presspot with the raging water. 'Seriously, though, that's messed up. Buh I guess I don't know what's going on between you two.'

'Aye, Ah know,' she said, tenderly, pleadingly. 'And tha's my fault. Ah've been a mess. Ah never phoned ya after Curler's, and Ah never said wha' ha'ened.'

I pressed the plunger down against water's resistance. Nicole grabbed two mugs, wiped them out on her shirt, and put them on the tree stump seat to be filled. 'Well,' I said, pouring, 'what happened?'

'First off, Ah had a fab time wi' ya when we went out. Ah ded.' I sat down beside her. 'Cheers,' she said, raising her mug. We clinked. 'An' Ah'm sorry Ah never phoned or nothin'.'

'You were down here – there aren't any phones.'

'Juz shuh yer gob a wee minute. Ah'm noh finished.' She drank from her coffee and set it down and zipped up her coat and dug out her packet of Holborn and started making a roll-up. 'It was surprising hearin' about you bein' divorced and all. Buh it was all ri'. Ah was okee wi' it. Then the day after, Ah was havin a bevvie wi' Sophie and Deb – you know, my roomies. Ah was tellin' them about ya, and they could see Ah wuz well chuffed, but they flipped when Ah told 'em you'd been married. Ah couldnay keep it from 'em, they're my best mates. They were like, "Och, Nic, it's noh on. American, an' only livin' here a wee while, now divorced as well?" Took the wind out my sails ri' enough.

'I goh stroppy wi' 'em, sent 'em away. Stayed in bed watchin' crap telly,' she laughed.

'Been there, done that,' I said.

'Dohn hold it against 'em, like. They were only lookin' out fer me. At the end of the day, though, Ah came round to wha' they were sayin'. Seemed like gettin' involved wi' you, Ah'd only wind up gettin' hurt. After all, Ah'd just finished with Ruaridh, Ah shouldnay be bothered with blokes – juz go out dancin' once my foot's sorted, and have a snog.

'Then my mum phoned, and Ah told her about you. Ah tell her everythin'. She went mental ri' on cue.' Nicole put on her mother's voice, reedy and broad-accented. 'American here fer work? Are ya daft?' She's so old-fashioned, Ah didnay dare mention divorced. She was callin' me a stewpid wee girl. "Juz mind yer studies,

Nicole." Tha's her favorite one there. "Juz mind yer books." And Ah goh the whole lecture on the fees and Ah'd be lucky to be hired as a secretary and all that carry-on.'

SEC-ruh-tree.

'When Ah rang off, Ah thought, "She's ri", Ah'm juz a wee girl from Dumerferline and Ah'm noh meant tay be datin' an American wi' a swish job and Ah'll pro'ly never live in America or even *see* it.'

'Whoa? Live in America? Did you think you might?'

'Ah have an active imagination. Ah tend tay get carried away.'

'Well, I'm sorry about your mom. What a drag.'

'Cheers. Ah wanhed tay see ya, but Ah was needin' money, an' the girls could only cover so many of my shifts. An' there wuz schoolwork as well. So tha's wha' Ah ded. Ah wuz juz glad to have my life back – no protests, no Ruaridh and his fits. Takin' the tube to the GSA, doin' my crap sculpture, havin' my crap dinner, workin' my crap job. All wi' a busted foot, mind you. Then Ruaridh turns up in the café, on one of his recruitin' jags.'

'No.'

'Aye.'

'Funny, he never mentioned seeing you.'

'Funny ha ha. Aye, he's selective in wha' he tells folk – a bit of a politician hissel'. He begged me tay come back. Ah dohn know wha' ha'ened. He's goh this way of bein' sweet an' forceful. "Wha's the use of art?" he says. "You should be doin' somethin' real, somethin' tha' has tay be done ri' now. Yer tubes of paint will be here when you get back." Och, why'd Ah listen tay'm? Guess Ah never learn.'

Lairn.

'Do ya think he's ri', though, Mel? He says, "Yer on the downward slide to the bourgeoisie. Yer young, you've goh no weans, no job, yer a bloody student, fer fuck's sake. If you wonh sacrifice the wee bit you've goh now, you're only gonnay get more apathetic. The more you have later, the less you'll be willin' to give up. You'll look back on the M77 and think, Och, it's okee to just give up an' mind my own."'

'Holy guilt trip!'

'Ah know! Buh is tha' how it is?'

'Well, I don't believe in fate like that. But that's the struggle, isn't it? Doing something meaningful that's not too stupid, taking a chance on what you believe, being true to yourself, while not pissing off your family, betraying their expectations.'

'Aye.' She stared at the ground a minute. She took a drink of her coffee. 'This is lovely, by the way. Cheers.'

'Glad you like it.'

'Ah guess Ah went back wi' him to spite my mum. Ah thought about uz gettin' arrested, her seein' uz in the papers an' shittin' hersel'. Buh I s'pose, as well, he wuz familiar. You know, a Sco'ish guy. Ah knew wha' tay expect. So Ah came back here. Then Ah really couldnay phone ya, even if Ah'd wahned to. An' Ah *did* wahn to. Ri' away. Ruaridh hadn't changed, he'd goh worse. More militant. More domineerin'. More criminal. Now he was nickin' buildin' supplies, knifin' tires on the diggers. No behher than the crooks he's fightin'. Fuck's sake, he wahned tay make Molotov cocktails! Then the whole thin' wi' the bairns from Corkerhill. Ah regretted it. It was cold an' miserable an' borin'. Ah was missin' my lectures and workshops. Joe at the pub was gonny fire me if Ah missed again. "Wha' am Ah doon?" Ah thought. "This is mental!" Buh Ah knew Ruaridh'd go mad if Ah spoke up – smokin' hash every night an' always goin' on about raisin' the level of resistance. *Direct action* this and *direct action* tha'. Then you and Klang came round.'

'Nicole, I had no idea. I thought you were happy.'

'Ah was makin' eyes at ya – buh couldnay say nawt in front of Ruaridh. Couldnay take you aside. Ah didnay know wha' tay do. The next mornin' Ah went away home. Snuck off wi' everyone still in their beds.'

'So you were back at your flat all this past week?'

'Aye.'

'Nicole! I went to every tourist trap in town to keep my mind off you. I had dinner alone every night. I must have walked seven hundred miles. I thought you were out of reach.'

'Aw, yer dead sweet.'

'I got an answering machine and everything.'

'An answer phone? Oh, brilliant. Buh Ah thought Ah'd mucked things up, sayin' you'se were welcome back anytime, then noh being here. Tha's like the ultimate blow-off.'

The sun had sunk but not set entirely. The foggy, low sky reverberated with a purple blend of city and diffuse natural light.

'I don't blame you,' I said. 'You were torn. I can relate. You have no idea how much I can relate.'

'Really?'

'Sure, I've mucked some things up in my time. Nicole, I need to tell you something. But it kind of depends on what I've already told you. And I'm not entirely sure what that is.'

'Whadja mean?'

'Well, when we went out, I had a lot to drink.'

'Aye. An' me as well.'

'I don't necessarily recall what was said. Or what we did. Say, after the chippie.'

'Ri'. Well, let's see, we bought chip suppers, and took 'em to the Botanic Gardens. You were sayin' about bein' married, bein' divorced. You told me a wee bit abou' Margaret – wha' she was like. You were pretty blootered. Seemed like it was hard for you to talk about. Ah walked ya back tay yer flat – bought you IRN-BRU on the way.'

'That was a lifesaver in the morning, by the way. So, was that all?'

'You sortay goh me tay come inside. Buh just for a fag. Remember, we had a fag in the lounge? Wha' else? You were talkin' about yer bed – the loads of sheets you'd bought. It wuz quite funnay. You wahned me tay see 'em and swore you weren't tryin' to have it off wi' me. Then you laid down on the settee, and tha' wuz you finished.'

'Oh dear.'

'Is tha' wha' you have to tell me?'

'No, no, no.'

What I had to tell her was the truth.

Though I'd added logs, the fire was dying. Night was on us, wet and chilly. I had to eat. I asked if there was a chippie around and if I could buy her dinner first. She said that'd be grand, and after could we have a lie-down in the tent? She was cold and knackered.

So we set off across the green where the Euros had played footie and Klang and I had tromped in silent syncopation. There was a chippie a few blocks in from the Welcome Centre. In a sweating brown bag, we brought back fish suppers and mince pies and IRN-BRUs. We sat in the tent cross-legged and ate by the light of the battery-powered lantern, dimmed and reddened by a bandana Nicole put over it to ease the glare. The tent smelled of new vinyl and the dinners of salt and vinegar. The ceiling was low, triangular and brownish, being green with red light cast on it. There was little noise – only rustling of trees, wind, and an occasional owl's hoot. It wasn't any type of setting I'd imagined prior to coming over. Not the setting Mrs Brown had spoken of over the fence, Mitzy sniffing at her feet. No heather hills, no otter-speckled bay, no Urquhart Castle. But then it wasn't any kind of history I'd planned on divulging.

We stayed up all night, which happened quite effortlessly; we'd had coffee, a meal, and IRN-BRU. There was also adrenaline, the rush of intimate connection. The rapt, electric giving of self and reception of other. All the chemicals flowing that cleanse the arteries and crispen sight. Sometime in the wee hours, we brushed our teeth out by the supplies, where the water was, and came back and undressed halfway and shared the sleeping bag. Nicole assured me that Ruaridh was spending the night in Barlinnie; he'd never agree to stay off park grounds. We kissed – a head-lightening, slow-but-too-fast kiss, her mouth small, her sexual aura reaching and devilish and foreign.

But there was a lot to tell. And so I did. With fingers locked behind my head, reclined, elbows out; Nicole on her back too and occasionally on her side with a word of comment, a hum of acknowledgment, a breathy gasp of disbelief, an appreciative laugh, a question about some Americanism, I told. It wasn't in these exact words. Far fewer. Far plainer. But the story was the same. Whatever abbreviated version spilled out – it was more of a trickle wrung than a dam bursting – this was the source, the one it drew from, the one I saw and felt in my mind, the one I'd lived 3,500 miles elsewhere. Nicole had told me about her confliction, and I'd had my own. That was the same. That's what I was driving at.

13   *The Reluctant Plunge*

I, Melvin Roger Podgorksi, was betrothed to Margaret Elizabeth
Irvine on August 22, 1991, at 4 p.m. Central time, before the cloth-
draped altar of St. Paul's Lutheran Church of Wynton, Illinois.
Senior Pastor Carl Hooper presided. My groomsmen were my two
closest friends from high school, plus my friend Jim, who'd been
my neighbor on Meadow Prairie Lane since I could remember, and
my cousin of eight, Jacob. On my own, three friends was all I could
come up with for my half of the wedding party, but Margaret had
deemed four maids necessary, and these things must be balanced,
I'm told, so I added Jacob, a bright and energetic kid, the son of my
mom's sister Jane. He looked up to me, and it was sweet, everyone
thought, to see him there, the short head in the row, along the
steps below the communion rail, adding a wholesome element
to the festivities that, looking at the faces of my pals, were mostly
about tying the knot and getting on with the debauchery. The
bridesmaids were more or less unknown to me. There were two
friends, Julie and Deborah, from La Porte, on the opposite side of
Chicago from Wynton, where Margaret had attended elementary
school and part of junior high. There was her half-sister, Ruth –
blood kin, yes, but in graduate school at Loyola and enwrapped, I
sensed, in an exotic world of academics and illicit cohabitation. I'd
met Ruth only once prior to the rehearsal dinner, and she had
regarded me with disinterest bordering on disdain. And there was
Margaret's dance co-instructor, Melinda. What would turn out to
be Melinda's long involvement with my neighborhood pal, Jim,
was begun, I believe, at the tail end of the reception, shortly after
last call.

Mrs Holmstead, my mother's bridge partner, took up the duty
of plunking out *Jesu, Joy of Man's Desiring* and something by
Pachelbel recommended by Pastor Hooper. Two angelic students

from Margaret's Tots Who Tap class tiptoed up the aisle in a state of blushing euphoria, scattering white rose petals from their tiny hands. Cousins Dave and John did the ushering. Greg Esposito, my cohort from the *Gazette* of Wynton High, had made the tri-fold program, inserting playful credit to his 'G-Man Productions' on the back cover. Greg was my photographer, too, committing to film, with the school's borrowed lenses and light canopies, this day of holy union.

Many people thought Mr P., with his imperial, exacting baritone, would do a reading, but we opted instead for a figure mutually fatherly to Margaret and me, Monsieur Drummond, our inspirational and expressive French teacher, in whose classroom we met. Mr P. was happier in the front pew anyhow – to the extent that he was comfortable in a pew.

Somebody knew somebody for flowers. Somebody knew someone who knew someone who catered. Someone had a something that got us a package deal on a deejay and drinks. And all this pleased Mr Podgorski, who wrote the checks, Margaret's father being 'out of the picture' (my family's euphemism for his drunken desertion), and her mother on a teacher's salary.

I wore a forty-four long Perry Ellis cutaway tuxedo over a wing-collared shirt and white bowtie. This white on white was supposed to connote a formality beyond formality, or elegance understated, but to me it seemed to admit to some inauthenticity in its wearer, a forcedness. Margaret was natural in her strapless gown with floral embroidered bodice, scalloped back, and a Duchess satin skirt under a shimmering organza overlay. The train was of moderate length, which surprised me. I had expected, given that her flare was for flare itself, and that she'd run herself ragged in preparation for this event, to see something rivaling Princess Di's 100-foot-long train. Selection of the gown had been carried out with limitless circumspection throughout the summer. Maybe that's unavoidable in a first-time bride. Luckily for me, Margaret's maid of honor shouldered the onus of consultation and devil's advocacy. Saved by tradition: 'You don't get to see it,' Margaret insisted, 'until the *Big Day!*'

Only thirteen weeks before, we'd both been attired in gowns – and mortar boards, tassels and stoles – stomping across a dais in the Wynton High gymnasium towards a congratulatory Principal Mullroy. And in truth, the white gown flattered Margaret more than WWH's royal blue; she was a vision. Gleeful, radiant, her smile broad and bashful, her youthful skin tantalizing, like a lavish gift peeking through lush ivory wrapping-paper. Her spectacular clavicles were bare, her auburn hair braided and twisted upward into an intricate bun, seen to throughout the day and evening by bridesmaid Julie, who flitted like a sparrow from across courtyards and reception halls to primp and pat it, saying, 'Hold on, hold on, hold on. There.'

I was not so much a vision, I felt, as a spectacle. The tuxedo is a laughable contraption, for one thing. A man cannot look dignified, much less at ease, in a cummerbund. I felt like a Czech-American masquerading as an Englishman, attempting a regal comportment throughout a nerve-wracking ordeal. In frequent trips to the men's room, to wash my sweating palms, I saw an ashen, zit-dotted face: the product of anxiety and an immune system beleaguered by bachelor-party booze and a few stressful days finalizing arrangements and tending to arriving relatives. Under the fluorescent lights of the sacristy, where I and my groomsmen were sequestered for dressing and cuff-linking, my sandy blond hair appeared, in a mirror on the pastor's wardrobe door, thin, flat and directionless. My eyes were baggy, my broad chest meekly concave, my tall frame cowering, my long legs unsolid. I was happy under it all, determined to proceed and never doubting my love for Margaret, but the disparity between the church's solemnity, its singular will to God, and the multifarious lives of the assembled guests seemed to manifest in me. Repeatedly I drew breaths to steel and calm myself, and repeatedly the odors of incense and the vellum pages of hymnals clashed with colognes and hairsprays, creating discord in my lungs. I was shaken.

Margaret stood poised on her trained, nimble legs, her bearing confident and elated. Clutching a bouquet at her waist, slow-stepping up the aisle on her grandfather's arm, she drew on a girlhood's worth of recitals – the electricity of being on display, the effortless seizing of attentions, striking poses and freezing in sync with the final crashing beat. She raised her chin, pressed back her shoulders and locked her eyes forward. It was all second nature. Throughout the introduction and homily, the vows and exchange of rings, the lighting of the unity candle, she was assured, as she always was, but with delighted restraint, following her role with stillness and grace. My embarrassment while fumbling with the ring box and clumsily lifting Margaret's veil felt large enough, under the eyes of every Podgorski I knew (and every Irvine), to fill the whole sanctuary, and I had no bouquet to hand back and forth, or train to fuss with, just a solitary band of gold to maneuver to its penultimate destination. Only beholding Margaret's presence of mind appeased me. Blurry in my mind, like the stained-glass rose window behind her, was the thought of unwrapping her from all that silk and satin.

I do! I do!

We honeymooned not in Cozumel or Hawaii or even Orlando, as Margaret wanted, but on the Door County peninsula, Door County, Wisconsin. Washington Island, to be exact. It was all we could afford. My father had flipped the bill for 80 percent of the ceremony and reception, and announced apologetically, as bills began to total in June, that he would not be able to provide for our getaway. This was extremely fair – no question. I had taken Sunday-school trips to Chicago's south side as a kid, to pick up trash, getting us suburban kids to see how the inner city lived. I knew even our modest Meadow Prairie Lane rambler was not a birthright. Margaret and I were both happy to be marking the occasion at all. The only amenity Mr P. had refused was special coffee, which I paid for myself. Whole-bean Ethiopian Yirgacheffe from a market downtown, because, let's face it, you endure a wedding, a long, slow reception line, a flimsy chicken dinner, the last thing that's going to sustain you through the Hokey Pokey and the dollar dance is a cup of thin church-basement Hills Bros. The beans were roasted that day, the catering staff instructed to grind medium-fine, to brew with distilled water in small batches (no vat-burn), at a two tablespoons per six ounces. This was me putting my stamp on the festivities, and in a way that wasn't tacky or overbearing, I don't mind adding. It wasn't like I insisted on a Monster Truck limo. I just wanted world-class brew for my wedding night. The guests benefited: win/win, as they say.

Margaret didn't drink coffee, and in the life of our marriage she never would, so she was indifferent, though, knowing her, she would have rather spent the money on a visual flourish. But once she grasped that this touch was important to me, she didn't argue. 'Have your espresso or whatever it is,' she'd said. 'I'll be drinking Cap n' Cokes.'

Anyway, Mr P. knew that, after this indulgence, Margaret and I had little more than a thousand dollars between us, a paltry sum largely spoken for: security deposit and first month's rent on an apartment that we would inhabit as husband and wife. 'You know, your mother and I didn't have a honeymoon at all,' Mr P. told us, with a kind of predictive assurance. We were seated around the patio table behind the house, the four of us. It was a hot evening and, having grilled steaks, we settled into more planning over margaritas. In classic Podgorski fashion, Mom and Dad didn't assert their ideas and preferences for the flourishes and frippery of our wedding, and didn't claim rights of choice by virtue of writing the checks. Rather, they went at it sideways, and the four of us often found ourselves kicking around ideas and considering things us 'kids' hadn't considered, such as what the guests would expect. 'Did we, honey?'

'No,' Mrs P. answered, 'we sure didn't.'

Mr P. looked knowingly at Margaret, an implication of parallel of outcomes twinkling in his eyes. 'And look at us. Twenty-two years and going strong. It's what you have between you that counts, not your first vacation together.' Since accepting Margaret into the Podgorksi fold, Dad had adopted a fatherly tone with her, embedding tidbits of wisdom on everything from finance to household duties. Though he sympathized with her having been raised fatherless, he underestimated her resilience and mistook her enormous will for foolish enthusiasm, and so the soft instruction of his tone often condescended.

'Oh, we know that,' Margaret stated, clutching my thigh. 'Right, honey? Besides, you're paying for so much already. We're very grateful for that, and we wouldn't expect you to buy us plane tickets or anything. It doesn't matter, we can take a better honeymoon next year, when we've got money saved up.' Much of Margaret's efforts with my parents aimed at proving her suitability. She grasped how my father vehemently valued level-headedness – that what he deemed most rare in a woman was foresight and diligence. Mrs P. expressed appreciation for lovely things but, by professing nothing contrary to Mr P.'s practicality, tacitly agreed with it. Though I know Margaret thought of him as dour and rigid, there was one tenet of his that she gradually adopted during the summer of wedding planning: his view of matrimony as a continual navigation of a ship into ports of preparedness.

'With two of us working,' Margaret continued, 'we can go to Florida in winter, which is a better time anyways.'

Silence followed what Margaret said, including from myself, since we hadn't spoken of such a trip in winter – though I did remember Margaret saying she wished she could do a fundraiser and take her entire 'modern' class to Disney World. I sent a quizzical look in Margaret's general direction. Mrs P. guarded her downturned mouth with her rose-red frosted glass, guiding the straw to her lips and sipping. Her hazel eyes looked to Mr P. as a signal for him to speak and, when he did not, she put her drink back on the coaster and said, 'Dear, that's only a few months away. How much do you think you can save by then? Plane tickets are expensive, and then there's the hotel and –'

'Oh, I know. It's just an idea,' Margaret said, looking around. 'It'd be fun! Go to Epcot, Space Mountain. Everybody loves Space Mountain.'

'Well, there's a lot to think about between now and then,' said Mr P., always guiding back to the tangible.

'Anyway, for the honeymoon,' I offered, 'we did come up with some plans – low-budget options. We thought we'd get a room downtown at the Plaza. You know, a honeymoon suite. For the weekend.' I had to look away from my parents, to my fiancée instead. The activities implicit in getting a honeymoon suite, even when unspoken, cannot be acknowledged in a mother's eyes. 'Maybe we'll take a ride in a horse-drawn carriage or, I don't know, see a show. Something fun.'

'That sounds nice,' Mrs P. echoed.

'Cirque du Soleil will be in town, in Grant Park,' Margaret said. 'But he doesn't want to go to that.'

'It should probably be something we'd both enjoy,' I explained.

'That goes without saying,' Mr P. agreed. I looked to him. He seemed lost in thought, absently creasing a napkin on the diagonal.

And a week later the object of his rumination was revealed when he summoned Margaret and me up from the basement. 'Leave that for now,' he said of the mints we were hand-wrapping in foil for the reception place settings. Upstairs, Mom muted CNN and sat with Mr P. on the edge of the fireplace hearth. Mr P. gestured to the loveseat. 'I spoke with a colleague,' he said, a look of what passed for excitement overtaking his round face. His thick glasses were of an old design, frames shaped like Boss Godfrey's in *Cool Hand Luke*. On Mr P., they were nerdy and dated, but some earnestness had seized him, so I kept his gaze despite the distortion that cast him as manic, disbelieving. 'Name of George Colville. A fellow with another firm who is ... indebted to me. I've known him many years. 3M has shared research grants with Plunkett for some time now. He's a good man and a clever chemist.'

'I've met him several times, at functions,' Mrs P. noted. 'His wife's an alto in the choir, if I remember right.'

'Be that as it may,' Mr P. continued. 'I recalled that he owns a cabin up in Wisconsin, near Green Bay. He often talks of boating and fishing there in the summers. So I called in a favor. George says he'd be pleased to let you two use it for your honeymoon.'

'Oh, cool!' Margaret said, springing from the couch to Mr P., leaning down and hugging him with force. Understand, hugging was the rage for Margaret. She had done it with her girlfriends from school since I'd known her, even when their separation promised to be no longer than a class period or two. Her dancers were showered with hugs – but that was different: children needed hugs. She hugged me constantly, sometimes to the point of excess. I mean, candy is sweet, but if you eat it all day, you'll get sick and lose your liking for it. The abundance of Margaret's hugs diminished their value. And while Mrs P. is an affectionate person in a Christian, consoling-hand-on-shoulder kind of way, I believe she had been taken aback by Margaret's reckless distribution of her body's tenderness. Mr P., too, of course, but it seemed to grow on him. He wasn't arguing with the nineteen-year-old dancer throwing herself on him in gratitude all summer. *Reception hall is booked?* Warm hug. *Limo is reserved?* Warm hug, with giddy smiles and copious thanks. *Bouquets and boutonnières and table centerpieces are paid for?* Tight clasp in low-cut, sleeveless summer dress, exposed neck smelling muskily of sweat and Calvin Klein's Obsession. Yes, there were lusts to be awakened in Mr P. and, while it was ostensibly innocent – an ages-old tradition of a family planning and paying for the wedding and a simple gesture from a buoyant girl – it was mildly perverse to be party to this exchange of cash for flesh. At these moments, Mother would look away and exclaim, 'Oh, weddings are so exciting!' as if to emphasize the sanctity of it all.

'That's so cool!' Margaret chimed now. 'We can go swimming, Mel!'

'You'll be expected to invite Mr Colville to the wedding,' Mrs P. said.

'Now, it's nothing fancy,' Mr P. cautioned, as Margaret released him and sashayed back to the loveseat in funky short steps. 'But it's remote and scenic, and I thought it'd be better than downtown. I mean, sure, find a hotel for your wedding night – then head up. It's yours for the week. It's wired for electricity. There's plumbing, phones in case of emergency. But that's about it. Just a few rooms, a kitchen, a deck.'

'Whatever – it sounds great, Dad,' I said. 'Thanks a lot. You shouldn't have.' I mustered a warm smile at Mom, while thinking that secluded in the woods was better than sharing a headboard wall with some tourists or conventioneers – on account of the sound effects. 'And be sure to thank Mr Colville for us.'

'Well, you'll have your chance to thank him personally. Like your mother said, it would be customary to invite him to the wedding.'

We talked more about the cabin, its location, how long it took to drive there, what we'd need to bring. Mr P. got sidetracked, excited with mechanical descriptions, as he got talking about facilities, amenities, activities, directions. Mrs P. grew bored, checked the clock, then went to the kitchen and started dinner. Margaret had been up to Madison and Milwaukee for dance competitions but couldn't visualize the geography, and when Mr P. got up to fetch an atlas from his den, we all shifted to the kitchen counter, where Mrs P. put out vegetables and dip and poured everyone ice water. I went down the hall and used the bathroom, and when I came out Margaret was waiting outside the door, looking at old family pictures hung there.

'Hi,' she purred, as I stepped beside her.

'You've seen these before, haven't you?' I asked, putting my arm around her.

'Yes, but they're still cute. Especially the one with your wee-wee showing.'

'Oh, that's the worst,' I said. Why pictures of me in the tub as a kid needed to be on display, I didn't know.

'I think it's the best,' she said, patting my crotch. Coy chuckling merged into kissing, then groping each other a little – only as much as we would be comfortable getting caught at. Aroused, Margaret pulled me into the nearest doorway, Mom's prayer room, and out of sight of the family room.

'Hey!' I hushly warned.

'Just for a minute,' she said. We made out some more, her hands exploring my chest under my shirt, her hips grinding mine. She was intent, uncharacteristically assertive, in fact. Usually at my parents' house, she presented her angelic side, which was 80 percent of her anyway. I opened my eyes several times, and saw, in the constant but dipping light of the votives, Margaret's own eyes remaining closed, two 'U's skirted with dark lashes. Eventually I broke the embrace and we straightened our clothes. She was pleased, her body hot and pulsing, her face flush with blood.

'Come on, let's get back,' I said. 'My dad's gonna show us how to get to the cabin.'

Looking down, Margaret laughed. 'Look at you.' She pressed at my bedenimed bulge with her hand, as if that would calm it.

'Holy shit,' I said. Margaret looked to me to see if I was perturbed that she'd forced that on me here, at a time like this. I let her know I wasn't by saying, 'I guess I'll need a minute. Hmm, hmm, hmmm,' I hummed casually, rearranging my package in a way that it could settle inconspicuously.

'Is there a mirror in here?' Margaret asked, producing a tube of lipstick from the pocket of her denim skirt. I flipped on the light. 'Oh, the shrine!'

'It's not a shrine, baby. It's a prayer station.'

Capricious with lust and the progress of planning, she said, 'Let's pray for something.' She stepped to the kneeler, and crouched down. 'How do I do this?'

'Oh, don't do that,' I pleaded.

'Don't be a fuddy-duddy.' This was a word I'd heard her mother use. She kneeled on the carpet and tried to put her elbows on the top rail.

'No, no, no. Like this. Back up.' The knee pad was in the up position; I pulled it down. 'You kneel on that.'

'Much better,' she said, in place like a proper Catholic now, complete with a moist, neglected pussy. She formed her hands into the more pious and archaic of the two praying positions, fingers like stolid figures facing off, not an orgy of intermingled digits. Her gold-capped lipstick tube lay nestled between her palms. 'Oh, baby Jesus,' she said, her eyes closed, 'thank you for the free honeymoon cabin, where we can knock boots as man and wife.' She opened her eyes and looked to me, gauging.

'You're gonna burn,' I said, smirking. 'If my mom doesn't get you first.'

She resumed her playful piety, facing the wall and the framed

Jesus. 'Please inject our car with your holy juices and guide us down the freeway to the promised land of cheeseheads–'

'Okay, that's good,' I said, trying to interrupt. 'Sacrilege has its limits.'

'So we may water ski on the Great Lakes that you made by peeing a lot out of the sky.'

'Oh, my God. Sorry, God.' I grabbed her arm.

Giggling, she clutched the rail and clenched her eyes shut. 'Just don't let me get pregnant yet, Jesus, because I can't dance with a big baby in my belly! Eeee!'

She screeched when I pulled her off the kneeler and she toppled over onto the floor. She grabbed my arm and pulled me down on top of her.

'What's going on in there?' Mrs P.'s voice came from the kitchen.

'Nothing!' I yelled back. I stood over Margaret and offered her my hands to pull her up, but she ignored them and instead flashed me a view up her already up-riding skirt. 'Mmm,' I groaned. 'No fair. Come on, let's go.'

'Okay, let's go. On the honeymoon.'

'Right now?'

'Right now.' She put her arms behind her head and did a bridge up, the white triangle of her underwear mound in full view.

'Oh, Lord.' I turned away. I put the kneeler back up and grabbed Margaret's lipstick off the floor. I stepped over her bridged body and set the plastic tube on her exposed bellybutton. 'Here you go,' I said. I bent over her upside-down face, a deep red now. 'I can see up your nose. Let's go.' And I returned to the kitchen, where my father had a Goode's Atlas open to Wisconsin and a paper pad ready for scrupulous notations.

Looked at aerially, if Wisconsin was the profile of a rotund man's torso, facing east, its flat southern border delineating his waist, the Door County Peninsula is his up-angled erection, and Washington Island his splash of spunk. Rock Island State Park would be a smaller dab that got away. That about sums up my mindset studying the tri-state map and my father's numbered steps and setting out from the hot-metal, grease-on-the-air downtown blocks at the Plaza in my 1985 Accord hatchback, groggy from a short night's sleep but buzzing with a newlywed's excitement, which is basically the pheromonal hangover of recent love-making tweaked with the anticipation of another session.

And it wasn't long before we christened Mr Colville's queen bed in the drafty back room of his humble lake home. The drive was only a few hours, along the unscenic Highway 43, past Green Bay, interrupted by a ferry passage – a new experience for both Margaret and me, in which we leaned on the rail of the ferry's top deck, facing into the afternoon sun, looking down at the chop and the faded red roof of the Honda. The solid conveyance that had gotten us this far now rested like a dog in the shade on the car deck below, its weight lolling effortlessly over water as if it were a Hot Wheel in a bathtub. It was *our* Honda now, no longer mine. The boat's grinding motor and the wind buffeting our ears made conversation impossible. We looked out on the water and the gulls swarming overhead whose squawks pierced the pulsating din of gears, and watched the mainland recede. Several times wind threatened to lift Margaret's lightweight dress, and I flex-raised my eyebrows suggestively at this possibility. We smiled at each other and I put my hand on her lower back and we kissed in the bright sun. An older couple clambered up the steep iron ladder and emerged on the platform triumphantly. The woman observed our obvious amorousness with a shy smile and, bolstered, clutched her husband's arm and escorted him to the opposite rail.

Soon I pointed north, over the ferry's bow, at the appearance of a sliver of brown on the horizon: Washington Island.

'What's that?' Margaret yelled in my ear.

'That's the island!'

'Oh!' she gasped, showing me her surprise. She then cheered, 'Yay!'

We held hands, squeezing love signals back and forth – our silent conversation. We fiddled with each other's wedding bands. Margaret recognized the characteristic way I tilted her outlaid fingers as the search for a diamond's glitter. She watched me study it and waited for my reaction. It was a small stone and we both knew it; but on this bright day it reflected and twittered as brightly as Lake Michigan's ripples. I nodded at Margaret, impressed. She squinted and scrunched her shoulders with pleasure, as if clasped by one of her own liberal hugs. Happy, we watched the approach of solid ground.

The island's size was hard to ascertain as the boat nestled, churning brown backwater under its keel, against the dock. We had moved to the lower deck and joined the line to disembark. The map showed us to be on the south side of a more or less round, symmetrical and largely barren piece of land, but with no cities, I found the proportions misleading, only the narrow lines of the few roadways to gauge dimension. My eye was inclined to interpret roads' widths as literal and proportionate, in which case Washington Island could be traversed in half a minute. I looked out the filmy window to the parking lot and the wide tarmac that led away from shore and up a slight hill and remarked, 'I wonder how big this place is.'

'It's big enough, honey,' Margaret said.

We watched two men in hunting-orange vests tie off the moorings and kick into place the hanging car tires that acted as bumpers. When I looked to Margaret again, she was smiling coyly, and her cheeks were flushed deep with red. 'What?'

'You're my honey now. I've always wanted a honey, and now I have one.'

I held her close, my arm around her waist, and buried my nose in her brown hair. At five eight Margaret's head tucked neatly under my nose, and my hand naturally found her opposite hip – a comfortable resting place where it could study, by means of fingertips, the waistband of her underwear, so tantalizingly accessible to the touch under summer's wispy dresses.

We followed Mr P.'s hand-written directions to the house, over poorly marked gravel roads that had not been graded recently. Some signs were rusted and nearly illegible, others low-standing and obscured by overgrowth. The sun glared on them and the faded black inset lettering blended with the weathered walnut grain into which it was sunk. The late August air was hot, and the croaks of frogs and chirps of crickets throbbed up from the grassy ditches into the open car windows. The sight of Margaret, her feminine lightness in the heavy heat, was a pleasant contrast. She was not shaded by the tube lights of Wynton High's hallways, not blue with the flicker of TV in Mr and Mrs P.'s living room late on a Saturday night – Mr P. rustling his newspaper loudly from the den to make sure we knew he was still up and might walk in at any moment. Driving, I was frustrated by my unfamiliarity with the landscape and the seeming endlessness of the flesh-colored gravel roads on an island that I had envisioned as small. In places, there was nowhere to put the tires to alleviate the resonant frequency made by the sun-baked ruts, the road's hard ripples. My navy jeans, and no doubt our cooler of food in the back window, absorbed the piercing heat that entered the driver's side. On top of this, disinterest hindered my attention to driving: I was drawn to Margaret's face with the passing trees and fields behind it. I was impatient with wanting to reach the cabin and sink into a bed – sink into contemplation of my new wife, my new self, my new life. Out of school, out of 8460 Meadow Prairie Lane, and I hoped out of Wynton. Maybe even out of Illinois.

When the third road shown on the map didn't appear, my annoyance peaked, and I lashed out, yelling, 'What the fuck is this? These directions are horrendous! This map – is this even the same island?'

'Oh, my God!' Margaret shrieked, as I stopped the car in the center of what was supposed to be Jackson Harbor Road. She was startled and mortified. She had seen me go from zero to irate in three seconds before; still, she hadn't yet learned – and she never would – that it was not a personal attack but a response to circumstance. Anger was for her a weapon against meanness, and against meanness only. Personal, intentional malice, as of name-calling, as of judgment: this she abhorred and proudly raged against. Whenever I became angry, Margaret was swift with her insistence that I had no reason for it.

'Calm down!' she said, a confused snarl on her upper lip. 'It's just a map. Let me see.'

Limited options in this case acted in lieu of ingenuity. Margaret pondered the map, the crickets thrummed around our idleness, and she concluded that the road we needed must be ahead. But we'd already passed Deer Side Road, I explained; it was shown to be beyond the intersection said to take us to Mr Colville's cabin.

'This is where we are,' I said, pointing. 'Or should be.'

We disagreed on the scale of the map. 'It's ambiguous,' I said. 'All we can do is drive on.'

'What's ambiguous?' she asked, as I put the car back in gear, and gravel crunched again.

'The size of the island.'

'No, I mean, what does *ambiguous* mean?'

At this point my brain simmered like an egg in a frying pan. 'Let's just find the cabin,' I said with a deep breath and, spotting a gravel inlet on the left, I nosed into it with the intention of making a U-turn. A silver mailbox appeared, on a long post like a beckoning arm, reading COLVILLE.

'Holy shit!' I blurted. Dumb luck and relief flushed the air of disagreement.

'This is it!' Margaret screamed, and she leaned across the center console and kissed my cheek repeatedly, with copious humming jabs.

We never bothered making sense of how we'd gone wrong, how the map had misled us. Probably it was just outdated. Or maybe I'd been too distracted when I should have been driving. Two ruts and a weedy median formed a sharply dipping driveway shaded by cool dense pines on either side. I slipped the Honda in neutral, and we rolled down and up again, me yelling 'Wooo!' Through the shade-black air, panels of stained timber and the familiar apparatus of an electrical meter appeared. As we glided onto a grassy clearing beside the house and stopped, the windshield was filled by narrow white birch trunks over blue-black, sun-twinkling lake water. We'd reached the other side of the island.

We fell onto the bed, a bundle of gropes, our bags unopened, the cabin uninspected, the Honda ticking towards coolness. Without a place of our own, our love-making in Wynton had been not infrequent but not indulgent either. Certainly clumsy in the early going, then, though more practiced, it had been hurried, and often tainted with the threat of unwelcome interruption – Margaret's mother, Mr and Mrs P., the school janitor, a park-goer or, worse, park patrol. Now I took my time, traveling with my lips up and down the smooth lanes of her outstretched limbs, and returning teasingly to the central concerns. I pinned her arms gently and worked across the beams of her collarbones, under her chin and into the cavern of her neck until she twisted and huffed with anticipation. Then I descended to her taut peaks and onto the valley where man's drinking is the stream's delight (if you do it right). There I stayed for a shamelessly long time, until Margaret issued me up, stone-hard and swabbing my face with the back of my hand. Margaret said, 'Oops' – not a word you want to hear from your new bride in this situation. I looked down and saw a viscous strand, like spider's silk, connecting me to the Colvilles' flowered bedspread. I reached towards the mess, and Margaret laughed, saying, 'Never mind,' and pulling me into position. Her brown eyes fixed on mine as she brought me hungrily into her. Forging this mere and quintessential distance, the memory of the two hundred fifty miles we'd traveled over Illinois and Wisconsin highways, the half a dozen knots of Lake Michigan and the unknown lengths of gravel we'd kicked up in search of this destination, all coiled and contracted to single point. Pumped into a fury, they evaporated into nothingness.

Unwittingly soon I flopped on my back, the buzz of ecstasy numbing the ache of travel in my bones.

Also too soon was Margaret's leap from bed and gathering up of clothes. Nude, she had always assumed a child's shyness after the act, and though our union would change many things, as I expected, none would be instantaneous. 'Come on,' she said, 'let's check the place out.' She stepped into her briefs, slid the dress over her head and left the room.

'How about a nap?' I called to her. 'I haven't had any coffee since the hotel!'

'Oooh, let's go down to the lake,' came her voice. 'We can get in a swim before dark.'

I said nothing, but breathed in the must of the stale bedding and the sticky sugar scent of pine needles that seeped through the thin walls.

'Mel!' She returned carrying her suitcase and set it on the bed.

'It'll still be warm after dark. We can skinny-dip at night. Oooh,' I appealed to her, 'Skinny-dipping at night.'

'I wanna go now. I'm hot.' She laid her bikini on the bed, and stepped out of her clothes again.

'Okay.' I stretched out limply and let my head drop under its own weight. 'I need a kiss, though, for strength.'

'Oh, just get up.'

The donning of bras and bikini tops is fascinating business to men, especially young men unaccustomed to seeing it done, as I was then. The quick ease with which the cups are draped in place and the arms' deft reach behind for clasping. Or the clever but inelegant method of clasping in front without the shoulder straps mounted, then twisting the garment roughly over the sacred mounds. Then pop, pop, both straps up, a quick adjustment, disappointing in its unsexual abruptness, and away we go. It's distasteful for a man to see breasts treated without ceremony, at least it was for me. Perhaps it's just the fact of them being put away rather than uncovered. These were the discoveries of partnership, however base and unflattering, and there would be more.

Suited now, beach towel over her arm, she looked down at me. 'Melvin, come on.'

'Coffee . . .' I groaned. 'Need . . . coffee.'

A minor battle of wills played out, until she agreed to wait while I unpacked the coffee maker I'd brought and brewed up a cup. Margaret found mugs for me in the kitchen cupboard but was not entertained by my exaggerated grogginess as I staggered around naked, the maker burbling and sputtering. She ignored my playful dragging of feet and, as if to create a deliberate contrast, rapidly narrated her thoughts as she moved my untouched suitcase, looked around and prepped this temporary nest.

'We might as well put our clothes in the drawers, we'll be here five days. No use living out of suitcases – I hate that. I've lived my whole dang life out of a suitcase. We can put the empty ones in that little closet in the bedroom. They'll be out of sight. Oh my God, this deck is great. I'm gonna get a killer tan. Will it get sunny back here do you think, Mel? Which way is this facing? What's the best way for tanning, east?'

'Grrr, east,' I moaned like Frankenstein's monster, lumbering back and forth before the kitchen counter, watching intently the accumulation of the holy black syrup. I'd used a lot of grounds and not much water. 'East good! *Coffee* good!'

'I noticed the fridge light is broken, maybe you can see if there's a spare bulb around. Maybe under the sink.'

'Fridge not on!' Even desperate for caffeine I was alert to the mechanics of a second home. A father's influence. I knew we might expect bursts of air from the faucets, a gas valve in need of opening and a stove with no pilot light.

'What? How do you know?' Margaret said. She opened the fridge, thrust her hand in, waved the air out at herself.

'Me hear no motor . . . Grrrr.'

'Oh, yeah! You're so good!' She unstooped and raised her lips to mine. I remained stock tall, monstrously rigid, primitively un-responsive. 'Kiss me, monster boy.'

'Grrr,' I purred. 'Woman gooooood.' I put my sleepwalking arms past her ears and puckered roughly.

An encouraging smack was placed on my hardened lips, and the quick withdrawal of its giver signaled the necessary end of my performance. 'Yes, woman good,' Margaret said, and walked away. 'Now pour your coffee – let's go swimming!'

I took only a few revitalizing sips in the house and carried the entire pot and a mug down the railroad tie steps to the water's edge. Margaret carried an extra towel, the radio, a bag of pretzels and a soda for herself. On the dock, I sipped heartily, the black jolt surging until I could bear to leave it behind and make the reluctant plunge.

14   *The Advent of an Age*

Hargrove is twice the size of Wynton, and more sprawling. It has the same Jewel-Oscos and White Hen Pantrys, but they are unkempt; the tarmac parking lots are buckled and littered with flattened cigarette packs and Mountain Dew bottles. In Wynton you see the managers Windexing the front doors and touring the lot, collecting trash in their blue vests and tidy, side-parted haircuts. In Hargrove, the managers are high-school graduates with flabby guts and ratty hair, who lurk in the store and hover in the back-rooms, smoking. Outside in the lot the Asian kids hang around their souped-up Civic hatchbacks smoking Camel Lights and throwing their tinted hair to the side with rebellious flicks. The Hargrove manager, if he strayed outside for garbage duty, his vest unbuttoned, name tag askew – even if he smoked, like them – would surely be heckled and perhaps even attacked with a fizzing Molotov of nuclear-green soda.

This is what I knew about Hargrove before Margaret and I lived there – impressions from passing through and from visiting a friend who ran a store there. Then we started shopping for apartments, and our understanding grew. Glaring to me was its flat, homoge-nous character. Fewer brick houses, more with fiberglass siding. No scenic lanes curving under oak canopies alongside private golf courses like they have in Wynton, the ones that entice teenage drivers to race over their rapid dips and drops, creating the stomach-hanging effect of a rollercoaster. Instead, the broad Ogden Avenue, which we would come to call 'the strip', with its glassy black pavement and freshly poured median, and the lesser arteries that drew traffic from it. Oak-less Oak Streets and elm-less Elms. The barrenness of yards, houses unshaded and sun-faded, grass scorched brown, the sidewalks unbroken by roots. I had hoped to find more tucked away, more landscape, more character but, looking back, I see, as with everything, we got what we paid for. It was affordable and, crucially, a marital starting locale equally new to us both.

That was the prerogative: to keep us neither too close nor too far from both in-laws. Mr and Mrs P. of course remained on Meadow Prairie Lane, and Margaret's mother, Janis Krantz (she had taken her maiden name after divorcing Mr Irvine, when Margaret was four), was nestled in a Wynton townhome. When Janis cried *Oh, no!* at our choosing Hargrove, there was, to my ear, an undertone of duplicity, as if thinking instead, *Oh, finally!* Having raised Margaret mostly on her own, Janis seemed eager to have the place to herself so she could entertain her dopey boyfriend, Alex. She was often exasperated at planning meals around her daughter's fickle tastes, loaning out her car to her, leaving herself stranded – and stranded socially when Margaret's hogging the phone line blocked Alex's calls. I'd seen it in her eyes, the anticipation of dipping her toes once again in the shimmering pool of independence and youthful larks.

That's how I saw it, but every observation was now subject to the new physics of coupledom. We resided now in the marital structure of joint identity, where differing opinions, tendencies and preferences are stacked up on one another like a house of cards' fragile assembly. Margaret didn't believe her mother longed for an empty nest. On moving day, as we carried boxes, I remarked to Margaret that I thought her mother was excited to have some space, eager to reclaim habits of the single life. 'Please!' Margaret scoffed in her animated way. She carried so much of herself in her lively face. Forget heart on her sleeve – Margaret's pulsed subcutaneously, submerged only millimeters below her luminous skin. All photos I'd seen of her showed an extravagant, almost painfully broad smile; when she cried, I comforted the embodiment of agony – an angry red forehead, scowling mouth, miserable pained eyes. When she disagreed, as she did now, it was absolute. The cockeyed squint and affronted lean that followed her 'Please!' befitted mortal outrage more than variance of view. 'She's gonna be miserable without me. She'll be calling all the time.'

'Of course she'll miss you,' I agreed. Always agree first – the credo of the politician's Q&A. 'I'm just saying, she's gonna crack open some wine, make a fire and put on a nightie. Then she's gonna call Alex, get him over there –'

'Eww! That's disgusting. That's my mom.'

'What? You don't think she *does it*?'

'Yeah, but I don't want to think about it.'

'Well, it's a reality. Why deny it?' I said.

'You're gross. You're sick. You're perverted – that's what you are.'

Margaret was prone to prudish streaks. But I couldn't resist goading her. 'I don't know. I just think she's ready to break loose a little. Get busy on the bathroom floor.'

'Mel!'

'No, seriously, you don't think she'll enjoy it? To me, she's never seemed that crazy about being your mom.'

'Mel! God!' She slugged me on the shoulder, hard, with knuckle. 'What a horrible thing to say!'

'I mean *a* mom. She's never been that, you know, active in parenting.'

This exchange soured moving day. Margaret was insulted, I was led to deduce as I was drawn into the vacuum of her silence, by the insinuation that her mother didn't love her, didn't dote on her. But that wasn't my suggestion at all. Janis, in fact, had always praised and fawned over her daughter; it was the circumstances of sharing that townhome that nagged her. But Margaret couldn't differentiate, evidently. She answered my every attempt to converse with 'You're a jerk.' Was I wrong? I tried to think of Janis as the mother Margaret knew. But I could not bend to this perspective. I saw Janis Krantz, near-fifty schoolteacher ready to do some living again. Once the rental van was emptied and returned, alone in the apartment and facing an evening of unpacking, I found a way to apologize.

When I think of this now, and Margaret's recalcitrance, her unwillingness to allow innocent fact to contradict her purest hopes – these moments seem like fissures that only widened.

Despite all this, in Hargrove we were to be near to Janis, and near to my folks. Our Wynton friends would not be far either.

'We can have Megan and Brad over,' Margaret mused, filling cupboards with plates and cups. 'We can make 'em dinner. Or go over to their place.' This was a central tenet in Margaret's vision of married life: couples' nights, movies, dinners, Pictionary, Trivial Pursuit. 'The drive to the studio will be a piece of cake. The only question, I guess, is where are you gonna be for work? You're not gonna be at Clix much longer. I mean, once you're working downtown, it won't matter – here or Wynton, it's the same distance, right?' Ports of preparedness.

That was the question, and Margaret was right: it was the same distance. Clix was a film lab – I never called it a camera store – where I'd worked during my senior year. It was a franchise operation making most of its money on mass photo-processing, but had managed to retain the cachet of an expertise shop, particularly when it came to hardware. While it was more than a drop-off joint for the family vacation shots, and while a few of its customers were actual talented professionals, it was no future. Not for this Podgorski. Part-time cash and small-time experience, but that was the extent of it. I had plans – plans that Margaret alluded to often and threw into conversations with alacritous certainty. I would be working downtown. Somewhere. Somehow.

The apartment was in a five-building complex on South Wright Street, over by North Central College. It was a claustrophobic's nightmare and a miser's wet dream: a garden level. The security deposit had been paid and the lease signed prior to the wedding, so we were able to share the news, at our reception, of where we'd be living. Relatives were terrified at the garden-level element, acting as if thieves and rapists could saunter right through ground-floor windows without so much as ducking their heads. Uncle Mark bellowed with authority, 'Oh, yeah, they get broken into all the time.' Aunt Lizzy, too, was aghast. We stressed, Margaret and I, that security bars were installed outside the windows, and the landlord had assured us there had been no break-ins. But it hardly mattered: visions of the double homicide of a newlywed couple, blood pooled in the beige carpet, glittered in people's eyes.

'Well, it's only temporary,' Aunt Jane said. 'You'll be buying soon anyway, right?' But home ownership wasn't on our radar. Perhaps it was prescient that we never thought that long term. We agreed blankly, as you do when you want the subject to change. Aunt Jane took care of that. 'They have these things now,' she said. 'Gated communities.' Even the way she'd been tucking crisp ten-dollar bills in my birthday cards since I was a boy seemed to bespeak her obsession with wealth.

September in the Midwest. The days shorten. One day you're driving home, thinking you have time for a sit-down meal, to clean up, watch some TV, then turn your attention to something quiet and thoughtful, the new wife or a hobby or the pursuit of some fleeting interest, maybe drift with the underseas programming on the Discovery Channel. But then it registers. Your assumption that the kitchen will be filled with natural light as you rinse and rack the plates, that afterwards when you plop on the couch for a post-dinner smoke and hear voices of walkers outside the building, you'll look out and see silhouettes against the streaked rays of a low-hanging but still-intense sun – these are wrong. Your dashboard clock, as you gas and brake from one stoplight to the next along Ogden Blvd, says 7.15, and it's nearly night. The air ruffling in the window carries a chill and, sure enough, in the house after dinner, goosebumps sprout on your legs and you change out of summer's well-beaten shorts into jeans and a sweatshirt. Flipping around the channels – the new sitcom season is being hyped for launch – your new wife suggests a cup of hot chocolate. You make hers, and for yourself you prepare a steaming mug of black coffee.

It was mugs such as these, meant to prolong the shortening days, that also shortened my nights, when I suddenly found I had to wake at 6 a.m. and be on the floor of Hughes Distribution Inc. at seven sharp. Hughes was a warehouse managed by Dan Johnson, the brother of my friend and groomsman, Brad. I had to get out of Clix, and this was out. The Monday after moving into the apartment, I punched in (using that relic, an actual punch card) as a forklift driver. The position was a favor, to help me out. Dan knew I didn't have any experience, but said that if I possessed an iota of common sense and was at all reliable, I was 'miles ahead of the pack, compared to some of the yahoos I get in here', as he put it. I bypassed the application process, just showed up, signed the W-4, shook some hands and got a tour of the break room, 'shitter', first-aid kit – and then The Floor.

The Floor was 15,000 square feet of vitreous green-grey concrete streaked by tire treads and segmented into numbered rows, 184 in all, of prefab pallet racks, five shelves high, each capable of holding two stacked pallets. The Floor is where I spent the next five weeks, after a shotgun driving lesson and mandatory safety video, spinning around on a lime-green electric forklift, clanking over hydraulically adjustable lift plates connected to docked semi-trailers, bringing in goods from manufacturers and sending them out again, to retailers.

'I needja on The Floor,' Dan would say, and I'd get to The Floor.

It wasn't glamorous, but it was a paycheck while I searched for work. Meaningful work. Photography work. The work was painless to acquire and effortless to keep. Dan was an overburdened manager, responsible for the swift, errorless movement of millions of dollars in merchandise daily, as well as a staff of sauntering, laughing, Kool-menthol-smoking employees, some partially toothless, some ex-cons. In this context, with my high-school diploma, reliable car, and ability to stay alert and sober for eight hours, I was a solid cog in an often failing apparatus. Dan started me at the pay level only earned, according to Hughes' official policy, by employees who had logged ninety days of service. 'Jobs like these, you get truancy problems all the time,' Dan explained. 'So, you scratch my back, I'll scratch yours. Shit, you just got married, so you need the money, right? I figure you'll at least show up. Otherwise, it's the doghouse, I know how it is.'

This view of husband as breadwinner may have been primitive, but it wasn't extinct.

The other reason Dan needed dependable help was because an

attempted efficiency leap had him mired in troubleshooting. This was late 1994 and, with the advent of Windows 95, Hughes was in the midst of transitioning to new 'user-friendly' inventory-tracking software. At times when Dan was hunched over in the office clicking helplessly at inventory logs, a phone cradled under his chin, I was put in charge of the FFUs that were normally his bread and butter. 'Fixing fuck-ups,' that is. Filling delayed orders. Recounting shipments. Rewrapping, using an enormous whirling contraption that would crush me if I misstepped, pallets that had been speared by errant forks. Restacking cases of Huggies that somebody'd dumped in a remote aisle while stoned.

I was Dan's right-hand man, and therefore something more than lowly grunt. Yet the exposure to this life of manual labor, Zen-like though it could be to operate the forklift under gravity's sure and easy rules, was enough to light a fire under my ass, as they say. In the evenings, I revised and polished my résumé and scoured the classifieds, reading those with potential aloud to Margaret, who was tickled to see me arrive in our home dusty, scuffed, haggard, armpits of my T-shirt sweat stained; to see me accept this as a passage, a rite, and then turn my attention to concluding the rite. I wrote cover letters, printed them and wrestled with the buggy emerging technology. The ink-jet printers that devoured twenty papers at once into the mouth of its feeder then promptly jammed. The finicky word processor that skewed the entire contents of my carefully aligned document upon the insertion of one additional space in an early bullet point. The floppy disk that suddenly went unrecognized and grinded angrily, refusing to save, until I ejected it – yielding a quick demand from the mercurial mind inside the machine to 'Insert disk MELSSTUFF', followed by the bitter refusal to perform any function whatsoever once I'd refused this request.

It was at the computer that the contrast between mine and Margaret's temperaments was revealed and accentuated. She seemed to believe that, because she'd once expressed her surprise and distaste for my outbursts, as when I had searched for the unmarked roads to Mr Colville's honeymoon cabin, that I would never flare up again. That since she'd proffered her perspective – 'Don't get so irate, it's just a . . .' – I would internalize and integrate it with a superhuman celerity made possible by my unequivocal love for her. The logic seemed to be that my vow of 'in sickness and in health' implied an unflinching estimation of her advice; and if my vow was true, and my intentions were pure and I was committed to the relationship, then I'd reform. But things don't work quite that way.

I'd be knee-deep in a pot of some home-brewed supermarket roast, trying to print the address of an art-book publisher on Clark Street downtown – trying to print on the marble-speckled envelopes I'd bought with matching résumé paper so it'd look professional and I could get a decent shot at an interview, during which I hoped to charm my way around the fact of my in-experience in the professional-photography field, pour on a little Mel-esque knowingness and articulation, my passion acting as a smokescreen. The damn wizard would prompt me to insert the envelope in the Epson's jaws as seen in the on-screen diagram, the stamp corner in the upper left. I'd do so, and it would emerge printed upside down. So I'd throw that out, and spool it again, and wait for the prompt, and study the diagram again, and realize they were showing the printer as being at the *bottom* of the screen, which made no sense, since that was opposite to how it looked when actually using the printer, unless you hovered over it like some kind of paper-inserting hummingbird. So I'd prep another precious envelope (there were only ten in the pack), certain of its correct orientation, but now the little plastic claw with the rubber foot would try to grab it and pull it into its clutches, and wouldn't take, so I'd feed it gently a little further, and it'd grab hard, so hard the envelope would be pulled in at a slant, and I could hardly send that off to an employer as a first impression. I suffered all this through imagining. Imagine! Taking the El, wearing a tie, eating a pita for lunch at my charmingly disorganized desk, careful not to drip tzatziki on contact sheets! Imagine! An office in a high-rise downtown, maybe looking out on the lake, approaching freight ships in the distance dim and speckled, hazy like an idea forming in solution to a particularly challenging project. Or – 'Fucking printer!' I'd blurt – imagine driving a forklift the rest of your life and taking over for a post-operative Dan (heart blockage? hypertension?) and pissing off one of the ex-cons and being stabbed to death with a Hughes pen from your own clipboard and left for dead in aisle 102, behind a crate of chewing gum.

Margaret would be on the couch nearby, our apartment's small size necessitating that the dining room moonlight as an office, talking to a friend on the phone about someday opening her own dance studio. She'd hear my tantrum and say, 'What's your damage?' This was a phrase of hers, born of Franglais, evolved to English, from *Quel dommage?* (colloquially *What a pity*, literally *What damage?*).

'What?' I'd question, feigning ignorance.

'Hold on, Julie. What are you spazzing about?'

'This thing's misbehaving,' I'd say, trying to paint it in terms she'd sympathize with – maybe it was like one of her kids giggling or picking her nose while she instructed.

'Well, don't blow a vessel. It's just a printer.'

That's the part that got me. *It's just a printer*. No, it's not just a printer. It's everything this printer is denying me access to. But I couldn't say that, I'd think, gulping heavily from my coffee to gain patience and calm. Every smidgen of energy spent explaining this was lost on getting the résumés out the door. I'd look at Margaret. Her nimble fingers would be idly tucking hair behind her ears, innocent optimism in her eyes as she described to Julie how, once her own studio was up and running successfully, she was going to spend her time off, what kind of house she and I would have. And I'd be warmed, thinking of the hope and trust she'd put in me, how happy she was to have found me, as she'd told me lying in my arms during the wee hours one night at her mother's townhouse when her mother had gone for the weekend. How we'd taken shelter in each other from the stupidity of high school and sworn not to be like the leaders of the cliques we didn't fit into. And I'd think, what am I getting mad at her for?

By the time I got the résumés right, I'd have cussed plenteously and ripped up the flubs and huffily swigged my coffee and glanced at Margaret with wild eyes to see if she was measuring my ire. And she would have been – absorbing it in furtive, distasteful looks that incensed me, overlooking as they did appreciation for my job-hunt efforts, which was, in the end, for us, not merely me. With tension in the room, she'd go to bed, and I'd stay up to outlast it and settle into restfulness, wait for coffee's nimble buzz to subside. It would be quite late when I'd shut down the PC and its affiliated contraptions and join her in bed. She'd be sound asleep. We wouldn't make love; we both had to be up early. In the morning, I'd drop Margaret off at the Culkin School of Dance, find a mail drop for my pristine letters and get back to Hughes and the vapid expanse of the warehouse floor and the ripped leatherette cushion of my forklift's seat, the incessant whir of its forward thrust and cautioning peals of its reverse indicator.

Dan was lenient in letting me dash off some afternoons for what he knew were interviews for office jobs as long as I stayed late and filled my eight hours. The regular guys knew that Dan favored me with a leniency they didn't enjoy, so my interview excursions always began with an ironic guilt as I jaunted, car keys in hand, down the concrete stairs by the open truck bays, hoping for a brief interview to get me back soon and keep me in good favor with co-workers I hoped to leave in the dust. A few blocks out of range, I'd shake it off. I'd stop at home, shower and change and mount Chicago's gray and grim Interstate 88 focused, rehearsing answers to the questions all the books had prepped me on. *What are your strengths? What are your weaknesses? Describe a situation in which you applied creative problem-solving.* The generic language of self-promotion nauseated me, but you had to jump through the hoop to get your foot in the door.

In the back of my mind flickered a dim awareness that accepting the world for what it was, one big marketplace, and me a piece of functioning meat, would make everything a lot easier. But I wasn't ready to resign to the notion that there were no avenues, short of immense talent and uncommon luck, around the barriers between a man and his passions.

I interviewed at a local newspaper, the *Oak Forest Journal*, with an aged hippie editor-in-chief wearing hiking pants and a silk shirt. He wanted a beat photographer with three to five years' experience, his own equipment and page layout skills in a software program I'd never heard of. He gazed at me, behind the comfort of his desk, with patience and equanimity, giving no indication of being impressed one way or the other. My responses swayed towards abstractions: drive, eagerness, learning potential. But the hippie saw through that tactic, evidently, and his office manager sent me a form-letter rejection. Oak Forest was too far from Hargrove, anyway, and would have created a tricky car-sharing arrangement with Margaret.

Next, a water-filtration company on the murky edge between downtown and the northern suburbs. Their expansive line of pipe connectors, seals, housings, cone-filters, spigots and seemingly endless doodads to fit ever-changing but seldom-retired models of office coolers and wall-mounted bubblers was cataloged in thick volumes printed in four-color processes which were provided for my perusal during the interview. Suppressing yawns, I attempted to persuade a dyspeptic Mr Samson, Marketing Director (and myself), that photographing said geegaws would be a compelling career indeed. I never heard from him but hardly regretted it.

There was an assistant position at a photographer's studio that excited me greatly: direct, hands-on photographic experience. I committed special attention to my cover letter for this position, infusing it with references to high-end products and the generalized implication of proficiency in darkroom techniques and lighting methods. But I was never called, and my clear-voiced inquiries left on the man's answering machine asking for 'confirmation of receipt of my letter of application' went unanswered. Fucker.

At Valley Shopper Inc., an excitable woman jabbered statistics about the demographics of households reached by the company's direct-mail products. Aiding in the production of junk mail didn't exactly thrill me, which worked out on balance, as I wasn't given the chance to impress Valley Shopper with my 'quallies'. The lady enjoyed hearing her own voice so much, her self-absorption lapsed only long enough to ask what my career goals were. Then she launched into a monologue on her sympathies with the trials of finding work in creative fields. Ending on that high note, she stood and shook my hand. When I didn't hear from them, I resolved to not inquire. I didn't think first-degree murder would look good on my résumé so early in my career, had I been installed as her subordinate.

Then came Nexis, a major stock photo-licensing company. It was a name I'd seen in sideways print alongside photos in the *Sun* and the *Chicago Tribune* going back years, since I'd first been captivated by photography's story-telling potential. With its sonorous suggestion of centrality, I understood they served an important role in furnishing images but never knew exactly how the business worked, how it was that '© Nexis *slash* photographer's name' came to be imprinted beside so many compelling images, in a format that lent slight importance to the company over the very person who'd made the exposure, whether an exploding space-bound craft, hungry African child, or Reagan on the ground with bullet in him. Never knew either that it was Chicago-based. I'd lived a sheltered life in Wynton. Turns out Nexis is head-quartered in the One-Eleven East Wacker Building, literally in the shadow, from late morning until mid-afternoon, of the titanic Sears Tower.

Nexis was going digital. A mammoth investment was being made, and staff were being brought onboard to support their newly launched distribution method: the Internet. That is, they hoped it would be the method of choice for their existing customers: ad agencies, design firms, news media, book publishers – anybody who needed a picture. If they didn't believe it themselves, it didn't matter. They had been advised that they could either build this ship now or sink when the flood came. 'Double yew double yew double yew dot Nexis photo dot com,' said James Schwartz, Sales Manager, Internet Division, to me, with a throaty confidentiality that alerted my prospector's radar. His firm gaze was like none I had seen span the interviewer/applicant chasm. I felt this adventurer on technology's expansive seas had decided to bring me aboard. My love of photography I had easily and openly conveyed and, since that exchange in our meeting, James had been conversational, asking no other pointed questions. Given the scope of what he described, it seemed to me he needed bodies, and he needed them fast. Phone-answering bodies to explain to the licensors of Nexis photographs how easy it was to 'log on' and 'download' their photographs 'online'. It is a sign of the times that I didn't comprehend this terminology then. He may as well have been speaking Mongolian. But it didn't matter to me. James described Nexis's impending leap: doing away with the mailing of returnable slides and paper invoices, and that I understood. Paced to the pauses in his practiced spiel, I nodded and mm-hmm'ed, daydreaming of the upcoming Podgorski Christmas fête. In it, I was casually relaying, *'Oh, hey, Uncle Mark, I'm at Nexis Photo now. That's right, at the headquarters on East Wacker. Oh, yeah, great company, Nexis Photo. Huge. Huge stock agency.'*

I sensed when James double-checked my résumé for the inclusion of my phone number – 'You got your digits on here?' – before thanking me and seeing me out the door that he honestly intended to use it. Back at the warehouse, a delivery of Clorox bleach had toppled and burst, and the stinging stench of antiseptic put the tingle of renewal in my nose. My aggressive slinging of the gearshift without regard for the instruction I'd received to be gentle on the intricate Japanese transmission was a small measure of abandon heaped on the scales of fortune. This grunt labor was a financial stopgap, and I itched to pull the plug. I had left James Schwartz's office at noon thirty, and now I had four hours remaining in my Hughes shift. I made the irreversible choice to admit enthusiasm, to get giddy and risk disappointment. It's a wonder I didn't crash ol' 'Green Machine', as I'd dubbed her, in my feverish zipping and filling of Dan's backlogged afternoon orders. But with hope comes clarity of thought and precision of movement. The *mondo* Burback's dark roast I'd picked up didn't hurt either.

Truckers who normally cast dead eyes on me and X-ed off pallets one by one on their pink purchase orders as I clanked in and out of their precious rigs today pondered my liveliness, my animated dumping of goods, with suspicion.

The rewards for getting hired were twofold. One from myself: a secondhand Meopta Axomat 5 black-and-white photographic enlarger, which materialized a few weeks later, after some research, the approval of a credit-card application, and a drive to Shutan Camera in Vernon Hills, with my photog friend Greg, who had recommended this out-of-the-way specialty shop as worth the twenty-mile jaunt up the I-355. The other was not from myself but from Margaret, and more immediate.

One full day elapsed; on the second, I was greeted at home by my wife's coy grin and a wordless escort to the blinking answering machine. 'Play it,' she said, standing close to me. James Schwartz spoke, from within a sonic sphere that seemed to convey the height and prestige of his downtown office. 'The position is yours if you want it.'

'Holy shit,' I whispered. I kissed my wife.

I reached him right away and accepted with a racing heartbeat and a wobbly voice, poorly concealing my eagerness. Impromptu plans took us to dinner with Wynton friends Megan and Brad, during which I tempered my disdain for the Hughes experience out of gratitude for Brad's favor. I treated to It's Greek to Me's Kotopoulu Gemisto, a signature dish Brad and I had been ordering since we'd discovered it together, at sixteen, while record shopping nearby. Elevated in spirits and back home in our sunken apartment, Margaret took me in her mouth in an uncharacteristic bout of sexual impatience. This was the reward, bringing me off with my jeans at my knees and herself still dressed. A more searing, raunchy shudder than through the usual channel, free from the considerations of timing, thrust, endurance. An indulgence of male member and ego. After returning from the bathroom, where she spat and replaced carnal tang with mouthwash's minty innocence, Margaret untied my shoes and tugged off the pants pooled at my feet. I lay, limp as a noodle, awash in physical release and the relief of earning one's self-improvement, of reaching that next corner on the blocks of advancement. I sat up, raised my arms; she took my shirt with motherly affection. Changed into her flannel pajamas, she crawled over me (the bed sat flush against the east wall in order to maximize space) and reiterated the pride she'd expressed all evening amongst our friends, whispering, 'Congratulations again.'

Shortly she asked, 'So how much are they going to pay you?'

15   *You Can't Teach Grace*

The red glow of a darkroom safelight soothes me. Working under a fraction of the complete color spectrum, the rainbow array taught in high-school biology by the mnemonic device ROY G BIV, takes the harshness off. Paper known to be white is seen as inky-black maroon but is processed by the ever-accommodating mind as its true white. The value of things is perverted and the perversion nullified, and thus a kind of falsely tempered moral equilibrium is attained. The world's objects are soaked and edgeless, unthreatening. The skin of one's hands, sliding a T-square into position or nudging a hot-water tap to achieve the optimum wash temperature, is thoroughly crimson, visibly veinless, as if no harm could be done by drawing blood. It would leak and hover but not run. You could toy with it like astronauts do with their weightless Jell-O. Blood would wobble coolly in the red air. All would be as one. Soothing.

Margaret and I had a system for laundry. She didn't like hauling, and I hated folding. So I made the frequent trips to the lint-dusted room at the back of the building where the coin-operated machines chugged and sputtered. To our apartment I lugged baskets of finished garments clicking with static electricity and returned, pockets jangling with quarters, to purify another load of the dim odors and tiny spots that passed for filth when your workspace is a sterile office and a featureless dance studio, respectively. The machines were aged and feeble, and the dryer in particular had been deprived of its former powers. I was waiting for it to tumble a few more minutes one Saturday morning when I began nosing around. The doors of an ill-used cabinet, yanked to overcome stickiness, opened upon tins of varnish and lacquer, spillage streaked down their sides like tears, paint-stirring sticks crusted to yellowed pages of the *Chicago Tribune*. Then an inconspicuous door I had assumed concealed electric meters or janitorial storage revealed a room bare but for a stone basin sink, single casement window and an empty light socket: the perfect beginnings of a darkroom.

Thus began my brainstorm about having my own printmaking facility in this, our first apartment. I had fantasized aloud to Margaret about having one someday, but having a house that could accommodate it felt far off. Now, suddenly, this dream could materialize. Immediately, I told Margaret.

'Why don't you just take them to Clix?' she offered. 'They'll still give you a discount, won't they?'

'That's not the point. I want to make my *own* prints.'

'Okay, if that's what you want to do.'

'It's perfect. A water source for rinsing, a socket for the safelight, window for ventilation. I couldn't make it better myself. I could use our bathroom, but this way you won't have to smell the chemicals.'

'The chemicals – oh, I forgot,' she frowned.

'I was thinking maybe I could use the high table in the corner, the one with the stools. It's the perfect height. We don't eat on it anyway.' This was the mode of discussion that had formed between us. It would be hurtful to slander the attempt Margaret had made to functionalize an impossibly narrow 'breakfast nook', but in fact this space had proved best for stacking the cases of Margaret's flavored sodas and for holding the open grocery sacks where the empty cans were left for me to tote to the recycling bin. Of course, I would need more than a table. There was a lot of equipment I wasn't mentioning.

'Would it stink like the one at school?' Margaret asked. 'That was terrible.' She had visited me at WWH's lab and found the pungency of the stop bath's acetic acid unbearable, even though the trays were kept under a vent hood.

'Well, there are some so-called odorless solutions, but they're more expensive. And the chemicals are still harmful, you just can't smell them. If anything, that makes them *more* dangerous. You get lulled into a false sense of security. You still asphyxiate, it's just not as unpleasant.'

Margaret had been sitting on the edge of the bed, facing the portable TV her mother had given to us for keeps recently. She snarled up at this morbid joke, showing her patented curled upper lip.

'I'm kidding!' I yelled. If people have no shared experience of death, learning each other's feelings about it can be surprising. Margaret found it a grave matter, I discovered, no pun intended. Her mother had ruffled her once by saying Grandpa Krantz had 'gone to the big casino in the sky', which earned a scold. 'Well,' Janis had answered, 'if there's a heaven, he's playing blackjack right now.' Without her having a religious upbringing, it was hard to place this reverence for life in Margaret – and, more confounding, too, to see it contradicted in the coming months by the emergence of self-destructive tendencies. In this instant, I took it as a newly-wed's shock at the morbid thought of her recent groom departing the corporeal world.

'Won't that be cool,' I said. 'I can make prints, frame them, and hang 'em around the house. It'll be better than the clichéd framed art we have.'

'I got you that Ansel Adams for your birthday!'

'I know, I know, and I love it.' She continued to process the bundle of clean clothes I'd brought in, sorting matching socks in her lap: my size-thirteen tubes draped over her right thigh, her petite pastel ankle socks on her left.

'Well, what am I going to do if you're hanging out in that musty back room all the time?'

'Oh . . . funny.' I laughed uneasily.

The TV announcer's voice elevated suddenly, and Margaret and I both turned to see the completion of some deft figure-skating maneuver. It was Saturday afternoon in America's pre-holiday season: the glory of winter and festivity of the free world was being showcased to Midwestern couch-dwellers by trim ice athletes from across the globe. A pair of handsome skaters arced around in unison, curving in reverse, each with a leg skyward, the man in green sequined pants, the woman airing a Christmas-red gusset to the tracking camera. The double-axle throw was over, and now the duo slowed into the anticlimactic arm waving and spinning. Margaret turned back to me with a realization: 'We can't afford that darkroom stuff, though!'

'You don't even know how much it costs,' I reminded her, picking up one of my heavy sweat socks that had evaded Margaret by clinging to a shirt and falling free under its own weight.

'Yeah, but I'm sure it's not cheap.'

She had me there. 'Greg says I can get a used enlarger for a couple hundred bucks.'

'Couple hundred? I wanted to get a microwave for two hundred, and you said we couldn't!'

Statistics abound on the matter of couples fighting about money. X percent of American couples polled, magazines tell you, say it's their number-one source of conflict. Whatever that X is, in our short-lived marriage, I often felt like we were clocking for a surplus in case the rest of the nation fell behind. Certainly once the Culkin School of Dance let Margaret go, the strain of money woes felt constant, like a palpable tension in the already dense air of our bunker apartment.

I got an enlarger anyway, as I said. Call it a sanity expense. Nexis turned out to be a lot of data entry, filling out forms and filing invoices. Not much different than life at Hughes, except instead of a mobile green desk, I sat stationary in an ergonomic chair before a monitor, a witness to the advent of the Internet age. Without a creative outlet I would have gone mad. In February, I would start an unpaid internship at a photographer's home portrait studio, after the stun of Christmas with the Podgorskis had left me with an even more pressing need not to wind up as unhappy and stagnant as them. But the internship, too, would prove to be little more than a bartering arrangement, my time and subservience to someone else's artistry in exchange for résumé credentials. The darkroom let me roam metaphysically. It was a gym in which to test my creative fitness.

Up until this time, I knew I enjoyed making things. I knew I liked the feeling of the hardware in my hands, the compact heft of an SLR's housing protecting the precisely angled pentaprism inside, the delicate iris diaphragm. I liked the feeling of power, knowing that spooled up in the darkness of the body was film that would react to beams of light allowed in on my terms, whether 1/8 or 1/200 of a second, through apertures of differing diameters. Empowering, too, was the vastness of choice over what to imprint on the virgin film: anything the world offered. If I could capture an event by its essence, even so mundanely as the story of a high-school wrestling match in an image of the crucial pin, then I was boiling down the world to essences as it did to me. Finally, there was honest declaration in photography – something not well-received in the Podgorski world.

I set it up, without consulting the landlord but with Greg's help, during a cold week in early January. Greg, a wiry kid with a hard, narrow adult nose and impenetrable black Italian-American hair, was fluent in the techno-speak and the trends. The photography magazines that had always been so dense with advertisements as to be off-putting to me were a fixture in his white-knuckled hands. I, on the other hand, liked the analog nature of film. What I wanted to accomplish by having my own kit and setup (two terms I latched on to through Greg's usage) was to locate my strengths and weaknesses, identify my prejudices and tastes, shine a flashlight into my blind spots. I wanted to see if I had any talent. While installing the darkroom, I explained what I wanted to achieve and the methodology. 'It seems to me,' I said, 'photography requires mechanical abilities, such as calculating an f-stop. But when you're out shooting a roll, you want all the math to be innate or unconscious. Internalized. So instinct, "the eye", can be alert.'

We were finalizing the room and the gear. Margaret had conceded use of the table from the glorified closet she'd hoped would be a cozy eating space. It was now placed against the longest wall, the enlarger mounted directly into its top with four woodscrews, since the mounting boards that came with the bulky Meopta were splintered from a previous owner's chemical spillage, an accident that allowed me to afford it. In fact, many of the implements we'd gone the cheap route on, and I'd shown these to Margaret out of the bag as examples of my frugality: kitty-litter bins for bath trays, clothes pins and clothes line from Mom's garage, a $1.49 red-dyed 'Party Lite' rather than the freestanding Duplex fixture that topped sixty dollars even secondhand. The cheap bulb, though, created a danger of leaking white light, so we were going to test it by exposing blank paper in segments without a negative. Of course, the room had to be entirely sealed from sunlight's chemical-triggering rays.

Greg stood on a chair and draped black Hefty bags across the casement's dusty frame. I handed him strips of duct tape which he kept fixed to a single finger, preserving their adhesive powers, as I distracted him with my talk. But he was a pig in shit. He loved commandeering this room – the renegade arts – and loved talking shop, even when it was rudimentary to him. He listened even as he made taut the slick plastic and planned the placement of the next sealing silver strip.

'Right now,' I went on, 'when I'm shooting, I tend to futz with the camera a lot. I want to get it in focus and get good depth of field and high contrast so I can make a good print – make different *kinds* of prints from the negative. I know only practice can make me quicker with adjustments on-the-fly. A lot of practice. But purpose-ful practice. That's what I want to do. Just work on things freeform but not mindlessly.'

'That's great,' Greg said, smoothing the tape. 'The thing is, you're aware of your limitations.' He stepped down from the chair, and looked up at his handiwork. Satisfied, he turned to me. 'Certain decisions about composition and about your subject can be made with the camera. Others you make in the print. You're totally right – only practice is gonna help you figure that out.'

'And *I know*,' I said, wanting to impress him now, and get him interested in working with me, 'that there are technologies out there that will simplify things and make shortcuts. But I also know that technology is not foolproof. So I figure –' I was aware, dimly, of adopting Greg's popping precision of speech to win him over, the exacting pronunciations like whitecaps on the waves of his repeated phrasings – 'the best thing to do is to learn the machines and the materials of the craft from the ground up. The nuts and bolts first. You know, like my dad taught me to drive: first with a stick shift, so I got the feel for what was happening in the gearbox, the torque on the drivetrain, the pull of the tires on the road.'

'Yeah, yeah!' Greg agreed excitedly.

'I mean, take Brad, for example. He's never driven a stick, I know he hasn't, and he's a terrible driver! You've ridden with him.'

'It's true!'

'To me, that's no coincidence. I mean, I think of apprenticeships like they used to have in England and stuff. Like in Charles Dickens or something. Even before that – a cobbler or a blacksmith in the Middle Ages. All a thing of the past now, and it's a shame. Craftsmanship is out the window. I don't want to get crappy results in my prints and wonder is it my film speed? Should I be using multigrade paper? Is it the lens – what?'

'Exactly. Exactly,' Greg said. 'So many guys will just go and buy the latest camera and hope that fixes it. You gotta have that *Karate Kid* mentality. Start with wax on, wax off. Stand on that post, and get your balance. Isolate each movement and hone it.'

So we had the same aesthetic outlook; now what I was hoping for was his companionship. I hopped up on the edge of the sink (poured concrete, rock solid) and motioned to the adjacent countertop for him to sit on. I put a cigarette in my lips and held out my pack to him; he plucked a butt with a thanking nod. With the incandescent bulb in the socket, not the Party Lite, the room had the aura of an arena prepped for a concert. 'Look, Greg,' I said. 'Here's what I wanna do. I've been out of school – what? – not even a year. Nexis is cool, but not all it's cracked up to be. I don't even *see* any photographs hardly. I just talk to customers all day.' I lit up. 'Why don't you come here and do whatever work you're interested in doing. You can use my gear, use my setup. And we'll feed off each other. You know, I'll pick up things from you, maybe there might be something you can pick up from me.'

'That sounds righteous,' Greg said, pointing his exhaled plume away from the enlarger table, thinking, I knew, that the particles would find their way to the lens we'd shined with a fine-grade cloth and pressurized air. The diehards behind the counter at Shutan Camera had advised not to use even a freshly washed cotton cloth – the minuscule granules of undissolved powder soaps possessed the power to scratch.

'You know what would be great?' I said. 'To have a showing. Even if it's just in a coffee shop.'

Margaret woke before me every day, though her schedule didn't require her to be at Culkin until eleven. Coping with the sound of *The Today Show* from the living room at 7 a.m. was one of the many adjustments cohabitation brought. I'd trudge from bed, start coffee brewing and give her a kiss, her mouth already grape-flavored. In her flexibility, she crouched on the floor before the TV like a hermit around a fire, bare feet flat to the carpet, knees under her chin, in perfect comfort. Her favorite plastic cup, one that commemorated a trip to 'nationals', rested in the crook between her chest and thighs, a straw just reaching her lips. She'd tilt her head up to me like a chick receiving a worm.

I don't do breakfast, and driving with a tie on, it's too hard to check the blind spots – so, except for shaving days, I could be out the door within fifteen minutes of waking. I'd depart for Nexis in slacks and shirt, clutching a thermos of coffee and absorbing Margaret's instructions for that day.

'What do you want for dinner?' a typical conversation began, signaled by the jangle of my car keys.

'Oh, gosh, I have no idea. I'm not even awake yet.'

'I know, but think about it – I've gotta take something out to defrost.'

'Burgers?'

'I was thinking chicken.'

'Okay, chicken.' And, after another kiss, I'd be gone. If you have to be up for work, then get to work, that's how I saw it.

Weekdays, she worked six hours, teaching four of them. In the daytime, two hour-long classes, one a basic mobility and stretching clinic for seniors, the other a smorgasbord of dance basics for beginners: the two-step, foxtrot, polka, salsa, with special attention to steps that went with Top 40 hits. (I was alerted now to these imported techno abominations ignored in my single life.) In the evening she had her 'girls', pixies as young as five trained in syncopated routines invented by Margaret from a playbook of spins, kicks and poses. The youngest wore tutus, used props such as star-tipped wands and danced to cheery sing-along music. The middle-schoolers, some on, some over the cusp of womanhood, in their twice-weekly two-hour evening class, did *numbers* as opposed to routines, and in these they sought, with every beat, to escape the clutches of innocence. Gyration, mane-flipping, over-the-shoulder pouty stares, shimmying and sassy ass-slapping were mainstays. These displays shocked me at first; I felt old and lecherous, though only a handful of years separated the girls and me. I found myself thinking, weren't the girls I knew then flat-chested and shy? And if they had had such hips, where had they hidden them? I'd endured back-breaking study-hall slouches just to glimpse a bra through the porthole of a blouse's short sleeve. Now, here, these girls thrusted, bent and sashayed under the paid instruction, culmi-nating, during performances, in rounds of applause from family members. Absurd. Times move too fast. Some sense of decency creeps up on you.

This was Margaret's milieu, this attendance to physicality, move-ment, timing, expression. She was witness to the whole scope of it, its inception, progress and deterioration. I'd seen her laboring patiently just to get a throng of impish toddlers to touch their toes in unison. And coming in on a winter evening, the studio glass foggy, being met by a hot blast of sweat and floral perfume, I'd witnessed post-class horseplay of Margaret and her girls competing at high kicks, throwing their ankles up over their heads, falling into the splits with confident sass. (At the close of this move Margaret's trademark gesture appeared, a sucking in, a hollowing of her cheeks when all eyes were on her.) Far removed in tone, I'd seen her in the sexless role of leading a cluster of gray-skinned geriatrics in arm circles, like a copse of aged trees shaking in a wind, she a sturdy figure under no threat of breakage, her smiling face unfazed by the women's decrepitude which was to me shocking and repugnant.

I admired how she took it all in stride. The thought of instructing horrified me – everyone awaiting my directives, listening (with any luck) to my every word, scrutinizing the order of my thoughts, the soundness of my methods, expecting to be taught their money's worth. Not Margaret. Margaret was a natural, a self-professed 'people person'. Indeed, she didn't merely instruct but related to people – and never condescended. She didn't hoard her knowledge and was never bored by repeating movements that her body had long ago committed to muscle memory. She seemed to remember more clearly than I did the difficulty of being young, when gangly limbs rejected the mind's orders and the torso and head still struggled with balance. And she understood the converse of this, the body's mirrored return to limited control, without fearing it. This amounted to a seer's wisdom for me, who doubted the validity of anything not experienced firsthand.

'Of course, you can't teach grace,' she often said. 'You're either born with it or you're not.' You hear this kind of summary made in sports to account for the limits of an athlete's accomplishments, but in Margaret it was a creed about personal acceptance, and for me a new concept. 'You're not patient enough to be a teacher,' she told me once, and I remembered it long after we parted. It seemed to me she meant I was not forgiving enough, and in that she was right. At Nexis, the support staff I was a member of was sectioned into teams, and some of my co-workers were inept, unqualified, outright dim. Initially, I harboured scorn for them; it was through talking with Margaret over hurried dinners and through seeing and hearing her interact with her students – even five minutes at a time, when I drove to pick her up and stepped into the studio to keep warm – that I absorbed some of her patience, the charitable nurturing I understood at the time, mistakenly, to be an exclusively feminine trait.

Weeks flew. Before I had finished begrudging the hassle of putting it up, the small Douglas Fir that was our first Christmas tree was taken down, brown and shedding. One by one, at weekend meals planned for their use, we christened wedding gifts received in the fall: a waffle maker, wine carafe, linen placemats and napkins that Margaret had deemed 'for when we have guests'. The luster of assimilated items rubbed off. Time was marked by the hyper-industrial-strength UPC stickers on the bottom of our tableware, against which knives and thumbnails had been no match, as regular dishwasher scaldings brought about their disintegration. Each time I emptied the machine, fewer reminders of newness remained.

Also before I was ready, the interval of privacy afforded to newlyweds expired, and my mother's suggestions of dinner at Meadow Prairie Lane turned to insistence. We had seen Mr and Mrs P. at Christmas, of course, but that was amid the chaos of seventeen other kin tearing into presents, tipping Bailey's on the carpet. On a Friday night in early March, when the sun's continued presence in the sky past dinnertime began to feel like a significant omen of spring, we put on nice clothes and drove to Wynton. But only after one item of business.

I had been toiling in the darkroom with Greg for weeks, regularly – every weekend night. Our setup worked brilliantly. But I'd never asked the landlord for permission to use the room, lest he turn me down, and it was, after all, public, just off the laundry; I lived always with the possibility of someone following their nose and discovering my equipment. Anything could happen – theft or sabotage or simply someone tinkering with the dial that raised and lowered the enlarger head, which I left focused, from session to session, precisely as it needed to be for the negative in the carrier. So, every night, I had been hauling the enlarger back to the apartment. It was tedious. The arm had to be unbolted from the top of the table and the thing carried and stored carefully. I was tired of it. So, already dressed in slacks and loafers, I set off for the hardware store, Margaret calling after me, 'You're obsessed, you know, with this darkroom!'

Returned, I hastily pre-drilled, guessing at the best bit size, and screwed a latch and hasp into the frame on the darkroom door. The wood was spongy and there was nothing stopping anyone from simply unscrewing the latch, but it was better than nothing.

I tore open the packaging on a Master padlock and snapped it into place. I regarded my quick work with pleasure, eyed the shiny hardware as if I were the landlord or another tenant. Would it catch my eye? Was it suspicious? Could it pass for having been there all along? It would have to do.

'Now we'll be late,' Margaret said in the car.

'Just a few minutes,' I said. 'You want me to protect my investment, don't you?'

'I wish you'd invest some time in *us*,' she said. This was not playful ribbing.

'What does that mean?'

'You're in that darkroom every weekend from the time you get home Friday till late Sunday night! You're worse than your mom and her shrine.'

'I told you, it's not a shrine. It's a prayer station.'

'Whatever, you worship in there like it is. When are you going to spend time with me?'

'Am I in there now?'

'Your mother had to beg.'

'Well, *am I*?'

She didn't answer. We drove to Wynton in that horrible nagging silence, the tension accentuated by every tick-tock of the turn signal, every squeak of the brakes. Why did fights always seem to erupt when we went to see my parents?

16   A Standard Play

'How are things at work?' my mother asked, over steaming chicken and wild rice casserole. Her concern was genuine and her charity Christian, but she seemed to be on a let-down since the excitement of the wedding.

'Not all I had hoped,' I confessed, heavily buttering a roll to make up for the healthful insubstantiality of the entrée. 'It's a lot of busy work, not so much creative.' I turned to Mr P., seated at the head of the table in a way his meek demeanor did not befit. The house's best window view lay over his left shoulder, a field of wheat-like weeds – the 'Meadow Prairie' – bordered by a copse of Norway pine, flattened by perspective into an odd remove. I turned to Mrs P., offering her my forced smile. 'But there's talk of a big project getting underway,' I continued, 'and I may be able to get involved in that.'

Margaret had reacted with something like a depression-era panic the times I'd spoken bitterly of the Nexis position, on suspicion of my quitting, I suppose. She had stressed that it was a good job, I was lucky to have it, and I should make the best of it. For fear of worrying her, I had not spoken again of my bored hours there entering eight-digit photo ID codes into a database and hand-collating mailers. She was belligerently curious now to hear what plans I would confess to my parents that I hadn't to her. Her expectant face awaited me, the third in the trilogy that circumferenced me at this table and, it seemed, in my life.

'It'd be more interesting, get me closer access to the pictures.'

This was something of a fabrication. Management, I'd heard, would be selecting a couple people, one or two, to train on a high-speed, high-resolution flatbed scanner for the conversion of prints to digital. Mrs P. cheerfully asked for clarification – 'A promotion?' – and I fed her something vague, throwing in technical terms to confuse her. Her attention returned to her meal, agitated by uncertainty. This was what I wanted. I could see her thinking, *So can I tell everyone you're being promoted or not?*

I'd spent my teenage years watching TV and doing homework within earshot of the kitchen telephone; the pitch of her enthusiasm was still fresh in my memory, and I imagined her boasting, *A promotion already! He just was hired, not three months ago!*

'You didn't mention any position to me,' Margaret said.

'I know,' I said. 'Sorry. It's very much up in the air whether they're gonna hire internally for this conversion thing.'

'That reminds me,' Mr P. said. He set his fork down and got up from the table. 'I read in the paper something about your company. Nexis, right?' he asked, as he squeezed between my chair and the wall. He knew damn well it was Nexis. There had been endless conversation at Christmas about Nexis. A scientist to the core, he saw things as being comprised of traceable stages, an order of operation, and couldn't allow for any error. It drove me mad! Regimented thought! Wasted time! This was his fact-checking stage, which bore the same hallmarks as senility, though he was too young for that.

'Yeah, Dad,' I said, rolling my eyes in exasperation. He was in the kitchen already.

'It was in the Business section,' came his level voice, muted by distance.

'This casserole is so good, Rose,' Margaret interjected, seemingly enlivened by the way this interchange annoyed me.

'Oh, thank you!' Mrs P. cooed.

It felt unjust that Margaret should like her mother-in-law. Her father being absentee, rumored to be living in Atlanta, no equivalent same-gender in-law existed for me to chum up to.

Mr P. returned. 'I don't know if you read that section . . .'

'Never. Just the Arts,' I said.

'Well, here it is.' Sitting down, he set it beside me, the narrow, one-column clipping of featherweight newsprint matching in density the lace placemat it lay upon.

'What's it say?' Margaret asked.

I nudged the clipping with my pinkie, indicating greasy hands.

'Talks about Mel's company acquiring some smaller companies,' Mr P. said. It rankled me, this implication of pride through association. The growth of Nexis was not my doing, and I didn't want to shoulder it, as a lowly customer-services grunt. Being so omnipresent and one-sided – nothing but benefits, revolutionizing commerce – the hype around these things called Cyberspace and the Information Superhighway struck me as suspiciously roseate. Kind of how they had boasted of a certain unsinkable ship. I didn't want to shoulder its failures either. The machine advances, let's acknowledge the cog. The machine breaks, let's blame the cog.

'Oh, wow,' Margaret said, meaninglessly.

'And plans for expansion, if I remember correctly,' Mr P. said, trailing away, leaving wake for my input.

'Yeah, expansion,' I said quietly. 'Okay, I'll read it later. Thanks.' I smiled at my dad.

'Read it now. Read it aloud,' Mrs P. urged.

'No, I'm not gonna read it aloud,' I said, returning to my meal. 'I'm eating.'

'Oh, you can't swallow your food a second and read? Come on, we wanna know what it says.' She elbowed Margaret around the corner of the table. 'Don't we, Margaret?'

'Yeah, what's it say, Mel?'

'Here, read it yourselves.' I crumpled the paper in my fist and threw it over the table – it passed between the two women onto the floor.

'Mel!' they both yelled.

'Oh, who cares?' I barked.

'Mel, really,' Mr P. said.

'Testy . . .' Mrs P. said.

'What is your damage?' Margaret asked – the upper lip raised in disgusted disbelief.

I looked to Mr P. His de facto demeanor was on display: objective observer. He chewed calmly, mouth shut. His eyes, warped behind his glasses into a false impression of deep excitement, were pools of evenness masking timidity, even fright.

'He's such a spazz,' Margaret said, leaning into Mrs P.

'A spazz?'

'He blows up at nothing.'

'Oh, a hothead. He is sometimes, isn't he?'

'You didn't tell me that about him,' Margaret said. Both women kept their chins down and eyed the corner of table between them conspiratorially.

'Well, he started out a nice boy,' Mrs P. said.

After dinner, Margaret and I did the dishes, pretending at warm partnership. Mrs P. tested the center of a lemon meringue she'd baked. 'It's not quite set,' she said over the shishing tap and clanking plates.

'Perfect,' I said, in a joking tone of evil connivance, 'then we've got time to brew a pot of coffee.'

'Have time? I should hope so,' Mrs P. said. 'It only takes two minutes to make coffee.'

I knew she typically brewed a cup or two for herself and herself only, because Mr P.'s level constitution extended to his diet – never foggy with drink nor lucid with caffeine. And she made it weak. Passing water through a few pinches of dry Folger's grounds could be done in a matter of seconds. But I had anticipated this moment: a slow evening, sitting around chatting or playing board games, and Mrs P. offering to make coffee, her way. My body – and its great hunger for caffeine – had grown accustomed to saturations of thick, tar-black coffee in the evening. I had come prepared.

'Not with this it won't, Ma,' I said, bringing out the sack of ground Costa Rican beans I'd stashed in her cupboard when we first arrived.

'What is that?' she asked.

'Some of his *expensive* coffee,' Margaret said. The last dish was washed, and she mopped up the sloshed water around the basin.

Mrs P. wiped her hands on the towel slung over Margaret's shoulder, Margaret holding still for her. Women and their little conspiracies. Chin up, peering down through her bifocals, my mother inspected the black package, her angled head recalling long-gone days of her nurse-like inspections of cuts, crusty eyes, swollen glands, though now I towered a head higher than her.

She was dumbfounded by this whole-bean coffee, what it was, how I had ground it, why I didn't just use 'regular' coffee.

'Mom, this is what coffee *is* – it comes in beans. I don't use Folger's because it has no flavor.'

'Since when do you drink coffee anyway?' she asked, as if I'd betrayed her.

'Since when? What, do you have Alzheimer's?' I felt pestered, cornered in the small kitchen, claustrophobic. Mr P. chimed in, giving me an opportunity to step away from my mother.

'Rose, he got that special coffee for the wedding,' he said, from a stool at the counter. His tone was brightly incredulous, which was the closest to fevered I'd ever known it to get. He'd always enjoyed correcting his wife. 'Remember, I said I wouldn't pay for it?'

'I thought he was showing off for company,' Mrs P. said. This was her hiding behind her wavering forgetfulness.

'No, actually that was mainly for me.'

Margaret hung the towel on the oven handle and shelved the casserole dish that was too big to balance on the filled rack. She left the kitchen and took a stool next to Mr P., who smiled at her. Silence expanded over us, from my epicenter to the corners of the house.

'He drinks that stuff day and night now,' Margaret said to Mr P. 'Like it's going out of style.' Mrs P.'s crinkled features announced that such extremity flummoxed her.

Mr P. patted Margaret's back warmly. 'Thanks for cleaning up,' he said, his pats bordering on caresses.

'Oh, no problem. You cook, we clean – that's how we always did it in my house.'

I got a pot going that would sustain me through however we spent the evening – which would not be print-making and therefore boring by comparison. Mrs P. poured ice waters for herself and Mr P., soda for Margaret.

'It's very popular now,' Margaret explained. 'A lot people hang out at coffee shops instead of bars.'

'Oh, so it's like a trendy thing,' Mrs P. said with relief, as if this meant I was not perverse after all.

'God forbid your son should be original,' Mr P. joked.

'Thank you, Dad!' I said. 'And it's not trendy. You have no idea. People have been drinking coffee for centuries, if not longer. Dad, back me up.'

'I'm not saying I've never heard of coffee,' said Mrs P. 'I've just never seen you buying full beans of Costa Rican, like it mattered.'

'Just be glad he's not boozing it up,' Mr P. said, 'like your brothers.'

'All right! Fine!' Mrs P. yelled, throwing her hands to the heavens, letting them flop with a slap to the sides of her matronly thighs. But she wasn't angry. She didn't get angry. Growing up under three brothers had taught her to concede absent a sense of defeat. She was the girl outnumbered by the boys. Sitting on the third stool, next to Margaret now, while I alone monitored the Mr Coffee's burbling, Mrs P. faced her daughter-in-law with her lighthearted *whatever* look, a clowning, frumpy frown and a high shrug. 'Sheesh!'

I stood in the corner, leaning against the countertop, my arms crossed. Habitually, my right foot found the cabinet handle near the back of my left knee, where I'd propped it during many a teenage snack session. In a soft, teasing voice I said, 'You just need to get with the times, Mom.'

'That'll happen!' she snorted.

'All right,' Dad asked, pleased somehow with the outcome. 'How are we going to pass the evening here, folks?'

A game was decided on. We shifted to the living room and set up camp, balancing our beverages and pie plates. It was a game requiring partners and, when they were chosen, the couples and genders split. Margaret's comment from the car ride still lingered between us, about devoting energy to us, and there was my testiness over the newspaper clipping; I didn't think we'd fare well in a game dependent on reading a partner's bids and responding to leads and sloughs. When she praised Mr P.'s every swept trick and called me nasty names any time I trumped (a standard play), my feeling of swimming against the tide made me morose. This game of moral King of the Hill was wearying. Now the ride home would be ugly, and probably the whole weekend. I could see from a mile off that my plans to work in the darkroom with Greg the next night would look, in the shadow of tonight's fight, like escapism. Maybe that's what it was, a reluctance to engage. This added a stewing self-resentment to my gloom. And it cemented my resolve to keep my plans.

For Mr and Mrs P., however, this was an exciting night, hosting company – an infrequent occurrence for the socially withdrawn pair with one child. So I tried to be upbeat and conversational. Margaret seemed to follow my lead, but in the wrong way: as if this too was a battle of wills, a contest: who could maintain pleasantries most convincingly. She was wrong; I wasn't trying to draw her into this. I only wanted not to sour my parents' social night. But, knotted by these complications, my voice refused to untangle into chipperness.

Margaret and Mrs P. gossiped, the goings-on of Wendy Culkin, the owner of Culkin School of Dance and Margaret's boss. The speculation about her love life became so heated that Mr P. could engage me in his strategy commentary without interrupting them.

'I didn't know my partner had the joker last time,' he said, while his hands nimbly shuffled the deck. 'Otherwise I would have led something else, probably clubs.'

'What, she didn't have it?' I asked, distracted, envying and hating at once Margaret's ability to pour on the cheer with my mother and pocket her antagonism towards me.

'She *did* have it,' he stressed. 'She trumped your king, remember? But she sloughed under my right Bauer on the first trick, so I assumed she wasn't holding it. That's pretty routine, wouldn't you say? If you've got it, play it there.'

'Yeah, I guess so.'

'Just a given,' he muttered, authentically annoyed. Margaret hadn't followed the stages – and we'd played this game before. He rolled his eyes at me. He drank his water and replaced the glass carefully on the cork coaster. Uncomfortable with conflict, Mr P.

became terse when he felt adamant, and clipped his sentences. 'Standard play. A courtesy. Let your partner know what you're holding.' He offered me the cut.

'Thin to win,' I said, picking off a slim portion of the deck, whose backs showed an aerial shot of a resort and the words 'Fort Myers, Florida' in a bloated cursive.

'Gotta teach her the rules.' Thumbing off three cards at a time, Mr P. cleared his throat and spoke to the table: 'Okay, ladies, let's play.'

'If she can *get* a man!' Margaret's sassy sentence ended, offering again the gift of her attention to the table. 'Who's winning?' she asked with the sudden, accosting airiness of the inebriated, though she was stone sober. She hadn't drunk since our wedding. Drinking was something she enjoyed at occasions and then over-indulgently, like candy at Hallowe'en.

Mr P. read the score card, which he kept in a careful pencil, the column's margins dotted with asterisks and secret codes signifying made and set bids. 'We're losing, partner,' he said. 'If Mel and Rose make any bid, they win. If we get set, we're out the back door.'

'Geez, Dick, we better get our act together,' Margaret said, for his sake.

'Geez, we *better*,' he mimicked affectionately. 'Bid high and sleep in the streets.' He filled the down in the center with five cards, picked up his hand and looked to Margaret. 'It's do or die.'

Sunday, I kept my plans with Grey, though the results were not the best. Monday, the sterility of the office, with its gray predictability and unwavering recitations from the sales script, was welcoming. Even maneuvering through the computer systems was pleasantly abstract; with the magic of Windows and Administrative settings, no matter where you clicked, you couldn't break anything, you couldn't do any harm. Worse comes to worse, you simply reboot. Just as I prepared to log off the phone system that tracked my call volume and average times, a familiar sequence of digits appeared on the display: our home number. A minute later, I would have been on my way to lunch, and who knows what would have happened. Margaret's voice barely trickled through my headset. Taking my work more seriously than I did, she usually asked, 'Can you talk now?' 'Sure.' Today, though, she didn't ask that, apologize for interrupting, or ask how my day was going. Alarm bells, all three. Sniffling, she asked if I could come home.

'What's the matter?' I asked, matching her quiet gravity.

A pale silence seethed on the line.

'Are you all right?' My heart rate climbed during a long blankness. 'Margaret, are you ... *all right?*'

'No,' she murmured. I had never heard her so meek. I had seen her despondent, when pent-up pain over her flaky, inconsistent father grew, but this was different. She sounded physically crushed somehow. Flat on the bedroom floor, I pictured her, as if decked.

'Holy shit,' I barely breathed.

'Can you ... come home?' she asked. It seemed to take half a minute for her to say.

'Yes, of course. Where are you now?'

'Huh?' she slowly whimpered.

'Are you in the bedroom? Where are you?'

In her answer of 'Kitchen' was the faintest perking-up, as when a child sees that his pouting has roused concern.

'Just stay there. Don't do anything. I'll be right there. Okay?' She made me ask again. 'Okay, baby?'

'Okay.'

I bounded down the back stairwell three steps at a time, the slaps of my loafers echoing up the thirty-story cement shaft. I nearly scraped up the Honda's fender descending the narrow spiral garage ramp. Once on the street, I clicked the radio off and never even lit a cigarette – just drove, one hand guarding the stick, ready to gun it or downshift as traffic signals changed. One yellow light, at Grant, kept me from making the expressway unstopped; halted and powerless, leisurely afternoon traffic of boat-like Buicks and taxis boxed me in, their encompassing languor tipping me towards thoughts of when I'd last known any kind of peace.

There had been a tension ever since I had taken the unpaid

internship, and it had worsened when I built the darkroom, of course. Margaret couldn't understand why I put myself out for long hours, no concrete career opportunity, and no pay. Being gone a lot had strained things. 'How long does it last, again?' Margaret had often asked. My driving her to and from Culkin ended, leaving her to take the bus or bum rides from Wendy or call her mother or mine, surely suggesting to her a regression in our marriage which strove, however tacitly, for a bigger apartment, two cars, vacations, new furniture, all the things I was expected to desire. Then when the internship did end, I had made myself scarce again. That it wasn't football or billiards that she lost me to, like some of her friends' husbands, was no consolation to Margaret. Then five straight weekends or more had been spent in that chemical rear room. I had tried to involve her in the work, showing her the best prints, explaining how I'd burned the sky and dodged areas in the foreground for contrast. I told her about the places around town where I'd taken 'studies'. But nothing reassured her like watching cartoons together on Saturday morning, for example, or any of the things she liked to do, where my attention was undivided and the giving over of my will indisputable. Then I got a cold that was obviously worsened by hours spent under the vented vinyl window, and when she learned that I'd done a little print-making during my sick day home, things reached a head. That led right up to dinner at Mr and Mrs P.'s, her suggestion of my neglect, and the inevitable fight during the drive home.

Everything offended her, everything was an indication of my disinterest, my disaffection. Why didn't I want to be her partner in the card game? Why was I such a crab ass, not even reading her the newspaper clipping? I wouldn't even help with the dishes, she claimed, not when I have to make my all-important coffee. Everything I did, she said, was about *me*! Did I even *like* her? Did I even *care*?

'What are you talking about? I dried right up to the very end!' I argued. 'And *you're* the one who picked those partners!' There were reasonable answers for everything, it seemed to me, and

I defended myself vehemently, even as it became clear that these things were all beside the point. For the things at the center, I had no answers. Only fatigue ended the bickering and accusations, that and perhaps my change of tack, to apologizing despite not knowing what exactly I'd done or whether conceding compromised my flickering integrity, and if so, if it mattered. The fight lasted the entire drive home and persisted, oddly, even as I courteously held our apartment door open for her. Dispirited, I flopped on the sofa chair, and she on the couch. She cried, and we rehashed the same points that had been made in the car, until there was no fire left in our attacks, no strength remaining behind our defenses.

It was late, we needed to sleep. I moved to the couch, put my hand on her leg, the foot of which was tucked under her butt, how she always sat. I apologized for being critical of her, and she reciprocated. A timorous peck concluded the discussion, though certainly it didn't resolve it, and we agreed to stop fighting and go to bed.

Margaret went down the hall to our bedroom. I hung our coats and returned to the solitary recliner, feeling drained and unsure, not knowing if I was right or wrong. I had left a few black and white prints on the coffee table, and I wanted to pick them up and study them in the light of this mood, but I felt if I were to be seen taking an interest in them I would be accused of callousness or duplicity or something that had not been named in our fight. The sounds of tooth-brushing came from the bathroom, and I remained slouched where I was, just breathing, thinking. When she was done, she came out and made a few remarks about the evening meant to neutralize the acidic air between us. I appreciated the effort, but felt too conflicted to join her in bed. 'I think I'll watch some TV till I get tired,' I said. 'You know – coffee.'

'All right,' she said.

Saturday was a wash. Despite our congenial close of the evening, we were both chilly and withdrawn. We all but gave each other the silent treatment. I hadn't intended to do this, but once she showed her reluctance by not saying good morning, I was steeled not to offer a word either. I made coffee and worked at the computer until she took the cordless phone to the bedroom and made plans with Megan. The fact that Margaret showered and dressed without showing herself or informing me of her intentions until her purse was in her hands was a drawing of battle lines. Without our usual equitable rigmarole over the car keys, she left, saying nothing. Stunned, I didn't move. From outside, as if expressing her own growling anger, the gnashing of the gearbox reached my ears, as out of habit Margaret jammed the shifter in the lower right, where reverse was located on her mother's Toyota but not on the Honda she'd married into.

As the whirring engine faded up the block, I sighed and picked up my coffee-table prints.

In the evening, I made a point of being out, rescued by Greg and chauffeured around to cafés and coffee shops I knew that doubled as art galleries for the unheard-of and amateur, the flagging and flailing. We didn't have starving artists in the western Chicago suburbs, just people looking to set themselves apart from all the sameness, spurred by the dim hope that they could put a burgh on the map as Hemingway had Oak Park. When I returned, a few managers' phone numbers and 'mere formality' applications added to my folder of best prints, Margaret's purse greeted me in the entryway. Beside it, shopping bags whose contents were none of my business this day. I looked down the hall at our shut bedroom door. The hum of silence in which she did not call my name pained me.

Sunday was no different. Laced with coffee from my café tour, I had stayed up till the wee hours watching a TNT run of *Young Frankenstein*, barely chuckling throughout, a sure testament to misery. Around sun-up, clanking and rustling woke me, and I shuffled from the couch to the bedroom, pausing along the way to behold Margaret hunched over, rummaging in the kitchen junk drawer, up to her elbow in masking tape, nails and picture wire. She did not acknowledge me. She had a class to teach at noon and was gone when I woke again.

We avoided each other throughout the evening and began the shutdown of our daily lives – lights, thermostat, dirty dishes and soda cans put away – having said nothing but the bare minimum. *Did you eat? Going to work tomorrow?* When I took a pillow from the bed and headed to the couch, she did not question or protest. The living room was insufferably cold and our short, flimsy couch murder on my tall heft. Not wanting to be a zombie even at a job I didn't value but needed, I moved to bed during the night, feeling her glib satisfaction beside me as I settled in, as if she had scored a point. A wide path of untouched mattress opened between us, and we both slept straight and stiff as planks. Monday morning, she was not up before me, not watching *The Today Show*, not crouched on the floor like a monkey, drinking grape soda. She was in bed and did not stir (though I knew she was awake) neither when my alarm sounded nor when I climbed over her, on my way to the shower.

I left the steamy bathroom and returned to the cold bedroom to dress. At the jangle of my belt she shifted, and I sensed her confliction, not wanting to acknowledge my hurtful presence, yet yearning for me to make things right. Walking out on her grated against my principles and, after brewing coffee, I returned and kissed her goodbye because, despite any circumstances, I feel this is a requisite. That was how I had left her.

Calling on all the available horsepower of the poor, belabored Honda's 4-cylinder, I floored it off the line to get ahead of the lumbering taxis and Towncars, and darted madly down the I-88 on-ramp. I could drive aggressively when I needed to, and I did now, weaving from lane to lane around the timid Midwestern drivers spaced politely apart and humming along only slightly above the speed limit. Clasping the wheel at ten and two and glancing regularly to my rearview for blue and red lights had me feeling like an urban outlaw rather than merely a frantic newlywed racing through the unfamiliar landscape of daytime outside Nexis's walls. Ogden Avenue was eerily bare. Rolling through a 'right on red', cutting early to the inside of our neighborhood's corners, fanning wide, I slammed up in front of 825 South Wright in record time. The queer and inconsequential fact of 402's lower level status, which normally tickled me with a perverse unease every time I descended our lobby stairs – I liked to imagine that we lived in a bunker-like enclosure sealed off from reality and time – surfaced and was drowned under the sound of my thumping pulse. As I put the key in the lock, a violent premonition passed through me in the form of an image, perhaps influenced by having seen Hargrove's strip malls vacant, as if in a town ravaged by virus or zombies in one of those ghoulish films Margaret was always dragging us to – though perhaps a quick vision of carnage served to make a relative improvement of what I would find inside. That old trick where your teacher hands you your graded essay, and you tell yourself, 'It's a D, it's a D,' so the B+ doesn't look so bad.

It worked. It wasn't as bad as I imagined, though it was bad. Margaret sat on the kitchen floor, back against the cupboards, in a cowering, dejected, exhausted pose. Half concealed by the hand that propped her up on the linoleum was a utility knife, spotted with blood's alarming black redness.

'Honey!'

She raised her head to me as I crossed the room and slid down to her on my knees. Her eyes held no fervency, no vitality, only a sulking transparency. They were like the shells of hollowed eggs, her pupils black punctures into a deep, peculiar fragility.

'Baby, what happened?' I asked. Kneeling beside her, I clasped her shoulders – they were flaccid and lifeless, all her dancer's muscle tone unaccountably drained. Her hair was shockingly mussed; I stroked back the brunette locks, that fell down her forehead. I tilted her face towards me. The rims of her eyes were pink with salted agitation, and her eyelashes clung in moist clumps. Her glossy cheeks and nose were inflamed from crying. Between the neckline of her green cotton pajama top and the shelf of her chest, darkened splotches where tearful runoff had landed.

In a languid motion, her eyes swam up and met mine, then fell away, down to her right hand, which she shifted off the tool it limply gripped.

'What is this?' I asked her, trying to remain non-accusatory.

'I couldn't help it,' she said through a soggy voicebox, using the merest puff of breath.

'Oh, my God, Margaret . . . ?' Releasing my wife's shoulders, I picked up the utility knife. She leaned back against the cupboard doors, behind which were the cake pans and cookie cutters and icing tools her mother bafflingly sprung on her at Christmas, even though Margaret, whose favorite dessert was Double Stuff Oreos, had no interest in baking. She let her head flop back, like a junkie. I held up the triangular blade, smudged with dried blood, that poked from its handle – held it up to her face, imploringly. 'What is this?'

Though I knew.

She looked at me with stillness, as if to incite a search – a smuggler saying rebelliously, with relish, go ahead, search the car. I saw myself – a teen who once dared his mother to find the alleged stolen schnapps in his cluttered closet of reeking hockey gear.

I picked up her wrists from where they lay in her lap, and pulled up her sleeves until the elastic cuffs stretched into the folds of her inner elbows. She submitted willingly and, I felt, with secret enjoyment at my rough, frantic care. One and then the other, I bared and turned over each wrist. Clean and untarnished, her forearm hair wispy, her twisting ulnae flexing the smooth beige flesh of her inner arm.

Her mouth now flattened out of its slight smugness; her eyes seemed to regain their native brown even as she replaced, throughout her whole façade, any trace of the satisfaction at being apprehended with a pitiable morbidity.

I backed off and rose from kneeling to a crouch. I turned over the utility knife in my hand. She had used this implement on herself – did I want to know where? How? If I uncovered it, I'd have to learn why and consider my accountability. I retracted the blade and put the tool on the countertop beside me and, turning back to her dejected slump, saw a tear stream down her cheek – and a dark line caught my eye, announcing itself by finer definition amid similar creases, which were the shadowy folds in the fabric of her green pajamas, halfway up her thigh. This line, though, was not shadow. Purple and straight, blood soaked through from underneath.

Margaret saw my eyes dart, and she moved her hand atop the discoloration, changing her game – or continuing it. She had called me here, she had not hidden the knife – now this unconvincing effort. These things played at the back of my mind but, despite her tactics I foremost wanted to help her.

'Come on,' I said, standing up and offering her my hands.

'Where are we going?'

'Let's go to the bathroom. You have to show me.' She put her fingers in mine. 'I need to see.'

She paused, then pulled against me, still more lifelessly than I'd ever seen her do anything, but some spark returning to her athletic body. I stiffened my arms, took her weight and brought her to her feet. I took her down the hall, turned into our closet-sized bathroom and put down the lid on the toilet. I stood her in front of it. Her immediate response to my vague gesture towards her lower half, of pulling down her pajama bottoms, signaled a deep-down, and perhaps long-dormant, willingness to bare her pain to me. There they were, the cuts, shallow gouges only – my heart eased at this – half a dozen or so on each thigh. She had pushed her pants down only to her knees, and the sight of her shackled there and open to my scrutiny demeaned us both.

'Sit down,' I said, like we were friends who'd just met in a diner for lunch – taking now as normal a tone as I could muster. Clearly, her life wasn't in danger. This was something else. Something or someone would have to lead us back to normality, and the sooner it began, the better, even as a future with therapists, anti-depressants, perhaps some type of monitoring by an authority loomed.

Margaret sat, naked to her French-cut briefs. As a boy, I'd devoted inordinate amounts of time to envisioning girls and women in their underwear. In school, on the bus, or in church, there seemed to be no stopping my imagination from eradicating garments of all types in all weather from any lithe body that passed in view. So much so that I wondered if there existed anything that would stymie my libido, any barrier at all that would place the sight of a girl in her skivvies out of the realm of the erotic. Now

I had my answer. The white triangular mound was snugged between her warm thighs, the nest of hair bristling under the cotton. My pose – I crouched before her again – was familiar, and yet nausea encroached at the thought of sexual touch, of parting her lips with my finger. They would be dry – not riled by grinding foreplay but stinging and sour with the opposite of sex. It was a reflex to think of this, but it was the nearness to her cut flesh that churned my stomach – thinking of her pressing the razor's edge to this skin that, for me, touching, gripping, stroking had so often aroused. No sane man would put any sharp implement near his privates; a sickened wave swelled up, knowing that the compulsion to defy this instinct was in my wife. What perversion took place that urged her to, if only mildly, destroy herself? Her mother, Janis, and her portly self-centeredness came to mind – she must have known of this. This must have happened before.

I swallowed the saliva that flooded my mouth and examined the cuts more closely. I smelled the tearful heat of Margaret's skin, the sweat in her clothes – a soddenness – mixed with the mildew of bathroom tiles. 'Okay, let's fix you up,' I said, as if I understood.

Each was between an inch and two in length. Horizontal, on the tops of the thighs, crossing the quadricep, a muscle that in Margaret plateaued when flexed. With so little fat, there seemed to be a thin margin of error between opening the epidermis and hitting muscle. Some were ripe and wide; blood had smeared on her left thigh, but she must have wiped the others. Some were dried already, closed and rimmed with pink inflammation that mimicked the rims of her eyes.

'Did you do this all today?' I asked.

'Some yesterday,' she answered, her clear throat and full voice indicating a resurgence in her natural buoyancy.

I dabbed the cuts with cotton balls swished against the open mouth of the hydrogen peroxide bottle. Bubbles frothed at the edges of the narrow gorges. I patted the cuts with toilet tissue, smeared antibacterial goo into them and, one by one, sealed them over with a mishmash of strips and squares from a variety pack of Jewel-Osco brand bandages.

Margaret was calm and patient as I attended to her, receiving the empty wrappers from me in a cupped palm. When I finished, I told her to go out to the living room and sit on the couch – she was no longer melancholic but had an aimless, eager air. I packed away the first-aid kit and wondered what to do exactly. Do I call 911? A doctor? My parents? Her mother? I stood at the sink and ran the tap, waiting for the water to heat. The mirror showed me crouched over, as if leaning on a fence gasping for breath. I certainly felt depleted. Blood tapped in my temples. All my tendons felt taut, like someone was pulling them across my chest from behind. I rubbed my eyes, cracked my neck, filled and emptied my lungs a few times, deeply, from the diaphragm. Nothing would be the same from here forward but, remarkably, my long Czech-American mug and square chin were unaltered – it didn't seem possible. This same boy I'd always known, edging towards adulthood, always a step behind where he needed to be – case in point today. I leaned over the basin and splashed my face – water would not change it – then buried my face in a towel as I stood, turning away from the mirror.

The bloody tissues in the toilet leaked red whorls like those frozen in the center of agates. My ragged yellow stream broke the trance. I had to decide something. Maybe the cordless phone was in the bedroom – I could reach someone without Margaret knowing. But it seemed a betrayal to alert anyone to her secret.

'How about a soda?' I offered. No, she said. She was cold and asked for hot chocolate. I fetched the blanket from the sofa chair and spread it over her, tucking it delicately alongside her legs. I pressed a smile at her and said, 'Just stay put.'

The kitchen's dingy sink and stained linoleum countertops emanated dreariness. The microwave hummed hollowly, nuking a mug of water to a boil. I longed for the crisp order and unthreatening sameness of my parents' home. The painless predictability. The ancient toaster my mother inherited from her mother with its herringbone-cloth electrical cord and prongs of a kind that were no longer made. It was perfectly good. Look what flailing around for some grander attainment got you.

Going for the cocoa packet, I came across the utility knife where I'd placed it earlier out of Margaret's reach. I scoured it under the hot tap and shoved it deep in the junk drawer it'd come from.

I brought Margaret her drink. We knew we had to talk. We couldn't just go to bed on this one – run out the silent treatment and hope some reconciliation arrived.

She had done it before and she didn't mean to kill herself. These were my two main questions, answered openly by Margaret sitting curled in the corner of our couch, a brook of excitement burbling – puzzling to me – among the stoic flats of her tear-recovering voice. She had first done it when she was fourteen after a fight with her mother. She didn't know where she got the idea, it was just instinct. She had wanted to make a physical equivalent to her inner turmoil and, once she had, she felt balanced, like she had created something tangible, recognizable, manageable, replacing the vagaries of parental conflict, how she needed her mother but hated the flippant treatment received from her. A blade from a disposable razor plucked from the trash was used – not upsetting the count of new ones in the bag in the linen closet. Janis hadn't found out that time; Margaret had kept it to herself. I asked where she had done it, and she said coolly, 'My legs. Only lower. On the outsides – here.' And she indicated the side of her lower thigh, just above the knee. 'But that's too low for shorts,' she said, cleverly.

I didn't like the lighthearted treatment this was getting. 'Were you trying to find a vein? Did you want to bleed to death? You know, when they talk about suicide, they talk about slitting your wrists.'

'Yeah, I know that, Mel. I'm not trying to kill myself. I'm not *stupid*.' she said. 'It's not about that.' She was never one to act out, she said. Throwing things, breaking stuff, having tantrums. The cutting took the place of all that. For a moment, as I listened to her explanation, the act appeared to have a kindly societal considerateness: an unobtrusive way of siphoning off anger or pain without affecting anyone else. It had a perverse but advanced logic to it that, for a moment, I saw as a crystal orb hovering – an unmoored, tidy, self-contained thing.

'You know, it's just . . . when I feel bad' – a tear dashed from her eye, without warning, without welling, 'it feels good.'

I leaned over and snagged the bead from her cheek with an upswept finger. On the momentum of this gesture, I moved to her, grabbing both her ankles in one hand, lifting her legs and sliding my lap under them. I unburied her arms from the blanket's cavern and nuzzled my hands around her guarded waist.

I kissed her, then retreated. 'You scared me there,' I said. 'This is not . . . this is not something you can keep doing.'

'I know.'

I stroked her hair, as she pulled a knee up under her chin and clutched it.

'Maybe you should see someone about it.'

Her mother had sent her to a counselor, she explained, after she'd been caught – after another time when her marks were found. A 'dippy' woman, she called her, named Helen, who told her she was depressed. It had been easy, Margaret said, simply to cheer up for the sessions and act sunny around her mother. After a few weeks she was allowed to stop going.

'My mother didn't care. That's all she ever said. Never said a word about it again. She was too wrapped up in herself.'

'She probably didn't know how to handle it,' I offered.

'Her boyfriends were always more important. *Mag, honey, I'm going to the movies with Alex! Going dancing with Steve! Mag, honey, don't stay up too late.*'

'Doesn't it scar?' I said, after a stillness in which Janis Krantz's terse, hearty spirit, evoked by Margaret's impersonation, came and left. 'If nothing else, you don't want to scar yourself for life.' I was surprised by Margaret's cunning, hiding her depression from her mother. That she'd been lonely was news to me too. I'd always envied her freedom in that townhouse. But what followed put another notch of estrangement between myself and my wife. She knew just how to cut it, she said, so it wouldn't scar – just how deep, just how long.

'It's like an orange rind,' she said. 'You just stay on the surface.

And you have to treat them afterwards. I found that out early on. You can't just leave them.'

'So you have some – or one – that scarred?' I asked. 'Where is that?'

She laughed with satisfaction. 'If you don't know, I guess it's not that bad.'

'Jesus.' I slid back to my end of the couch and threw my head back, pulling my hands through my hair. 'So did you do this when we were going out?'

'You can say it. *Cut yourself.*'

'Well, Jesus, Margaret, you don't have to be so proud.' I looked at her intently, probably queerly to her. My physical perspective of her seemed to broaden and fluctuate in depth – like Scorsese's trick of tracking in while pulling the camera back. The computer, desk and wall drew forward and flattened as if leveling into 2D. I held her gaze to let her know I meant to have an answer. 'You hid it from me?'

'Well, obviously.'

I tried to think back to times when that might have been. Times she wore pants in summer or wouldn't undress, or had refused to be seen.

The tone of our conversation changed. I felt I'd been duped and misled, even toyed with. I asked her, when she'd done this, had she always cut herself on her legs? I tried to think. Did she wear long sleeves at odd times? Had I seen bandages in places before? Irritation, a shortness, entered my voice. So many questions came up all of a sudden. Did her friends know? Weren't they alarmed? Didn't they advise something? What about her mother – did she know it went on still? Margaret seemed to treat it like a game; had others played along? Did she expect me to? Then a certain injustice appeared, one that seemed to trump all: this was more than I'd agreed to in marrying. Margaret was speaking, but my mind lofted away on an updraft of righteous panic. It was like I'd made an error, like I was walking away from a car I'd parked and realizing I'd left the engine running, the gear in Drive. And now it was too late – it was getting away from me. I'd said *I do*. Till death do us part, yes. But not small deaths every few weeks, or however often she took out her dissatisfaction on herself rather than dealing with it, like everybody else had to. Not small deaths that I was responsible for resuscitating her from. Not small deaths that wore off on me and worked against what I strove for.

Margaret was hurt by my anger and cried again, then became irate. I was saying how this was unfair to me, how I hadn't known this about her and she'd been keeping it from me, when she was set off and began screaming about things that were unfair to *her*. How I never spent any time with her. How I was always complaining about every little thing, like a tyrant – the pop cans she left out, things she forgot, things she didn't understand. How I would pick up after her because I had to have everything spotless all the time. Then I'd rub it in her face, she said. We were arguing properly now. I wasn't rubbing anything in her face, I bellowed. Empty aluminum cans go in the recycling bucket, that's all, I didn't make up that law of the universe! Well, none of this would have happened, Margaret yelled – we were both standing now – if I'd just pay attention to her. Listen, do some things with her, not be always so wrapped up in my fucking pictures and bitching about my job. 'I want a career too, you know! You're not the only one who's unhappy at work!'

And so on. But soon this felt painfully wrong. 'Okay, okay,' I said, interrupting her. 'This is not what we're here for. I'm sorry. I'm sorry. Let's just stick to the problem at hand.'

'What? Me cutting myself? You'd like that. Then it's all my fault! Then I'm the only one who needs to change!'

My will left me at that point, I suppose because there was some truth in this. Or perhaps I felt helpless to convince her otherwise. If Margaret was threatened by my personal ambitions, I figured she always would be. That was immensely disheartening. It was deadening. The sad and pointless part of it was that these aspirations that somehow worked against me felt rinky-dink in the big scheme of things, laughable. Minuscule. A grain of rat shit in a wheat silo. Like that bumper sticker, 'If you want to make someone laugh, tell God your plans.' How could I say to her what I felt? I didn't mean to make her miserable. I didn't mean to hurt her, alienate her. I didn't care anymore about a photographic exhibition. I'd gone around to café galleries, shopping my prints, thinking it would make a difference – either to spite her or prove something to her. But seeing Margaret now – *my Zoë* – and how my selfish way of loving her aggravated her vulnerabilities, I would have trashed my darkroom, never touched it again, if it had to be. Guilt is a powerful force, as powerful as love.

I sat and was silent. I was out of things to say. Too many thoughts. I admitted as much. I said I loved her. 'Maybe that's not good for much. Maybe it doesn't help,' I said. I asked her what she wanted to do – what she *wanted*.

'I just want to be happy,' she said, weeping again. 'I just want *you*.'

Well, she had me. She had me.

17 Percolating, Kneeling

In the week after Margaret's wound-making, she was 'let go' from Culkin Dance and came home in a tempest of black malice. Wendy had taken her aside after locking up and made a garbled declaration about shifting the focus of the school's instructional offerings, which meant she couldn't keep Margaret on anymore. She was sorry, she said. Margaret was like a daughter to her. Margaret pleaded, got angry, cried, then left. She relayed these details to me, pacing back and forth in the kitchen, her jacket still on, packing her favorite 'Nationals' cup with ice, pouring a diet cherry cola over it till the caramel-colored froth mounded over the rim and spilled to the countertop – where Margaret sucked it up with a straw.

'"Take care of yourself," was the last thing she said, with this look in her eye. What's that supposed to mean, *Take care of yourself*?'

Wasn't it obvious? She spent two days in bed, watching the portable TV with the lights off, sleeping and percolating in a cloud of contempt. Or was it self-hatred? I couldn't say exactly. Periodically, I came in and asked how she was feeling, what she was going to do, if she needed anything. But all conversation led to vitriolic rambles about Wendy. 'How could she do this to me? She thinks she's so fucking great? I could have a studio ten times better than hers. Nobody likes her. They only take her classes so they can get into mine. She can't even get a man!'

Margaret made no mention about her cuts, whether a student had seen her in the locker room, or if she'd bled through her tights – what kind of example that might set for the girls.

By the second day, a pile of wet tissues took shape at the bedside. I offered to cook her something – scrambled eggs, toast, anything. I drove to the White Hen for whole milk at her request, made her heaping bowls of Fruit Loops, then left her alone, to brood, to process in her way, though it certainly wasn't mine. At the computer, I tallied our expenses against our income, minus Margaret's, and tried to put a cap on how long we could reasonably manage without her contributing. We had about two weeks. One pay period. When the time was right, I would bring it up.

A call came in from a café called Kuppernicus. They would let me show my prints and sell them on consignment. The news was bittersweet, like the coffee: I couldn't enjoy it but certainly couldn't expect Margaret to. There was only one thing that enlivened her now, but it seemed antithetical to my artwork. In swings of hopefulness between harangues against Wendy's (perceived) unfairness, Margaret talked about opening her own studio. Maybe in Aurora, where it could get really big. Did I know there were three high schools there! She could easily put a team together that could contend for titles at state competitions. I should get a promotion, like that scanning thing, or work overtime and start saving for this. This was what I was trying to achieve with the prints, a livelihood with more promise, yet I didn't feel she wanted me out of the house pursuing any ego indulgence. I felt like she expected some kind of masculine vigilance, a husbandly heroism, to simply make something materialize without neglecting her. Her need for me felt palpable. Unspoken signals conveyed that, if I left, she might seek the solacing pain of self-harm again, though I tried to show to her a face that trusted she wouldn't. Wouldn't need to do it. Wouldn't occur to her to do it.

Kuppernicus was one of these organic-oatmeal-cookie type of hangouts where quasi-urban sub-professionals in cargo pants came and went with Dead Kennedys stickers on their tote bags, making a living downtown without conforming overmuch. There was six hundred square feet, Robert, the owner explained, as he walked me around, pointing to the walls where someone else's swirling oil paintings hung. Slender and tidy, with silver hair, he had the requisite rimless rounds and the peaceful manner suggested by them. He was one of these people who liked excellence in everything – I was thankful for his choosing me and eager to please him with my work. My being numbed by the state of things at home played into his unharried demeanor.

We rounded the room and returned to the service counter, where the encouraging odor of roasted beans was lifted on steam. He offered me anything off the menu, on the house. I had just eaten lunch and felt like something sugary, like a dessert. I also felt, given the reduction of my household's income by 50 percent, I should milk this freebie I could get for all it was worth. I got a caramel macchiato. The cloying sweetness sickened. It was the first and last time I'd order anything other than black dark roast.

It was also, unfortunately, the last time I saw Robert. He told me how long I'd be able to display my prints, what tools and equipment of his I'd have available to me in the shop – wire, hooks, a ladder, a level. He advised me to not overcrowd the walls or overprice the prints. 'It reflects badly on the store,' he said in his curved, quiet voice. 'People feel insulted. It puts money on their mind, and they end up skipping the muffin or the biscotti. That's where our margins are.' And be sure to label them 'silver gelatin prints', he said – that's what they're called in museums.

'But mine are just made on regular paper, store-bought Agfa multigrade.'

'I know, Mel. But you have to market yourself. The silver nitrate on that paper is held in a gelatin glaze. So,' he said, cheerfully. 'People won't pay $150 for a *black-and-white photograph*. But they will for a silver-gelatin print. That's Art, son!'

I didn't know if he meant the print became art by naming it such, or he was saying Marketing was an art. Marketing: that tradition of well-intentioned deceit.

Robert pulled out a planner from under the counter and selected a day for me to return with my work matted and framed. We shook on it, and I thanked him heartily, feeling his equal, feeling recognized. But when I next returned, and every time after that, Robert would be out, not working that day or at one of his other stores. He also owned a couple gas stations.

*

Greg joined me for the installation on a Saturday morning in early June and, afterwards, I bought him a coffee and a sandwich and we sat at a table surrounded by the product of our winter sessions. We reflected on the display – which images were most striking, stood the best chance of selling, how the arrangement worked. 'The skater is still my favorite,' Greg said, referring to an action shot of a skateboarder grinding on a railing in the plaza of the World Book building on Michigan Avenue. The rubber strip on the underside of his skateboard met the railing at a single point and the trucks and wheels hung loosely, as if an afterthought. The rail divided the composition into two blocks, one a third wide, the other two-thirds. The boy's arms, akimbo for balance, made a contrasting line that led the eye along a slant, as if mimicking gravity's pull on the skater, in which he was, here, forever in suspension. His face was obscured by flailing blond hair, swished beautifully by motion into a gelatinous slurry. There was the suggestion of flight, overt but unforced, and through this an intimation of youth's majesty. The tone and balance were exquisite, down to a faint cloud in the far background that I'd burned ever so slightly. It was my favorite too. Looking at it sometimes, just as I turned away, I thought, if not for the obvious dating of the subject, it could pass for a Walker Evans.

I thanked Greg for his help, both instructional and inspirational, and, without giving him time to linger in embarrassment, said, 'There's something else I've got to tell you.' I hesitated. 'Oh, shit, I don't know.' But I had to tell someone. It was like a worm in my gut, writhing around, seeking an exit. 'It's about Margaret.'

'That's messed up,' was about the extent of Greg's reaction. I felt foolish – I'd overstepped. He tilted the legs of his chair back and glanced towards the door.

'I don't know why I said anything,' I quipped. 'It's my problem.'

'No, no,' he backtracked. 'I mean, it's messed up. You know . . . I'm sorry, man. It's harsh.' He scrunched his thick, black eyebrows and studied his coffee absently. 'Maybe she should be . . .'

'Locked up?' I joked. He clearly hadn't been prepared for this heaviness, and I wanted to relieve his discomfort.

'Well, I didn't want to say that, but yeah. I mean, what if she comes after you next?'

I had forgotten this side of Greg – that, in addition to the photography magazines, there'd also been the *Guns 'n' Ammo* and *The Anarchist's Cookbook*. He had a paranoid side, a self-protective streak. He didn't want people to fuck with him. I nodded along to his ideas – separation, name change, restraining orders. 'Next time, man, background check.'

'I'll figure it out,' I said. 'Thanks.' I changed the topic, and Greg never returned to the subject, not ever.

Margaret emerged from her mini-hibernation to get her hair and nails done. She needed something to make her feel better, she said. I didn't argue, though our checkbook register did. She asked how the thing at the coffeehouse went, and I said fine. I suggested, as placidly as I could, that she pick up a paper with the jobs section.

'Can I just enjoy myself for one day?' she cried. Anguish poured over her face. A small peck was all we could muster between us before she stepped out, purse in hand, keys chiding. Within an hour, my anxiety mounted, and nothing brought relief. I went to the darkroom, thinking I'd do something fun – play around with dodges and burns or something. But being in the room sickened me, and the guide I'd made and taped on the enlarger to mark the f-stop positions looked outright perplexing. I couldn't even think which allowed in more light, 2.1 or 6. I went to the breakfast nook and started peeling an orange; when the sections wouldn't part neatly and juice stung a papercut, I slammed the handful of pulpy mess into the trash. I made coffee and clicked around the files in my computer, looking for something to occupy me, till the sight of its flickering screen gave me nausea. Before I knew it I had my mother on the phone and was telling her our drier was too old to handle our blankets and comforters.

'Come and use our machine!' she offered, cheerfully seeing an opportunity for me to visit.

'The only problem is, Margaret has the car. I was really hoping to get all this stuff washed today. Maybe you could come get me.'

Mrs P. was suspicious but willing. Her mother's instinct hadn't gone dormant just by my leaving the house. She knew something was up but was tactful about it, saying, 'I was just going for a walk with Mrs Brown, but I can do that any night. I've had enough of her gab lately anyway.'

I tore off all the bedding and heaped it into our laundry basket, and stuffed the living-room blankets into trash bags. On a notepad I wrote, 'Took laundry to M&D's. No quarters. Back later, Mel.' I reached for the notebook I sometimes write things in, but left it. I glanced at some photography books I'd bought secondhand, thinking of bringing one, and glanced just as quickly away. I stood over the cigar box on the desk where I kept my wallet, spare change, gum, cigarettes. I didn't want any of it, didn't want any material thing weighing me down. I lugged the bedding out of the apartment, letting the door slam behind me unlocked, and sat on the front step waiting for Mom's Nissan to appear.

At the house, she lingered around, conversationally elbowing but not prying. She watched closely but uncritically as I loaded the washer, then lay nearby on the couch, waiting like a loyal dog as I flipped around the TV channels. She seemed to understand, and I was unspeakably grateful for that. There was nothing on, so we went to the kitchen and scrounged. There Mr P. showed up, and had to make sense of my situation. 'Well, how have you washed big items so far? You've been there, what, eight months? You've washed your bedsheets before, I hope.'

'Yeah, of course.'

He had come in from the backyard wearing jeans white with age and a sweatshirt from his alma mater, the University of Urbana-Champaign, sleeves rolled up, revealing his bone-narrow forearms. He stood, brushing dirt off himself with irritation. Before he went back out, he would clean his glasses on a tissue and adjust the gardener's kneepads he wore which looked like bulbous swollen joints halfway down his scrawny legs. 'Well, how'd you dry those?'

'Leave him alone, Richard,' Mom said. 'Are you still on a coffee kick? Look at this – I bought some whole-bean coffee at the store to have around for you. You want to make some?'

'Not tonight, Mom. Thanks, though.'

'How about iced tea? I made a pitcher in the sun today.'

'Well, I have to finish up outside while there's still daylight,' Mr P. said.

'What's going on out there, Dad?' I asked.

'Oh, just fixing up the landscaping,' he muttered as he drew the sliding screen door aside: the squeaky wheels in the track recalled many summer days coming in and out from dusky games of Kick the Can and Nerf football with neighbor kids. Mr P. shut the rickety frame behind him and said through the screen, 'If I'm not done before you go, I'll see you later.'

'All right, see ya, Dad,' I said. Mom sat on a stool and leaned over the countertop. 'What's this about landscaping?' I asked.

'Don't even get me started. He's losing his mind. You know what he's doing? He's washing the rocks in the beds – in the – in the edging.' She began stacking the junk mail and magazines on the countertop. 'You know, around the house. Washing them by hand! A bucket at a time with Palmolive and a scrub brush! Can you believe it?'

'I really can't,' I sighed. 'I really can't. Why is he doing that?'

'Why?' She got up and went to the refrigerator. Speaking into the open door, she said, 'Why does he do anything he does? God knows.' The abundance inside the fridge was staggering, every shelf packed to capacity: tubs of synthetic margarines, breads, tupperwares of deli meats, English muffins, pitchers of juice, gallons of two kinds of milk, two cartons of eggs, jams and pickles and huge jars of mayonnaise, two kinds, one Lite, one regular, and two kinds of mustard in the door, one yellow, one brown, and tubs of wheatgerm and containers of E-Z Wipp topping and a pie tin balanced atop a head of iceberg.

So they had their own problems buried under excess, avoid with preoccupation.

I changed the loads and returned to the TV, clicking aimlessly. Mom asked after Margaret. I'd been on the brink of telling her before, seeking her consolation and counsel, but had lost the gumption. Now was my chance. 'Oh, fine,' I said, not seeing how she, and Mr P. once he returned, could react with anything but fright and worry. I wanted there to be understanding between us all, but saw only inevitable panic and confusion. The washer chugged mutely from the basement, and the talk turned to the sitcoms, the news, a cleaner with a money-back guarantee that didn't work for beans, Mom knew, because she'd tried it.

I sunk into numbness with the smells of home all around me: the carpet-freshening powder Mom'd been vacuuming with for a decade or two. The tingly concocted odor of newness and purity that was on my fingers after handling the fabric-softener sheet – the one with the fluffy Bear mascot who clutched a towel to his cheek on the box and smiled with erotic bliss. I clicked and clicked, looking for something we could drown in, and the voices from TV seemed to fade, as if originating from far off in the stratosphere. I imagined saying to her, 'Mom, there's something I need your advice on. And Dad's . . .' The confiding, natural tone I tried to hear my own voice produce wouldn't come, wouldn't solidify in my imagination. I twisted the words and phrasings – casual, cagey, candid.

'Listen, can I ask you something? It's about Margaret . . .'

'Okay, I can't keep this to myself anymore . . .'

'All right, Ma, I know you know something's happened . . .'

Mrs P. kept watching TV, not speaking. Each moment was like a lashing whip, repeating. With a lump in my throat, I got up. 'Nature calls,' I managed to say, before a pang seized my larynx. I dashed to the restroom. That every shelf, the countertop and toilet tank were crammed corner to corner with heart-shaped glass tea-light candle holders and ceramic Danish trolls and dried potpourri enshrining her woodblock cut saying 'Love is Everything' struck me like a fist, dizzying. I wanted to swipe them all aside, throw them on the tiles and into the tub. Such abundant effluvia wasn't brought into life by anyone who trusted the world to just be. This room, this house, was like someone repeating a lie they had to convince themselves of, and now the lie had closed in on me, and stolen my breath. I'd stayed stock still so long for fear of upsetting the careful order of it, the preciousness, it was like I had gone dead, stale, like I was mired in quicksand, about to vanish.

On the way back down the hall, the sight of Mom's prayer room stopped me. One votive was lit, as always, deep within its tall, tubular glass. The Venetian blinds were down and slats turned open, providing a sliced view of an oak tree's heavy bark and Meadow Prairie Lane. From the aging Sanyo console set in the living room came a woman exalting over galloping banjo: 'Save big money! Save big money! When you shop at Lenard's!' Then a *tschht* and a new soundscape – Mom had the clicker now and was trawling. I stepped into her sanctuary, closing the door silently, using the trick I'd done as a kid, twisting the knob, bringing in the latch, pulling the door flush with the frame, and slowly untwisting the knob. I walked to the prayer station and knelt.

Kneeling is universal. It's supplication. It's saying, I'm out of ideas. This is beyond me.

The rich old boards of the kneeler creaked, and the vinyl upholstery with the brass rivets let out a hiss of air as my knees sank into it – the foam springy again now that Mrs P. had restored it with new batting. I brushed my finger over the black leatherette cover of the missal that rested in the holder, and I pressed the spring-coiled coat hook as I'd done obsessively in mass as a boy, when I'd dare myself not to let it snap (then accidentally let it snap, and receiving a scold).

I took a deep breath, and looked down at the rail – a few scratches in the golden varnish. I put my elbows upon it and made the sign of the cross.

'Dear God,' I whispered, my eyes closed. 'Forgive me for my sins. Forgive me for my . . . apathy . . . greed . . . lust. Vanity. Mostly vanity. Wanting things for myself. Pride, too, I guess. Thinking my work is more important than my marriage. Thinking I'm better than others, that I don't have to work hard and sacrifice, be responsible and support the wife You brought into my life.' I paused, the memory of my voice in my mind like the smell of a dirty, wet sponge. Why couldn't I have one of those deep, earnest voices? Mine was all sinuses – dully resonant septum, cartilage and snot. 'I don't know,' I continued.

I heard a muted clatter and opened my eyes and turned to the door. Closed. I turned my ear out: TV's vague cacophony and, in a moment, another shift in its manner. I could sense my mother's reluctance to stay seated; she was a fidgety person and not an avid TV watcher. I didn't have long.

My eyes met speckled darkness again. 'God, please be with Margaret. Give her strength and clarity. Take away her pain. Let her have peace in her heart. Show her . . . whatever it is she needs to see. Oh my God, that's stupid.

'Um, sorry. God, tonight I pray for change. Please show us the way to be in union with each other and with You, like the pastor said at the wedding. Even though Margaret doesn't really . . . know You. But mostly, God, in Your mercy, please bring an end to her suffering – our suffering.'

I stopped there before I got any more jumbled. Prayer was not a regular practice for me. It was a rarely visited aunt; I never knew how I'd be received, what I'd mutter at her doorstep to gain admittance. I thought what came out was passable, and I hoped it would suffice. Mom would be wondering what was keeping me, listening for a flush. 'Amen,' I said and, as I touched my fingertip to my forehead again, a muffled crunching startled me. A nearer noise this time, the direction clear – away from the interior. My head whipped around and my eyes met Mr P.'s through the Venetian blinds. His hair was mussed and his face sweaty. Seeing it was only him, and impelled by a natural momentum, I continued the sequence I'd started: touching my chest, my left shoulder, and my right. The series' end came instinctively too: both hands atop the rail again, knuckles interlaced. Mr P., for his part, raised into view a Schwaan's ice-cream bucket filled with edging stones – the gray, maroon and white rocks I'd tromped through as a kid chasing stray baseballs, the same I'd butted against with the lawnmower in their weather-beaten two-by-four frame-beds. This was his purpose, his gesture said. This was his reason for being there outside the window, split by slats into segments. A flash of understanding passed between us about that, his eyes admitting instantly to the obsessiveness of his project, but unapologetic, saying it cannot be helped, the path has been made. Then in the space where I might have made a reciprocal gesture towards the kneeler, votive and portrait to convey my purpose, or where we might have exchanged a reassuring smile, Mr P. instead offered an expression of nothingness, a flat neutral look, before crouching down, his head dipping below the window frame. The sound of stones rattling against the cement foundation came through, like a squirrel in a wall, from where my father, on the other side, knelt in the stones.

18   *The Grand Canyon*

I should have known, should have taken it as a sign, when Margaret insisted on buying an atlas from the bookstore. I'd had an itinerary mailed to me from the travel bureau, ordered under Mr P.'s membership number, at his insistence. I'd just stuffed the bulky packets into the glove box, a hair's width in front of her bare knees. But she wanted nothing to do with it; or, so shaky in her self-confidence, it was too prescribed. She wanted to chart her own course. One mile down, seventeen hundred to go, and we were fighting.

'We don't need a road atlas,' I said. 'We have the Triple A maps.'

'I just want to see what they have,' she said. I knew this euphemism: I want to buy something, I just don't know what. An American vacation starts with needless spending.

'What's wrong with these?' My guess was, coming from such a utilitarian agency, the itinerary wasn't glamorous enough for her.

'Just stop into Barnes and Noble. I'll pay for it,' she said, irritated, as if I was the one annoying her. 'It's on the way.'

It was not on the way. The ramp to Interstate 80 West was south of us; the mall was towards Chicago. And her paying was the same as me paying. I drank deeply from my travel mug of iced coffee, watching the road over the lip.

'I want to navigate,' she explained a few blocks on, softly now and looking out the window as if in practice for her passenger-side duties. So this was about her sense of purpose – wanting to chart her own course, control her destiny. 'Plus, I can make sure you don't screw it up!' She smiled her teasing smile at me.

Behind every joke . . . I thought.

It was shortly after 9 a.m. The lot was barren. I watched Margaret enter between the oversized stippled portraits in the display windows – Virginia Woolf's bunned head, a pensive James

Joyce. I waited in the car. It was a brisk, sanguine July morning. The sky was bright, and the shadows morning-long. The grass and mall-planted trees sparkled with remnant dew. Even the pavement was pleasurably tight, not overheated yet, not driven upon and greasy. I let the cool air in the windows, the air that, in a few hours, on the highway, we'd seal out and temper through compressor and vent. She returned with a spiral-bound jobbie showing the whole damned country and Canada too. $14.95 printed diagonally – eye-catchingly – in the corner.

'That should do the job,' I said levelly. I put the car in gear and began driving.

'Yeah, it's huge. It's got everything!' Her satisfaction agreed with the ineluctable brilliance of morning. Morning is possibility, hope. And hope feeds the mind and a hungry mind devours hope, converts it to energy as the body converts food to fuel.

I got us onto Hargrove Road and made note of its posted county road number, 23, which was information ignored daily and useful now, since the AAA materials used this nomenclature. I hoped to get us to Topeka by evening. I had the route memorized, easy with its symmetry: Interstate 88 to 80, then 35 and 335 for the turn southwest. Depending how much drive we had in us, we could plug on after dinner and reach Oklahoma City. The next day, we'd pick up a state highway for the slide into the desert. There was a new number for that, and it was my system, and my nature, not to learn it now.

Margaret studied the book's features, the mileage charts, points of interest, emergency phone numbers and so on, listing them to me as if each item added to the value of the purchase. She looked up just in time to see the green and white crest-shaped signs, 80 West, 80 East. 'Which way?' Margaret asked, with a rousing, team-spirited vigor.

'Which way?' I asked. I did not laugh. I was incredulous. It was a secret incredulousness, and concealing it blurred the edges of my vision. Life seemed like a narrow tunnel closing in. We passed the ramp for East, and I entered the turn lane for West.

'West?' she concluded.

'Do you know where we're going?'

'I know *where*. It was my idea!'

'You do know that the Grand Canyon is west of Chicago, though, right?'

'Melvin, don't start. I told you I was not good with states. Geography was one of those classes I missed a lot of. I told you.'

I kept my mouth closed. We sat in the turn lane, the blinker *tick-tocking* at a murderously slow pace. Margaret's head was down, devouring her acquisition. I saw her flip from Illinois to Missouri and back. The green arrow lit, and I accelerated down the ramp. I attempted apology in my tone when I chimed, 'Here we go.' Margaret looked up and around – a white flag of a gesture within the war-like rules of intimacy, where excitements are shared and slights must be brushed aside. I brought us to 65, and Margaret returned to the spaghetti of blue, red and black lines on her lap. With a fingertip she traced along the familiar curve of 39 south from Hargrove to Springfield, the route AAA had recommended initially. It was a course that no doubt looked more direct on paper. Even though I didn't think it likely that Margaret would inquire, I had an answer ready defending my choice to set out westward through Iowa: because the highway to St Louis was two-lane, while the interstate was four lanes, divided. I rehearsed it in my head. *This'll be faster. On those country roads, if you get caught behind an eighteen-wheeler, you're screwed for the next hundred miles. More time to spend at our destination.*

The truth: a neighbor girl I'd played with and had a crush on as a boy lived in Peoria now, which was along the southern Illinois route. Jill Herbert. She'd had a round bright face, an expansive feminine forehead and sandy hair cut in a line of magnificent straightness across her back. I'd known her from the ages of five to nine. We'd rode the bus together, ran through sprinklers in summer, had birthday parties, hunted crayfish in Wynton's little stream, the Vermillion, kissed before we knew why people kissed. Her family had moved back to Peoria, where her mother was from, when her father was laid off. This was all fine. I hadn't seen her in over ten years, never knew what became of her. The last awkward letters had arrived amid the terrors of puberty, when friendships were lashed by violent hormonal waves. It was behind me. She – Jill – was behind me. The problem was, I'd had dreams about her lately. They were unaccountable, but had recurrent force. In them I'd be with her, and engulfed in her angelic aura, free from all earthly worry. In the peculiar manner dreams afford, I'd be simultaneously young and my current age; Jill would be in spirit her eternally young self inhabiting a dream-warped adult body. There were never any storylines, just a nondescript landscape, expansive and open, a representation of edenic possibility. I'd wake feeling like a ship had sailed, like I'd suffered a horrendous, sorrowful loss, like I'd grasped bliss and let it slip. I'd keep my eyes closed, the smell and feel and awareness of Margaret in bed with me unfathomable. How did I arrive here? What brought me to choose this? Eventually, I'd drag myself to the shower, hiding my eyes from my wife, terrified they showed the lingering confusion and ache.

The dreams were ridiculous but persistent; the last had come only a week before, after an evening of planning this reuniting trek. I didn't actually believe we'd run into Jill if we stopped for gas or lunch in Peoria, though at the office I had daydreamed of that. I simply didn't want to see the word Peoria at all. I feared that the real Peoria, even merely passing through it, might awaken me to the real significance of Jill – why was I dreaming about her in the first place.

Speaking with the AAA rep, ordering the itinerary from my Nexis cubicle, I had told a little white lie: 'I want to visit a relative in Des Moines on the way. Can you make it via 88?'

We were on 88 West now. Near Rock Falls I finished my coffee, and Margaret opened a soda, broke out the breakfast we'd packed and draped napkins on the center armrest. The windows were up, shutting out the morning air – too noisy at freeway speed. The car whinnied at 3,000 rpms and the tire roar of freeway pitch had settled into our ears. The car drove comfortably even with the weight of our luggage and food in back and ourselves up front. I spooned up yogurt and steered with my knee. Margaret kept the atlas open on her lap, looking as if she intended to wear it there the entire 1,700 miles, tracking our journey towards togetherness. She occupied the bucket seat with her characteristic sporty lightness, an ease the same as if she were paused on a park bench during a relaxing stroll. She wore her hair in a ponytail and a new sleeveless shirt she'd bought for the trip. I'd put away the thought I often had about new clothes for occasions: that these events typically happened away from home, with seldom-seen relatives and strangers, none of whom knew whether your clothes were new or old. The atlas, though, had pleased her, and I didn't mind it now. It had lofted her into a carefree exuberance. She possessed an active mind, and it had something to work at now as she happily munched a granola bar. Her joblessness, her pain, her mismanagement of it, my detachment – she had arrived at this word to describe what I had been exhibiting, and I hadn't felt entitled to disagree – it was all forgotten now.

That was the purpose of this getaway, to forget. And to remember. Remember what we'd felt not so long ago. Margaret had proposed the idea in June, saying, 'Why don't we go somewhere – get away? I feel like if we could just be together and not have to worry about things . . .'

How could I refuse?

We reached Kansas City that night. She never asked about the southern route to Springfield. She was too interested in the scenery, which across Iowa wasn't much, though it was pretty – faintly sloping fields, peaceful silos peering out of copses, skeletons of barns and rusting tractors. Some grooved hills, in and out of the Mississippi River valley, that could have passed for Germany or something grander than Iowa but for the faded vintage ads which were irreducibly American. On the flats again, rows of beans and alfalfa, just popping out of brown soil, whizzed by with psychotropic effect. The outlet malls outside Des Moines shocked Margaret – fashion names that one associates with New York's Fifth Avenue, I suppose. We ate and stretched and laughed at the gifts in the truck stop attached to the restaurant – she snapped my picture wearing a green foam and vinyl cap. (We had borrowed her mother's snapshot camera and left my Pentax at home.)

There was still plenty of daylight, so we pressed on, curving south on 35 and putting the sunset over Margaret's right shoulder.

Our distance from home put me at ease, as if all the open land had the properties of a confessional. At the motel, there was trouble with the phone line dialing in to authorize my credit card. Tired of waiting and ever eager, Margaret went to the car to unload while I sweated it out. Thinking the card might be declined, I made confident chitchat with the clerk, traveler's talk, some offhand remark in reference to the 'You Are Here' map of the state behind him. He gave me a confused look and answered obtusely, then did not meet my eyes again, only watched the machine for the 'approved' message. Only once I looked closer at the grid of Kansas City did I piece together my blunder and blush. Walking the long corridor, I laughed at myself, and voiced what the clerk might have been thinking: 'Welcome, Yokel.' Flopped atop the thin, floral bedspread of our Best Western room, within reach of diesel fumes and burning road rubber, I piped up 'So!' in a way I had that let Margaret know I had a little story.

'Yeah, babe?' she called. She was reading the fire escape plan on the wall.

'I didn't actually know there was only one Kansas City.'

'What do you mean?'

'Well, you know when you do capitals in school, there's Kansas City, Missouri. But there's also Kansas City, Kansas. I always thought they were two separate cities. I always wondered, Was it a competition? Who was there first? Was it done in unison, in tribute? I thought it was quite a gaffe. Like, how do you overlook that?'

Margaret laughed and teased me. I guess it was a rare thing I was saying somehow. She joined me on the bed with her well-studied atlas. 'No, see, dummy,' she said, opening immediately, via a bent corner, to the grids of downtown and spiraling developments of Mission and Overland Park. She traced the state line snaking in from Leavenworth on the Missouri River.

'You didn't know that?'

'No, like I said, I knew there was Kansas City, Kansas, and Kansas City, Missouri.'

'Oh, that's funny! No, there's only one.' She lay on her back, the spiral-bound book above her, angled towards lamplight. In the chill gush from the air conditioner, her hair flickered over her forehead. Her breasts spilled beautifully towards her armpits, but were dammed up by her upraised arms. 'I noticed that right away,' she said again. 'The whole metro sprawls across the state line. And then look at this –'

'No, you look at this,' I joked, taking the atlas out of her hands and rolling on top of her. 'That's about enough geography for one day, there, Magellan.'

A familiar voice – male, soft, thoughtful – prodded me out of sleep, brought me into the world, a world of fleur-de-lis wallpaper borders. 'Sorry,' Margaret said, 'I turned it as low as I could.' Bryant Gumbel addressed the screen from a chair, Katie Couric beside him, jubilant Times Square faces behind, sealed and silenced by glass. A woman held a sign reading, 'HI LUANN!' An awareness of America's enormous breadth fell over me, impressive but obnoxious. Granted, we hadn't traveled very far and were only in a freeway motel, but the media's tentacles, with their slimy, comforting caress, seemed far-reaching, squiggling over to whatever corner you backed into.

Margaret sat in the wooden roller-chair in the corner, legs up, soda in hand. She'd slitted the curtains just enough to see her way around, and the morning light that fell on her reflected the gray of the parking lot and highway outside. I rose and kissed her. 'So, is there a coffee maker in here?'

There was not, and I had to survive on a cup of free stuff from the motel lobby – flavorless swill, Maxwell House was my guess.

Margaret drove the first leg to Oklahoma City. Nervous compulsion kept me watching the road. I hadn't experienced this riding with her at home, but I yearned to be in control of the car. It wasn't that I distrusted her. She was an above-average driver, though lacking in foresight, impatient, unforgiving. An assiduous monitoring of other cars' lane usage occupied her, and the slightest show of aggression she took as a snub. Narration was her way of coping and, though cute at first, it got tedious. 'Okay, Mr White Van, what're ya doin'? I don't want to go 58 miles an hour here. Let's go! Okay, I'll go around you. Oh, now you decide to pick it up. What is your damage, buddy?' Inevitably, people came racing along in the fast lane, and if they did as she was passing, she took great offense. 'Oh, my God, settle down, jerk! Geez, I'm going! I'm just trying to get around this slowpoke. You people! I don't want to go 45, or 85. Give me a break here.'

As wingman to Margaret's captain I got no rest from the stress of road awareness – always ready to referee a skirmish or shout instruction. I had no recourse to relieve my edginess. I tried reading (*USA Today*), tried an early snack (PB&J), tried educating myself with study, in the atlas, of parts of the country I'd never been to (Seattle, Boston), but it was also my job to navigate, and Margaret asked often, 'How far now?' I was hostage to her mania. The enclosed cabin shrank. Even her approving monologues grated. 'See? Maroon Boat Lady knows how to be nice. Hello! Thank you. Yes, go on by. Oh, you're from Texas. How nice. Everything's big there.' As the theater played on, despite my best effort, inexorably I began to see this feistiness I had adored in her as reminiscent – and symptomatic – of the ups and downs of life at home. Would it always be like this? Would there be any proverbial open road, any peaceful stretches?

That's when I asked for a pee and a fresh cup of coffee. And offhandedly offered to drive.

For better or worse, the rest of the trip, I was in the driver's seat.

We trolled the radio stations, catching talk shows in southern twang, self-satirizing Christian music, lots of country and western. We entered stretches of road jagged with gaps in the concrete, making a train-like rhythmic *clack*. We got irritated and begged for it to end; we worried about the tires popping; we laughed as the jarring jolts to our butts turned ticklish. Finally, it ended, and we joked about the state being poor. *You suck*, we said. *Fix your roads. Yeah, you suck.* Margaret gnawed truck-stop beef jerky with indulgent pleasure, and I teased her with the old saw that hot dogs and the like are made of cow-lips and assholes. It is not, she said. Just to be safe, I'm not kissing you the rest of the day, I teased. Sunflower seeds delivered my oral fix, a bag parked in my lap, the floor littered with shells until my lips were salty and numb. We overtook semitrailers of dumb-faced cattle, their snouts and eyes visible between slats, the tang of manure infiltrating our air-conditioning intake. Bikers on hogs wearing goggles and bandanas thundered by in adjacent lanes, beards flapping, arms up, and Margaret called me a perv for musing on the effects of such powerful, prolonged vibration. We wondered at billboards, strange places like Shoney's – *'Authentic grits, biscuits and gravy!'* – and were chilled by the twenty-foot-high fetuses of pro-life ads, with their reminders about when heartbeats begin.

The conversation swirled on natural winds at a pace not found at home, where a few hours after dinner or moments before work were what you made do with for squeezing in the depth of your disparate experiences. We talked about our friends Megan and Brad, how we figured they would be having a kid soon, were probably trying right now. Not right that second, but probably had been for a few months, judging from intimations they'd made. Would they make good parents? We guessed so – as good as any we knew. Would Brad give up weed? Probably not. We wondered why it always comes as a surprise when someone gets pregnant. People celebrate like it's a miracle, but people are constantly screwing, I said, it shouldn't be a surprise. Margaret said it always marks the beginning of the end of friendships, pregnancy, drawing on girlfriends from her other schools before Wynton who she'd kept in touch with. I couldn't relate to that, I confessed.

'Kids should only come when there's money to feed them and time to care for them,' Margaret said, retracing a well-trod trail. 'Don't you think?'

'Yeah, of course I think so! You know I think so.' Not sure if this was what she was looking for, I said, 'We'll get there. When the time is right.'

Margaret squeezed my hand, which rested on the gear shift. My family was a natural extension to the topic of kids. 'What's the deal with your mom and dad?' she asked, the mental segue seeming to be: And when that time comes, will Mel father the way his father fathered? Mr P.'s mysterious passivity puzzled her too, as well as Mrs P.'s unquestioning complicity. Over the past year, whenever we left their company, she'd try to figure them out. She had no problem lovingly entering my mother's confidences, being warm to her and then, when alone with me, turning on her, intimating dysfunction. No problem charming my dad with her smiles and hugs, then holding him up unfairly against her non-existent example of fatherhood. My answer was always the same: I didn't know. They'd always been like they were.

'But your dad,' Margaret mused now, 'I can't figure him out.' I tensed. The salty seeds gurgled in my belly. She talked about how at first she had thought he was shy and sweet and nerdy. 'But now he seems distant, withdrawn.' I recognized this in a deep, unexplored part of my mind – how his kindness can seem forced, not so much timid as effortful and contrived. 'He used to be hit and miss with his moods, but now he's usually on edge.' Yes, I thought. Yes. 'He always asks about my dancing, but never has anything to say about it.' Yep – his paternal cares had a superficiality about them going back a few years in my memory, to an age when I was old enough to notice it. 'Then I ask him what he's been up to, and it's' – Margaret tucked down her chin and made a vocal foray into Mr P.'s dry bluntness – 'Oh, cleaning the garage, returning a garden hose to the hardware store.' Indeed, his conspicuous omission of meaningful dialogue was nothing new to me. 'What is that? What is that about?' she said – a verbal jab in my direction to either block, duck or return.

Weariness surged. 'Oh, I wish I knew,' I sighed. 'What makes him tick is a mystery to me.' Trying to see through his disguise was a burden on me – perhaps I didn't want to carry it. Perhaps the truth of it would crush me.

'Are we at 44 yet?' I asked. We were coming into Oklahoma City. I knew we had to circumvent downtown, and hook up to this artery. Margaret gladly consulted the map. With that satisfying feeling of predestiny unfurling, I followed the signs and took 44.

Development started to thin, so I figured we should get dinner, but all that materialized were truck stops and golden arches. I cussed at the thought of having to backtrack; but a restaurant arose and we ducked off the next ramp. The sun was still high, and we wasted no time getting into the air-conditioned building. Afterwards, I checked the dipstick, smoked a cigarette under a shade tree, and we were off again. The familial talk, all this tire spinning trying to suss out my father, was forgotten. Margaret read the Grand Canyon brochures to get her excitement up. The intrigue of passing country had faded. She was ready to see the main attraction.

We entered the Texas panhandle under a cloudbank. A fittingly mammoth sign greeted us in the silvered light. 'Welcome to Texas, Drive Friendly – the Texas Way.' Soon it was like dusk, though we were a few weeks short of the solstice and the sunset came around nine. The air pressure dropped. A greenish smell seeped through the vents into the cabin, which I opened my window to inspect. A violent, electric vibrancy. My neck hair stood on end, and my eyes scanned instinctually for danger. But traffic proceeded as normal, save for cars in the eastbound lane approaching with their headlights on. I felt keen, like a coyote. I swear my sight sharpened. Margaret was alert now, too, eyes up from the dimming brochures.

'The Triple-A stuff has a list of weather stations,' I said. 'Get that out, will you?'

When she found and focused, amid the patches of static, the unmistakable tin-can timbre of the weather report, she looked to me with searching pride, like we were partners in a conquest now. The man described – was it a man or a computer? – cold and warm fronts meeting in counties I presumed to be in the vicinity but whose names were meaningless to us out-of-staters. 'Custer County,' I entreated Margaret. 'See if you can find that on the atlas.' I turned on the overhead light for her and told her the last big town I'd seen signs for: Weatherford.

I also turned on our headlights, as a dual King Cab truck with tinted windows barreled past in the fast lane, like a rocket fired to break up the clouds. A clinical diatribe of wind speeds, temperatures and barometric pressures issued from the dashboard speakers. 'Why doesn't he name a city or something helpful?' I sat up straight and maintained a steady distance behind the brake lights in front of me, gleaming a fierce red in the vivified desert air. The steering wheel began to kick around under my grip, the car buffeted by growing gusts. I pointed out to Margaret the writhing of the roadside trees and the occasional upstart sand tornado. We passed a bar – people scurried towards cars holding their hats. The sky was gunmetal gray now and black at the horizon, swallowing up the straight, flat freeway ahead of us. In the rearview, minute by minute, the last sliver of baby-blue sky was swept under the rug of the advancing furor.

'There's no counties on this thing,' Margaret said, her voice tight. A crack about her atlas would have been most unwelcome. She clicked off the radio and watched the darkening road ahead. She was nervous – this was the first time we'd been in a situation like this. I don't know why, but thoughts of her fatherlessness crept up. I felt she trusted me, but perhaps only up to a point. Maybe we were nearing that point. I was in doubt too.

'Mel, maybe –' She swallowed. 'Maybe we should pull over.'

'Well, that semi up there seems to think it's okay. He can see further along from that cab, up high.' What a bunch of bullshit, I thought. It was the kind of thing my father would say. I laughed to myself.

Then a single raindrop hit with a startling *thwap* on the windshield, a grape-sized blob that scattered the dust into rays. Then another and another – and within seconds the wipers couldn't keep up. The tail lights ahead of me flared – braking – and rushed towards us. The driver had panicked. Margaret screeched and braced against the dashboard as I stood on the brakes. Unable to slow in time, I swerved around, assured only by a fleeting look over my shoulder that the fast lane was empty. Our car lurched left, I quickly straightened it under my grasp. In the rearview all I made out was a head of white hair, short stature, and a hulking hood, as of a Lincoln or Cadillac.

'Holy shit!'

'Oh, my God!' Margaret yelled, craning to look back.

My adrenaline spiked – my forearm muscles twitched and ears flexed up in readiness through no effort of my own. The white side line in the lower corner of the windshield guided me. 'You all right?' I asked.

Margaret cussed out the old driver.

'We're fine, we're fine,' I said. Fear had left with a jolt, been scared out. Through the silver-black slurry I could discern that the road was clear before us. Our speed was safe – we weren't hydroplaning. The road was straight. 'It's just water!' I said, loudly, over the chaotic machine-gun pelting. 'Lots of it!'

'We should pull over, I think!'

I was considering this when I saw hazard lights ahead, off to the side. Cars were stopped, probably under a bridge. As I neared, I saw I was right. 'Here we go.' I checked behind me for anyone who would be thrown by my reducing speed, and eased off the gas.

'Yeah, stop here, babe,' Margaret said, doubling over, peering out the edges of the windscreen and making out the scene. She sighed heavily.

The wipers flapped madly at everything, then in a stroke, at nothing.

It was a wide bridge, divided by round pylons, and two other cars sat on the shoulder. Three adults stood by, and a young boy crouched up a ways on the concrete embankment. I parked our Honda well off the roadway, and left it running. We climbed out and up the sloping concrete a few yards, gaining some type of dominion over the vehicle that had held us captive to danger. There we crouched like the boy on the other side of the pylon, the concrete's grade just right for balancing with arms over knees. The invigorating air swirled with warm and cool in every gust, a microcosm of the larger intersecting fronts, winds at the edge of our newfound roof blurring the division between shining pavement and dusty dry. The curtain of rain rippled with waves of density.

Lightning flickered, not crooked branches spiking downward but high flashes behind towering cumulonimbus heads. Seconds later the muted popcorn pops of thunder. The slapping water was a cacophony of individual sounds – a warping soundscape, an aural vortex. I filled my lungs with the ripe air that was seemingly tinged with the sated thirst of sagebrush and long-dusty ground – the vicious, satisfying kindness of nature. The aggression of the storm leveled. We watched a while more.

Clouds galloped over, pulling up cleared sky behind them like a boat's white wake. Eastbound pickups and wagons on the other side of the median roared through, yet to encounter the blinding winds and water. Heads turned as if thinking, Taking shelter for a little shower? The winds were calmer now, the crackling drops sparser.

'Mom, look!' called the boy opposite the abutment. Margaret and I both turned: he had climbed to the height of the slope and stood wedged under the bridge, his hands bracing against its underside. His mother called him down in a southern accent: 'Hon, it's dirty up there. Come on down now.' The boy lingered, flexing his resistance, then shuffled down the slope. His restlessness contagious, I turned to Margaret and said, 'Well, it'd probably be all right to go on now.'

As I was fetching a sweatshirt for Margaret from the back hatch, a man's voice spoke up, bright and directed, 'Ya'll pressin' on?'

'Yeah, pressing on,' I agreed.

He was a sturdy tan southerner in his forties, knotty forearms like tree branches, thumbs actually hooked in the pockets of his too-tight jeans. 'Looks pretty cleared up now,' he said, nodding at the sky. 'Was coming down in buckets for a bit there.'

I handed Margaret the sweatshirt and shut the hatch.

'We couldn't see a thing, I know,' Margaret said, zipping up.

'Cooled down some too,' the man remarked, eyeing Margaret's extra layer.

Southern charm is infectious. 'We almost got in a wreck,' I added, matching his no-hurry delivery. At home I probably would have said we almost crashed. 'Driver in front of us slammed on the brakes when the rain dropped.'

It was impressive, the man agreed. His heavily creased face

scrunched into a form of amenable languor. He was just a curious road soldier making talk with out-of-staters. 'Illinois, huh?' he prompted, with a nod at our plate. He asked where we were headed, and a kind smile formed as he listened to the straight facts of our journey. Maybe there was more to it – his brown eyes did drift down occasionally to Margaret's knock-out legs, on display in shorts. But he seemed all right; his candor and warmth engaged me, and I returned it as best I could.

A little too well, it turned out.

The man was saying what magnificent storms he'd seen in the south. 'Big black thunderheads rolling in. Showers falling in another county. Whole arced rainbows. A storm's a beautiful thing.'

'Oh, I know,' I agreed. 'I just wish I had my camera with me. That's the first thing I thought of.'

And when we finally shoved off, pulling onto the soaked road again, Margaret was icy. She huddled upright in the passenger's seat, shoulders tense, eyes pinched.

'What?'

She couldn't believe I had thought about my camera. About taking pictures.

My fuse shortened in a flash – scorched to a nub by this sudden blast of hers. 'Let's just get this in the open right now,' I said. 'You never said so, but I knew you didn't want me to bring it. I *knew* every time I got it out. I'd feel your glare. So I left it at home. Only brought your mom's piece-of-crap snapshot. I mean, think about that: a photographer not bringing his camera to the Grand Canyon. It's ludicrous. It's criminal. But I left it at home, no questions asked. And did you give me any credit?' Righteous indignation, it was all I had left. The creative will to come up with anything else was tapped. But, believe me, it wore on me as much as it did on her to be so pedestrianly cantankerous. 'Now I can't even say in passing to a *fucking stranger* that it'd be nice to have my camera with me during this epic display?'

'You said it was the first thing you thought of!' Margaret cried. 'Not *What is this gonna do to my vacation with my wife?* Jesus! Not

273

Are we gonna crash into that car? Not even *Are we gonna get sucked up in a tornado?*'

'Obviously, it wasn't literally the first thing I thought of, Margaret. What is it with you? I thought you might be glad I saved both our necks back there. I thought you might be impressed with me for getting us to safety. I thought you might be thankful I put aside my own interests on this trip – to work on us, as you put it.'

'Thankful?!' she shrieked. 'If I have to thank you for paying attention to me, I don't want your attention. I shouldn't have to beg you for it. I mean, how sincere is that? If you loved me, you'd drop everything for me. If you loved me, you'd – you'd –'

'I'd what?'

'You'd do –'

'What? What would I do?'

'Anything! Anything to make me happy.' She was crying now, tears that looked tiny compared to the pellets that had spanked the windshield earlier, compared to the water everywhere around us. 'But you don't! You don't do anything for me.'

'What am I not doing, Margaret? Tell me. You named a place you wanted to go, just named it, and I made it happen. With money I don't have, by the way. So we could be alone, so we could be together. Now here we are, having a good time, not even *there* yet, and because I say one thing, you get to decide the level just goes back to zero. All Mel's effort down the toilet. No points for Mel! Sorry! It's a single-elimination tournament! One slip, and it's all nullified. And it's not even a slip! I don't know what you'd call it. My attention wandered for a millisecond.'

'First of all, I said I wanted to go to Florida! I had to settle for my second choice.'

'Disney World is for fucking children! Okay? *It's. For. Children.*' I stared her down, longer than I should have had my eyes off the road. 'We do not have children.'

She shrank at my forcefulness, my patronizing – these secrets revealed. The deadening glaze of fear, like in a dog cowering, settled on her eyes.

Calmly, I continued, sitting up, watching the road. 'What else?

You said "first of all".' Headlights encroached in my rear view – provoking me like I was provoking her – and I patiently applied the turn signal and moved to the slow lane. 'Hmm? What's the second thing I did wrong? Please, enlighten me.'

But there was no more. There was not another word said. Not for the rest of the way that night, which was another eighty miles to Amarillo. At first I waited for her to recapitulate, and when she didn't speak I considered that she might be constructing something. Like what? A whole catalog of offenses? I looked at her a few times, and smelled the hurt and anger rising off her, steaming up the windows. She looked away to the ditch, the coming of night. Minutes of silence passed, agonizing. After a while, she sat back, head against the headrest, but I couldn't tell if it was a posture of fatigue or contemplation or regret or resolve or just avoidance of setting eyes on me. Maybe she was realizing she made things impossible for me sometimes. Or maybe she was waiting for me to apologize. That seemed likely. But there was no way in hell I was going to do it. I had to set my resolve. But maybe that's what she had done. A sinking weight like a cannonball dropped in my gut, as the idea formed that she might have decided something, her reclining being a sinking into this conclusion. Maybe she'd had enough of me. As in enough – finally, period. But then I was glad, though deeply hurt and terrified of the failure. I couldn't drive like that; it blinded me; like tunnel vision, everything but the center of the road blacked out. I cracked my neck, forced a deep breath into my shallow lungs. I sat back, though I wasn't exactly comfortable. My senses were dulled now and I didn't look at Margaret anymore. I just stared out at the road, lit by our feeble headlights. I retraced everything up to her getting mad at me – and I stayed there, stayed with my derailed sense of justice that a person could be at fault for wanting something that they naturally wanted, and my outrage and self-pity that that person was me.

In my guilt and indignation, my eyelids grew heavy. The weight of my head increased, and I felt my shoulders slump, my chin begging to meet my chest and in resistance not lifting up but turning out to the side as if pensive. A hotness grew around my heart, as if the fluid around it – what was it called? I had learned it once in biology – were in a kettle on the stove. As if my heart were a smoldering ember.

There was no more rain, just endless gray road, straight as an arrow, and the flashing center line. Signs counted down to Amarillo: 78, 67, 59, 42, all the way to 10. At about 30, I noticed Margaret was asleep. I didn't need the itinerary or her atlas. I certainly didn't need her to navigate. I remembered the Texan and his signs of age, the crevices in his face, his weather-beaten neck. He was so restful and at ease. And his wife behind him, like a fact of himself. That's about all I thought about. That and the headlights coming at me, going east.

19 *Katsina*

In the morning, in Amarillo, we said only enough to agree on a place to eat. We'd checked in, showered, watched a little TV and gone to bed, all without speaking. And when we did that, it was with our backs to each other, riding the mattress rails.

Blinding Texas light showed me she'd shaken something off that I hadn't. She ate pancakes heartily, washing them down with chilled milk; my eggs landed on a gurgly belly and, worse, so did the coffee. That added insult to injury: already in a bad mood and now nothing to prod me out of it.

All too soon we were back on the road. There was communication of sorts between us. I checked my maps, confirming that Interstate 40 would take us all the way to Flagstaff, then folded them away in the glove box. Margaret thumbed open her precious atlas, studied it the first few miles away from the motel, then slid it in the doorside cubby, away from me. In that way, we communicated that six hundred miles was all that stood between us and our destination.

We lunched in Albuquerque. I was settling the bill when out the window I saw Margaret striding across the gleaming tarmac. I had a cigarette by the car, watching the door to the gift shop across the road. When she didn't return, I reluctantly crossed. These places were all of a sort. Fake log-cabin walls. Hokey woodsy signage, like grooves burnt into a plank by a Boy Scout, mustard coloring poured in. Tacky T-shirts.

A Native American woman sat on a stool behind the cashier counter. She greeted me, then returned, chin in her palm, to her magazine. I found Margaret looking at a display case labeled 'Hopi Katsina dolls' – gaudy figurines with feathers glued to their arms, headdresses on, crouching, pouncing, dancing, treading somewhere between human and animal. Margaret peered in, transfixed.

She saw me but didn't acknowledge me. There were books on Pueblos, Navajos, Zuni. Chief Geronimo keychains. Mugs with pictures of mesas and cacti. Fridge magnets, posters of cowboy art.

I was torn. I would have liked to buy something to commemorate the journey, but feared I would regret having it around, the way things had soured. Margaret no doubt desired a trinket, but I felt I had to be consistent in my message about spending and therefore couldn't appease her.

Why not just surprise her – I wavered – and offer to get something? And some things for people at home too. I sauntered around, imagining the painted porcelain wares on my mother's shelves, imagined cactus magnets on Janis's hopelessly cluttered refrigerator. Nothing quite fit. I was reading T-shirt slogans on a high display at the back of the store when I collided with a table, jabbing my hip on its corner. It was Plexiglas, with bins set in the sunken top, each filled with chunks of different minerals – pink rose quartz, purple amethyst. I picked them up and studied their crystal ridges, the haphazard angles of their growth. That these had been plucked from the dusty ochre ground seemed miraculous. There were books about them for sale, but I didn't care to know anything more. They were mysterious and beautiful, and a reminder of that potential in the world was what I needed after shelling out twenty-five bucks for a tasteless meal eaten in silence with a woman I couldn't reach.

The malachite's green was vivid and scintillating, especially in a buffed piece in which the lighter and darker shades formed rings like those of a tree trunk. But azurite was my favorite: blue, so densely blue I held a piece to my nose, sure I would smell its essence, like a ripe berry. The blue spoke to me. There were some that had been made into jewelry, but I liked them in stone form, glossy, just existing, not contorted into something vainly functional. I dug to the bottom of the bin until I found my favorite, the perfect size and shape, with an appealing pattern. I put away all the others and held it in my palm, looking as closely as I could. The rings on this piece wrapped over the face of the stone in repeatedly dipping lines, like how a child draws the surface of water. I stared a long time, thinking about this thing coming out of the ground, a pebble in one gift shop in one city in one American state, in one country on one of the seven continents, but here in my palm looking like a world itself.

I looked up and around. I spotted the cashier, chin still in palm. I dropped the azurite in my pocket and went to find Margaret.

'I wanna get one of these,' she said as soon as she saw me. I had taken on a numb neutrality in order to endure the ill feeling that had no hope of being reconciled soon – not, it seemed, until we reached Grand Canyon National Park, and I spread my arms and presented to her the gaping pit of earth like some kind of monument to my devotion. Margaret, however, seemed oblivious to the fact that we were in the midst of a fight with momentous implications. In her carriage, her stance (she stepped lovingly close to me), she was open again.

I said nothing. Inside, part of me was clamoring to rise out of the pit and meet her in the expanse of forgiveness. But it was like the stunted efforts of a dream, like when you dream of sprinting and only lumber at a snail's pace, straining mightily and losing ground to some undeserving competitor. Reconciliation called me, but I was unable to answer.

Just put it on the credit card. You'll pay it off some day far from now. It won't mean anything.

'Okay,' I said.

'Check this out, it's so cool,' she said, and started talking about the dolls in the case. I didn't listen. I thought about her making a point not to say thanks, to treat it like she hadn't been asking. It was a foregone conclusion. Of course I would agree to buy it for her, I had to. Prolonging the fight was my other option. She knew all this and played it cunningly. She'd woken with this steely plan, and gulped down her breakfast without a worry. It was no consequence to her if the misery continued. She was used to being miserable. She expected it, as she expected men to disappoint and hurt her. She made sure they did. The only consequence was to me.

She pointed at the dolls in the case, talking about them. I put my hands in my pockets and rubbed the smooth azurite.

'They represent spirits,' she said – I caught that part.

'Of course,' I said neutrally, wanting to scream it with venom. Of course they do! All Native American stuff represents spirits. Everything they do is about the spiritual. Dream catchers. Folklore with gods and animals. Their respectfully thorough use of the bison's body, whose spirit is sacrificed. Everything you ever learn about Native Americans is spiritual. Margaret moved to the cabinet, and waved me down to her bent-over level. 'Aren't they cool?'

Notecards named each one. There was Supai and Hilili and Mudhead, all colorful and hideous. I expected something more generic: a rain god, a tree god, a mountain god, a river god. Their strange forms offered no hint of meaning. Most had a basically human shape, with legs and a torso, topped by enormous heads like barrels or discs, but sometimes they were animalistic, like the one with a monkey's wild grin and half-circle ears.

'This is the one I want,' Margaret said, pointing to a standing female form.

'Qoqle?' I asked, reading the card, and the phonetic, *kwo-kull*.

'Yeah, Qoqle,' Margaret said, owning it already.

She was wood and cloth, about eight inches tall, and the least figurative, by virtue of her skirt with Native American patterns and mukluk-style leather boots. Her head was a block, with a cylinder like a pencil eraser for a mouth. She had no nose, and two black rectangles painted on for eyes. Gargantuan red ears and hawk's feathers for hair, mussed and spiky, giving her a wild, hip look. While some of the others held drums, weapons and instruments, this doll's hands were triangular wooden fists, painted lines representing the gaps between fingers. They aimed outward, empty, doing nothing.

'Qoqle it is,' I said, fishing out the credit card. 'Let's ring it up.'

Heat. Oppressive heat. Southwestern, landlocked, red-earth heat. All the way to Flagstaff. No Lake Michigan gusts taking the edge off. Cactus and sagebrush and creosote bush from horizon to horizon, simmering under a blue-baked sky. On the road, that black warping of light that makes it look like you're headed straight into a lake – a lake that dries up under your inspection, that creeps off over the hill, waits for your next approach, then scuttles away again.

Buttes and mesas – magnificent and otherworldly at first, then dulled of their wonder by abundance.

The car strained and struggled under the double burden of hills and full-powered air-conditioning. At a service station on the edge of the Cibola National Forest, checking the oil and coolant levels, I felt such pity for the engine, with its dusty hoses and heat-sagging belts, that I searched for a car wash or a water line. I wanted to douse it down and see the satisfying rise of steam, hear the tinkle of stress-relieved steel. But I didn't really know if you could do that to an engine. Probably it would flood some critical part, like the carburetor. And I suffered, too, out in the sun, and all I could do was take the driver's seat again, and press on, leaning on the accelerator, dumping in gas to power the vents aimed at my glistening face and Margaret's golden thighs.

A modicum of civility existed between us on this stretch into Arizona. The satisfaction of arrival lay ahead. The only thing stopping it would be a breakdown. If that should happen, it was important to me that it not come as a surprise. Overheating would be an agonizing setback; I would want to deal with it swiftly and efficiently; I didn't need Margaret's panic and confusion contributing. I didn't need her saying, Did you forget to fill something up, forget to check something? So I explained the mechanics of the internal combustion engine, how it powered the alternator that powered the condenser that cooled the interior, however feebly. (It was probably 85 in the car, an improvement over the 97-degree temps outside.) The duress in this heat was enough to cause a parts failure, I impressed upon her, regardless if all precautions were taken, all fluids filled and monitored properly. I'm no gear-head, obviously, but I knew the basics. Mr P., in his shrewdness, had forcibly given me a tour under the hood and taught me, at sixteen, how to change the oil and filter myself. I had learned the location of the oil pan, how to pop the nut and catch it and the ensuing stream of dirt-black oil, how to grease the gasket on the new filter so it wouldn't dry up and crack. Driving was a privilege, he said; learning maintenance earned it.

My knowledge was just enough to be dangerous, as they say, and I spoke with enough informed authority about it to Margaret that she took on some of my concern as we crept across the flats and over the Arizona border. In this way, though our courtesy and regard for each other kept gathering and dissipating, like the pavement's heat mirage, our interests intersected and formed a wary alertness to the fate of the car. This was no cake-walk for our aging Honda, and I was pleased after my talk that Margaret's posture adopted some rigidity; she no longer read her magazine with abandon, but looked up from time to time with pestered curiosity, holding her hands to the vents to test the coolness of the air. She looked out to the landscape as if to weigh the threat of the summer sun to our safety, to find in its stunning brightness the dangerous ferocity I implied was there. Because of this I felt connected to her, like I had gotten through to her on a level deeper than ever. My respect for her resurged as she appeared to realize there was no guarantee we would reach the Grand Canyon at all.

We passed behemoth RVs weighed down with bikes and towing small sedans. And we were passed by fitter cars, by luggage-laden Taurus wagons or boxy Mercedes sedans, comfortably sealed up, their German-engineered motors unfazed by the conditions. Our engine's whir and roar, though strained, remained constant, and the engine temperature gauge held in its intended zone. At the height of afternoon, we passed a sign: *ARIZONA. THE GRAND CANYON STATE WELCOMES YOU.*

It was after five when we pulled up to the Ramada, just off the I-40 in Flagstaff. Hotels must know what travel does to couples – they always give you two beds when you ask for one. We collapsed, each of us on a double bed. The heat, the wearying rhythm of the road, the nagging insecurity of possible breakdown, and the energy it takes to stay mad at someone – all caught up with us. The cool sheets and shaded room were heaven. I lay there, veins pulsing, body still swaying internally, adjusting to inertia. I opened my eyes a crack to see Margaret's brunette ponytail, her bent arm clutching the Katsina doll. She was cheek-down on the bedspread, facing the bathroom.

I stripped off my socks using the big toe of the opposite foot, burrowed my bare feet in the fresh sheets and sighed with pleasure. I merged onto the highway of sleep.

I woke with my cheek on a sponge, the coverlet, soggy with drool. The room was mottled by darkness, though the curtains were thrown wide. I rolled over in search of a clock. 8.20. I'd been asleep over two hours. Margaret's bed was empty, only ruffled duvet remaining. I rose, dabbing my mouth with a sleeve. I crossed the room and turned on the light, revealing vaguely Native American décor: repeated triangles on the lampshade, like you see on quilts and ponchos. Atop the dresser nearest her bed was Margaret's suitcase, and draped over it were the shorts and shirt she'd been wearing earlier. The air smelled faintly steamy, soapy. She'd showered. But where was she now? I stood and thought a moment, catching sight of my gut, heavy with road food, in the mirror. She usually told me when she went somewhere, even when I was sleeping. Of course, she hadn't done so at the gift shop.

I lifted the lid of her suitcase, standing at a distance from it. I don't know what I thought I'd find. Perhaps if I'd seen something spotted with blood I would have felt better, would have understood her running out – her period had struck while she'd been asleep. But there was nothing untoward in sight, just folded clean clothes topped with toiletries. I shrugged it off and let the lid fall.

Funny that it should bother me even at this point.

In the bathroom mirror, I found sleep grooves on my cheek and, on the counter, a plastic shopping bag. I picked it up – Skippy's Superette. The cloudiness of sleep still hung in my mind. All that occurred to me was what I had dreamt just before waking. Something about having an exhibition, a photography showing, at a big gallery in downtown Chicago. The walls were white and bare, and my pictures were hung on them. There were adults, people in suits, teachers, married couples with silvered hair and nice physiques and elegant gowns. They admired the work with pleasure; they were neither ecstatic or harping; impressed but not fawning. It seemed a realistic depiction. The only problem was, I knew they were not connecting the work with me. They didn't know my name, because it was not on the walls by each work or on a program or sign as it should have been. I never saw myself in the room, and I was powerless to make myself present.

I found another item on the countertop. A tube of Sure brand underarm deodorant. Must have been what Margaret ran out for.

Showered and changed, I made my way out to the lobby, in search of a big coffee. And I meant big. I wanted a quart if they had it, though a couple pints back to back would do. I brought my swimsuit and towel in a backpack in case the urge struck. But being inside the air-conditioned hotel, the need had faded for instant, plunging relief.

From inside the hotel restaurant I spotted Margaret in the pool courtyard. She was dancing, of all things, tangoing cheek to stomach with a young girl in a swimsuit, while the girl's mother looked on with forced patience. The girl's wet head was pressed against Margaret's flat abdomen, and her flip-flops dragged to keep up with Margaret's long strides. Margaret wore black cotton pants and a red spaghetti-strap top. It was evening now, and wobbling light from the pool was tossed up on them. Plastic trees and wrought-iron tables and chairs decorated the seating area. The courtyard was open to the sky, which clung to the merest shade of blue and offered a few dim stars, nearly drowned by the lights of town. Two kids floated around silently in the water and a couple was eating a meal, but mostly the place was deserted. On a table behind Margaret I saw her purse, her Katsina doll, and two drinks with umbrellas in them, one empty. I watched from inside the restaurant, sipping my coffee.

She and the girl, who was about nine, stomped with their chins up, arms extended, back and forth in the noble stride of the tango. Their laughter pecked at the windows. The posture of the girl's mother, standing by in a waist wrap over a one-piece suit, clutching a shoulder bag and shifting her weight between hips, said everything. They had finished swimming and were drying off. The girl, stir-crazy from travel or juiced up on Coca-Cola, had been dancing around idly. Margaret had spoken to her, maybe complemented or corrected her steps. A conversation had ensued. Do you take lessons? What do you like? Oh, good. Neat. Well, guess what – I *teach* dance. The mother, on vacation and relaxed, had not discouraged this interchange with a stranger, though she had probably noticed the empty drink and Margaret's loudness, almost bossiness. Margaret prodded, and they got to talking. Then they did a few steps for fun – maybe it would burn off the girl's restlessness, which the short swim had not done. They'd done some move from a popular routine in a music video, and a few others. But with the tango, it was getting to be a bit much.

I stepped out to the patio and headed towards them. Margaret saw me right away, and bobbed her eyebrows at me flirtatiously. She and the girl tangoed left and right once more while I approached, then stopped and separated. Their giggles subsided.

'Hi!' Margaret said.

'Hello,' I answered.

'Erica, this is my husband, Mel.'

The girl said hello, and I was introduced to her mother, Sybil, too. 'Erica's from Dallas, and she's in Dance Line at school.' I was told how they'd started dancing there just now and given all sorts of background, sloppily arranged by Margaret, who picked up her drink from the table and slurped, stirring the ice with the umbrella.

'We're driving to California to visit Erica's uncle,' Sybil said. 'Aren't we?' She looked down at her daughter, waiting for her to agree.

'Uh-huh,' Erica said, by rote. For her, the spontaneity was over now.

Margaret said thanks, that was fun, and good luck and have a safe trip and nice to meet you, Erica, keep practicing and bye – Bye – Bye. It seemed to last about two and half hours. I drank my coffee and smiled between rich mouthfuls. It was black and strong. The bartender had made a fresh pot for me.

I sat at the table by Margaret's purse and Qoqle.

'She's sweet,' Margaret said, flopping into a chair.

I said nothing and looked at Margaret. She had never been a composed drinker. In high school, we had drunk sometimes with friends at parties. Of course, in high school you drink explicitly to lose your composure, but Margaret had always been the first to act tipsy, slur her words, get squinty-eyed and flit around the room picking up knick-knacks and doing cartwheels. She'd change the music and crank it up so loud the speakers distorted. She'd get sick sometimes, too, and soon learned not to drink so much, eventually not drinking at all except with close friends in small groups. Tonight, there was a recklessness about her. Her clothes seemed to hang crookedly. She sat in her usual pose, heels on the seat, knees under her chin, but only one knee up, the other leg dangling as if dead. She was only half herself.

Her eyes steered away from mine, and she brushed a stray curl off her forehead with imprecision – it fell right back. Sloshing her drink, she asked, 'Doesn't the waiter come out here?' She didn't give me the satisfaction of showing her my response to her performance, and by doing so told me she didn't want it. She would only hear approval now. *That* I could empathize with.

The pool water lapped delicately, responding to the two remark-ably well-behaved children who still bobbed around quietly in the shallow end. Warped light was tossed upwards and onto the plastic palms. If Margaret's needs were waves, I was prepared to ride them. It didn't seem like she intended to speak of her trip to Skippy's, or why she was out here drinking alone. I was glad, though, that she had forgotten about sightseeing in Flagstaff, an idea she had floated in the car during the day. It was a beautiful night – I'd finished my coffee, and a cold beer sounded like just the thing.

I stood up and said I'd go find a waiter, and get some dinner menus. 'What are you drinking?' I asked.

'Cap'n Coke,' she said, smugly.

'With umbrellas?' I asked.

'I asked for 'em,' she said.

I smirked.

She hit bottom – rattling the last dregs with her suction. 'Got a problem with that?' she asked, holding her empties out for me to take.

'Shit, no,' I said, matching her toughness. 'They'll pick those up, though. That's what waiters do.'

I walked away, into the restaurant.

We ordered burgers and salads and drinks, and they came quickly; there weren't many other guests around. Our conversation was cryptic and clipped, though sincere. It felt as if one of us would be boarding a ship at the end of the night and sailing off to another continent. Margaret made remarks about Erica that were intended to be pointed – I just wasn't sure in what way. She kept returning to the girl, her promise, her youth. 'She could be a great dancer,' she mused. 'Oh, I hope she sticks with it.' There were long silences in which we didn't share the satisfaction of eating – didn't ask each other how the food was, didn't signal via pleasurable moans, didn't lock wide, indulgent eyes. I ate slowly and purposefully, without trying to detect her thoughts. After a while, she'd return to Erica. 'Did you notice her legs? Probably not. They're very long. But strong too. She should do ballet.'

After the plates were taken away, I remarked, 'Kind of hot for pants,' eyeing her covered legs.

'So don't wear them,' was her advice.

Without asking, she tasted my beer – then took another approving sip and said, 'I want one of those.' When the waiter didn't come, I went in to order at the bar. The guy who'd helped me before was nowhere to be found – just the CNN anchor reading down to empty stools. I took the opportunity to fetch my cigarettes.

In the room, seeing the bedside clock, I remembered the time difference to Chicago and the pestering memory that I still hadn't called Mr and Mrs Podgorski, as I had said I would. It was nearly midnight at home. Mrs P. would be asleep, but Mr P. was a night owl, often doing giant crossword puzzles until the wee hours, racking his brain and our dated World Book encyclopedia over obscure clues. I decided to get the call over with. I'd probably continue to put it off otherwise.

I got Mr P. Indeed, he was up on his own, the satisfying loneliness of the living room enveloping his voice.

'Everything's great,' I told him. 'No problems with the car. We're on schedule. We'll get there tomorrow. Margaret's fine. I'm fine. Nothing to report.'

'Well, have fun,' he said. 'Let us know when you're on the way back.'

When I got back Margaret was fixated on Qoqle, whose feathers she brushed against her forearm. 'Isn't she pretty?' she said, receiving a beer from me. She was so cool. Where would she keep it at home? She wanted to give it a new name – what should she name it? But she gave me no time to answer. In fact, it was as if she didn't want me to. 'What took you so long?' she said, remembering to ask this.

'I called home,' I said.

'Oh, home,' she said. 'Your mother.' She laughed, without completing the thought.

'What about her?'

'No, no. "If you don't have anything nice to say, don't say anything at all."'

I didn't get vindictive; she didn't have to like my folks. Besides, she was drunk, and it wasn't a question of liking or not liking. I asked, 'Are you gonna call *your* mom?'

'Ha!' she snorted. 'What the hell for?' She had taken a drag of my cigarette earlier and lit one for herself now. I filled my mouth with fizzy ale. 'I doubt she remembers I'm gone,' she said.

'Oh, that's not true.'

'Isn't it?' The scales had been tipped. She began talking about Janis, telling stories I'd never heard. How she didn't want kids in the first place, or so Margaret believed. How she'd ignored Margaret and her sister when they were young – working, coming home, getting ready for dates. The two of them were always left alone in the house, which they rented from a sleazy man, Mr Kimball, who came around at weird times and stayed too long, talking to them, when Janis was away. How their mother never believed them when they said Mr Kimball had been over, leaning in the doorway, asking questions about their boyfriends while they tried to watch TV. How she never brought it up with him, never told him not to come around or come in the house when the girls were home alone. 'She loved men's attention, any man. She probably figured we would too.' Margaret was reflective and petulant now. She smoked unconvincingly, taking small puffs and blowing them out of her mouth as soon as they arrived. But her feelings were real; I saw eyes grow glassy as she stared at the tiki torches the staff had lit. 'The selfish bitch,' she said into the distance. 'God, I hated living in that house.'

Had something happened with Mr Kimball, I wondered?

'Then there's my dad,' Margaret went on. The tears came and her voice seized up, squeaking like the pinched mouth of a balloon. She reiterated all I'd ever been told – that he'd stuck it out for the first four years. 'Then, gone.' Her shoulders shuddered, and her chin dipped to her chest. Her hand forgot about the beer glass and let it tip, spilling beer onto herself. I rose and went to her, snatched the glass and rubbed her leg.

'Hey, hey . . .' I said in my softest voice.

Snotty rasps staggered from her throat. Her torso heaved. Her heel slipped off the seat, as her body lost the critical tension of its being. The effortless tautness and natural uprightness of her frame – the assertive opening statement in the presentation of her self – went limp.

Her words came out muffled. 'He . . . didn't . . . even . . . live . . .' she sobbed, face down over her lap.

'Shhh, shhh,' I implored, looking around. The deck had been empty for a while, save one rent-a-cop ambling through a half-hour ago. I pulled my chair near hers and rubbed her shoulders. I tried to lift her chin with my finger, but she wouldn't allow it.

She lowered her voice. 'He lived . . . in Gary . . . twenty . . . minutes . . . away.'

'I know, I know.'

'Asshole . . . never came . . . to one . . . recital.'

I thought pushing her hanging hair aside would clear an avenue for her to look up to me. She kept her face buried in her palms. 'One fucking . . . recital.'

She was inconsolable. She sat up and showed her face, only to reach for the beer. She was slow with drunkenness and I grabbed it away. 'You don't need any more of that,' I said. Then her sobs stuttered up again and her weight flopped forward.

'Hey, listen,' I offered quietly in her ear, 'You got screwed on the father deal. I'm sorry. I'm really sorry. He was a real shit. But it's not your fault. There's nothing you could have done.'

'I was . . . a good . . . kid,' she said.

'I know you were. '

'He would have . . . liked me.'

'He would have *loved you*,' I whispered intensely. 'But he obviously wasn't capable.'

This went on for some time. Why do people have kids when they're not gonna take care of them? she wanted to know. Pointing out that this was an age-old question didn't seem like a helpful reply. I just wanted to get her outflow of pain to stop. I suggested we go back to the room, get her sober. Maybe a shower.

'No,' she demanded.

She talked and wept, and held her vulnerable body at a distance from me. All I could do was put a hand on her. And, eventually, I didn't do that; I sat back and smoked a cigarette. She talked about feeling empty, like nobody cared about her, no matter what. Even though her mother said she did and I said I did. It was getting late, the patio would close eventually. 'Come on, let's get you to bed,' I pleaded. 'We can't stay out here all night.'

She looked at me, no hands over her face, in all its red, swollen-eyed glory. It'd come to look pretty familiar. The corners of her mouth seemed turned irretrievably down. I smiled at her weakly, not asking too much. 'Don't make me carry you,' I said. I would carry her if I had to, but hoped the amusing image would cheer her.

She stared back, flickering with blankness like the surface of the pool. After a moment, she stood up, leaned over the table and lunged, as if underwater, at the glass of beer I'd moved out of her reach. I didn't react, but let her do what she wanted. She leaned too heavily on the table, which was round, and nearly tipped it, then over-compensated and fell back in her chair. She had kept the glass upright and not spilled, and she made the slightest recognition of this to me by cocking her eyes as if to say, 'See?' Then she looked closely at the glass and brought it to her mouth, gradually tipping it until the amber liquid sloshed forward. But her motor skills were not up to speed and, by the time the beer reached Margaret's open mouth, she needed a breath – and so breathed, and breathed in beer. A cough erupted into the glass, and she blurted forward, letting spillage out of her mouth. She set the glass quickly in the direction of the tabletop, but missed – it hit the concrete and shattered with a piercing *kccheee!* Margaret then drew breath – or tried to draw breath – and instantly alarm bulged in her eyes and she sprang from her chair. I lunged at her from behind and slung my arms around her waist and pulled, and she lurched and I heard a vocal projection bearing the stamp of her voice and a splatter on the concrete. Then she was breathing again – at first one desperate intake, then small breaths between wet coughs. Panic-alerted adrenaline must have sliced through her, because she seemed considerably more sober when she turned and faced me, speechless, still coughing, but controllably, purposefully, to clear the way for air.

'Y'allright?' I asked, and she nodded as she coughed.

In a few minutes she was recovered, and was about to speak when she hesitated, then dashed to the potted palm and threw up into it. I held her hair back, and did what I could until I got more nods in response to my questioning, 'Okay?' After copious spitting and groaning, she sat back on her heels, looked up and smiled about one percent of a smile.

I left a big tip on the table, and did honestly look for someone to apologize to, but there was no one around. For once I was glad to be in a third-rate hotel. The walk to the room was slow, with Margaret on my arm, unsteady, growing queasy when we took it too fast. We went each to our own bed again, because we could and because it seemed right. I undressed, tossed my clothes by my suitcase and slid under covers. Margaret flopped atop her bed, face up, spread-eagle. After a few minutes, she got up and threw up some more, in the toilet. There was flushing, then silence.

'Margaret?' I called.

A groan.

'You okay?'

She cleared her throat. 'Yeah,' off porcelain, echoed back.

Soon there was water running, brief tooth-brushing. She flopped again, still dressed in her cotton pants and tank top, and I turned off the light.

20   *The End of the Road*

I was standing in the shade of a Joshua tree across the lot from our room, smoking a cigarette, when Margaret finally emerged. She was dressed in pants again, as she had been the night before, and a Culkin Dance T-shirt. She carried her purse, the Skippy's bag, and can of root beer I had retrieved for her earlier that morning. She had said she couldn't be seen without make-up, even to venture down the hall for her breakfast soda. Indeed, she had looked rough, like a Mack truck ran her over, backed up, and ran her over again. Now her wet hair was tucked behind her ears, and her whole body tensed, scrunched up as if in resistance against its own diabolical aching. Her movements were ginger. Stepping into the sun, she flinched as if struck.

It was hot. Not even nine a.m. yet, and pushing 85 degrees. The sky seemed to reflect infinitely, making the piercing sun omni-directional. I had the car idling and AC blasting.

I was surprisingly alert and feeling strong. Prolonged, distressful dreams had made waking a pleasure. The calories of last night's alcohol and the lightness of dehydration had me feeling un-commonly peppy, energized. It made me wonder why I didn't drink more often. The answer shuffled across the lot towards me. 'Here, I'll take that,' I said, opening the back hatch.

'I got it,' Margaret muttered, stepping past me and leaning into the vehicle secretively. She wedged the bag between the cooler – we hadn't replenished it since Topeka – and the emergency road kit Mr P. had assembled. Everything I'd need for the day was packed already; I slammed the hatch. Margaret squinted up at me and drank from her soda.

'How you feeling?' I asked. Twice already that morning I'd asked this, and twice she'd insisted she was well. Her head must have been pounding. Or maybe, since she'd ejected her stomach's contents, she felt all right. After all, she had been the one to wake me, saying time to get ready. She had given me about thirty seconds, then flipped on the clattering *Today Show*, cranked up the shower and asked me, from the bathroom doorway, a towel around her waist, to go on a soda run for her.

'Fine,' she said now, eyes creased, blocking out the stinging sunlight. She'd put on so much beige foundation, to put color in her face, that it crumbled off her, like a thickness of dust. She wore lipstick too – a crass, glinting maroon. 'You know where we're going?'

I shook my head half a turn in disbelief at her doggedness. She hadn't complained at all – not so much as a moan, a yawn, or any hint that she needed sleep or aspirin. 'Pretty much,' I said. 'There's a county highway – takes us right up to the South Rim Entrance Station. One-eighty. Or One-eighty-one. Just have to double check that number. I'm sure there'll be signs.'

'Well, let's figure it out,' she answered, and tipped her root beer high, draining it.

I asked if she needed some breakfast. 'I couldn't eat anything right now,' she said, oddly upbeat about such an occurrence.

'How about some water on the way out of town?'

'I'm good.'

I paused, and watched her a minute. If I had waged a staring contest just then, she would have won. I could read nothing on her. Whether she recalled her outpouring of grief and was embarrassed by it or unburdened of the sadness; whether she half-recalled an incident and not the particular trauma; whether she was preoccupied now with an urge for motion, a craving for external stimuli to supplant memory; whether she clung to the happy minutes of tangoing with Erica, whom she had identified with so deeply, as the capstone of the evening – I was clueless. Clueless Mel rides again.

'You know, we don't have to go right now. It's July – the days are long. If we reached the canyon in the afternoon, there'd be lots of time to see it.'

'Mel, no way. I didn't come this far to see Flagstaff.'

'I'm not talking about seeing Flagstaff. Come on, you must be wrecked. We could sleep a few more hours. Take a refreshing swim, have a nice breakfast.'

'I'm fine, Mel! I'm ready. I got up before *you* did.' She winced – at her own volume, it seemed – and took a deep breath. Looking away, she seemed to focus on something within, surely trying to steady the uncentered nausea of a hangover.

'How about this? I saw a brochure in the lobby. There's a bus tour that goes to the South Rim. First run is at eleven. We could take that. It'd be cool. We'd just have to sit there.'

'Let's go now. Why would I want to wait two hours?'

'Maybe I'm sick of driving,' I snapped.

'Too bad. We have an itinerary. We have our car. We're not paying to ride with a bunch of old fogies, getting on and off whenever they say. I want to see House Rock. I want to see the crater thing. And Point Sublime.'

She was ahead of me on these secondary sights. Given the magnitude of the canyon, I hadn't considered other attractions. First things first, that's my method. Mine was a singular focus. Margaret now inserting these other destinations into our plans – like releasing fresh hares ahead of tired hounds – so enraged me that I couldn't even fathom it. *The one day we should be easing our pursuit, being charitable to ourselves in terms of pace, and she wants to ratchet it up, make the whole day even more pressured, up the odds of unraveling, exhausted, car-sick and broke, around sundown.* I was getting awfully close to delivering her the canyon, to not letting her down, and it seemed to threaten her.

Sweat beaded on her upper lip.

'What about your outfit? You're going to roast out there. Why don't you wear some shorts, for Christ's sake?'

'I'll wear what I want to wear, thank you. Don't worry about it.' She strode around me to the passenger side and poised her hand over the door handle, leering sarcastically.

'It's open,' I said, getting into the all-too-familiar driver's seat.

We nosed out of the lot and made a continuous arc into the neighboring gas station. I filled up, and got Margaret a bottled water, though she hadn't asked for it. In town, I got a cash advance on a credit card, because the National Park Service didn't take plastic, and a Burback's – twenty ounces of succulent, fortifying French Roast, hotter than even the Arizona air – because one cannot appreciate epic sights on a diminutive buzz.

Outside Flagstaff, men in polo shirts and visors gathered on glassy greens in the unified patience of putting order. Leaning on clubs or tending the flag pin, they seemed like less adapted versions of the cacti around them – similarly armed figures who would not last a day in this sun. Massive gated communities of Spanish Mission estates sprawled past under a fortune's worth of red clay roof tiles. Other homogenous spreads – beige brick, ostentatious pillars and three-car garages – were piled over the land, inciting a confusion of envy and despair in me. I was glad when the housing ended, replaced by bromegrass and prickly desert shrubs, some crowned in spikes like the Statue of Liberty.

We had sixty miles to cover before we'd reach the entrance station – exactly an hour's drive. Margaret read about Sunset Crater National Monument and peppered me with its geological statistics, operating hours of the site, and so on.

'We have to stop there after the Grand Canyon,' she said.

'Is there really going to be time? I know it seems like we have all day, but the canyon is huge, we'll want to get some lunch, I'm sure there'll be gift shops . . .'

'Hey!' Margaret blurted, distractedly. 'Have you seen my Katsina doll?'

'Sure, I just saw it.' It seemed like I had; its image was fresh in my memory.

'Where? I haven't seen her this morning.'

'You've had it with you ever since you got it.'

'Is she in the car? Did you see her in the car this morning?' She put down the booklet and began twisting around, clawing between the seats and peering in back.

'I don't think so. In fact, I straightened up the car while I waited for you, and I never saw it.'

'Shit! Mel!'

'I can picture you holding it – it's around somewhere.'

'Last night! What if I left her outside, by the pool?'

'You think you did?'

'I must have. We have to go back!'

I looked at her, keeping my foot pressed to the pedal, gauging her seriousness.

'Turn around. Come on, let's go back.'

I said it would be fine, someone would hand it in to the lost and found.

'What if a maid picks her up and decides to keep her? Or a kid. Some little girl'd love to have her.'

'Maids can't do that, they'll get fired. And what does a kid want with an ug– I mean, her parents would wonder where it came from. They'd know she found it.'

Margaret asserted that she didn't care, she'd paid good money for that doll, and she was one of a kind. She wanted me to reverse course at the next side street. I refused. 'It'll be in the lost and found. Don't worry. Or in the room somewhere, like under the bed.'

She wasn't satisfied until I agreed to her ultimatum. 'If it's gone, you have to buy me the expensive one that I really wanted.'

'We didn't get the expensive one?!'

'No, remember the tall one with the drum?'

'So if I'm wrong, I have to get you that one? Because you lose a hundred-and-fifty-dollar doll I have to buy you a new one?'

'Well! You won't turn around! She could be sitting there right now, just waiting to be taken.'

'We don't know that.'

'But if we go back, we'll know.'

'Well, I'm not turning around. You wanted to go bright and early, I'm not doubling back now.' What I would have given to see, beyond her profile, instead of a blur of cacti and rusty sand, Hargrove's strip malls, Lake Shore Drive, even Meadow Prairie Lane's oak canopy. 'I'm sure dear Qoqle is in a cardboard box behind the reception desk. Someone noticed it and turned it in.'

That appeased her, except for the occasional mutterings issued towards the side of the road: 'Knew I should have kept her in the room.' 'Better be there.'

With twenty miles to go, she took out her purse and checked her face in a compact, then returned to the guides. She flipped through the section on greater Arizona, beyond the canyon. Window Rock. The famous corner in Winslow where you could stand, just like in the song.

We didn't have far to go, but when a rest stop turned up, I took advantage. The twenty ounces of French Roast felt more like a hundred and twenty now that it was all competing for bladder space. An Arizona Highway Patrol car was staked at the top of the ramp. I slowed dramatically, taking the speed bumps at a crawl. A mustachioed officer nodded at me, and I grinned back. His head turned, following our slow-motion passing. The heat was climbing, and I left the car and the AC running. Margaret and I marched side by side up the pavement to the building, splitting just inside the entrance to opposite doors, men's and women's. Back in the foyer, I studied the posted map of the state, with its 'You Are Here' arrow and network of colored roadways like jumbles of nerves. Ten minutes passed before Margaret appeared. I pointed to our location, on the assumption it would widen her understanding of the distance separating the sites she so whimsically took interest in. She made a meaningless gesture of acknowledgment and walked away. I recognized this: starting now, she was withholding her affection. Qoqle would decide my fate now. Qoqle was part of a fable never imagined by tribal elders.

Margaret got back in the saddle behind the windshield with its double arch of dust and bug splatters beyond the wipers' jurisdiction. I stretched and surveyed. The roar of rubber on road, dopplaring. Industrial cleaner and fetid chewing gum on the air. An RV hulked at the end of the scorching blacktop; under nearby shade, a slope-backed couple leading a leashed Pomeranian about, its white coat parted by the wind. Plenteous signage communicated, via the symbology of the Stick Man and his universe of civic comforts, the park's dictates. Picnic tables over there. Emergency phone, restrooms, beverages that way. Litter disallowed. Bold text accented the last: 'NO LITTERING – $500 FINE.' My scan of the compound ended at the patrol car, hunkered still at the entrance, decked in sirens, antennae and lights. I could make out the officer's stern jaw from the distance. Over his territory he presided, alert to a catalog of offenses, many of them unrecognizable to the civilian eye. I imagined his nightmares: punks screeching in after dark, parking over handicapped spots, pissing in the grass and dumping trash. Unleashed Great Danes dropping gargantuan shits on the State of Arizona's sun-seared grass. I retrieved my empty Burback's cup from the car, where Margaret wordlessly waited, and toted it to a trash can. Garbage was heaped to the brim, and I wedged mine in securely so it wouldn't get blown out. The trooper and I – the tassels on the brim of his hat visible, through his tinted windows – exchanged another nod, as if in recognition that the monetary deterrent was working.

Though the mechanics of the combustion engine probably do not bear this out, I believe something happened under the hood of the Honda during our pit stop. Something malfunctioned. Something failed. Something gave up the ghost. What that something was I don't know. I didn't know then, because I did not have the car much longer. And probably will never know, because it is something that, for my sanity, must remain unanswered. Yet for a long period, a period of inertia and doubt, a period of much shiftless coffee drinking, I speculated and wondered.

When we resumed highway speed, the air conditioning seemed feckless. It became hot in the car, and I became irascible. My back sweated until my T-shirt was soaked against the cloth seat. I became dry-mouthed, and the previous evening's alcohol caught up with me. A headache surfaced, niggling at first, then piercing. The vents fired their fullest but were impaired. The engine temperature gauge told me nothing, hovering where it'd been the entire trip, well shy of the dangerous red zone. Probably it was just the midday heat. Yet the sun was above in the east, and we were driving north – I remembered this later – so Margaret bore the brunt of its rays, not I. So I don't know how to account for my suffering. Arizona in late July – there was nothing I could have done.

We neared the National Park. I turned to Margaret and asked her to hand me my wallet from the glove box. I wanted to have the cash nearby when we approached the booth to buy a pass. I felt if I had pulled up and suffered any delay or disorganization in producing the price of the tickets, any hitch in the execution of bringing us through the gate and into our destination, I might erupt with furious impatience. I was pleased to have gotten the cash advanced in Flagstaff.

That's when I noticed Margaret's legs. She had changed into shorts at the rest stop. She must have pulled out a pair from her bag in the back seat at some point – either when looking for her Katsina doll or perhaps when I had been preoccupied by the sight of the trooper and his cruiser. I thought about it many times later. I hadn't noticed. If I had, I might have said something. Might have stopped sooner. But I noticed now: Band-Aids peeked out from under the hems of her baby-blue shorts, midway down each thigh, like flat worms wriggling out of a bait can. The gauze pads of two of them – oddly symmetrical, one on each leg – were speckled red. As if I wasn't hot enough already, my chest ballooned with a searing pressure. Fatigue tunneled outward into my extremities, like an explosion down an alley in a movie. My first thought was to ask, 'What happened?' But the words didn't emerge. Nothing did. Margaret saw me looking at her legs; in my peripheral vision, I could see her watching me, awaiting my response.

When I faced her, she was holding out the wallet – I didn't even recognize it as the object it was. Meeting her eyes only a moment, I took it, put it in the center console, and turned my attention back to the road. There I steered the car and waited until I knew what I had seen in my wife's eyes, because it was different than last time. Two or three miles passed. The road quit being road; its form bent, in my vision, and also in meaning. It changed from a linear man-made slab into a rubbery slide, curving away over the arching earth leading you on to nothing, then more nothing, only more of itself. It required my sitting up and forward, peeling my sweat-soaked T-shirt from my back, to shake off this daze and focus on what to say.

I knew the complicated answer, but the simple question came out anyway. 'What happened?'

And then we fought. The particulars of what was said are gone now; I left them where they were uttered – and not many *were* uttered – on Arizona Highway 180. She had done it in the bathroom of the hotel the day before, while I'd been napping. What she had bought at Skippy's was bandages. The deodorant was to throw me off the scent, no pun intended. She had showered and was shaving her legs when the temptation overcame her, she said. She couldn't help it. After our fighting, she had felt so bad, and cutting promised reprieve. She couldn't help it, she said more than once. She knew how to crack the housing of the disposable razor and remove the blade. Once she began thinking of it, the draw was irresistible. The idea did occur to me though – again after the fact, when I had the time and opportunity – that the thought of cutting herself must have been tickling at her as she had gone to shower, knowing she could lock the door, knowing I was dead to the world, knowing whimpers or cries would go unheard – if these she made – drowned under the shower's noise.

Then there was the confused point of her pants, how I'd questioned her choice the night before and again that morning. I knew what she'd done, I said. It was obvious. That's why I'd commented on the pants. Why else would she wear pants in such heat? Did I ever notice what she wore at other times? No, but only because it didn't matter to me – she always looked great and fashions couldn't be less important. That was just it, she wailed. Nothing she did mattered to me. Why, if I knew what she'd done, if I knew she was in so much pain inside that she'd cut herself on the outside, why didn't I say something? Why didn't I care and want to help her? That only made it hurt worse, to see me just ignoring it, even teasing her with comments about wearing pants. She was hysterical. I wouldn't help her. I didn't care. Why didn't I do something?

My frustration reached its greatest heights when what got me in trouble, what angered or hurt or confused or upset my wife, was a choice made precisely so as *not* to worsen a situation. Somehow my most careful instincts led most precisely to Margaret's injury. Because, I screamed, she'd broken down bawling, drunk. Glasses had been shattered. She'd nearly choked and puked, she'd wept abjectly, all about her father and mother. All these deep pains she'd never let out before finally, mercifully, were being brought into the open. Speaking of the illicit, morbid side-effect of her repression was the last thing I would have dreamt right. The topic of how she'd been dealing with this had been taboo, judging from how much she discussed it. Now that she was giving voice to the cause, the last thing I thought to do was to remind her that she hadn't coped well to date. Though I knew nothing wouldn't be immediately resolved, I figured the memories of whatever neglect and misuse she had endured at her parents' hands might be blown away by the force of the release, the yen to cut purged.

What Margaret said to all this I don't recall. Only that it did not console her. All she saw was neglect and obliviousness to what she considered obvious cries for help. She had believed that I just didn't care or was incapable of empathy or too self-centered to attend to her problems during my vacation and, having settled on that, my version of things changed nothing. What I would come to comprehend later – many cups of coffee and many miles across the Atlantic later – was that I had been hurt too. Perhaps this would have fulfilled Margaret: that her turning away from me, to the secrecy of the bathroom and to the lonely deadening relief of self-harming left me raging within myself around a core of inadequacy. Every cut on herself was in a way a cut on me.

But perhaps that would not have consoled either, only fanned the flames. We were mired in misunderstanding. Angry, I demanded she cover herself back up. Why? She wanted reasons. There were several. General decorum. For our own sake – putting it out of sight so we could enjoy the Grand Canyon. She had a rebuttal for each. Okay, I confessed, loudly, bluntly, I was embarrassed by them.

'Do you think,' I asked, 'I want people looking at me, looking at you, and wondering, "Oh, what happened there? What's wrong with her?"'

But she didn't care what I wanted, and understandably so. Seeing my hypocrisy, she seized on it with a relentless attack, reminding me how I had prodded her the night before, then nearly insisted that morning that she *not* wear pants. 'Why do you always have to disagree with me? Do you want me to be unhappy?'

'Of course not. But we can't go parading your cuts around the canyon for the world to see.'

'It's hotter than hell out. I'm roasting.'

'What will people think, Margaret? You don't accidentally cut yourself several times on each leg like that.' How I managed to keep the car on the road throughout these miles is a mystery. My consternation grew; the heat grew; the air conditioning faltered. It's unclear to me how much of what burbled in me reached the surface. The possibility of lining up along a railing at one of the scenic overlooks we'd seen in the brochures, of having some child at eye-level with Margaret's bandages, seemed real. The child would catch sight, cling to his father's leg in revulsion, ask an innocuous but attention-drawing question. What happened to that girl, Daddy? Now a well-meaning bystander is drawn into our drama. He sees it too – a series of cuts, their placement grouped as if calculated. He shushes his boy, puts himself between him and the girl. Look at the canyon, he instructs, eyeing Margaret – eyeing me.

I gave voice to some level of this fear, I recall. 'People will wonder, Margaret,' I said.

'What do you mean?'

'I mean they'll wonder, "What's with him?"'

'Oh, my God, you're not serious.'

'Well – I mean, you're walking around puffy-eyed, cut up. What are they going to think?' This only scratched the surface and was not getting at my deeper meaning. They would think it was a shame. A shame to see all Margaret's evident beauty from ten paces negated by the crying eyes and glaring dysfunction announced by the bandages. They'd heard about people like her, they'd think. Heard about this curious tendency, grouped in there with bulimia and anorexia. Perhaps they'd know more about it than me. If they didn't, they'd guess, fling the dart of their judgment at the board. He gambled and lost. He married the arm candy and it turned out to be sour inside. Or maybe he's abusive – who knew what drove people to self-mutilation? Maybe somehow he's the victim, her cutting a manipulative tool. Whatever the case, they're sick.

These fears drove me. However unbalanced they were doesn't matter now. Or, rather, it does matter and continued to matter, but for a long time nothing I did was able to bring about a change. Margaret was livid, seeing my concern as a continuation of a pattern of self-centeredness.

Once I struck on the idea of the photographs, I stuck with that. 'Forget about what I think then. What are we going to do, bring home vacation photos with your sliced-up legs showing? Your mother will recognize what's going on.'

This shook her a little; she stabilized by reiterating that my flip-flopping – egging her when she had worn pants, now egging her back when she didn't – was inconsistent and cruel. But we could just not take pictures, she offered.

'Oh, that's normal,' I said, getting sarcastic. 'Aspiring photographer goes on vacation, leaves 35-millimeter at home, then opts not to shoot even snaps. You're putting something back on to cover those,' I demanded. 'So you better get used to it. I don't care if it's pants or a skirt or what.'

To my surprise, she seemed to respond to this forcefulness. 'They're half covered by these shorts anyway,' she said, mildly.

'Not enough. Where are the pants you took off? Reach back there and get them.'

'I put them back in my suitcase.'

'How did you do that?'

'I went in through the hatch at the rest stop.'

'When? I didn't see you.'

'You were throwing something out or something.'

'Well, crawl back there and get them.'

'I can't – my suitcase is under yours. I put everything back the way it was so you wouldn't notice.'

'Shit,' I said. Amazingly, we had been making good time and were not far from the park. Signs for upcoming campgrounds, gift shops, family restaurants, were more frequent. I didn't want to stop – I recalled how the car seemed to get agitated idling in the heat last time – but I wanted this settled. For the next mile, I looked for a convenient turn-off, a gas station, anything. When nothing appeared, I became impatient and pulled onto the shoulder, startling us both by grinding over the ruts they scrape into the tar to awaken night-time drivers – *brrrap, brrrap*.

Bewildered – I suppose by my boldness – yet deferent, Margaret collected one sandal from the floor and stepped into it. The other was not in sight. She moved languidly, fiddling with the sandal's buckle straps.

'I'll get it,' I said, checking my side mirror hastily and bursting out. I left the engine running, the transmission in neutral. The heat outdoors made it apparent that the air conditioning was working after all. The asphalt throbbed. Wind gusted, dry but close and suffocating, thick with the breath of foreign flora and fauna – iguana and cacti, prairie dog and anteater, or so I imagined. If there was in it a western ruggedness, it was probably just dust, grating in the nostrils like hardship.

'What do they look like?' I asked Margaret through the hatch into the cabin.

'Get me the white ones. They're rolled up. Under a pair of jeans, I think.' She was genial now, evidently owing to my efforts on her behalf. They say in love it's the little things – maybe they were right after all.

Unzipping Margaret's suitcase – the larger of the two and therefore on the bottom – was manageable, but the pyramid of luggage atop it, though orderly, made access difficult. My forearms were in, but I groped blind, bearing the weight with my elbows and leaning awkwardly. A wide stance gave me leverage, but exhaust sputtered hotly on my shin. I was about to disengage, hoping somehow I might suddenly feel a balled whiteness in my hands, when noise from behind startled me.

Brrrrap, brrrap.

I stood quick, scraping my wrists on zippered edges and thumping my head on the hatch.

The jaw line like symmetrical angular L's. The stiff brim of the hat, the gold tassels. The wind blew my utterance of 'Holy shit' straight into the car.

'What?' Margaret said, turning around.

The cruiser was stopped, its grinning grill and wide-eyed lights, its side-mounted spotlight ears and flattop of siren-colored hair belying its driver's sternness. Trooper Reynolds – he'd prove to be a tender, considerate man in my dealings with him, the affidavit, the subsequent investgation – lumbered out and rose, his haunches sturdy as a horse's. He approached, the batons, cuffs, and gun strapped to him swinging like toy boats on the waves of his stride. I could cling to his shoulders from behind, he could wear me like a cape – and probably fly too. I preened to my full height, put on my most civic-minded countenance, feeling every bit the pudgy, un-sophisticated tourist I was. Probably well aware of his intimidating stature, Officer Reynolds opened with a disarming question that nevertheless encompassed his duty.

'Have to pee again?'

'Pee?' I was relieved at the kindness in his voice, but confused.

'You just went not fifteen miles back. Must be all those tall lattes.' The rugged approbation conferred by his badge and radio met me at eye level. His eyes were brown and intent, his face crisp like a stretched tarp. His thin lips disappeared when he smiled.

'Oh, that,' I answered, laughing. 'That was you in the – by the – you saw . . .'

'Yup, that was me.' His smile dropped. He turned duteous. 'Public urination's an offense.'

'I wasn't, uh . . .' In the officer/driver two-man play, I had been cast as the bumbling buffoon, the nervous offender covering up.

'Okay, what's the stop for then?' The wind swirled, and I held my hair off my forehead, though it hadn't been in my eyes – a self-conscious attempt at tidiness under his order-inciting watch. Before I could answer, I saw him complete his appraisal of me – me as an element of the traffic situation. He moved onto the other concerned party, peering through the hatch at Margaret, who sat sideways, clutching the headrest to keep her body twisted, listening. 'Ma'am,' Reynolds acknowledged with an upraised hand.

'Hello,' Margaret quavered.

My bumbling ineptitude continued. 'Actually, we just needed something out of the back.'

'Couldn't wait? What is it, drugs?' I could not read this softball suggestion. Perhaps he'd saved a lot of time that way, catching the unsuspecting off-guard in a comradely confession.

I held my tongue from repeating 'Drugs?' with a snort. 'No, sir,' I answered. This seemed to satisfy him. What were the legalities of car searches? my mind flashed. The hatch was open – could he just begin one? Did he have to ask? Was it within my rights to refuse? You live in a country and don't even know its laws. Did it differ from Illinois here in this char-broiled Arizona? But I wouldn't need answers to these questions. Reynolds would be the one needing answers from me. What had I seen? A make of the vehicle, a color, the driver, the license plate, anything? Now he didn't even ask what I most feared him asking: what we needed out of the trunk.

'Everything else all right?'

'Yes, fine,' I said. 'Let me just shut off the engine.' He nodded okay, and his hand moved, open, over his gun as he watched me. I tiptoed around him, shut off the car, and returned, a forced grin emerging.

In Officer Reynolds's ducking down again and asking Margaret through the hatch if everything was all right – 'Yes, great,' she answered in an aloof monotone – was suggested the necessity of his inquisitiveness: the macabre and violent scenarios he might encounter on any given day. Abductions, kidnappings, robberies. Things that when taken across state lines became felonies. Various other perversions that don't make the papers or the news. An awareness of these dealings blew over us momentarily, like the shadow of a fast-moving cloud. Thankfully, these activities were outside our realm. Or rather – my blood surged with gratitude – we were outside *their* realm. I was sure of that. Dead certain. On those counts, I was not guilty, no evidence, no question, case dismissed. In keeping our orbit from intersecting with the likes of Reynolds and the muscular girth of the law, I had done something right. The whipping breeze suddenly felt pleasant, and I released my hair to it and unbraced my stance against its swirling machinations.

Reynolds took my license, saying he would run a routine check. Then he advised that next time we need something out of the rear of the vehicle, unless it's an emergency, we should pull over at the next filling station. A parking lot was better than the shoulder.

'Okay, sure,' I said, giddy with relief. Reynolds walked away, my Illinois ID in hand. Head under the hatch again, I set about clearing an avenue into the depths of Margaret's luggage for her pants.

'Did he know us? Is that what he said?'

'He recognized me from the rest stop.'

'Oh.' I looked up at her. She was practically climbing over the seats to get in back. Her knees were on the seats, and she leaned into the back area.

'What are you doing?'

'I'm coming to help you,' she answered. All the kindness I had ever known in her was shining. Something had sparked it, but what? She smiled at me.

Margaret reached back, trying to hold things out of my way. The officer had unnerved her. She didn't like the law. She didn't like strange men, especially domineering ones. She was relieved and perhaps even proud of how I'd dealt with him, though I hadn't done anything remarkable. Just followed the elementary laws of man-to-man dealings.

'I got it,' I said, waving away her outstretched arm, which was not positioned right to hold open the suitcase lid anyhow. 'Sit down, I got it.'

Then I made a mistake.

The Zippy's bag was among the things I shifted around. 'Here,'

I remarked. 'Take these.' And I removed the box of bandages and tossed them up to my wife. It must have been a latent bitterness, my sense of competition; I couldn't give her the satisfaction of being pleased with me. Not so little so late. When the chance to remind her of her own shortcomings appeared, I threw it at her, a token of 'I told you so.'

'What for?' she asked, her smile diminished.

'You'll need more later. You've got some bleeding through.' I threw a suspicious look back to the cruiser, as if, ridiculously, Reynolds might hear and apprehend me for cruelty. Then we would be seized, the jig would be up and, ultimately, Margaret's cutting – the morally impertinent leniency she had taken with her body – would be culpable.

'Let's just get the pants,' Margaret said, pleading for mercy.

'Yeah, I will,' I barked. 'Here –' I lay over the luggage to hand her the keys. 'Start the car. Turn the air on. Just make sure it's in neutral.' I watched her jiggle the gear shift loosely.

'I can start it from over here?'

'Yeah, sure.' She reached over, inserted the key from the passenger seat. The whir of ignition clicked into soft sputtering. Margaret *whee'd* at the novelty and raised her eyebrows at me to indicate feisty pleasure. To the last, she enjoyed the novel, anything haphazardly revealed.

The last phase of Operation Rearrangement neared. 'We're gonna have to stop anyway ...' I grunted, seeing now into Margaret's bag. 'I'm gonna need a cup of coffee ... after this.'

'Always awake,' Margaret mused, arranging the AC vents that bellowed air again. Bless her that it always took so little – she was awash in the bliss of our common goal again, uniquely edified by my trust in her. We would be off again in moments, and at the gates of the canyon soon. 'Always staying wide awake.'

Rolled up white pants. 'Got 'em!' They came out and like a thorn, like a pimple popping, the pile snapping back into place. I tossed the pants up front, stepped back and dragged an arm across my sweating brow. Looking up, I saw the Zippy's bag leap out of the car on an updraft. It curled out from under the hatch and darted up over the gully. I spun around – there was Reynolds poised with pen and clipboard, his eyes trailing into the sky as if watching a Hail Mary pass. **Littering. $500 fine.** I slammed the hatch shut so nothing else would get blown out and sprang after the airborne litter – over the guard rail, then aflight, arms flapping, blurting 'Holy shit!' in midair at my underestimation of the ditch's depth. Luckily, the ground was sandy and loose. A soft landing. I scrambled to my feet. The bag puffed and curled over my head; one eye on it, I dodged among the brambly tangles that passed for plants in these parts. In the sand I spied tracks made by something clawed and tailed, and the chasm between its existence and my own was instantly horrific – bypassing comedy to the tragedy. This instant was one I would revisit often in my upcoming coffee-numbed life hiatus. I saw in that flash a space, like the space between my feet, clumsy in the sand, and the sure marks of this critter's pace, huge with potential. I wanted to know how I had gotten so far afield of any kind of purpose – how man had. It was an instant's pang, proportionate to its later size like a grain of the sand I skipped upon to the acres around me. As the bag alit, I scurried and caught up with it. Reynolds I was sure was ready with his pen and pad to scribble a littering ticket, adding $500 to the county coffers, so I was eager to hold up my spoils to him. While unsnagging the plastic from the thorny jumble of stems and prickles that had captured it, I was startled by a sound like a shotgun's sharp retort. Two, in fact.

Two, and so alike and adjacent – and yet just dissimilar enough – that my first impression was of an echo. The initial was louder, the second flatter, like a popping. But they were too near to be echoes. As fast as a person can open-hand slap another person on one side of the face and return with the backhand to the other cheek, that's how quickly the two retorts cracked in my ears. I turned and was puzzled to see a green mini van about forty yards past. Just how far – using the known location of the bush and its distance from the road, by having me point with my arm to make an angle representative of my line of sight – was approximated by the experts later.

The 'rate of travel' they called it. Of the mini van. Of the suspect. The offender, the perp. All these things I never took to calling him, or her – I hadn't seen the driver at all. To me, the force remained what it was from the beginning: abstract deliverance manifest in the form of green quarter panel, an ironic benediction and tinted parallelograms of side window. A tire. No other details to be coaxed out by tricks of hypnosis or mental revisitation, because it was a blur. Which is much like what my marriage came to seem, until I realized it wasn't that at all, that it had a form, a pattern and a reason for its pattern. But that would be a while. In the meantime, the Flagstaff detectives concluded for their reports that the rate of travel was upwards of eighty or eighty-five. This figure jived mathematically with the two snap-like retorts.

The first sound had been the mini van clipping the spotlight on the driver's side of Officer Reynold's cruiser. The one two feet from where Reynolds sat at the time, having finished calling in a look-up for my record. The second sound, the too-soon echo, the backhand slap, was the rear windscreen of our Honda shattering, having been punctured – also at 80 miles per hour, the experts informed me – by the spotlight that had been severed, cleanly, by sheer force, from its mounting arm on Arizona State Patrol cruiser No. AR844-E and rocketed into the cabin of the vehicle, where it struck Margaret in the head.

21 Getting Away

Ruaridh's voice woke us. 'Mel, y'in there? Eh, coffee man? Rise and shine!' Thwaps on the walls shook the whole pole-and-peg structure. Sure enough, my eyes open, there was his silhouette on the green vinyl, rear-lit by late-morning sun. I don't know what was stranger, having told the truth about Margaret, lying beside Nicole while her ex who was supposed to be in jail flailed at the walls, or the sun coming out in Glasgow.

Holy shit! I mouthed to Nicole, whose eyes were partly open. As rude awakenings go, this one ranked right up there. *Fuck*, she breathed with a roll of her eyes. I sat up.

Thank God for the ample credit line of the Plunkett's Citibank Visa. I'd bought the deluxe tent, complete with a luggage-sized padlock for the zippered door.

'Mel! Come on! Ah ken yer in there. Ah heard ya snorin'.'

Haird.

Nicole grabbed my arm and shook her head, no, no, no. She pointed to herself, and crossed a finger over her lips, miming *Shhh*. I nodded agreement but shrugged helplessness.

'Yeah, Ruaridh,' I said, clearing my talked-dry throat. 'What's up, man?'

'Come on,' Ruaridh said. 'The zip wohn budge. Let uzz in. Gi'e uzz tha' film.'

'Um, gimme a minute, will ya? Why don'tcha put on a fire, I'll make us some coffee.'

'Coffee, coffee. Naw, time's a-wastin', ma'e. We haftay get the photos of Douglas to the *Herald*. Ya lazy git, what're ya hungover?' His shadow moved to the corner of the tent – he crouched and tugged at the zipper again. 'The wolf's at the door. Ah'll huff, and Ah'll puff –'

'Hang on! I'm coming out.' I found my jeans and slipped them on – sweatshirt too. Nicole bit her lower lip and gave me a petrified slash 'good luck' look as I climbed over her. The cozy warmth of her neck and hair wafted to me soft and sweet, slightly morning-sour. While she wormed down inside the sleeping bag, making slithering rayon hisses against the tent's vinyl floor, I froze into soundlessness. After she went still, I undid the lock and stepped out, blocking the door.

The cold, wet grass on my bare feet, though bracing, put me at a disadvantage. I felt defenseless, like a knight without armor. The low-hung sun stung my night-adjusted pupils. Ruaridh wore a gray wool jumper and jeans – the Sandinista poncho on siesta for the day. His hair was tied back as usual, and his sallow, parchment-paper face was bloated in the cheeks and sunken under his eyes in gray-blue pools of fatigue.

'I thought you were in jail.'

'Ah spent the ni', the wankers. Those CJA laws are bollocks an' they know it. If they wannay bring charges against me, leh 'em. Buh they cannay keep me off the park. I've goh a ri' tay be here.'

'Mmm,' I groaned.

He said I'd done a brilliant job with the camera, that we'd have the Tory bastards on their heels. Douglas on page one swingin' an ax was just what our side needed. He reckoned they'd give me a by-line and a couple hundred quid.

I imagined Carson ordering the Plunkett PR machine into action: how to spin the conflict of interest between its employee's eco-activism and its client's expansionist aspirations.

'Who will give me a couple hundred quid?'

'The *Herald*. The police report'll be available today, which means the story'll hit tomorrow. I've goh a mate in the newsroom. If we get the spool to him strai' away, they can pair it up. It'll be sensational!'

'Exactly – sensational. I haven't even seen the negatives yet. I don't know how they turned out. Someone might've stepped in the way. It might be out of focus. I'll tell you what – I've got the know-how, I can make prints myself. That way we can see what we're dealing with here, before we get too excited.'

'Mel,' Ruaridh said, taking breath for patience, squaring his shoulders. He spoke softly, earnestly. 'This is no time tay drag our feet. Another phase of tree-fellin' is slated fer Monday. No disrespect, ma'e, buh we've been out here fer months, and you havenay. We've been waitin' for somethin' like this fer ages. We gottay act now!'

'I understand that,' I said, hugging myself in the cold, shifting one bare foot atop the other, subjecting one sole at a time to the icy grass. 'But don't you want to see the photos first? I mean, we don't want to misrepresent what happened, what Douglas did. Do you? Because I don't. Yeah, he made a mistake. But he was pressured. He –'

'Pressued? Are ya daft?'

'Let's just make a contact sheet and see what we've got. If there's a shot of him with the ax up, snarling, you can bet the papers are gonna run it with some inflammatory headline – *MP Goes on Murderous Rampage*. I'd rather make a deal with the editor, a contingency clause that my shots aren't paired with some tabloid headline.'

'Wha'? Are you on their side now?' His hackles were up now, I could see – his eyes narrowing, thin mouth setting.

'It's not about sides, Ruaridh.' Standing up to him, adrenaline surged in my veins like mainlined espresso, doing more for me than coffee would've at that moment. 'Things aren't always as they appear, that's all. Taking a single image and saying, That's the man, that's what happened, that's how things are – who needs it? Yes, Douglas is an ass – a righteous ass. But he was surrounded, and I didn't see what happened, but something sent him to the ground – it may have been you.'

'Hey, Ah didnay touch the fucker!'

'Regardless, the ax was there, grabbing it was largely self-defense. It was a bad decision, no question, but I won't hand over my film so it can be reported that he came down here knocking people six feet with a poke in the chest and swinging away like a bloody ax murderer. He had it in his hand ten seconds.'

'Yer mad. The camera doesnay lie. Wha'ever's on there ha'ened,' and it's fact plain as day. And – and – and if you wannay do anythin' – anythin'! – buh get the photos to the *Herald* strai' away, you've goh shite fer brains!'

'Things aren't always what they seem, Ruaridh.'

He paused, iron-jawed, studying me eye to eye. 'Okay, where is it?' He came at me, pulling my crossed arms apart, grabbing at my jeans pockets. 'I knew it – yer a fuckin' stoolie! A double-crosser!'

'Get off me!' I grabbed his bony wrists and pushed him away. He stiffened his arms and fought back.

'Ah'll get it mysel' then!' He drove at me, digging his boots in. I tried to brace and counter with my weight, but my feet gave out on the slippery lawn. My legs went under me, and Ruaridh shoved me aside and ducked into the tent in one swoop. I hit the ground, knees and palms in the mucky earth.

'Oh, fuck me!' came his cry.

Before I'd reached my feet again, I was socked in the gut, then tackled and toppled, getting a face full of wooly jumper.

'Fuckin' ungrateful cunt!'

We scrapped, him maneuvering to land blows on my face. But I got on my back and again was able to grab his wrists and hold him off. I was bigger than him, and stronger. Though his red, clenched face loomed, strands of hair flying free of his ponytail, I was casually aware of my bare feet and of Nicole having emerged from the tent, shouting at Ruaridh, who himself kept up the abuse. 'Ah welcome you here! Ah give you a passport! Fuck! Ah never shoulda trusted ya! And Ah never shoulda trusted *you*,' he said, throwing a look at Nicole standing by in her long overshirt, palms out-turned, twitching to assist somehow.

'Ruaridh, geh off him!' she yelled. 'Leave him be!'

'Shuh up, you! Ah knew ya had eyes fer him from the word go. Talkin' 'bout this American bloke with his taxi rides to hospital! So nice! So sweet! A photographer!'

'Come on, Ruaridh,' I said, trying to shove him off. When I let go of his wrists, he swung for my face. I blocked it. We scrapped again, me rising up and tipping him off. He charged again, head in my midsection, powered by his boots' traction. I steered us away from the tent and we hit the ground again – at least it was soft – him swearing, yelling rambling accusations. Corporate pig! Earth-raper! Capitalist tycoon! Nicole screamed at him some more and I think pounded on his back a few times, judging from his hiccupped bellowing. I didn't try to hurt him – just shifted him, gagging on his patchouli stench and annoyed by his Brillo-pad jumper. He was like an outsized dog humping my leg; I could feel the force of his desire. He was a hairy, smelly, clambering nuisance. His contact, compared with the fresh memory of holding Nicole, was clammy, pudgy, languorous. At one point I rolled out of his clenching arms, which put him behind me; he put me in a headlock and cut off my air. Only then did I seriously consider using my size to pop him one – an elbow to the groin or upside the head. This wasn't needed though: Fosters, Sweden, and Arsenal, hearing the fracas, ran over and broke it up. They yanked Ruaridh off me, stiff-armed him back and played buffer between the beet-faced Scot and me.

Separated, Ruaridh smoothed his hair and looked around, as if expecting a crowd's reaction. It was a phony kind of posturing. He was glad to be done with the brutishness and pleased, even surprised, with neither losing the contest or suffering a single blow.

Fosters lit him a fag and advised him to stay cool and not to get himself in trouble. The resistance needed him. Ruaridh nodded, eyes darting between me and Nicole. 'Aye, she's noh worth it,' he scowled.

'Oh, noh worth it? Ri'! Ya tosser!' Nicole said. 'Do wha'ever's necessary, ya said. Yer a *user*. We're finished!'

Arsenal winced playfully – feeling Ruaridh's pain. Sweden pulled the corners of his mouth down like a kid hearing a swear from a parent. Both bit their lips against laughter. Fosters stood with hands in pockets, looking at his shoes.

'Aye, that's uzz finished,' Ruaridh spat. 'Two-faced minge.' To me, he muttered, 'You can have her. Take her and yer film and fuck away off.'

But that was a conditional offer, ultimately. A swap. When the interlopers learned I wasn't sold on giving the press the Douglas photos, they aligned with Ruaridh.

'Hold on,' Arsenal said, his five o'clock shadow somehow the perfect stylish length for the lager and *Loaded* set. 'He's got the film? Why ain't ya turnin' it in?'

'He doesnay wannay tarnish Douglas's reputation,' Ruaridh said.

All the gel-heads questioned this, in an avalanche of niggling protests, an array of accents. *That's a load of shite. He was gonna crack our skulls. What'd you take the pictures for in the first place? Don't you wanna stop the M77? You think a representative should be allowed to threaten his constituents?*

They circled around me now, forgetting about keeping back Ruaridh, who prodded, 'Wha' you have tay say fer yersel' now?'

I'd hardly stuttered a response when the terms were put to me, compliments of a puff-chested Arsenal: 'You and her is leavin'. Either the film or yer teeth is goin' as well.'

I thought of opening the spool, exposing the roll to daylight, but I had no tools and had to act fast. The whole cadre was waiting outside the tent for me to fetch it. Anyway, it probably would only have gotten me in more trouble later. Receiving the intact Agfa cylinder in his open palm, Ruaridh said cheekily, 'Cheers.'

I left the tent behind – considered it a donation. I packed my ruck-sack and sleeping bag, put my shoes on, and set off, Nicole's hand in mine. 'Slag,' Ruaridh scoffed, as we passed the campfire area, headed to the cleared strip around the threatened copse.

'Twat,' Nicole answered.

We crossed the Pollok green one more time, angling toward the train station. Reaching Barrhead Road, I suggested taking a cab.

'Tha'd be brill. My card's empty,' Nicole said, referring to the ScotRail pass she put credits on to get to her mom's in Dunfermline. 'Ah canh be arsed wi' the train anyway.' Waiting at the cab stand by the chippie we'd gone to the night before, we kissed, in a show of solidarity. I thought, given the facts – awake till God knows what hour and woken so brutishly – I really could've used a cup of coffee. Yet it wasn't urgent. Usually, *sans* morning mug or three I felt as if I was sliding down a wall like a glob. But not now. I was alert, centered, steady. Nicole stood close to me, my arm around her shoulder until a Citroën hatchback taxi picked us up, not the traditional black rig. The driver swung us onto Barrhead Road to get to the M77, the regular section that wasn't extended yet, and I saw Pollok Park – the Maxwell House, the White Cart footbridge, the sheltering copse – pass and recede. In a matter of blocks, it vanished behind a row of council houses.

Nicole looked agitated, weary, unsure. 'Sorry for the trouble back there,' I said.

'Och, nevermind Nirvana,' she said, going straight to her well-worn phrase of dismissal. 'Wha's he like anyway?' This saying was familiar to me now; it was rhetorical, a flexible assertion of either *He's great* or *Fuck him*. 'Ah'm sorry abou' yer film. Maybe it'll be put in the papers, though. Tha's no bad, eh?'

'Yes and no. Nothing I can do about it now.'

'Aye, no worries,' she said, looking no less worried.

The cab dipped beneath an overpass and looped into a roundabout, an array of carats indicating routes to the Airport, Ayrshire, Paisley and City Centre. Our driver put us on the last of these.

'Ah didnay know that's how you felt,' Nicole said. 'About Douglas and yer photos.'

'Me neither. I didn't have time to explain.'

'Ah was surprised you could talk at all, strai' outta bed, no coffee or nowt.'

The elevated five-lane motorway looked down over industry's conflagration of warehouses, pipe-laced towers, oil storage drums strapped with precipitous ladders, and the squat cylinders of a sewage-treatment plant. Among all these, of course, were the chimneys, fire escapes, roof-mounted billboards and street lamps of the endless residential / commercial zones of outer Glasgow. In the wee hours of morning, when I'd finished telling Nicole of my prior life, we'd both drifted to sleep with only a few words. *Ah'm so sorry*, Nicole had whispered into the stillness of the night-surrounded tent. *Nevermind, Nirvana*, I'd joked. She'd smirked at this intimacy, my borrowing her language, then acknowledged my seriousness with her own straightened lips. I'd meant it, in a way. Nevermind:

Margaret and all that'd happened was well behind me; I didn't want it bothering me anymore. Indeed, having told Nicole the whole truth, it felt further in the past than ever, like wake behind a ferry, once churning, now still. Life had settled. Seasons had passed. The whole roiling had smoothed and iced and hardened, then thawed. Now it was glassy and sparkling again.

Yer a gewd mahn, Nicole had said. *Yer all ri'*.

With that, we'd slept. But I could still hear her words now: *Yer a gewd mahn*. The Scottish flattering understatement. *Yer all ri'*.

'Nicole,' I said, 'I can't just drop you off, go home and go back to work. What am I gonna do, sit in coffee shops till I have to go back to America? Every minute I'll be thinking I could be with you. Let's go somewhere. Show me the Highlands, or Loch Ness, the Shetlands – anything. You and me, let's get away.'

'Like a holiday?'

'Holiday, vacation – whatever. Let's just get away. Let's get out of the city, do some hiking, get some fresh air.'

'Sounds brilliant! Ah know wha' ya mean. Ah was thinkin' tha' as well. Going back to lectures and bar-maidin' – it's juz noh *on*.' Not on. Meaning off. Meaning the thought put her off. 'Buh wha' about yer job? Wohn you geh in trouble?'

'Nah. Klang is in London. Carson's in Chicago. It's a long leash. I can visit coffee shops in any little town we go to. I'll write reports and fax them in. They won't know the difference.'

'If you say so. Buh Ah havenay goh the dosh fer a holiday.'

'Well, I do. My job pays well. I can cover us both. Whadya say?'

'Mmm.' Her eyes showed something else.

'Nicole, I'm sorry I lied, and said I'm divorced,' I said. 'Are you mad at me?'

'Naw, Ah'm no mad. Ah've no ri' to be. Ah don't tolerate lyin' as a mah'er of course – juz ask my da. Buh you had yer reasons, Ah reckon. Ah cannay imagine comin' over here, meetin' folk – "Aye, my wife's just been killed in a car wreck." A bit depressin', no offense.'

'But I wouldn't lie to you otherwise. You know that, right?' The cab coasted off the motorway and slowed into Charing Cross's five corners. 'I mean, I never would. Not some bullshit lie to get away with something, to deceive you. This was different. There's more to it.'

'Wha'dja mean?'

'I mean, I said I was divorced because that's what I've been doing. I told everyone after Margaret died that we were divorced. Well, not everyone. People it didn't matter to, you know. It was out of habit. An unfortunate habit, yes. It's a family tradition. A Podgorksi family tradition.'

She looked doubtful. The car was moving again. We'd be in Kelvingrove, her neighborhood, in a few minutes.

'How do I explain?' I mused. 'It's the most demented thing. I've lived with it so long, it's become normal. It wasn't until coming over here, getting away from it, meeting you, that I've gotten any perspective on it. It's pretty backwards, I can see now. Counter-productive. Harmful, actually. They have these rivalries, my parents and aunts and uncles – with the world, really. Everything's sugar-coated. All ugliness is subverted. They don't talk about anything real. Strife, conflict. It's all glossed over. They did the same with Margaret's death. It's like they're in a happiness competition, and they think any difficulty means you've lost. You know, *Life, liberty and the pursuit of happiness*. They take that a bit far, I guess.'

'So they lied abou' it?'

'Well, yeah. Nicole, you've got to understand, I had prayed for a change to break the deadlock. I prayed for the Grand Canyon trip to help, to get me out of the mess. Then I got it. That was a mind-fuck. There was a lot of guilt. I felt like God was fucking with me, playing a cruel joke, telling me, Be careful what you wish for. Once I got over that shock, I had to deal with the fact that Margaret wasn't coming back. Every time I talked about it, every time I told someone that my ex-wife was dead now, I was reminded of why she died. That in a sense, I'd hoped for it. I guess that's just a way of saying I blamed myself.'

'Tha's the tradition then?'

'Shit,' I laughed. 'No, but in a way maybe it is. I'm sorry, I'm not making sense. You have to know my family. You have to know what it's like in America. It's nothing like here. See, this is what I mean. This is why we should get away: I have so much I want to say to you. And we have to make it happen now! God, I sound like Ruaridh, I'm sorry. But it's true, we don't have much time, and I don't know what'll happen once I have to go. I don't know when I'll be able to come back. So will you go away with me? Just for a couple of days, however long you can.'

'Okay,' she said, smiling now. 'We'll go tay Campsie Fells.' She sat forward.

'Yes!' I said. 'What's that?'

'Aw, there's lovely hills there. We'll have a nice walkabout. Buh yer noh to spend loads of money on me. We'll take the bus and stay in a hostel.'

Nicole guided the driver through the last circuitous blocks to her flat, and I paid with the Plunkett's Citibank. It was a long drive, and the fee was astronomical. Buoyed in spirit, I tipped generously.

'Soph?' Nicole called, stepping inside. 'Deb?' But her roomies didn't answer, and I followed Nicole into the lounge, dropping my bag and flopping into a chair. She called again and continued through to the kitchen. From there came her voice saying, 'They must be away.'

Nicole's flat was much the same flavor as mine, only bigger, naturally, holding the three of them. The ceilings were high and sooty, the carpet thin, the windows water-warped and the appliances a generation removed. The tiles were chipped, the linoleum dirty, the Formica worn, and there wasn't a surface in sight, high or low, that a pencil wouldn't roll off. But it was cozy with heartening belongings: women-things transplanted not long ago from teenage bedrooms, some of them Nicole's. Framed pictures of family, shelves with books and candles in wax-weeping wine bottles, a stack of CDs on a lace doily, mismatched furniture, some rattan, some highback, a small dusty TV, magazine pictures of Hollywood hunks, a poster of the Firth of Forth rail bridge and another saying something in Gaelic. It smelled of incense and breakfast sausages.

'Fancy a cup of tea?' Nicole called. I answered yes and joined her in the kitchen. She asked me to start some bread toasting, and after some somber filling of the kettle and washing of the tea pot, said, 'Och, they'll think Ah'm mental.'

'What's that?' I was seated behind her at a picnic-style table, manning the toaster and holding a geode I'd found on the center-piece placemat.

'Soph and Deb. It's juz as well they're noh here. Listen, Ah'm noh gonnay tell 'em we're goin' away together.'

'No? How come?'

'Ah've just said to 'em a coupla days ago Ah wasnay gonnay see ya. Like Ah told ya, they thought it was a bit much, you havin' been married, and American and all. They're only lookin' out for me, understand. Buh last they saw me, Ah was headed back wi' Ruaridh to the Free State.'

'Oh. Well, do you think I should leave? They have a problem with me?'

'No, no, it's all ri'. Yer welcome here, of course. It's juz they can be a bit thick sometimes. Ah love 'em tay death, but they dohn understand.' She threw two Tetley's bags in the teapot. When the kettle switch tripped, she poured and brought the tea pot to the table and sat across from me. I asked what she would tell them then; she couldn't tell them nothing, could she? Wouldn't they worry? Wouldn't that cause more trouble and confusion? I wanted her to feel confident enough in me to stand up to their resistance, but it wasn't my place to say so.

'Aye,' she said, her chin in her hand. 'Ah reckon yer ri'. They'll see ma bag's packed and Ah'm gone. They'll only worry. Course, Ah didnay come home last ni' either. Och, wha' a hassle.'

When the tea was steeped, she filled two mugs, filling one a third, then the other, then the first to just over half, then the other, finally topping them both. This was to get an even distribution of the thin tea in the top of the pot and the darkly steeped at the bottom. I commended her on her care and technique. 'You could work for Plunkett's,' I said.

'Aye, and you could be a barmaid – fetch uz the milk.' She indicated the back door, which was nearer me.

'Outside?' I asked.

'Aye, on the ledge.' There was no refrigerator in the flat. I opened the door and stepped out. 'And the butter – mine's the small one,' Nicole called. Under the eave were three stashes of perishables: cheese and margarine tubs and short cartons of milk. The bags were pocketed with icy rain water in their folds. It was raining now, and the crackles of roof-streams meeting cold bricks echoed around the back alley.

Over tea and toast, she got out a leaflet for the Campsie Fells and the phone. I read her the number to dial for information.

'Wait a minute,' I whispered – she was in a queue for a person – after looking at the Campsie Fells material a minute.

'Wha'?' she asked, holding the mouthpiece away.

'This is only a few miles from here! At the start of the Highlands.'

'Aye, Ah know. It's dead close.'

'Hang up, hang up,' I said. 'We'll call back.' Puzzled, she put the phone down, and I explained that I wanted to go up into the Highlands proper, where the big mountains were, and get well outside Glasgow. I hadn't studied Scotland's geography thoroughly, but I knew some of the major slices: the Lowlands, the Grampians, the Highlands. I'd oriented myself prior to coming over, and I knew that where I wished to be was farther from Glasgow than the Campsie Fells, described by the leaflet as 'standing guard between the broad farmlands of the Carse of Stirling and the northern fringes of the City of Glasgow'. Pleasant rambles could be enjoyed, it said. I didn't want a pleasant ramble so much as a total seclusion and Nicole's undivided attention.

She was warm to the idea of a longer trip. Fort William was lovely, and she hadn't been since she was a wee girl, but it was three hours by bus, which meant it was only worthwhile to stay a few days, which meant more money: nights hiring a room, meals and drinks. And this worried her. 'Thing is, Mel, Ah'm skint. Ah've enough fer *one* ni' out.'

I insisted she forget all thoughts of expense. This was my idea and my treat.

She mulled this over. Being fiercely independent, her reservation was with being reliant on my funds. A supplicant position, reminiscent of the dynamic with Ruaridh. Also, a self-described Libra through and through, her strong sense of justice didn't agree with *not* sharing the expense. But student life and Glasgow and the recent events at the M77 wore on her, and the offer was too good to pass up. 'Oh, dear,' she said after a bit.

'What?'

'Em, well, the hostels are divvied up. Men and women are kept separate.' She blushed. 'Mind you, Ah'm no bothered. Ah dohn need anythin' swish fer my kip. Buh, seein' as we're goin' together. A coupla ni's . . .'

'We'll get a B&B,' I said, an inferred understanding between us of what this inconvenience engendered.

'Are ye sure?'

'Positive.' I punctuated this certainty with a kiss.

We phoned the tourist board and got some numbers for B&Bs in the Fort William area, settling on one in Glencoe as our top choice, being removed from the bigger town, a place where hikers, kayakers and genealogically minded tourists flocked. Nicole reached the proprietress, Mrs Wallace, and a room was available. November was not exactly high tourist season.

'That's sorted,' Nicole declared. I was beginning to anticipate these conclusions from Nicole – when things were brill or fab versus a hassle; whether something would fall on the 'can't be bothered' or the 'Ah'm noh bothered' side of the divide; whether a thing would incite a cheerful claim of 'tha's sorted' or the sour assessment 'wha' a mess'; whether a person would be viewed as 'dead smart' or 'horrible', with the faint flipping of the R's and tonal lightness in her voice that was far too pleasant to contain any real horror. In a bed-and-breakfast lounge sometime during our excursion I would pick up a book of poetry by Hugh MacDiarmid and read in the introduction about the iconic lines from 'A Drunk

Man Looks at the Thistle' which also served as the author's epitaph:

> *I'll ha'e nae hauf-way hoose, but aye be whaur*
> *Extremes meet . . .*

Where extremes meet. Nicole seemed to embody this as much as Scotland itself with her passion and vehemence in one matter and apathy and indolence in another. Or maybe she was that centerpoint where extremes diverge. Inwardly, it fatigued me at times, her over-simplifying, all or nothing. Some of her nothings were cop-outs. It was jarring being privy to her reactions and interpretations; if you followed her lead, you sometimes suddenly skidded, no traction. You lost balance and had to recover. But then, I reasoned, I was no smooth ride myself, perhaps more predictable but nevertheless consistent in my many human flaws. Anyway, I wanted to enjoy my remaining time in Scotland, and the casualness that came with Nicole's 'noh bothered' side made enjoyment easy – as easy as picking a flower.

In her room, Nicole showed me some of her art. There were charcoal still-lifes. There were impressionistic self-portraits in oil on small boards. There were multimedia works incorporating snapshots, spackle, drawing, threads, found objects, leaves and personal-hygiene doodads. I looked them over while she packed – she had just finished when Sophie and Deb arrived home. I was introduced to the women, and we all settled in the lounge with another pot of tea and a plate of biccies.

Deb had a typhoon of red hair – ginger hair, as they call it – rosy cheeks and green eyes like ripe olives. She smiled largely, laughed loudly and said things like 'lovely jubbly!' and 'cool beans!' She came from a farm in Perthshire and talked about neeps and tatties, her Gran and Granda, and the lambing coming up. Deb's voice was an instrument, rising to shrieks, bursting with gasps and dipping to low, grave acknowledgments: 'Och, Nic, Ah know. Ah *knowwwww.* Terrible!' But powering it all was indefatigable cheer. She clutched her tea, listened, leaned in, leaned back, flung her hands in gesticulation – I thought she should be put on one of those BBC morning shows. That'd liven things up. Watching her, you couldn't help but have a good day.

I was largely silent, noshing digestives (plain cookies) and looking on as they flitted, topically, like mating dragonflies, around each other, catching up on goings-on in the flat, at school and, in the case of Sophie, also a barmaid there, with The Corn Exchange. Did this flood of conversation, given the censure they'd expressed, mean to drown their misgivings about me? If so, I didn't blame them. I hadn't been warm to Glasgow's strangeness at first. Now here I was in their college home-away-from-home, threatening the sanctity of their well-intentioned friend.

Sophie was a striking brunette with a cynical manner. To Nicole making a roll-up she asked, richly, if she was *gasping* for a fag. She wore jeans and a brown leather jacket, which she kept on, fingers drawn up into the sleeves like an insect's retracted proboscis. Her brown eyes were set under puffy lids like Ruaridh's. She was guarded and bit her nails occasionally. A warm smile spread when she shared that her Gaelic exam results were 'brilliant' and that she'd been selected for the team going on an archaeological dig to Barra, but otherwise she slumped in her seat and levelly doled out contempt. At a 'piss-up' at the Queen Margaret Union over the weekend (week – END), a bloke named Neil had been an arse, but she herself had drank too much, and probably carried on like a tart.

She was so real, this charmed the pants off me. In another life I might have fallen for her rather than Nicole.

These girls may have been suspicious of me, but they had no qualms revealing themselves. Maybe they meant to set an example, a message that disclosure is expected.

They asked about my work with Plunkett's, about Chicago, whether I missed home, how I liked it here, the food, the weather.

Deb said, 'And you do photography as well?'

'I dabble,' I said. 'It's a hobby.'

'Been takin' part in the M77 protest then,' said Sophie.

'Yes, a little bit,' I said. 'Nothing like some people – camping out there permanently.'

'Tha's grea',' Sophie said. 'Wha's she like, eh?' She looked at Nicole. 'Spendin' a week there.'

Nicole changed the subject to Sophie and Deb's studies. Deb was doing agriculture at Strathclyde, learning about potato blights and mineral soil concentrations and the workings of farm economies. She'd been wearing wellies and driving a tractor and birthing lambs since she was a wee girl; now she was writing a paper on co-ops in Peru. Sophie was doing Gaelic at Glasgow Uni. 'She's dead smart like,' Nicole informed me in a mock-aside, to which Sophie deadpanned, 'Aye, Ah'm dead smart.' I asked the difference between Gaelic (*Gal-lick*) and Gaelic (*Gay-lick*). *Gal* goes with the Scots, she said. *Gay* with the Irish, where it all started anyway.

'Soph, teach him a couple of phrases,' Deb said. 'Teach him *Kimmer aha hoo* and *Glay va tapula*.'

Sophie was writing something down when a knock came at the door.

Deb went to answer and, like a good farm girl in the big city, looked first through the peephole. 'Oh, dear!' she whispered, with her countrified artlessness. 'It's the police!'

Nicole sprang to her feet. 'Deb, no! Hang on!' She whispered too, a panicked whisper; and urgently indicated for Deb to take her hand from the doorknob. I didn't know what she was afraid of, what she thought they might want. It didn't occur to me to panic. In a move that stunned me, Nicole grabbed my arm and ordered, 'Get yer bag, we'll go out the back.' Standing, I saw the siren atop the car out front. To Deb she implored, still in a breathy voice, 'Juz wai' a minute or two. Then say Ah'm noh here. You havnay seen me. Or Mel!'

Deb, wide-eyed, nodded. The instructions were clear, and she seemed willing to follow them, like these were the parameters of a challenging lab experiment. In the rattan chair, still with her jacket on, Sophie calmly traced, in the notebook on her lap, the cramped block letters of the phrase she'd written for my instruction: *Ciamar a tha thu*? Hello, how are you?

'Nice meeting you,' I said.

'Aye, you as well.'

More rapping rattled the door.

'Buh, luv, where're you goin'?' Deb pleaded.

Nicole and I spoke over each other, both answering.

'The Highlands,' I said; Nicole avowed, 'Ah dohn know.'

We looked at each other. Quickly, Nicole conceded to Deb. 'Mebby away fer a wee while.'

'Oh, dear,' Deb said, watching us go.

I grabbed my bag, Nicole grabbed hers, and we bolted through the kitchen and out the back door, which I pulled shut behind us with that silencing technique, twisting the latch in, closing and releasing.

She took us down the alley at a skip, the long way, away from her flat's end of the alley. We came out on Lansdowne Crescent, curved around and emerged on Great Western Road opposite the Kelvingrove tube stop. In a minute, we were in a cab. I gave the driver my address.

We figured the police would track down my flat soon enough, but we had to chance it. We had the driver park around the corner, and I ran in and picked up some clean clothes and 27Gs. There was Qoqle on the mantle with her pencil-eraser mouth and vacant eyes. I shoved her in a drawer. The azurite was on the mantle too: that, I pocketed. I turned off the answer phone.

We went to the Buchanan Street bus station, in City Centre, down by the Royal Albert Concert Hall. Nicole didn't even fake reaching for her billfold to help with the fare – not that I blamed her. There were some pretty big digits on the red LCD display. I didn't even want to think about what it came out to in dollars.

The bus left at four, a tall coach three-quarters full with red cloth seats and closet-sized loo at the back. A single in-town stop was made before charging straight out Great Western Road. The driver came on the intercom with a jocular preamble ('Ah'm noh allowed to drink, so neither are you') and itinerary. We'd reach Glencoe by half seven, weather permitting. It was pissing rain. Nicole and I slumped into our seats holding hands and watching Glasgow streak by under the deluge and melt into the past.

After a while we took out some IRN-BRUs.

'So you were talkin' abou' yer parents being liars?' Nicole said. 'There's a tradition, like?'

'Well, liars, not exactly.' I reiterated that what they'd done was perpetuate the notion that everything had been hunky dory in my marriage and that the incident was accidental.

'Buh it *was*, Mel,' Nicole said. 'You didn't cause it. It was pure chance.'

'Ah, yes. *Chance.* How many times have I heard that! That's how Mr P. saw things. "It was chance. Bad luck. Freak timing. The intersection of forces." Mrs P. latched on to it too. She tried to peddle the idea that God needed Margaret to come home to Him, that old bit. But it didn't comfort me, so she fell in line. That made two of them selling that story.

'Their story went, "Well, it's just unlucky. A chance occurrence. What are the odds? It's been hard, but Mel soldiers on." This was the spiel given out on the phone, over the back fence, even in my company. But it didn't stop at that, you had to hear them say it. They'd grind the subject.'

I explained as best I could how Mr and Mrs P. would give it the full discourse, give it laldy, reconfirming the cause, asserting it with unnatural force, a false conviction – how they left out all the factors that brought Margaret and I to that angry, cantankerous moment, factors we had control over but didn't control.

'Let's say ... I don't know, let's say you're serving steaks for dinner. Okay? Steaks for dinner. Everyone's been invited for steaks. You don't mention it over and over. If that's what it is, you get the grill out, grill the steaks and eat them. You let it be and visit with your guests. But if something's amiss – if you're serving horse meat – you drive it home that on the menu tonight is steaks. *Mm, mmm, steaks. Everyone loves steaks. Bill, do you like steak? Are you in the mood for steak? How do you like your steak? Okay, good, then that's how I'll make your steak.*'

Nicole laughed, receptive to some levity.

'Buh, Mel, it's true.' She pursed the vowel in her Scottish lips. *Tdroo*. 'It *was* an accident. And if they didnay know about Margaret cuttin' and the problems you'se were havin', then especially it *wuz* an accident tay them.'

'Don't take this the wrong way, Nicole, but I've heard it all before. Yes, a car came by, that was chance. The driver was reckless, not paying attention – by chance. But *I* made us pull over. *I* insisted Margaret cover up her cuts. I was the acting agent. I had a hand in the outcome. That's indisputable.'

'Mel, ya cannay blame yersel'. Did yer folks noh tell you tha'? Did they noh comfort me?'

'Comfort me? Well, of course, in the immediate aftermath. But in the long run, Mr P. led the charge with his rational in-sistence. He's a scientific man; attributing Margaret's death to freak factors, slim but possible odds, comforted him. I guess he hoped they would comfort me too. Mrs P. has her faith, but she's of a generation and temperament where women don't think independently. She went along. Their intentions were good – hammering home this version of the truth meant that I was not to blame. Problem was, the more they said this, the more depressed and guilty I became, thinking of the real reasons. And, worse, they were relieved. They didn't have to address the complexity, that I'd been selfish, complacent, that I'd fucked up. That confused me, the shelter they took in this lie. I didn't see why they did it.'

'Why did they? It's mad!'

'They meant well. Saying it was a fluke meant I wasn't to blame. That was important to them. Mel didn't fail, Mel did nothing wrong. In America, there's having the right house, driving the right car, going to the right school. Marrying right. Too much of my shit didn't fit the picture. I didn't go to the right school – any school for long – and I didn't marry the right girl. A grisly death sure as hell didn't fit in. So it became known as The Accident, capital A. Before the accident. After the accident. Since the accident. It made it a blip on the family radar. No error on record. A statistical anomaly, throw it out.'

'Buh Mel, you didnay *tell them* about Margaret cutting hersel'!

Wha' should they ha'e done, read your mind? Pried in your lives? Looked in a crystal ball?'

'Asking would have been good. They saw our essential differences, they knew we were troubled. We were testy with each other around them, we had different goals, different backgrounds – these things weren't mentioned. Mrs P. relied on her "Love is Everything" motto and hoped prayers would deliver all I needed. Mr P. saw me praying but didn't inquire. He pulled weeds and washed rocks in the back yard well into dusk, until I yelled goodbye from the back patio. Then there was the road trip. What were we doing there? Margaret's out of work, we had nothing saved. Why the urgent need for a vacation?'

'Och . . .' Nicole sighed, skeptically.

'Actually, asking probably would not have helped. I couldn't have answered. We'd gone too long not speaking of anything real, and old habits die hard. That's why, privately, to people I dealt with, I began saying we were divorced. I was so tired of the misjudged pity. It elided the deeper truth. In a way, it felt natural to say we were divorced. That's where we were headed.'

'Maybe, maybe noh.'

'Maybe, maybe not,' I agreed. 'You know, Nicole, after Margaret died, I was really withdrawn. I didn't go anywhere. I didn't have a job. I didn't even do my photography. I hardly saw anyone. The only people I met were acquaintances. What were they to me? My version of the truth worked better with them. In fact, it worked great until I met you. You're the first person I've been bothered about lying to. I couldn't remember what I'd told you after Curler's, which version. I knew I wanted to come clean, just didn't know if I'd managed to. That was eating me up. You – this place – you've become synonymous with the truth.'

The bus spat us out on the side of the road like a couple of gumballs into a child's clammy hand. There was no shelter at the stop, just a wedge of raised pavement and a posted schedule. The horizon was black in three directions, with the sense, gleaned from the acoustics of rainfall and the air's brackish odor, that the sea lay swishing nearby; and from the surrounding starlessness that mountains towered. Down the road a single street lamp spread diffuse orange light slashed with rain. A building sulked at the street corner. We walked, hand in frigid hand, chill rivers streaking through the jungle of our scalps. The bus's tail lights disappeared further up the A82.

Nicole had phoned ahead from the rest stop halfway up, telling Mrs Wallace when to expect us. Mrs Wallace had said to go to the pub on the corner and ring them again; Mr Wallace would bring the car around and take us to the house. I was relieved to see, as the little building drew near, a lit window and a pub sign. *Twa' Corbies*. I'd seen that old Scots referenced in a newspaper or on TV somewhere. Two crows. I suppose it should have been foreboding, but you take what shelter you can find in a Scottish rain.

The pub's warmth met us kindly. I stood, over the floor mat, rain dripping off my Gore-Tex, paralyzed by my soaked state. Nicole dug up 20p and the number. Her ability to produce the most touching of voices, all respect-for-elders and insouciance, amazed me now, emerging from the doldrums of our bus conversation, all death, deception and blame. This was consistent with our dynamic as a traveling pair: I had the dollars, she the interpersonal tact, a fuller sense of the Highland topography, and of course a lifetime's fluency with Scotland's social customs. She also had something I didn't: that beyond-her-years fluency in the language of suffering that let her sweep between the two worlds.

We'd covered a lot of conversational ground weaving up the Highlands, gaining and losing altitude, sweeping around curves in that nose-led way of coach buses beside ever-rockier sheep pastures and over curving, climbing roads where the roadside brambles and hedgerows were trimmed to within a margin of a few inches to accommodate traffic. My ears had popped every so often. As loch-bottomed glens spread outside the window and fewer and fewer crofts and petrol stations dashed by, a world widened within me. Nicole talked about her divorced parents, the fallout, her troubled wee brother, the wrench of going away to Glasgow for art school rather than staying on with her Da, a self-destructive drinker who needed her. Her unwavering perspective on the grim realities of her own life cleared the view to the horizons of my past.

'Okee! Cheers! Ta! Bye!' she said now, putting the phone down.

'Sorted?' I said, cheekily showing her my Scottish idiom.

'Aye, sor'ed,' she said with a smirk. We stepped around a short wall sheltering the phone, into the pub. It was a one-room joint with darts, karaoke, jukebox and a gambling machine bedecked with neon £-sign enticements. Three or four tables were surrounded with drinkers and topped with drinks' detritus. 'Hi ya!' Nicole called to the barman.

'Just off the bus?' he asked, leaning, a fag in fingers, over an ashtray.

'Aye,' Nicole answered. 'Our ride'll be round in a wee minute.'

'Mr Wallace.'

'Aye, Mr Wallace.'

Mr Wallace's headlights swung in soon, and we climbed in his tidy, tight-running Vauxhall. It was hardly a mile to the house, but the combination of turns would have frustrated an out-of-towner on foot in the dark. Mr Wallace was as relaxed a man as you could ever hope to meet, asking after us and receiving our answers with a knowing smile. Didn't faze him one iota, Nicole being a student at Glasgow studying art, originally from Dunfermline, me being American and in Scotland on business. Like it was in sumptuous harmony with his expectations. I suppose he'd seen it all: backpackers from the continent, Scandinavia, the States, Australia, everywhere. He was sixty-five if he was a day, and flush with calm health in his light jacket, which hung on him so gently it could have been stitched under Eisenhower – or Churchill, as the case may be – and not have frayed a thread.

We could hardly see the house, night was so dark and the earth so freshly wetted and eager for the attention of our footsteps. It was set back from the road behind hedgerows, and the porch light showed the front doorway but little else, only a halo of swaying spider-monkey and pine boughs, the indistinct notion of mountains beyond. The air rippled with the seventh-sense smells of animal treachery and bliss. It was easy to imagine in the distance a forest filled with creatures and flora *Let's Go Britain* had listed as native to the region: hawks, thistle, heather, rams, wildcats.

Mrs Wallace received us, shook our hands and said how do you do, welcome, come in, come in, while Mr Wallace slipped into a high-back and flipped on the telly, his part finished. We were shown the lounge and its amenities, and the dining room, where breakfast would be served. She was a vivacious yet slow-moving matron, kind-spoken with a softer version of Nicole's up-and-down inflections molded by a mid-century politesse. The dignity of the short-statured aided her tour, which though certainly oft-repeated was not said by rote. Her only indiscretion was a moment, after the where's and what's were finished and we chatted, in which she seemed to size up, behind her yellow-iris eyes, the romantic reality before her: my accent, Nicole's rucksack carried still very much like a schoolgirl's. No ring on her finger, none on mine. But then this was a hazard of the B&B profession, wasn't it? Unlikelier couples had surely been ushered over the narrow hall with the braided pink runner into the bedroom where potpourri packets and a watercolor of a mountain scene hung on the wall. It was with the forbearance of the elderly that Mrs Wallace pointed out, as if they were completely impersonal matters, which pillows were feather and the sturdiness of the mattress, illustrated with a push, push of her knobby fingertips. I felt my face grow hot as a vision of Nicole appeared, sprawled there, lissome in undergarments, her supine head crowned by a spread of silken hair. I felt unwieldy, my size-twelve shoes, my gawky hands, my diminished-but-still-pudgy gut all hinting of other engorgement.

We were shown the pull cord that started the hot water to the shower and the hard-to-find light switch to the toilet. 'Most Scots say *toilet*, I've noticed,' I said. 'Rather than *loo*.' A little cross-cultural banter, a linguistics lesson to lighten the mood in these nudity-foretelling settings. I remarked that in America, *toilet* meant the appliance, not the room; for that we used the euphemistic *restroom*.

Our hostess was amused – or pretended to be – but Nicole blushed. 'Ri' – breakfast?' Nicole said.

We went out to the dining room. Our breakfast orders were taken, chosen from the standard Scottish menu of eggs, sausages or bacon, toast or potato scones, fried tomatoes, baked beans. I'd grown quite fond of this fare since my first breakfast at the Hilton – hard for me to believe it was only a few weeks ago.

'Tha' sounds lovely,' Nicole said. 'Cheers.'

'Let me guess, coffee for you, Mel?' Mrs Wallace asked. Scots were very good with using first names right away and sounding as if they'd known you a lifetime.

Nicole and I laughed and shared a look.

Mrs Wallace asked, 'What have I said?'

'That's what he does fer his job,' Nicole explained. 'Drinks coffees all day. He's mad fer it.'

I explained this absurdity in brief, not confident that the idea of an American chain restaurant would be well received by these old-timers. 'I work for a market-research company. We're testing the waters for a franchise that may open up.'

'My John loves his coffee,' Mrs Wallace said, looking towards the lounge, from where the sound of a BBC newsreader came from. 'First thing every morning for the last thirty-five years.'

'One of yer kind, Mel,' Nicole remarked. 'Yer noh so far from home.'

Nicole then asked to use the phone, and Mr Wallace insisted he leave the lounge to give Nicole privacy (PRIH-vacy).

The phone, like the faux fireplace at my flat, had been rigged to accept pound coins. A digital display showed a countdown of purchased minutes. We emptied my pockets to reach Deb and kept a stash of Nicole's at the ready to keep her on. Nicole's suspicion was confirmed: the polis had wanted to speak with me. She pulled me close to her on the couch and turned out the earpiece. 'What'd they say?' Nicole insisted.

'Well, Ah asked him in and offered a cup of tea,' Deb said, 'He was a nice wee man – muscles to beat the band. He started ri' in with the questions. "Does Nicole Marston live here?" I said yes. He asked is she home, and I said no, like you said to do, Nic. He showed me a photograph and asked if I knew this chap? It was yer man Mel. At least it looked like Mel. Hard to tell. It was from a video off a polis van. At the protest site. That's what he called it, "the protest site". Said an investigation was underway. A public figure was involved, so withholding information would be hindering justice – committing a crime! Oh, dear, it was nerve-wracking! Ah said I didn't have any information. Och, wha' else? Oh, Aye, it was one of the blokes in the fray that had said the man they were after was an American, Melvin Podgorski – could be found with Miss Marston at this address.'

Nicole and I looked at each other – *Ruaridh*.

'He said if I see him about, I should phone 'em up strai' away.'

'Deb, wha' else? Did they say why they wanted Mel?'

'Aye, they're after some evidence to do with the charges against persons involved. Nic, wha's all this about, eh? Are ya in trouble?'

'Nah, Deb, it's fine buh,' Nicole answer. 'It's a load of carry-on. Ruaridh's juz fucked off cuz Ah finished wi' him.'

'Did you? I wondered . . .'

Nicole told her not to worry, she'd fill her in later, she had to ring off, the meter was running down.

It was some news to eavesdrop on. Rather discomfiting to know the police were looking for you. Nicole was angry. I hadn't heard her cuss as much as she did on the walk back to the Twa' Corbies – the rain had let up a little and we refused to be driven – since she sprained her talofibular ligament.

Over a few jars, she set in on him. 'Ri', this is *pants!* Fuckin' tellin' the police yer name, where to find ya, like. The bastard. Why cahn he get on wi' his life and leave uz be?'

'And he lied about the film, evidently.'

'How's tha'?'

'The cops want to seize my film? I don't have it!'

'Fuck, tha's ri'. Buh after all that carry-on from Ruaridh about handin' it over, why would he tell the polis you have it?'

'To throw them off his scent. Of course,' I said, just piecing together myself how things must have gone. 'The cops didn't know. They just saw me in the van footage with my camera. They come down, start asking Ruaridh, never guessing the film's with him. Then he's clear to get it to his connection at the *Herald*.'

'Aye, aye, his mate from prep school is on staff.'

'The hypocrite. He slagged "journos" to Klang and me.'

'Aye, well, Ruaridh doesnay like the bloke. He keeps mates he can use.'

'I don't see why the cops even need my photos,' I said. 'If they have video footage and witnesses, how can Douglas deny it? Then again, what's the charge? He didn't assault. He didn't even attempt assault.'

'There'll be no charges,' Nicole said, sitting back with her roll-up. 'And no trial either. He'll get a slap on the wrist, if tha'. The polis –' She sat up again and leaned in, realizing she didn't need to broadcast all these iterations of *polis*. 'The polis dohn need yer film. They juz wannay hassle anyone havin' to do with the M77. If they can pin a CJA charge on you, interruptin' a lawful act or some shite, they reckon ya wohn return to the Free State. And that makes their job easier. The road gets finished quicker. Fewer security costs. More profit.'

'I wouldn't mind if they brought me in,' I said, swaggering in my seat a bit, pleasantly uninhibited with beer. 'Even held me for a night. I've got a right to protest. Everyone knows they're trumped-up charges. Might not go over too well with Carson though. Shit, that's an understatement.'

'No, no, Mel,' Nicole said, with gravity. 'You wannay be careful. They could send ya back to the States.'

'Deport me? I don't think so. I was there *one* night. I haven't done any tree-spiking or monkeywrenching or any of that stuff.'

'Aye, buh that's why they passed the CJA bill. They dohn need a reason. Dohn assume yer untouchable, eh. There muz be terms on yer visa sayin' yer to maintain order or follow UK law.'

'Well, there's a stamp that says I'm permitted to reside and work in Scotland until such and such a date. They rounded up to six months or something.'

The weight of inevitability, of this implied outcome, settled on us, silently; we attended our drinks. Contrary to the myths that circulate in the States, not all beer in the UK is served warm. These McEwan's were chilled – and hitting the spot. For all the stock I put in the sting and jolt of coffee, its alerting powers, its sobering virtues, as much as I'd come to equate the razor's-edge grind of it in me with the truest vitality of life, I had to admit with that jar in hand in Glencoe I could have sworn off the black and bitter then and there and not missed it. This impulse, I found, arose with growing frequency now. I felt more akin to Nicole and more Scottish. Less driven to my nerves' edges. Wouldn't last long though.

I fetched us another round and returned to Nicole with a plea. 'Listen, let's not worry about it, okay. We're out of there now. Look where we are. Our days are numbered – I mean our vacation days. Our holiday. So let's enjoy it.'

'Aye, yer ri', yer ri',' she said. 'Wait till ya see in the mornin'. There's hills all round. And we're noh far from a big inlet – the sea is juz there. It's lovely.'

We put aside Ruaridh and the police and the M77 and talked about the next day. A hill-walk was in order, no doubt. But I had 27Gs to fill out too. Just a few. I could rifle them off fast. As long as I had enough to fax Klang a batch in a few days. Whatever could be found, whatever degree of café, whether roadside stop or hiker's inn. Fort William was the best bet there, Nicole said. Glencoe's village center was but a few shops. So that was planned for after breakfast. Then we'd head up Ben Nevis by midday.

'It's the tallest peak in Britain, I read. You want to go to the top?'

'Och, no,' she laughed. 'That'd take ages. Not to mention Ah'm noh fit enough.'

'Okay, I wondered – I don't have any equipment or anything.'

'You dohn need ropes or anythin'. It's juz a long trail. Loads of rocks. Gets steep in places. Ah went up it with my Da when Ah wuz wee. Nah, unless we go up first thing, we'll run out of daylight. We'll wannay be back down for our tea.'

Tea was dinner, depending on context. Sometimes it was just tea.

The other consideration Nicole raised with some chagrin: her schoolwork. Her artwork. 'Bugger! Ah'm gonna havetay phone in tomorrow and let Mr Mongrain know Ah cannay make lectures.'

'Geez that's right. You have class. Nicole, I feel bad. I didn't even think about that.'

'Och, Ah did. Ah knew I'd have tay miss. It's allri', like. Ah didnay wantay let you down. Ah mean, Ah wanted to come.'

Asked if she would get in trouble, she said she could miss tomorrow's lecture and Tuesday's workshop. Nevermind, Nirvana – she could make them up. But what was doing her head in was a meeting she had scheduled with her advisor where she was meant to present a proposal for her Michaelmas project. She'd have to come up with a good excuse for canceling and rescheduling, and think up a brilliant idea for the project anyway, in case he wanted to hear her plan over the phone, seeing as how the term was getting on and it'd be Christmas holidays before she knew it.

I asked hadn't she started yet.

'Och, no. Ah'm horrible! Ah've been down at the park savin' the world.'

I knew a thing or two about art, and thought I might help. But she resisted, saying, 'Ah can't be arsed at the moment. Ah'll have a good think about it tomorrow while yer doin' yer coffees.' I took no offense.

Closing time, eleven, was coming up. No cars had passed outside in quite a while. There were remoter traveler's outposts, for sure, but this was no Grand Canyon either. Nicole slipped to the Ladies and I fetched new pints. I read a wall display memorializing the events of the Glencoe Massacre, after which the calm became more significant and the barman's jocular banter less frivolous, more like a triumph.

Nicole received her lager with cheers and made a roll-up and looked at me across the table. She said she hoped I didn't mind her asking, but she'd been wondering, what had happened with the driver, the bloke who'd hit the polis car? Was he jailed?

Reflexively, I sighed. Though I'd worked through it enough, beat it deader than any dead horse, and filed it in my mental cabinet under F for Finished, the stress of ambiguity still clung to the memory. He – or she – was never caught. Never identified.

I'd told select people these events, the real events. Not everyone had been given the easy gloss, the lie that Margaret and I had divorced. People like Greg, Brad and some friends I had made since had received the truth and the implications. It'd been difficult to tell then, being fresh. Now, with Nicole, I didn't have to relive it to tell it, and my being unemotional may have surprised Nicole. It certainly did me.

'In the immediate aftermath, I was confused. Since the passing vehicle didn't come to a stop, I thought the sound, the double bang, was backfire or blown tires. But then I saw the glass shattered. And Margaret – I went into shock, or something. Officer Reynolds kept me back, instructing me to stay in the ditch and not to enter the roadway. He checked Margaret, then I heard him call for an ambulance and backup for pursuit of a hit-and-run vehicle on Northbound 80.'

This was before troopers and squads were all rigged with cameras and computers, so nothing was caught on video. Reynolds didn't see much more than me, didn't try to ID it until it was a dot in the distance. Later, interrogators tapped our brains, even tried hypnosis, but the most we could come up with was a forest-green minivan, one of about five different makes and models.

It's funny, I told Nicole, before that day I could've named perhaps two minivans – Chrysler and Dodge. Turns out there were about nine on the market, and more every year. Every maker had a knock-off, all modeled on the big seller, the Dodge Caravan. Made to look just like it. Mazda, Mitsubishi, Toyota. I'd seen them all. The detectives got brochures from dealerships and did a lineup. They isolated features and asked did I see them? A sliding side door, faux-wood paneling, rear-mounted spare? Very little came out though. Nothing distinguishing. Only that the plate probably had a white background, though I couldn't be sure. There was a lot I couldn't be sure of. It was all, like they say, a blur.

'Mel, tha's wha' you had to think abou' after Margaret . . . ?'

'Died,' I finished for her.

'Tha's horrible. Did they noh chase 'em down?'

I told her how it went. How there were six or eight county roads that branched off the highway. Naturally, the National Park Service at the Grand Canyon had been alerted. But the driver didn't go there. At least, not through any of the major entrances or into any paid parking or lodging area. He would have been found – every vehicle needed a pass. A dispatch was put out, and police in the small towns sent on patrol. But he – or she – seemed to disappear. Or slipped through just the right crack before the cops went scurrying all over the grid of county roads. It was just too vast an area.

Without a license-plate number, or even a state of issue, finding the perp by his registration among hundreds of thousands green vans was impossible.

'My God,' Nicole said, getting a taste of vicarious rage, tapping her own sense of justice. Which wasn't necessarily what I wanted. I meant it when I said our holiday would be short and my Scotland stay finite and that I wanted to make the most of it. Recounting these events was out of kindness, closeness. I didn't need to tromp this trail again for my sake, though admittedly the sensations from sharing were akin to a descent to the sanity of earth – depressurizing, grounding.

'Ah'd be mad as fuck,' she continued. 'Did you noh wahn to find him and skin him alive?'

'To be honest,' I said, 'who it was, how it happened, was not something I put thought to until, I don't know, maybe a day or two later. Seeing Margaret's injury was traumatizing – she died at impact. And just coming to grips with the suddenness of it – the instantaneous loss. That it was irreversible. The body and mind go into protective states. You really cannot process much. It's like you hear people say, like a dream. You go numb. You weep, you're crushed, you're panicked, you're devastated. Then you have to deal with something, and you somehow manage. But you're wiped. You're slaughtered. You can't eat. You can't sleep. You just start the cycle over. It's funny' – but not funny ha ha, Nicole clarified, in one of her silly phrases – 'No, not funny ha ha. I recognized the textbook phases even while passing through them. Disbelief. Anger. Denial.

'But the people there were great,' I recalled. 'These professional care-givers are saints. They take care of everything. They towed my car, put me in a hotel, they literally held my hand. What could I do? I was a zombie.'

The barman at Twa' Corbies began his shutdown routine, turning off the telly and the armless bandit, wiping tables. 'After a day or two,' I went on, 'once my parents arrived wanting answers, then it kind of came to the forefront. Who was this person? What was he doing? How could he have been so careless? Was he drunk? Why didn't he stop? Did he realize what he'd done? Policing is not a science, it turns out. It's a lot of supposition. Informed guesses. They figured no, the way the squad car had been clipped, being just slight enough to make contact with the spotlight – they chalked it up to carelessness. Maybe he was watching me off in the gulley chasing the litter. Possibly the same gusting wind moved the van. Did he realize where the spotlight had gone? Probably not.

'Regardless, it was fleeing. And the best reason for fleeing a simple traffic accident is if you have priors. Serious priors.' (No cop-show watcher, Nicole needed an explanation of this term.) 'And, statistically, serious priors means more likely a male. That's profiling in action. Make sense. Your average tourist or a suburban mom, a decent person, is going to stop.'

The satisfaction of arranging these facts for Nicole was unexpected. It conferred for me the distance between the events and the present. It felt like how I'd been struck, sitting that night on the steps of my flat in Hyndland Circle, by the inconceivable miles between Glasgow and Chicago. Distance and time. Time and distance. Between me and Meadow Prairie Lane. How I'd marveled at that and taken it in and felt the release from proximity's grasp.

'Sorry,' I said. 'This is awfully morbid.'

Nicole gave me a warm, slight grin that brushed away my apology. Her mouth formed a resigned pucker that said, Death is morbid, no way around that. 'They never found the van?' she asked. 'Ever?'

'No, never.' I told her how of course it could have been identified by the damage, to the right-front quarterpanel, we assumed. A savvy criminal, if the driver was a criminal, would have disguised or destroyed this. 'I like to imagine,' I said, 'that it was parked in a shed or barn and dismantled, the parts mangled or melted, buried or scattered, burned or pounded into oblivion. I don't know why, that's just what I picture. It's not that I want this person tormented or anguished. He no doubt saw the news and knew what'd resulted. He had to live with that, whether I wished a guilty conscious on him or not. That's true to this day – I couldn't stop it if I wanted.' But what I liked, I said, was the idea of the implement of Margaret's demise not existing anymore. Rubber hoses burned up in black smoke. The frame rusted, the tires and seats shredded. A select few gears and gauges scattered around the country through a network of resales and scrapyards. 'That way there's no point in me looking for it – though I still turn my head at green vans. Every time I see one I do a double take and check the plate. I can't help it. I always will.'

Back in our hired room, I flopped on the bed and, a bit drunkenly, watched Nicole commence her night-ritual. I brooded on her physicality and in it found a clue to my disorientingly intense attraction to her. Nicole was shortish, below the curve by an inch or two. She was thin and light. She wore jeans and Doc Marten's, tops in basic shapes and solid colors. Her hair was straight and sensuous, but orderly, each strand descending forward, to the sides, or down the back like spokes from a wheel. Like a pure golf swing or an old recipe, very little could go wrong with it. She wore no make-up and had no blemishes that I could see. Her flat, but not completely flat, chest matched her boyish slang. Her walk: cocky, bouncing, her head remaining still while she flopped her feet and rose with each step high on her toes. This jaunty stride rebuked the idea of women aspiring to feline sultriness. She would have been laughed off a catwalk but laughed more herself if asked whether she cared. All this suggested to me an imagined sexual simplicity. No bouncing breasts, no broad-strapped, triple-hooked bras. No time-consuming hair-dos with curlers, sprays, mousses, gels. No clutter of mascara wands, lipstick tubes and compacts. Nothing to smear, smudge or run. Image was not 'everything'; it was nothing. Of course, this is easy for the young and pretty, which she was, with her pronounced jawline, sharp nose and wide eyes. But she neither took her beauty for granted nor coveted it. I felt a surge of confidence that being with her in a permanent sense would be similarly clutter-free. It had been so far. Now, loose with drink, I indulged in thinking long-term, despite the many unknowns around this idea. The desires I had not been able to manage in Margaret, the whims, the heightened emotions, the tangles of misunderstanding in things said and un-said, even allowing for some difficulties – everyone will have their differences, no doubt – I imagined would be easy to cope with in Nicole.

The sounds of tooth-brushing came from the bathroom. I liked that Nicole's way of moving through things involved some digging-down into the reasons and disappointments, hopes and happinesses, not just new aims. She had from the start let me in on her troubles with Ruaridh, voicing them within minutes of our meeting, as her sprained ankle throbbed. Ever since, she'd been flexing her vocabulary for life's foibles and follies. She was always saying *stroppy* for crabby or cranky, *naff* or *pants* for unfortunate or ill-timed. Dirty things were *mingin'*, the unacceptable *not on*. Troubles with her folks' divorce; keeping her boss happy at The Corn Exchange; the stress of art school, the self-pressure to be creative: conflict was central, not dispersed to the periphery. This realism seemed to guarantee success. What could complicate? If she was not perfection, there was no perfection.

Certainly imperfect was the romantic ambiance at the Wallace B&B. Too grandmotherly. The Wallaces, bless them, who had given us a key and left the light on and gone to bed, hung in the room like ghosts. They were present in the freshness of the bedding and the hospitable serenity of the place. And the day had been long and the pints tall. Nicole came from the bathroom shiny-faced and shy in a tank top and men's boxers. I washed too and got into bed in T-shirt and shorts. We fooled around and laughed quietly, me making wisecracks to fend off nerves and beeriness. But the room was steadier, perhaps for us both, with eyes open. We kept returning to our backs and the view of the lamp-lit curtains, with their hidden wilds beyond. I commented on the humble décor. Joking about it with a kind of appreciative derision was an outpost where we stayed safe from sex's entrapping mire.

Morning. A purplish peak caught light from the out-of-sight sun and bounced it down, over the forest line and into the Wallaces' back garden. There were no clouds. Opening the window, I received a faceful of air ringing with pine-dew. It was Highland air – no Glasgow bus exhaust, salt-and-vinegar breezes, whiskey vomit. And silent. Utterly silent.

In the dining room, we found a set breakfast table, from full toast rack to a covered plate of poached eggs. The black pudding and fried tomatoes arrived in the hands of a smiling Mrs Wallace, who enjoined us to sit, sit, and eat, eat, then dashed away. Mr Wallace turned up in his bonnet, having driven from town to fetch the morning paper, which he laid on the table between Nicole and me.

There it was. *Minister Lifts Pickaxe in M-way Clash.*

And the photo. My photo. I just about did a spit-take, spraying Highland brew all over it.

'Holy shit!'

Douglas had the ax over his shoulder. He was pouncing-eyed, hair fallen forward, accenting his supposed madness. He was in perfect focus. The stippled dots that comprise newsprint showed a shoulder in the foreground bearing the stripes of Ruaridh's poncho. At Douglas's left, the slick gray tone of his heftier henchman's suit. The photo had been cropped, Douglas isolated, the editorial emphasis put on his maniacal reaction. His eyes indeed were wild, his mouth obstreperous in mid-utterance.

The acknowledgment: *Photo: Ray Vaughn.* The asshole didn't even give me credit! My career as an international photo journalist thwarted before it even began.

'Wha'?' Nicole was asking. I turned the paper toward her. She knew right away and shrieked with delight, which drew the attention of our hostess, in the room now with a delivery of bacon rashers and a carafe of coffee. Mrs Wallace was a sharp woman, not at all fogged by age, and when Nicole said 'Tha's yer photo!' she pricked up, impressed.

'That's his photograph in the paper,' Mrs Wallace said to John, returning from hanging up his coat.

'You don't say,' Mr Wallace quipped, having a look. 'Ya look a fair bit older,' he joked, knocking me on the shoulder with such a gentle touch of his knuckles.

'Nah, he *took* ih,' Nicole said, laughing with the kind old man, who sat down with a cup of coffee and played like he was coming around.

'Oh, he *took* it.' He gave me a wink and filled his mug from the carafe.

A big fuss ensued, more than I cared to make. But explanations were in order. Photo hobbyist. Live in the West End. Got involved. Spent some time there. Douglas came around. Started snapping.

'Let's just leave it at that,' I said, looking to Nicole as if to say, no need to mention the police visiting and us absconding. Mrs Wallace called Douglas's outburst dreadful, and asked was I all right, was anyone hurt. Pleased with our presence no more now than before, she left us to our breakfast, urging her husband out too.

'Come, John, you can read your paper when they've finished. They're just out of bed.'

The article read:

Police yesterday sent a report to the Procurator
Fiscal after a heated clash between a Scottish
Office minister and anti-motorway campaigners.
John Douglas, a junior minister and MP for East-
wood, grabbed a pickaxe during the confrontation
on Saturday at Pollok Park, in a portion known as
Pollok Free State, in his Glasgow constituency.

Mr Douglas said in a statement issued yesterday
that he had armed himself after being 'rushed' by
about a dozen opponents of an extension to the
M77 as he inspected the construction site.

'A dozen!' I snorted.

> ... 'There was a pickaxe at my feet,' he said. 'I
> freely admit that I was afraid for my own safety
> and that of my companions, and I picked it up to
> prevent anyone else doing so.'

The rest was equally skewed, spun and propagandized. The
euphemistic line 'an exchange of views took place between Mr
Douglas and Ruaridh Gilmore, 21, of Bearsden' was especially
tickling.

> Mr Gilmore, an environmentalist, gave his version
> of the encounter, arguing that he and the other
> campaigners were the ones in need of protection.
> 'We were working peacefully on a project to save
> the last remaining trees, when we heard someone
> clearing down our banner. Here came this man
> shouting obscenities and racial slurs.'

'Racial slurs?'

> According to witnesses, Mr Douglas, accompa-
> nied by representatives of the contractors Wimpy,

then gave Mr Gilmore a few prods on the chest before pushing him so hard that he flew 6 feet backwards.

George Robertson, shadow Scottish Secretary, demanded an inquiry into Mr Douglas's 'bizarre actions'. The Scottish Conservative Party said it could not comment as it did not have all the details.

The closing paragraph was the kicker, but not for hyperbole.

As police carry out an investigation, an American businessman is wanted for questioning. The man, identified as Melvin Podgorksi of Chicago, is seen in CCTV footage photographing the incident. Immigration officials confirm Mr Podgorski is employed by Chicago-based Plunkett Research Corporation, which Mr Gilmore asserts is a front to sabotage the roadworks resistance. Mr Douglas and Wimpy Construction PLC representatives deny any connection to Podgorski. At press time, Mr Podgorski was at large and his firm unavailable for comment.

My blood pressure shot up. Mr Podgorski? Since when was I known as Mr Podgorski? I could hardly speak – just flipped the paper around and stabbed at the closing paragraph for Nicole's attention. My coffee cup shook in my hand.

'The fuckin' gall!' Nicole snapped.

'My firm unavailable for comment? Did reporters call Plunkett's?!'

'He tells the cops yer wi' me, then turns round and hands the film they're after to the *Herald*!'

'Shh, shh, shh!' I quieted her. 'Be cool.'

I gnawed on a salt-rimed bacon rasher, skimming the related insets. There was a short column on other Free State goings-on:

more tree-felling slated for today, with resistance expected. Campaigners had taken to treetop roosts, and more recruits of EarthFirst!, Friends of the Earth and the Corkerhill Schools were on the ground, cozying up with chains and linked arms to every available trunk. When Mrs Wallace came back through checking after our hunger, we praised the meal and insisted she bring nothing more. Asked of our holiday plans, Nicole coolly asked for the bus timetable to Fort William – which sent the matron away again.

'We gotta beat it!' I hissed. 'When they read this paper, they'll be on to us.'

'Ah know!' Nicole said. 'Buh Ah said we'd be on fer two nights. Och, this is naff! Can't we just explain –'

'No, no, no,' I insisted. 'They're old. They're wholesome. They'll panic and call the authorities. I know it.'

'Aye, Ah reckon so,' Nicole agreed.

We gathered our things and stuffed them in our bags – never even got to pull the novel hot-water cord. There was nothing else we could do. I wasn't about to trash our holiday by sticking around so the Wallaces could call the police on us. We'd be back in rainy, crowded Glasgow in no time, down at Barlinnie being questioned about Douglas's ridiculous blunder, having my passport scrutinized, my work Visa revoked, plus answering for our hasty departure. Was evasion a charge? Christ, was I even safe on the streets of Fort William? For all I knew there was an APB out on me, or the UK equivalent. How fast does news travel in these hinterlands? A functioning fax in Glasgow was no easy come-by. I couldn't imagine technology being more advanced outside the metropolis. On the other hand, this area seemed pretty fat with tourist money. Even an old-timers' B&B off the beaten path had a digital payphone. Was my mug shot on the 'Wanted' sheets up here already? Roadworks saboteur – gimme a break.

Nicole did the talking. 'Sorry, everythin's lovely, honest. Ih's juz we wannay go a walkabou' on Ben Nevis, then see the town as well, you know, in the evenin', so we sussed it out, and reckon we'll kip in Fort William.' Stunned, Mrs Wallace was still picking up the breakfast plates. Nicole didn't give her time to speak, explaining we had the forty quid just here. I handed over £50 – a tip for her trouble – from the maximum allowable withdrawal of £200 I'd made at the Buchanan Street bus station, not knowing if I'd see a cash point up in these parts. 'Breakfast was grand. Yer lovely, the botha ya's. Cheers! Ta! Ta!' I pitched in my thank you's, smiled and waved, and we nearly trampled dear old John scooting out the door.

I hadn't been smoking much but lit up now with a vengeance. To say I was agitated would be the understatement of the century. Aye, I was ruffled – and the Scots enjoy a tipple now and again. And the Highlands are a wee bit hilly.

Why was Ruaridh fucking with my shit? How the hell had my involvement with him and the Free State and M77 – and Nicole, really – gotten to this? Now reporters from a major London news outlet were phoning the Plunkett offices? Thank God it was the weekend, though for all I knew some nosy journo could have been sniffing that lead again, calling a second time in the coming hours, when it'd be Monday morning Chicago time.

What it really came down to – more to the point, as Nicole would say – was how had I let it happen? Why did I trust him? Why? Because I'm not really a cynic; I've just often wished I was, rather than naïve. Following other people's fancies had always gotten me in hot water. I'd followed Mrs P.'s – 'Love Is Everything' – in getting married, putting all my eggs in that basket, hoping the happiness, the fulfillment, would come. And I'd followed Mr P.'s model in floating along, stumbling over my ambition, tinkering with my developers, stop baths and silver nitrates – my version of adhesives and Post-It notes. He'd had his lab, I'd made mine. Then I'd indulged Margaret's fancy, taking a getaway for rekindling the flame, dim after only a year, rather than looking hard, asking the pertinent questions, having faith. Shit, if I'd let her pick, we'd have ridden Space Mountain, toured Epcot, and probably be in a condo in Aurora right now rotting happily. I couldn't regret that entirely, but if I'd have been more assertive and resourceful, and not gone at all but rather dealt with things head on at home, she'd at least still have her life.

Nicole got us to the bus stop, hustling left and right. The wait gave me time to regroup.

'Wha' if the polis up here have been told?' Nicole asked, once seated. 'They could have a photo of you. They could be out lookin'.'

'I've thought of that, Nic, and basically there's nothing we can do. If they see us, they see us. But the good news is, if we're apprehended, I can just say, "Oh, you're looking for me? I didn't know that. Yeah, I was at the Free State. Then we left, came on holiday. Didn't do anything wrong, didn't know you wanted to talk to me. The film? Gave it to Ruaridh. Talk to him." So you see, I've thought it all through and there's nothing to worry about.'

'Except my art project.'

'Now you're getting it! Except your art project.'

Pro-ject. Praw-ject.

The bus mounted a long, low bridge spanning an inlet. Sparkle-pointed chop surrounded us, one side leading to the horizon, the other to the foot of the mountains, whose Gaelic names on signs throughout Glencoe had me thinking of them as sage masses crouching with a godlike omnipotence: *Buachialle Etive Mor. Bidean nan Bian. Ballachulish.*

Fort William was built on a half-shell at the edge of the shimmering, too-blue-to-be-true Loch Linnhe. In town, the motorway looped into a roundabout, the rumbly Highland range towering behind. The bus depot was modern, clean and busy. On the charming High Street I found several cafés and patisseries wedged among the kilt-and-kitsch shops at which to fulfill my research duties. Only 9 a.m.; I was hardly late for work.

Only a few people were yet afoot – men in hard-soled lace-ups and hiking pants. Matheson's was just opening. Nicole and I took a table facing the cobblestone, a large black for me, and a tea for her. I got out my folder of forms, Nicole a charcoal pencil and sketchbook embossed with 'Glasgow School of Art'. The coffee was tourist-priced, as expected, but this had to be ignored when rating Value, since I'd be submitting as if from Glasgow. Palate-wise, it was nothing new. It was a synthetic kind of coffee flavor, like spray-paint and tree bark. A few sugarcubes helped the cause, for both my tongue and my brain, the latter struggling to overcome irritation and get to that place of bright clarity, to attain that souped-up inconquerability that only coffee brings. Contrary to popular opinion, alcohol doesn't do it; drunkenness is just a hollowing out of the wits, an abandon that's easily confused with spark. I was more sure of this than ever now that I needed its alerting properties so urgently. I derided myself over last night's flirtation with lager. That would get me nowhere in turning this pursuit on its head, reversing the polarity of circumstance, outfoxing by sheer energy the past stalking me. I had a holiday to have, a Scotswoman to love. I summoned my hunger and furiously completed the form.

The mug-bottom appeared before expected. It was just like old times in my apartment, when I'd scoured the classifieds for vindication.

I left my bag and camera with Nicole, gave her a kiss and dashed off to another establishment. All the high-street façades were adorned with enticements. Spend your pounds here. My next stop was called No. 12, named eponymously, unoriginally, after its address. Fifteen minutes was all I needed to knock off a fair-priced Guatemalan of surprising clarity and crank out a cogent 27G. After that was Redburn Café, up the curving mall by the shop selling tartan postcards and keychains. Then the Grog & Gruel, a typical pub-grub eatery doing brekkie fry-ups for the hungover anorak crowd, who were out of their hostel beds now. I made thorough reports. My Midwestern work ethic was still intact; only relocating these establishments was delusive, and that was academic, was it not? Merely semantics, subtracting a few degrees of latitude from the locales, placing these sunny Highland cafés in gritty Glasgow, to West End streets from memory. Dalrymple Lane. Lansdowne Crescent. All the same to the folks at home. *In an octopus's garden in the shade.*

This research rampage left me with a cramped writing hand, down about eight quid, and up about four notches on the 'juiced' index, as evidenced by my trembling fingers and wobbly vision, lighting a smoke afterwards. But my confidence was up. I soared over the sea of worry that earlier had me sloshing and listing. I was doing my work, and doing it well – four solid reports on the back of several weeks' worth that had impressed Klang and hopefully Carson too. As for a confrontation, should the long arm of the law reach me, should it tap my shoulder and try to hook me off-stage by the neck, I was prepared. The whole pleading-toned spiel replayed in my head. *Didn't know you were looking for me. Didn't do anything. Don't have the film. That's with Ruaridh, talk to him.* I was even ready to recite this to Carson, should the *Herald* pester Plunkett's. *It's a misunderstanding, Mr C. Don't worry, I've had no part in this – motorways, monkeywrenching, Wimpy and councilors. I'm a coffee connoisseur with a camera, not an eco-terrorist.* I even thought – piggybacking a second cig on the butt of the first, in the high-street sun – preemptively warning the Chicago office myself might be wise. Go on the offensive. *Word to the wise. There's been a media snafu. If you hear from any reporter, disregard. Everything's in order. Nothing to hide. I'm on task, business as usual.*

Only problem: I'd forgotten about the expense-reporting procedures. This was a 'Holy shit' moment. I was supposed to file my expenditures with Melissa, scheduler, greeter and mail handler extraordinaire. Corporate credit-card statements were her domain. Given the confounding differences in sterling and dollars, the US's routing numbers and the UK's 'sort codes', Plunkett's clunky paper paychecks, sent by poky post, and the simple ubiquity of accepted plastic, along with the bureaucratic nightmare of most British institutions – okay, yes, and certain other diversions, acrimonious and otherwise, the PFS, the M77, and N.E.M. (Nicole Elizabeth Marston) – I'd neglected to get my economic house in order. The prospect of phoning home on the premise of a personal PR counterattack and being answered by judicious Melissa brought to mind this actuarial oversight.

The last thing I wanted was to speak with her now and be interrogated about these trivialities. This monetary molehill didn't need to become a mountain; I had plenty real ones around me and more interest in them. Nevermind, Nirvana.

Yes, exactly! My sizzling mind seized on this.

Nevermind.

Nirvana.

And so I returned – at a trot – to the originator of this phrase.

'Hi-ya!' Nicole said. She was standing outside Matheson's with our bags. 'Well, Ah've goh it!'

'Got what?'

'My project!'

She was sitting there, going over ideas, she said. There was a sculpture she had in mind, but it was naff and would cost loads in materials. She wasn't that keen on mixed media anyway. Meanwhile folks are queuing up for lattes, cappuccinos, and all that, and she can hear them talking about what they're going to order. Not all English, and a variety of accents. She started listening in. What she noticed was that everyone's over the moon about their drink. *'Tha's wha' Ah geh every mornin'*, and *Ah'd die withou' my espresso*. They're totally zealous about it. And competitive. Yours is crap, mine's brill. Like it defines them.'

'What a minute here – are you moving in on my territory?'

'Juz listen. Here's wha' Ah wannay do. Ah wannay take photos of folk with their coffees. See cuz, take this wee gran who came in. Sco'ish, musta been seventy. She ordered a cup of tea and dug her change out her coin purse. She was such a dear. She'd no idear wha' a latte is!'

It was a generational thing, she said, and national. What she envisioned was close upper-body portraits, like Avedon. Black and white, candid. It would be dead easy and Mr Mongrain would eat it up! She said when she did the display she'd have a bit saying she'd gone round with a marketing company looking at Scottish beverage tastes. That would make it look like she'd joined up with this heartless corporation, and while they sussed out superficially what Scots like, she'd secretly made these really personal portraits going against the type of quantifying they were doing. 'It's just the type of crap the art world goes mad for. Subversive is like black, it's always in fashion. It's full marks guaranteed!'

It *was* genius. Was she mocking my work though? I didn't ask. I wasn't sure I wanted the answer.

'Well, I guess you've thought it through,' I said. I gave the plan my hearty endorsement and complimented her cleverness. Of course I would let her use my camera. Not wasting a minute, Nicole phoned Mr Mongrain at the GSA. She used a phone box in the center of the lane, a modern glass and metal BT box, not the red relic of post-war Britain. I smoked at a polite distance, until she emerged beaming.

'Sor'ed!' she said, her bouncy gait high as ever. We found a Menzies off the high street, selected rolls of film and a large sheet of white cardstock. Ideally, we would have had an easel-like contraption to hold up the backdrop. We considered taping it up to a wall, but that would be tedious and perhaps require the permission of each shop owner. It was decided that I'd hold the backdrop behind each subject with my arms. Simple, portable. The easier the better.

Nicole promised she'd get me back for these costs once in Glasgow again. The Corn Exchange owed her some wages. No problem, I said. What did pose a slight problem, however, was the semi-coronary, the stab of chest-panic, upon seeing the bored Menzies' cashier perusing the front section of the *Herald*. Depending how far along she'd gotten, how alert she was, she could easily recognize my name on the Visa as the same as the American wanted for questioning. Paying cash was an option but a threat to our mobility and freedom. If we ran out, we were stuck. Not viable long-term if we wanted to get home by some method other than hoofing the West Highland Way.

I took my chances with the plastic. No one really looks at your name, it's just swipe, bag, and Next please. Or as they say in the UK, First please.

We went right back to Matheson's, which was still doing a fine trade in java and related concoctions. Orienting Nicole to the camera was a snap; she'd used an SLR before. She had no shyness to overcome in asking for patrons' participation. Nor was there any shortage of holiday-makers willing to go on the photographic record. There were equal numbers Scots, English, Irish, and all manner of Europeans. Nicole asking them their names and the spellings, and scribbling in her sketchbook this info, and talking about the beverage in their hands made a natural ice-breaker, during which the subjects were eased by her impish conviviality. She complimented their choice in drinks, saying to each and all, 'Lovely' and 'Yeah, those are nice.' The photo came moments after, and even I, behind the screen, sensed that by this time the subjects were, if not smiley, endeared enough to offer themselves with open countenances. As I say, this was my sense. Behind the white tagboard, I could only hear. Hear Nicole asking them to hold up their drink about chest height. Hear her instructing, 'Okee, look at the camera.' Hear her probing 'Is that your favorite then?' or 'Do ye always geh tha'?' Hear the shutter snapping.

23 Beinn Nibheis

The quaking of my upraised arms should have tipped me off. The dry mouth too. The cigarette nerves and racing thoughts. But I was helping Nicole and was chuffed, as she'd say, about her and her project. My Scottish girlfriend, photographer. Not a dancer, not a teacher – a paragon of the capable, proving the positive half of the adage, Those who can, *do*; those who can't, teach. Determined to help, I held the white backdrop for two hours' worth of subjects, with only cigarette breaks between, for the weather proved unseasonably warm and Fort William bustled with Brits, who in their weather-watching ways must have anticipated this atmospheric turn. And who had evidently garnered, in their indoor, at-home, workaday lives, a taste – a hunger if you will, like my hunger – for caffeinated drinks. More so than Glaswegians, at any rate, who had no means to hone such a yen. The high street teemed with day-trippers of all ages, and Nicole captured their likenesses with undimming zeal, seeming to appreciate more fully with every shot the far-reaching implications of individual tastes vis-à-vis national character. All the while, I dutifully played my part of one-man studio backdrop, ignoring my growling stomach, my bean-roast- and Silk Cut-flavored mouth, my aching gums, my quivering limbs. We turned her subjects to follow the climbing sun, which was too bright, too pure, too rare to these parts for us to break from.

After three rolls of thirty-six, Nicole felt she had enough for the day. She was over the moon, though hoarse from chatter. She thanked me with a kiss. Thus encouraged, I urged us to Ben Nevis, where I could share her only with nature and fulfill my quest.

At the bus station, Nicole phoned ahead for B&B vacancies. She, also smartly, ate a sandwich and crisps. For me, with cops stirring in the crowds (none doing anything but strolling and observing so far) and the Menzies' newsstands so prominent and the Skye news showing on the pub TV– yes, the bus station had its own pub – smoking proved more pertinent than eating. Wondering, wondering, would we be nabbed? Was it safe to speak, to wag my inflectionless Chicago tongue? Were the Plunkett phones ringing? Nicole, across a café table, was a refuge for my eyes. A large coffee under my nose was a refuge to my senses, an elixir of my ambition and desires.

But also a diuretic. The more potent, the more dehydrating. The fuller of flavor, the meaner to the kidneys. And this Highland java had flavor, apparently elicited by market forces, by the monied crowds who flocked here in droves, even now in the off-season.

Beinn Nibheis, in Gaelic, meant poisonous or terrible mountain. Looking at it once we were off the bus, it did what mountains do: it towered with majestic, ineffable hulk. Green at the base, and creased like a hanging bedspread, looking gullied by runoff like arroyo mud, only lush and loamy; peppered granite and schist gray midway to the summit, where no grass grew but a cap of white shone in the splintering sun. It was a bald man's head, void of stubble. Scotland had been purged of its trees some time ago, beginning reforestation efforts only in recent decades. Coming from Glasgow, I had seen swaths of evergreen plantings with unnaturally precise boundaries – rectangles like farmsteads sectioning off the *braes*, as they called them. Grafting nature back onto nature.

We stood roadside and looked: specks dotted the lower third, human specks, on the trail, clusters of men and women moving slow with pack-weight. Moving up, the vein they flowed in vanished into the fold between Nevis and its neighboring summit, Càrn Mòr Dearg, the Great Red Peak. From there, everyone was out of sight. Whether we would wrap around the other side or continue into an imperceptible distance, I could not say.

To avoid advertising my name, Nicole checked us in at the B&B and gathered the guide sheets from the park employee. I lingered at a pamphlet rack within earshot; they joked about needing sunscreen. Across the road and through a gate, we mounted the trail, starting as rockless, smooth dirt. Leg-weary, I issued a desperate prayer. *God in Heaven, be with me now. Give me strength to climb this mountain if only halfway. Grant me . . .* I meant to ask for a return of wellness, for release from unwarranted pursuit. But I didn't get there, only tangled in the ideas. The Scottish police wanted a word. Ruaridh had co-opted my photo-documenting efforts. My rights to UK residency were in jeopardy. The whole prospect of my just-burgeoning career in market research was in peril, should Carson decide I'd mislaid my obligations or crossed a moral line in regards to my duties to the client. Melissa would soon try to account for my expenses. Then the penultimate terror: all the stripping down of lies and revealing of the misrepresented past. This frightful slew kept me from seeing through any plea to my maker.

Or did I fall in vanity's trap? Maybe I wanted no help. Who but the weakest man cannot conquer circumstances on his own? Who with splendor abundant around him, a tender companion at his side and the trail at his feet, needs guidance? I had sought counsel once and been misled; why not climb by my will alone, my human powers, to oblivious heights?

All of which is to say I was not centered. My mind was fragile and jerky and the trail ever rockier and subtly rising and my back sweating and Nicole's pace brisk ahead of me. It took all my concentration to maneuver my feet and match Nicole's eager conversation, as she, excited by her project, inquired about my print-making, her voice distant as if from another room.

My print-making. My print-making? I wasn't sure what she meant. Had I made prints? Was I all right, she asked. Yes, yes. Bottled water was offered to me – Highland Spring. I took a small sip: liquid glass. Fishing line down my esophagus. What did she want to know about making prints? How did I recommend she make hers? However she liked, I guessed. Would I come with her and help? The GSA had a darkroom in the Mackintosh Building, and the paper would be supplied as part of her course dues. That'd be great. But what about size? What size prints should she make?

We climbed a stone staircase now, clean and smooth with human wear, of knobby, sometimes colorful rocks, many times the size of one's feet. A misstep would cause a bad sprain. Nicole veered, as if by instinct, left, right and center, on this roadway, at places two feet wide, at others ten. She seemed to be following a trail remembered from when she was wee. My chin was up and down, my attention skittering between a study of her course, in an attempt to mimic it, and my own footings. Into this cerebral ping-ponging was thrown the added appearance of foreign feet: toes, bony shins, wool socks, red laces. People descending. I'd stop, look up. They'd smile, honk Hi with their mouths, swerve and leap into outside lanes, into the tufts of wind-twisted grass, or prance on gracefully, calves flexing, bounding onto boulders, leaving the main lane clear for doddering, skittish me. I was an old man suddenly. Unbalanced. Grimacing. Wheezy.

'I don't know what size, Nicole. I don't know right now.'

Nicole was ahead of me, looking back, waiting. Not ten yards ahead and a whole person taller, her feet at my head's level. I ignored the green vista opening below us, but for glimpses. With the descenders passed, I re-entered the rhythm. Focus. The negatives would reveal what size the prints should be, I said. This was true to the best of my knowledge.

Had I ever sold any, she wanted to know.

'Sold any?'

'When you had the show at the coffee shop?'

'Oh, right,' I remembered. Old slick-booted Robert, whom I had imagined to be avuncular, when he was merely smooth and knowing. 'Not a one.' I cleared my throat and found a register where my voice rang – up until now raspy and toneless rattles depleting my strength.

'Och, tha's a shame.'

'I never went back for them either,' I called.

'Eh?'

'I left them there. At the gallery.'

'Yer jokin'! Did ya noh e'en collect 'em?'

'No, I left them and never went back.'

'Mel, how could you?'

'I didn't care, Nicole. I wasn't getting anywhere with it.'

Coming off her own energetic shoot, she couldn't imagine abandoning the fruits of her labor. 'But it's yer art. Tha's all an artist *has*.'

I said I wasn't an artist. I wasn't meant to be one. I wasn't cut out for it.

She was in a challenging mood. 'Anyone who makes art is an artist.'

'Maybe I was for a little bit then.'

'No! An artist is always an artist!'

'You just said anyone *making* art is an artist. I made a few prints when I was married and haven't done shit since.' I stopped again, grinning embarrassedly at my open-air cuss, as a couple in Marks and Sparks knits glided past with turned heads like shoppers on a down escalator.

'It's noh like tha'!' Nicole insisted.

'No, then what's it like?'

'Och, you're so negative sometimes!' she barked.

Was this why we were up here, to argue semantics – what is, what isn't an artist?

'Being an artist is a calling. It's a vocation. It's wha' you *are*. It's a way of life.'

I groaned at this idea. Did I disagree? she asked. What was it then? My fatigued swelled, pressing up behind my eyes, and I stopped. Hearing my steps die behind her, Nicole stopped too. She asked what I was doing. I waved her down to me, and she retreated, descending to my height. I turned us to the view with my arm around her. The glen spread below us, the hostel and B&B and Welcome Centre nothing but Monopoly houses – pinchable frameworks of near-weightless significance. New peaks emerged on the horizons, behind nearer ones. A glassy sliver of Loch Linnhe glinted through to the south. There was more sky than could be seen at once.

'Brilliant, yeah?' Nicole said, not succumbing to it really. 'So come on. Ah wannay know wha' you think. Do you disagree? Is a person juz an artist when they're makin' art?'

I lit a cigarette and must have looked at her with some pleading, some call for mercy – into those green eyes. They were resistant eyes now, eyes not interested in absorbing bland majesty. She'd seen this before, the backdrop to her girlhood. Heather-strewn hill and dale, firth and glen. The promise of new learning was in this discourse, a part of her schoolwork, testing the ideology behind her project, bouncing theories off me, whom she mistook for having the courage to form a worldview. Unsure of what I'd managed to do here with my Plunkett's opportunity, with the M77 involvement, shaken by failure's imminent return, defeated, I couldn't venture an assertion on a truism of this magnitude.

That'd always been my problem. Hopelessly constrained by my perceptions, hemmed in among the personal, out of balance with the universal by the pointless density of my own microcosm.

The wind stirred and pulled her hair across her face, and she unthinkingly turned her head with the wind and tucked the strands behind her ear. Hi-ya. Hullo. Ruddy, fit knob-kneed men passing and me with so much envy of their integration into this world, in which they could flit to the top of mountains as if it were nothing, descend, have pints of stout and shepherd's pie and hearty laughs and go home and tell their families they'd had a lovely walk up Nevis and the weather had been grand – hugging their children and making love to their wives and dying happily, and that being the end of it. Nothing unclear, nothing regretted.

'Let's just have a nice walk,' I said, my knees twitching, as the Silk Cut undercut my remaining strength. I leaned to kiss her, but she pulled back, smiling abstractly. We continued, but a puzzlement came off her now. Less confident steps. Short-changed haste in her movements. Then a consternation, with quickened, agitated stomps, and bolder, thoughtless choices – barreling straight up, tackling all sizes of stones, leaving packed-dirt aisles at the sides defiantly unused. Guilt and turmoil seethed in me, and soon the storm was upon us.

Wha' had I expected then to come of my showing? she asked. Did I think people would snatch up my prints, the whole lot? I played dumb – was dumb. Hmm? What did she mean? While far in memory's drawer was an item filed, never aired to Margaret,

Physically, I was near exhaustion, yet oddly on the brink of rejuvenation, as if I might pummel myself into ecstasy. The trail wound into switchbacks and burrowed along open-earth banks, then crested over slow-arching flats, where the path rattled with pebbles darkened by thin streams cascading down from what sources I didn't know. Melting snowcaps? Spotty rain? Boulders occasionally hulked in the hillside, green-gray with moss and lichen. With so little vegetation, scents were few, not that any would have penetrated my smoked-up receptors. At one point, a sheep lolled on a crag, looking indifferent to the neon-orange spot on his coat that identified him as a member of some unseen shepherd's flock. He stood with pleading stillness.

'Did ya or did ya noh?'

The fact was, I said, it was my choice. We had talked, my folks and I. Of course, they wanted me to go to college. They had a fund, a small one. I could have applied for loans. But what it came down to was, I looked at Mr P. He had book smarts, reason, practicality – and he was unhappy. He'd been discontented since I was a kid. Of course, adults are boring to kids. But this went beyond that. He was not boring, but bored. Resigned. Cold. Distant. Detached. As I grew up, this perception deepened. Even the things he spent the most time with – his work, the yard – he did dispassionately. Sure, he was committed to his career, but it didn't seem to excite him. He was obsessive about the yard, but its perfection didn't seem to please him, either the physical exertion or the satisfaction of a thing well done. Nothing did. He was a displeased man, and it seemed closely linked with his cerebral life. On the other hand, there was my mom. She, though perhaps not fulfilled, at least had spirit. Given a choice, I figured I'd rather have that. Meeting Margaret sealed the deal. Or maybe that's what I was looking for, something to tip me in that direction. I decided to marry instead of go to school. Love seemed more important than knowledge, if it meant not ending up like Mr P., a put-upon crank. I didn't want to encourage any of my already strong analytic tendencies, which seemed to kill passion – and I valued passion more than a job. Of course I did – I was seventeen. I figured I could blaze my own career trail.

At a switchback, Nicole looked at me as I came beside her a moment. She was not accusing now, but had excusatory compassion in her eyes.

What I had really wanted, I said, apart from fantasies of being catapulted into wealth and success, what I really thought I could do was start a life with Margaret, get work in some industry related to photography and develop my artistic sensibilities to a point where I could get a scholarship to Harrington or Dupage – they have photography programs. Or, yes, I thought it was an option, too, that if I cultivated my talent, I could earn money from my photography, then when I'd become really fluent in still photography, move on to film.

'So yer dream was really to learn film?'

'Yes, I suppose. And write the screenplay.'

The screenplay?

The screenplay. The Scientist. The one based on Mr P. The guy with the dual life, adept in the white lab coat in the realm of the infinitesimal, but bumbling when it came to life-size, feeling organisms. A portrait of a purely unemotional person, really. Or repressed, or whatever he is. 'That was always my ambition, Nicole. That's what I wanted to do.'

'*Wahned*? Do you noh anymore?'

'I let it go, I guess.'

'Why?' She inched back towards pugnacity now.

'Do you realize,' I said, looking up now, 'I never even told Margaret about that screenplay? I never shared it with her, even though she was always asking, What is up with your dad, What is up with your dad?'

'Why noh?'

'She wouldn't have understood. She watched The Today Show – all this fluffy, reactionary realism. Her idea of interpretation was the strutting and sass of dance. My film was a complex portrait. She would have said it was weird or like one of these Eddie Murphy/Jerry Lewis knock-offs. She would have missed the point.'

Nicole laughed derisively. 'Come on! Give her some credit!' My mistake, Nicole said, was classic – she'd seen it loads of times at the

GSA. I simply couldn't articulate the vision well enough, because it was unformed. It was just an idea I was afraid to pursue. So I made out like it was beyond comprehension and kept it perfect by never doin' it.

The truth hurts, especially at altitude. Even though she turned back to me with a half-tender look to soften the blow, it was a pitilessly accurate assessment.

'You're right,' I said, out of respect for Margaret. I had always hoarded the idea, kept it private. Drafts I'd started, scenes I'd written, remained packed in boxes. It was deeply personal, and I was never sure it would mean much to anyone else. I wasn't sure if it really depicted Mr P. as I knew him. 'Maybe because I don't really understand him.' With this admission, other possibilities came in, like gusts through a cracked door. The fact was, I had always believed that the reason Mr P. discouraged my pursuit of an artistic field was out of fear that I might dramatize my life, which would naturally include him, and the more I grew up and came into my own and formed my own views and perceptions, the more he receded, as if to keep from being known.

'It was like an unspoken rule – I could not question him, his stoicism, his remoteness.' Like those tell-all bios, when abuse victims say there was an *understanding* between them and their captor that the cruel perpetrations were not to be spoken of. Which seemed absurd and insulting a notion for me to co-opt, considering I hadn't endured anything violent or horrific. No Sister Wendy Rulerwhacker, no commune dope smoke, no manipulative step-parents, not saddled with heirloom legacies of war-squelched glory. Just a middle-of-the-road, middle American upbringing. Every freedom and advantage in the world. Yet why could I relate? Why did this shine in my mind like a new insight, a keen tie to others who had been mistreated? Why had it never been discussed, how Mr P. had slept so late Sunday mornings while Mrs P. and I shuffled off, she chipper, me obedient, to St Boniface for mass? Why as we scurried to meet the weekly 10.45 departure had he been shut in the cave-like bedroom, Mrs P. keeping the blinds drawn and dressing in the dark, using barefoot, soft-carpet steps and opening closet doors slowly to minimize creaks? And why asleep still at 12.30, after mass, torturously long to me, never allowed to proceed from the communion line out the door as some families who sat in the back did, but always returning to the pew to kneel again with the dry host clinging to the roof of my mouth, to watch the others go down the aisle, then hear those blessed words, 'This mass is ended, let us go in peace,' and sing the recessional hymn, all five plodding verses. Then a donut in the basement of the school across the parking lot, and Mrs P. visiting with people and talking of me and my age and my favorite subjects in school, embarrassing me with pride, then home, finally. And there would be Mr P. in the bed, his freckled shoulder to the doorway, the lemony putridness of stagnant body heat spilling into the hall. The seventies-brown rattan blinds glowing dark, holding daylight at bay.

Why?

'Holy shit,' I repeated, not knowing what else to say. I'd forgotten, in fact, what had been said last. I felt very warm. My jeans were heavy, and I wished I was wearing shorts. My legs flickered between suffocation and leadenness. Hiking itself, the navigation, had become automatic, rhythmic, but now, self-conscious, toppling or buckling seemed a distinct possibility. My mental presence leapt back and forth between the rudimentary strain of motor skills, concentration and the foreign yet tantalizing peeling away – as of a scab edged with tight pink skin – the layers of accepted Podgorski wisdom. The slate gray of averageness had subtle depths, variations, after all. My nuclear family seemed less nuclear and more potentially explosive.

'Wha's holy shit?' Nicole said. 'Tha's what you say when yer freaked out.'

'Um . . .' I uttered, my feet heavier with every step. What could I say? That I was remembering things now, putting things together to frightening effect? That altitude, air and coffee overload, and her insistence, were conspiring to evoke disturbing realizations? That not only had there been no evidence of my family possessing the emotional resources and tools to handle Margaret's cutting, but that there may have been evidence to the contrary, that in fact my reluctance to present the predicament to them may not have been an elementary matter of keeping within the Podgorski bounds of gloss, superficiality, pleasantries and platitudes but something deeper? That within the recesses of memory were cases, incidences, indicating that the family itself hadn't dealt at all with its own deficiencies? And that the paradox of this non-functionality was the very thing that had incited me to keep Margaret's troubles to myself – to ourselves. That all Mr P.'s witty and wise sayings – *A man's gotta do what a man's gotta do* – *What's good for the goose is good for the gander* – *No harm, no foul* – *Getting one's ducks in a row* – were neither witty nor wise but self-contained nothings, like a fart in a jar, a pedagogy of endless mirrors, which was precisely what I had available to me when time came to draw on and apply to my wife's suffering some learning, some wisdom, some acquired lessons? Does one just walk up a mountain and say that behind the sweltering delirium and labored breathing the idea is forming that certain realities had led one to deal with his ex-wife's difficulties obtusely, rather than head-on? That what I had been wrestling with since her death – what had sunk me into depravity and inertia and, yes, depression, was not the loss of life only but resentment over this gross vacancy in myself, this hulking cavity, the inability to engage, to sort through, to deal with the real? Could I even catch up to and seize, in words, the next-surfacing thought, that in this popcorn popper of my emotional life was the kernel of *The Scientist* – a man capably engaged with sub-particle vagaries but incapably detached from human life, human *strife*. Was this the seed of my passion for photography – observing, *focusing on*, acknowledging, honoring the real – and the bean, if you will, of my coffee obsession – maniacal insistence on nothing short of total alertness? Alertness!

'Eh?' Nicole asked after considerable pause – though not pressing, just curious. Was I there?

'Oh, I'm *here* . . .' I uttered, sandwiched between short-breathed huffs.

Just then she called, 'Oy, we made it!' I didn't see what we'd made. The summit was seemingly miles above us still. She was mounting a rise and drifting left. As I breached the crest, I followed her off the rocky trail, wide and wavering here, onto trampled grass that fanned out into a bowl-like clearing. Up ahead, a few clusters of hikers sat in the field, some towards the base of Nevis's continuing side-slope, some far across the green where the earth rose again and became Càrn Mòr Dearg. I trudged behind, sweaty and delirious. Nicole stopped and waited for me to catch up. When I reached her, she took my arm in hers and smiled at me.

Then I saw the inset water appearing, what had drawn and separated the other hikers. A mid-mountain loch, sunk down in the earth, its glassy surface blue-black like a bruise, like coffee below the brim. But this was anything but, thank God. This was Lochan an t-Suidhe, the southern lake. On Meall an t-Suidhe, the southern hill.

I'd keep a picture at my office back in Chicago. I'd remember the name.

We approached silently. The other hikers were seated at the shore, their ankles bare and dipped in. They watched us draw near the water, gauging perhaps our exhaustion against theirs. Mountains brought out all sorts, and it was curious to see your place amongst others interested in a challenge; you could share the comfort of suffering and the camaraderie of willful exertion.

Nicole and I sat at the edge and took off our shoes and socks. My feet were white and swollen and pulsing. Freeing them was heavenly – the water something beyond that. Though cold. We both gasped, then settled into it. The lake floor was hard and empty – so unlike the mushy, milfoil floors of Midwest summer-cabin lakes. No turtles or tadpoles or minnows here either. Visibility was clear to a few feet, then darkened. I reached forward and wetted my hands, rubbed them free of sweat and tar stink. Then again. Then pushing up my sleeves and bathing my forearms. Then flicking drops at Nicole. Then scooting forward, plunging my calves deeper and scooping handfuls of the chill clearness onto my shins and arms. Then scooping a handful and sipping. Then crouching over and splashing my face and gulping.

And gulping again, tasting the salt of my own sweat. Then standing and lifting off my shirt and unbuckling my jeans and kicking off my shoes.

A smile kicked the corner of Nicole's mouth.

The submersion was total, excruciating, and irresistible. I heard delighted laughter and cheers at the lake's edges and smiled in these directions as best I could, for I was blind with cleansing ecstasy, near blackout, with the dizzying exhilaration of agonizing renewal. My heart pounded. I went under as if into the silence of death.

I held it. And held it. I leaned into the pain. Then burst out.

I clambered out and shook out my hair and dressed wet, letting my clothes absorb the lake water. My skin clenched taut with gooseflesh but I didn't shiver. Tucking in my shirt, I felt a lump in my jeans pocket – the azurite I'd grabbed from the mantle at my flat. I sat down beside Nicole and showed it to her.

She took it in her hand. 'From Arizona?' she said, remembering amidst all I'd told her in the tent. 'Albuquerque,' she said, finally repaying all my quibbles with Scottishisms. 'Wha' are you like, eh?'

'I'm like me.'

She held it close and studied its rings, which wrapped, like the stitches on a baseball, around the imperfect sphere. 'Lovely,' she said.

She returned it to me.

'Did you ever pay for it?' she said – a kind offering, telling me she cared enough to listen, that she recalled I'd pocketed it back at that gift shop that I told her about in the tent, but that she didn't judge.

I took in its smooth form once more. 'No,' I said. 'I never did.' Of course, the temptation in life was to say that you had, and to go on feeding this impression with whatever it hungered, pointing fingers all the way.

'Well?' she asked.

I shrugged. 'I think I ought to call home,' I said.

After a minute, she said, 'Sorry fer gettin' stroppy wi' ya.'

I said, 'Nae bothar.'

'*Yer* an artist, Mel. Tha's wha' Ah meant tah say. Yer an artist by nature.'

'Hmm, I thought I was a market researcher.'

'Nah, tha's only a job,' she said.

I stood, took her hand and pulled her up. The sun was still warm, but dipping. One of the other couples had left the lake. 'Aye, we'd better go,' Nicole said, and stepped away. I looked at the surface – undisturbed, thick and dense like mercury, reflecting Càrn Mòr Dearg and the dimming sky. I reared back my arm to send the gemstone sailing, then instead tossed it short, underhand, where I'd just bathed. It entered without a splash.

24 Klang's Second Coming

I was back in Clix, in Wynton, behind the counter, looking for a packet of prints by last name which were nowhere to be found. I wore the old blue shirt with the company logo stitched in it. I was a common proletarian dweeb, futureless, doomed to answering the same questions about film speed and red-eye and did they want four-by-six or five-by-seven, matte or glossy. My sense was of a Saturday, a three-to-nine shift, and it was after Spring Break or graduation – busy. Customers were lined up, though they didn't materialize, just emitted a pressing presence. I wanted to get the key to the lower cabinet to look for the missing prints – sometimes they went astray of the columned bin – but I couldn't find it. From the back area the ol' Minilab QSS beeped its error beep (the pitch, I swear, was true to life), which meant either the fluid tank or paper stock needed refilling. Then, in that way that it does, time shifted and I was going through the closing checklist: garbage emptied, floor swept, reports run, drawers counted and receipts put in the cash bag in the safe in the office. The crew was doing what we did at close: they vacuumed, restocked the film and straightened the frames for sale. I had the sense, one that had been a regular reality, of Mr P. waiting out in the lot with the car running. I pulled the chain on the neon OPEN sign, and hit the lights and let the crew out, then set the alarm. Outside was neither the Podgorski family wagon nor a dream-warped conveyance, nor even the empty lot; rather a sandy, arid expanse, endless under nightfall. The exciting limitlessness of this landscape shocked me to sentience. To Fort William. To a parched mouth. To Nicole beside me.

There's only one thing Brits love more than tea, and that's a scandal. London's *Independent* was a triple threat. There was John Douglas above the fold, the latest of Major's ministers resigning for 'non-political reasons'. There was OJ, in the sidebar with his defense attorney's rhyming appeal for acquittal. And there was me beneath the fold, that side parlor of newsworthiness. Not one but three CCTV camera stills: dotty, scan-lined images from tape. The police van at the Free State had me orbiting the melee with my trusty Pentax. In the Glasgow sporting-goods store I balanced mid-stride, clutching the tube-like tent, looking more surreptitious, via the overhead angle, than I'd felt breezily shopping. And one from the bus-station ticket counter, Nicole at my side. This last one flattered me by looking like a legitimate fugitive. Leaning coolly on the counter, a foxy female standing close, she devoted to my imprudent but winning brilliance.

Like the best scandals, this one was overblown, puffed up. The slant was political: not so much news as an argument for invasive surveillance, counterbalancing the flak CCTVs took from civil-rights advocates. The proof was in the pudding: me. I'd been detected and identified, my travels were known. These were the rewards of an omnipresent Big Brother. Yes, there were ongoing suspicions around my involvement in the Douglas event. No, my absence from police testimony despite the helpful forensic evidence I'd produced was not understood. But the threat of total evasion was contained. And because of that Ruaridh had owned up to supplying the photo to the *Herald*, which had taken heat but refused to reveal its sources. A conciliation, I figured. Ruaridh saving his editor friend's ass. He wasn't doing me any favors, though. A steady paranoiac, he still maintained I was in cahoots with Wimpy.

Both he and Douglas had been fined £250 for their roles in the disturbance. Douglas, trying to paint his attack as a defense of children's safety and 'family values', called Ruaridh the Pied Piper for having incited Corkerhill schoolchildren to join the protest. 'I don't even play the flute,' Ruaridh was quoted as saying.

I was too subdued to panic at all this, coming down off my privately tempestuous climb. I sat in the lounge of the B&B, break-fasting on scones and juice, waiting for Nicole. There was no attentive Mrs Wallace here, but a buffet laid out with à la carte Müesli, fruit, and other time-insensitive items. At the sight of a coil kettle and a jar of Sanka, I winced. Not even an option. This was no hair-of-the-dog morning, and I was still no hair-of-the-dog guy. Even if it had been organic Columbian, shade-grown, fresh roasted, burr mill-ground and steeped with Evian through gold filters, I'd have foresworn. Every cell in my body quivered and twitched, as if in their nuclei cowered little men, unburdened but vexed, cross and distrustful, cursing me not only for yesterday's abuse but for years of self-agitating.

How I would make the day's 27G quota was a humbling and ironic proposition now.

Yet that was the agenda, along with Nicole's project. She needed more Scots subjects. Staggering down Nevis in the dusk, we'd somberly acknowledged the need to head back to Glasgow soon and decided on hiring a car, the best and perhaps only way to make tracks while having the freedom to stop at coffee shops of our choosing. The added expense would sting, but of course I put the PRC Visa up for offer. At least we'd be sitting today. My calves ached. My quads ached. My glutes ached – it hurt just to sit on my ass.

As for the rest of me, my non-muscular parts, my brain, my heart, the inner Mel that I carried around, so it is with the parts, it is with the whole. I was a bundle of trembling atoms bound together around a core, glommed onto a skeletal structure by the force of their electric static. I was calm but pulsing. Like I'd been cracked open and was oozing. Like a blister popped. Like a bone snapped for resetting.

There was now the matter of looking at the afterspill, the blood on the bandage. I found myself thinking – and sat forward, attentive to myself, on the flowery sofa, my hands nerve-shaky holding the scone and juice – that when I'd said to Nicole I hadn't blamed myself for Margaret, not since leaving the US, that this was true but only to an extent. I had blamed. I had blamed this thing I'd been calling the Podgorski tradition. I'd blamed it harshly for miring me, and blamed myself for not rising out of it. I hoped to do that still, rise out. I felt mostly there, like the bulk of me was on solid ground.

Before rising anywhere, though, I intended to repay Nicole's generosity, her prodding me into feverish recognition, her seeing me off the mountain into a nourishing dinner (fish, chips and peas) and forgiving bed. For all she'd done, for who she *wuz*.

She came down, wet-haired and morning-fresh, I tossed the *Independent* on the side table, and we headed out. The car was hired under Nicole's name, with cash. Luckily, the rental agent was no newshound. At the Esso, pay-at-the-pump technology kept us shrouded in anonymity as I stayed in the car, and Nicole swiped the plastic. And while the pounds-per-litre to dollars-per-gallon conversion was beyond my *maths* capacity, I knew freedom wasn't cheap. I ballparked it at at least triple the cost of gas at home.

We were in the clear, if not in the black, in our right-sided Ford.

I drove. Nicole had ideas about medium-sized towns where good cafés could be found. She took watch duty. Adjusting to the gear shift's left-hand orientation and the reversed roadways was easy enough. Hardest was minding the road through the breathtaking Highlands. Mountains scrolled on either side, sharp, craggy, otherworldly. I was hyper-alert, hyper-attuned to steering, speed and depth, but dangerously so, with the unreality of a video game. After a few miles it was obvious that a tonic, a leveler, would be a wise choice. I swung us through a roundabout and into a Highland version of a strip mall – a few roadside shops in a small village – where Nicole ran inside and came out with two IRN-BRUs. The bean-head's bloody mary.

Perhaps overconfident, I bungled the second roundabout, picking the wrong ramp and sending us west to Kyle of Lochalsh. I never did learn a translation, but I wasn't so green to ask *who* Kyle was. I took it for a Gaelic landform word, on the order of *moor*, *glen* and *brae*. We arrived in a port town a stone's throw from the Isle of Skye, the most romanticized of the Hebrides.

'Speed, bonnie boat, like a bird on a wing,' Nicole sang as we rolled through a narrow lane. 'Onward, the sailors cry . . .' Seeing my puzzlement, she queried me on the source. '"Skye Boat Song"? Do ye noh know ih?'

She could be forgetful at times of our differing roots. For all her determined insights, little gulfs spread between us regularly. 'Aw, brilliant song,' she said, looking off. This seemed a matter of the tune's mirth concurring with her own buoyant feeling. She was doing her mother right, minding her books. A studious streak ran through her, deep as the fault-formed lochs. Aspirations surfaced too, perhaps revived by hearing of the derailment of mine. 'Ah can't be bothered' was put away now. She clutched the camera in her lap, eyes scanning for our next stop.

We reached a waterfront where a timeless sea-harbor-type stucco building with dormer windows stood, and a few cars awaited the ferry's return. There was that thing that Americans alternately seek and are nauseated by: quaintness. Old tires were used as bumpers here, as on Washington Island. As long as we were here, we got out and headed to the tea room next to a Royal Mail office. I ordered a small black coffee. Its coppery tinge, its medium-brown color, the way it swished limpidly like sea water – I knew this coffee. The 27G practically scored itself.

Only one customer materialized for Nicole, a woman of fifty, nonchalant about the proposition. I proffered the white tagboard, Nicole made palaver and snapped. As we waited outside for other punters to appear, I overheard the locals, leaning on their cars and pointing across the water, whinging – *griping* – about the construction of a toll bridge. We looked across to Kyleakin, the town on the isle – the crossing was that short. With the Cuillin mountains rising behind, the scene was inviting.

'Should we cross?' I asked Nicole. We were sitting on the cobble-stone wall beside the ferry pier. I fondled a cigarette, waiting for the urge to light it. Nicole held the camera, cupping the lens like a pro.

'Nah,' she said. 'There's nothin' fer us there.'

'No towns?'

'There's towns.' She looked at me sheepishly, apologetically.

I put the smoke back in the pack. When no café customers came, I tossed the pack in a bin as we returned to the car.

This was a verb to Scots. *Ah binned 'em.*

I said to Nicole that I wanted to see Castle Urquhart. I had a neighbor at home who'd appreciate me bringing home a picture or two. Though it wasn't directly back to Glasgow, it was moving on. Nicole said Okee but we'd have to be gettin' back the next day. There was an understanding here that we were stretching my finances, stretching her time away from work and school, but that it was worth it. This was a *one-off*, that Briticism for an unlikely but useful thing.

Invergarry. Aberchalder. Achnaconeran. Drumnadrochit. Our path sounded like a head cold but looked like perfect health. Fierce, austere mountains. The sky multi-layered, banks, indiscernible from fog or cloud, hanging over passes. Deciduous forest, unlike the regimented pines. Trees heavy with rain bare on some stretches, carpeting the roadway with slick leaves sliced by tire trails. Idyllic towns surviving on God knows what industry. Tourism, distilleries, sheep farming. Unmended walls sectioning rocky fields. Crofts with exposed beams and slate roofs enlivened by red, blue, yellow doors. A church spire. A high street. A gas station, a phone box, trimmed hedgerows. A café. Each stop was like a touchdown along our flight of the A82, before it climbed again, and we clung to hillsides on the edge of Loch Ness, that bottomless black gash.

In each place, an odd assortment of locals and passersby increased Nicole's tally, filling up the final roll of Fuji 400 ISO. My stash of blank 27Gs diminished, though I took only sips. Even those stung my tongue, tastebuds agitating into raised nubs, like stroking a cat from the tail end. I chased with ice water. Waitresses were contrite and overgenerous with offers to replace my untouched purchases, every displeased American a potential word-of-mouth demerit against the region's visitability.

As for the content of the Plunkett forms, mimicking the passion of previous batches came easily. I aped my own aged attitudes and, emboldened, made larger claims: the inferior product accounted for the slow business. In fact, this was self-reflexive. If you have fresh and flavorful, rich and dynamic coffee, you will move it faster. Stagnant product begets a stagnant ledger book. But how to get things moving? A simple Grand Opening can go miles in overcoming unfamiliarity. Marketing 101: on a cold, dismal Glasgow day – these reports were transmuted to Glasgow, remember – give out generous samples of hot, delicious coffee. Send punters away steamy and smiling, I wrote, seeing this now more as a business model than a life cure. Do it all week if you have to. You'll recoup the loss, it'll rain again, and they'll be back in droves.

I kept this hyperbole to myself – or to the page, rather. For Klang and Carson's eyes only. It seemed to run counter to the integrity Nicole sought to reveal in the Scots, her subjects, my subjects. Yes, she'd pitched her project partly as a kind of in-joke on the sometime gullibility, the hokiness, of the art world, but she couldn't carry out a falsity or just willfully abandon her heuristic interest. She trod the tightrope between irony and earnestness. This was our bond now. Paradoxically, our solidarity was in something otherly: the patrons whose lives we touched, though at divergent tangents; and art, whose purpose we'd both chased but had yet to tackle. Strangers brought us intimacy. Scotland, Nicole's homeland, my home away from home, was a common ground. An atmosphere of pointed seeking – seeking an aesthetic through which to regard and interpret this nation, this culture – pervaded the rented Fiesta's pine-scented cabin and the entire adventure which, from the outside, probably seemed aimless.

In Lairgmore I slipped away to the Bank of Scotland, telling Nicole I was going to Woolworth's for chuggy – chewing gum. After much negotiation and an overseas call to the Citibank Visa customer-service line, I was able to wire a sum from my personal checking account, which had some Plunkett's salary pay in it. This required knowing Citibank's 'sort code' and for some reason its physical address, as if the digital ones and zeros, if lost, would ask directions. Dealing some reprieve to the Plunkett expense account I'd been abusing I thought would show my intent to make good on the personal items – the camping gear, the cab fares, the B&Bs. Melissa, Plunkett's meticulous bookkeeper, might show mercy.

Nicole and I orbited around each other in our joint but exclusive operations. Even speaking of other topics disrupted the energy, the flow. When a BBC report came on the car radio, we listened, acknowledged, but did not remark. Events from Pollok Park were reported on in one of those savvy radio pieces with real audio and the intimate voiceover of a concerned journalist. They were calling it CarHenge. A caravan of Englanders had driven up from Manchester, 'To Glasgow With Love' painted on their vehicles. The cars were junkers: they were burned on-site and their corpses buried upright in the ground 'like the menhirs of Stonehenge'. This was the aim of some factions, the death of car culture, though politicians were keen to point out the hypocrisy of burning rubber and putting wreckage in ground in the name of the environment. Some people seeing the spectacle were confused by the message of celebration. Over background sounds of folk music, a scene of revelry was described: dancing, drinking – and drugs, allegedly. At the fringes, police and security. Wimpy and its forces had spent the day dislodging occupants of the rope-connected forts and razing a dozen trees. Protesters, awarded interview soundbites, came off as delusional, saying they would stop this process yet, if not at the legislative level, then at the brick-and-mortar level.

The laying of tarmac was slated to begin next week.

We reached Inverness around dinnertime and went for pizza at a place in town, a Pizza Hut, menus modified to Scots tastes, with corn and baked beans and bacon among the toppings. The most literal of places, you could not get lost here. The restaurant was on Bank Road, where all the banks were. From there we drove up Bridge Street, not much longer than its prominent bridge, and took a room off Castle Street, site of Inverness Castle.

Nicole, propped on the bed with a notepad, set to work on the text portion of her project. I went down to the lobby and faxed Klang. It was a large stack of 27Gs, and I stood by as each page was sucked through at a glacial pace. The call would be added to our room bill.

In the morning, we drove out to Castle Urquhart. Why, of all the dozens of castles in Scotland, Mrs Brown had mentioned this one, I couldn't remember. She wasn't a descendant of Clan Urquhart. Hadn't she said she was *née* MacDougal or MacKay? It seemed an awful long way to go to acknowledge a neighbor. But the imminence of my return was pressing, and it seemed like a normal thing to turn up with. Nicole took my picture before the castle, and a tourist took ours together. Sure, the scene was lovely, with low-slung Loch Ness slick alongside and edged by the ever-rising hills, but walking through it was like netting a ghost. Here was once the drawbridge, the dovecot, the smithy, the chapel, and the store rooms where grain was dried. Yes, fine. But here now is a tuft of sod, some crumbling orangish bricks, and me, who will soon be gone.

We were back in Inverness by noon. The legend of Nessie had turned this Caithness port town into a destination. It was sprawling and lively. The sea monster's appeal had persisted through stages of exotic attraction and pseudo-scientific inquiry. Now it was debunked kitsch, which should have been the death of it, but in fact had the opposite effect. You couldn't kill what didn't live. The abundance of retail proved it. You could drape your person in Nessie wear, feed off Nessie packaged goods, on Nessie plates. Take your tea in a Nessie mug, play whist with a Nessie deck. Whereas once there were Nessie hunters, now Nessie hunted you – you and your wallet.

Wearied by being prey, we wound out the day in town, listlessly going through my market-research routine – it was a work day, after all, and this my mobile office – in Inverness's bistros and tea houses. But when we climbed Bridge Street in the afternoon to fetch our bags and depart, the listlessness quickly shattered. There was Klang, at the bar, a pint in his hand, eyes on the only entrance.

'Holy shit!' I shouted. This was inevitable.

'Surprised?' he said, stepping down from the stool. He wore a tan overcoat and greeted Nicole with soft remorse, as if she were a soldier's mom and he an army messenger: 'Nicole.'

'Hi-ya. Whatcha doin'?' She was not cheery but suspicious.

'Yeah, what are you doing here?' I said, shaking his coolly offered hand.

'Well, Mr Podgorski,' he said, formal and coy, 'we need to have a word.' He picked up his briefcase and pint. 'Perhaps Ms Marston should wait upstairs.'

'I don't see why,' I said. 'Anything you have to say to me, she can hear.'

'Very well,' Klang said. He motioned to a corner booth. 'Shall we?' Seated, he took out a pack of American cigarettes and offered it to me. I waved it away, which surprised him. All his gestures were slight but pointed now, as with the curious cock of his head at my refusal. While nothing in Klang's manner indicated he was on a friendly visit, I threw out a genial flippancy anyway.

'So, Klang, how's it going? How'd you know I was here?'

'First things first, Pod. Before you get any ideas, I've got a mobile phone in my pocket. 999 is dialed, and my finger's on "send". So no funny business.'

'Funny business?' Nicole asked.

'Just remember that, both of you. Now – how'd I find you? Easy.' He lit up and exhaled. 'Every fax transmission is required by law to bear record of its origin. It's a security measure, enforced worldwide. Puts the kibosh on anonymous threats, ransom notes, things of that nature.' He produced what would be the first of many paper exhibits: the previous evening's fax. '"The King's Arms" is printed right at the top, Mel. I didn't even have to trace the number. A phone book will tell you, 01463 – that's Inverness. Really, you have to cover your tracks better.'

'But I'm not trying to cover my tracks,' I said.

'No?' Klang was very much enrobed in the aura of interrogator, and Nicole, who sat with me on my side of the booth, took my hand in solidarity against him. Klang's eyes noted even this. 'My dear,' he said, 'I hate to be the bearer of bad news, but your friend here is not all he seems.' He indicated me with a quasi-gentlemanly outlaying of fingers in my direction, like he was a magician setting up an illusion. 'Melvin' – he turned to me – 'is there anything you'd like to tell her?'

'Klang,' I said, pushing his hand away, 'I've told her everything there is to tell.'

'Is that so? Then you won't mind her knowing that you're not ... *divorced?*' He sculpted the glowing ember of his cigarette in the ashtray, forcing patience, then looked up with burbling glee to take in our reactions.

'Aye, wha' abou' ih?' Nicole said.

'No, he's not divorced at all,' Klang barreled on. 'Far from it. In fact, his ex-wife is no longer *of this world.*'

With a shrug, Nicole said, 'Aye.'

Klang was let down not to have shocked her, so tried again, aiming for the result he'd anticipated. 'She's *deceased*, Nicole.'

'Aye, Ah know.'

'And how do you know this?' he said, suspiciously.

'He told me.'

He paused. 'Ah, but too many lies have a way of catching up, don't they, Mel? Why don't you tell Nicole about the circumstances around Margaret's untimely demise.'

'I already have.'

'That it happened out of state.' He flipped open a notepad and glanced at it. 'In –'

'Arizona,' Nicole said.

'Arizona,' Klang echoed. 'Under strange circumstances.'

'Aye, strange, eh? Wi' his folks coverin' ih up an' all.'

'His *parents*? Of course! So you had your suspicions too,' Klang continued, ignoring me. 'When were you going to open your eyes, girl? Blinded by love, I guess.'

'Och, once he told me abou' ih, Ah could tell he was wracked with guilt.'

'You pitied him? Jesus! You're worse off than I thought!'

'Buh he's doin' *great* now!' Nicole said, with cheer.

Doon g'date!

'Oh, I see,' he said. 'He's doing great. He must have told you how it was an *accident.*'

'Aye. Wha's he like? He swears it's his own fault buh!' She

looked over her shoulder and with equal weight said, 'Is there a waitress abou'? Ah fancy a drink.'

'So you've admitted everything to Nicole?' Klang asked me.

'Klang, I have nothing to hide anymore. I can't ignore what I did.'

'You heartless bastard,' Klang said. He clutched at his chest, at the lapels of his coat. 'Look, Klang, I know I lied and said I was divorced. I'm sorry about that. That was my way of dealing with it – with my role in it. I mean, hell, I wouldn't have been so bothered if it was just an accident.'

With a squinting Barbara Walters-esque visage, with disbelieving persistence, he breathed, 'So it was no accident, and you admit this as freely as you admit your name is *Melvin Podgorski*?'

'Absolutely.'

'Aha!' Klang stabbed out his cigarette and produced something else from his inside pocket, a tape recorder.

'Wha' the fuck?' Nicole said.

'It's all over, you two – this little Bonnie and Clyde routine. This is the end of the line!'

'Yer mental!' Nicole laughed.

'Don't try anything! There's people who know where I am – Mel's parents for one! And there's witnesses!' He motioned to the empty room.

As if on cue, a waiter sidled up and took Nicole's order for a vodka lemonade and a lager for me. Klang concealed his tape recorder.

'Oh, okay, okay,' I said. 'I get it. You think you're onto something.'

'I'm onto *everything*,' Klang said sinisterly. 'I've got you nailed to the wall.'

'Klang, I didn't kill Margaret, if that's what you're thinking.'

'Kill her?' Nicole laughed. 'Dohn be daft!'

'No? Then how do you explain this?' Klang said, pulling out exhibits B and C and turning them towards me. One was a grainy copy of newssheet from the Arizona *Sun-Ledger*, the other a print-out with a strange bit of code at the bottom – strange at the time, though it would become commonplace to my eyes in my future employment:

www.courthouse.state.az/ record.asp?=945872.

Margaret's full name appeared in the header.

'It's remarkable, this World Wide Web thing. You should look into it,' Klang hissed. 'In London, the internet cafés are taking off. Now – don't think you can snow me as easily as the others, Pod. Reynolds's testimony says it all. It's so obvious. Arizona was the perfect spot. Retirement towns. Gated communities. Golf resorts. You can't swing a dead cat in Flagstaff without hitting a corrupt cop. He must have been bored senseless, just itching for a bribe, a little excitement. You two met at the rest stop beforehand. You had it planned to the letter. You'd called Triple A weeks in advance, asking specifically for this route. Before that, you'd confided to your friend Esposito about your wife's suicidal tendencies. This corroborated the marks on her legs in the autopsy and cast you as a victim, but it also spells *inconvenienced*. She was getting in the way of your career ambitions.'

'Jesus Christ, Klang!' I said. I couldn't help exclaim. This was the most preposterous thing I'd heard. 'You talked to Greg?' Nicole was speechless, looking at me a little funny. 'You don't *believe* this, do you?' I asked her.

'Those lies catching up with you, Mel?' Klang lit up again and sat back. 'Can't keep 'em straight, can you? What have you told her? What's she gonna believe now?'

'Look, first of all, how the hell would I plan to have someone hit the cop car and send the spotlight into the back of my hatch? How do you calculate that trajectory? And then to have Margaret sitting exactly where she needs to be?'

'Oh, right, the trajectory,' Klang said. 'From the green van that never materialized.'

'This is madness. I don't have to defend myself. The autopsy shows death by blunt force. Did you download that?'

'Right here,' he said with pleasure, pulling out another sheet of paper from his briefcase, propped open beside him. 'Sure, blunt force. You bop her in the head and place her in the seat. Reynolds – what is he, six foot six? – breaks off the spotlight and throws it through the back window. Wearing gloves of course. No finger-prints. Bada-bing, there's your crime scene. How convenient that no one saw the plate on the car that allegedly went by. What was it again? Right, the most generic, abundant vehicle on the road – a green minivan! It's the perfect story. Too unbelievable to be disproved. Who came up with it? You or Reynolds? My money's on you. Fabrication is your forte.'

I looked at Nicole again. She was slouched in her seat with a straw at her lips, taking this all in like it was an episode of *Law & Order*. She didn't look worried, but the gears were turning. She was enjoying the stretch of imagination. When her eyes turned up to mine, I saw in them strong belief in me, a confidence, a knowingness.

'Unforunately, no, Klang,' I said, softly, palms up. 'We were in the wrong place at the wrong time. That's all there is to it.'

Klang quaffed his beer nervously, puzzled deep within himself, letting the spool of improbability unravel.

'Wait,' Nicole said. 'Ya thought Mel wuz a murderer, and ya let him doss about wi' me in the Highlands. Ya didnay phone the polis or nuthin'?'

'Call the fuzz?' Klang laughed. 'That's the last thing I'd do, even if Mel turned out to be the antichrist.' He turned serious. 'No, cops couldn't find snot in a kindergarten, especially bobbies. Besides, we gotta keep a lid on this.'

'Hey, what's this about "your parents know where I am?"' I said, recalling his excited interjection.

'Well, you know. You must have talked to them by now?'

'No, why? Don't tell me –'

'Oh, Pod. You shouldn't keep a worried mother in the dark. No wonder she was so grateful to hear from me. Though she wasn't happy about everything I had to say.'

'Klang!'

'Admittedly, the suggestion of foul play may have been out of line,' Klang said, looking delighted to have agitated me. 'But they're fine. You can ask them yourself. They'll be here this afternoon.'

'What?!'

'Oh, dear,' Nicole added.

'I had to reach them. I had questions. When I saw the bit on the BBC, you know, the MP going ballistic at the park, and they mentioned your name, I got to thinking. That Ruaridh is a bright guy. A bit crazy, but bright. Maybe he was right about your allegiances. What did he call it, roadworks saboteur? It kind of made sense. I didn't quite get why you were at the protest site in the first place other than to see Nicole. That's when I got online. But some things are best straight from the source.'

'Jesus, Klang, you asshole.' He shifted from suspicions of homicide to pride in his own sly methods with disturbing ease. 'You're ignoring the glaring oversight of your investigation: I'm innocent.'

'Hey, you should be thanking me! Your folks were worried sick! Don't you know the wire picked up yesterday's story? CNN too. They broke in on an OJ pundit panel with those security pics. Nothing substantial. "American missing in Scotland. Wanted for questioning, whereabouts unknown". But that's CNN's bread and butter: hazy intrigue. Your parents saw you on television. They about had a heart attack.'

'Holy shit!'

'You're famous!' Nicole laughed.

'Yeah, great.'

Klang went on. 'I was lucky to reach them. Their phone was ringing off the hook. Your aunts and uncles, neighbors, old teachers, your ex-in-laws. They're all wondering what the hell is going on.'

'Oh, my God,' I said. 'But I didn't do anything! I took photographs!'

'Yeah, about that . . .' Klang said.

'Wait, though,' I said. I had things to talk about with my folks, but hadn't planned on dragging all the ugliness into the light just yet. 'They're coming *here*? To Inverness?'

Klang assured me they were. When he'd reached them yesterday morning, he said, they'd been frantic, trying to decide whether to book a flight or call Scotland Yard. 'Funny – they didn't exactly know what Scotland Yard was.'

'Funny ha ha.'

'What?'

'Nothing.'

Klang said again that I had him to thank, this time because he'd talked Dick and Rose – that's what he called them – out of contacting the British authorities or Carson, both of which they'd considered. 'They were going nuts. I said, "Calm down. I got a fax. I know where he is."'

'And I should thank you for that? Now I've got to deal with them on top of everything else?'

'Hey, you'd have your nuts in a sling right now if it wasn't for me. You'd be behind two-way glass under a hot light.'

'I've got nothing to hide,' I said. 'I just wanted to spend time with Nicole before we have to go back.'

'Mel, you idiot – that's not your only problem anymore. You're forgetting one thing. The most important thing. *The account*.'

'The account?'

'Burback's! We need to keep a lid on this! If you haven't blown it already. That was another reason to handle this myself. You may have screwed yourself out of a job, or you may be a mole after all – I don't know yet, and if I need to take care of you myself, I will. But I plan on cashing in on this. This place is ripe for the picking, and all we have to do is turn in our homework.'

'Now I'm a mole? What next, Hitler's illegitimate love child? *My parents*, Klang. How are they getting here? When?'

'They have my mobile number. I had to keep in touch so they wouldn't flip out and start alerting everybody. They called when they touched down, and they'll call again when they get to the station.'

'Touched down? What station?'

'At Glasgow airport. And Inverness train station.'

'Holy shit.'

'Och, ya nutter!' Nicole said to Klang, finally speaking up. 'He doesnay wannay see them. His wife's died, and his folks sound half mad.'

'Well, what do I know?' Klang said. 'He told me he was divorced! I don't know what to believe!'

The waiter brought more drinks and emptied the ashtray. Seemingly enticed, Klang took out another cigarette and, before lighting it, sighed heavily. He sat back and pulled his hand through his hair. 'Look,' he said, lowering his voice. 'Why don't you just tell me who you're really with. Greenpeace? Is Nexis a front? Mafia, right? Maybe 3M. Because I got your data.' He thumbed off the next few sheets from his briefcase. 'I know you weren't hired on merit, that's obvious. Something there hasn't seemed right from the start. But I can't figure out who's behind it.'

'Klang, I'm not with anybody,' I pleaded.

'Wha' hasnay seemed right?' Nicole asked.

Klang chose to reply to Nicole. 'From the beginning, his 27Gs were different. They don't read like an MBA's. Okay, I know MBAs, and Mel is not an MBA. Marketing people are not particularly thoughtful. They do not work tirelessly to specialize in one small area and get to know it inside and out. They are looking to apply broad concepts that they've learned by rote from textbooks and proven business models. If they care at all about originality, it's only in the sense of looking for a stroke of luck. They want to come up with that one unique idea, the right thing at the right time, the thing nobody else thought of. They're money-hungry leeches. They're opportunistic pedants. I should know – I'm one of them. I don't want to work particularly hard. I'm just looking to hit the big payoff. Which is why I need to figure out if you're out to wreck this Burback's contract. Because so help me God, I don't care if I'm the only one crossing the pond alive, I'm getting my commission and bonus.'

Klang looked to Nicole as if to incite her, but he could not get between her and what she believed. He could not undo what I'd done in telling her the truth.

'My 27Gs,' he continued, making a case to rouse her disbelief, 'the ones I fill out in London, I stuff them full of buzz words and meaningless marketing terms. That's what everyone does in product surveys. Mel's – his are different. He's actually paying attention. Not just kowtowing. Why? I don't know yet. But your ambition, Mel, is a giveaway. All this thoughtfulness and observation. And you're not exactly a shark at economics. Something's off. But what? There's nothing else on you on the web. No college degree. One year with Nexis. A photography showing at a coffeehouse.'

'Yer noh seein' the forest for the trees,' Nicole said, speaking Klang's language. 'No job record. No degree. He's an artist. That's all. Juz artists dohn care abou' the corporate world and salaries and diplomas.'

'An artist, huh?' Klang said. 'Isn't that high-falutin'?'

'It's not really,' I said. 'I'm just a guy with a stunted résumé.'

'Oh, and humble too,' Klang said. 'But I was ready for this pitch, and there's one more item.' He dipped into his briefcase again. This time, he kept the papers facing himself. 'See, when the trail goes cold, you have to check if they doubled back. Know what I mean? It's the oldest trick in the book. If you're not planted into Plunkett's, then Plunkett's is in on the plant. And your denial fits that bill perfectly.'

'What now, Klang?' I said. I was at the bottom of my second lager and about ready to dive into Klang's smokes, just to ride out this inquiry.

'My ace in the hole, that's what.' He laid out one sheet – another photocopy of a newspaper article. This one looked dated; the fonts didn't have the crispness of computerized typesetting, and the men in the small photo wore the medium-length hair, thick sideburns and the wide striped ties of the seventies. '3M VP Steps Down to Join Research Firm' read the headline. It was from the business section of the Chicago *Sun*.

'The past is never buried,' Klang said, blushing at the clumsiness of this *bon mot*. 'The big papers have their back catalog online already. Searchable by keyword and everything.'

'I get it,' I said plainly.

The simplistic caption read: 'Bob Carson (left) 3M Vice President of Product Development, with Richard Podgorski, Chemical Engineer, at a press conference'.

'That's my dad! And Carson!'

Their hands were locked in a firm businessman's grip, Carson with his elbow out and up, grinding down with leverage on my dad's.

Nicole sat up and leaned in, saying, 'Lemme see.'

'Carson was at 3M?' I said. Skimming the text, I picked up that he'd had a good, if short, run, bringing the stock price up to the highest it'd been since the company had put out – ironically – Scotch tape. The Carson era had seen the successful introduction of Stick-'Em Notes and Liquid-White and the dry erase board. 'What does this mean?'

'Little on its own,' Klang said, handing me another page of bygone characters reanimated into printed pixels. '"Plunkett Research Inc. Awarded Major 3M Contract".

'One year later,' Klang said.

Carson was pictured again. He looked a little chubbier, more like his current self. This was from *Investor's Business Daily*. The premise: the firm started little more than twelve months ago by former 3M VP was taking off, thanks largely to a contract from the founder's old haunts.

'Does the word *nepotism* mean anything to you?'

'Look,' I said. 'My old man may have had some problems in his younger days. I've got questions myself. But I don't know about this. I mean, where's the wrongdoing?'

25   *Sinecure*

I wouldn't have to tell Klang anything – not that I knew anything. Mr P. would do it for me. This was a first. Most of my relationships had featured me answering for Mr P. – his reticence, his remoteness – not him for me.

They arrived like a pair of social misfits to the junior prom: awkward, hesitant, but purposeful, entitled to be there. They just stepped in and stopped as if beneath a flowered arch awaiting their introduction over a loudspeaker. Only this was the King's Arms, Friar's Lane, Inverness, Scotland, UK. There were no corsages, but the smells of cigarettes and lager. In lieu of piped-in ballads, the bar telly's play-by-play of a Celtic–Rangers match. Announcing them, only my stunned inner-Mel: *Dick and Rose. Mr and Mrs P. Dad and Mom.*

It's tempting to say I couldn't believe my eyes. Actually, the vision was hyper-real; I couldn't deny my eyes. The fuchsia of Mrs P.'s windbreaker could only have come from an American department store; the color did not exist on the British Isles. Xenophobic displeasure sprang from her countenance, igniting the reality of her presence. Her eyes ranged and she clutched at her husband's sleeve, Mr P. expectedly more stoic. A fearful aspect was upon him too, tending towards skepticism and annoyance. Though he pressed out his scholarly self and almost passed for a Brit with his distinguished jaw, prominent brow and dapper wool sweater, alas, there were giveaways. The newness of his denim jeans, the gleaming penny copper of the brads, the hang of their cowboy cut on his desk-bound suburbanite's flat-butted body: he could only have come from America. Like Old Glory itself, the way he hung at the edge of the room was a reminder of duty.

I was speechless long enough to leave them lingering some uncomfortable moments. Klang stopped his paranoid rambling to interpret my bug-eyed involvement with something across the room, and Nicole too (sloppily) put down her drink and traced my ogling eyes. I climbed over her and out of the booth, crossed the room and threw the lifevest of my presence to my parents, asea in Scottishness.

'Melvin!' Mother called, embracing me.

'Hi, Mom,' I said casually.

'Oh, Lord! You're alive!' she wept. Over her shoulder, I met my father's eyes. He smirked with satisfaction as if he'd just found the missing tape measure in a junk drawer. Jabbing his weighty eyeglasses up the bridge of his nose was not a mere nervous tic but an indication that he'd been too preoccupied to tend to this. Now he was brought back to himself, seeing his son safe.

'Of course I'm alive,' I answered Mom, who continued to clutch me. Mr P.'s face now registered contempt for his wife's predictable display of unreasonable emotion. Of course I was alive; explanations abound, he knew that. I nodded at him, which made him stern. Don't cozy up just yet. This was a costly and inconvenient bit of transatlantic babysitting.

After all the articulation and challenging heart-to-hearts with Nicole, how instantly these glances and silent, uncertain exchanges resumed.

I pulled free of Mrs P.'s embrace, gave her a reassuring smile, and shook Mr P.'s hand.

'Mel,' he said, all business. He was always all business. 'You gave us a scare there.' He sniffed and looked down. 'Get your mother's bags, will you?'

He stepped aside of the door, adding, 'And pay the driver – here.' A fold of paper pounds, blue and yellow and pink, was thrust at me. Even the mathematically minded flounder to grasp the fractional value of the dollar on this green isle. Though too, this munificence bespoke his larger MO: he was here to bail me out, and he'd rather do it with money than talk.

The waiting driver sent off, I urged the newcomers into the room, where Nicole and Klang stood looking on from a distance, affording us the privacy of a distressed family reuniting. I drew the disparate duos together and made introductions. Mrs P. was charmed and alarmed at Nicole's accent: she flinched and squinted, showing her age and her shelteredness. Post-war outer suburban Chicago had not been a bastion of diversity. She was relieved to recognize Klang's boomy, cut-to-the-chase voice. 'I don't know whether to thank you or . . .' she said to him, trailing off, unable to iterate gratitude's equivalent action. 'This has all been so worrying.'

'Yes, you've got some explaining to do, Mel,' Mr P. said. His tone was serious, but there was hypocrisy in his censure.

But a civil face was put on everything. Upper-middle-class white Americans do not make scenes, much less public scenes in foreign bars. We sat and Nicole asked about their flight and train ride. Drinks and food were ordered, us three Scotland-acclimated people interpreting the menu for the two newcomers, though it was already fairly Americanized. The fish was likely haddock. Mince pie was a meat pie. What kind of meat? Well, ha ha . . . *Bitter* on the beer menu meant a pale ale. It was a surreal conversation given the questions hanging out there, the Podgorski gloss and avoidance tendencies more glaring than ever, like cigarette smoke's harshness after a period of abstinence. When finally the itch could no longer be left unscratched, Mr P. asked, 'So, what's going on, Mel? You're protesting a highway? You photographed a politician in a fight?'

'Dad, it was a misunderstanding,' I said. 'I was there. I had my camera. This MP came around, raising a stink. Things were getting tense. I took some pictures. That's what I do.' With surprise, I heard a Scottish tinge to my voice, 'around' clipped into 'round'. Rather than *stink*, I'd almost said *kerfuffle*.

Mrs P. asked what had I been doing there, had I broken the law? 'Your letter said you were just taking pictures. Why do the police want you?' I assured them I hadn't broken any laws, I'd just been there, and the police were pinning obstruction charges on people to get them out of the way. The protest, I said, was something I had gotten interested in because Pollok Park was supposed to remain public and then the city had taken it over and rushed through this measure to expand the motorway. This wasn't necessarily an unequivocal good.

'Motorway?' Mrs P. asked.

'Highway,' Klang said, a clarification met with a flash of recognition in Mrs P. Highway, Mel disapproving. Margaret was killed on a highway. Klang continued, to my surprise, in an obsequious tone. 'It's a hot-button issue, Rose. May I call you Rose?' he said. 'Very topical. You know, this is a smaller country than the US. There're fewer resources. And it's a nation that's been going through growing pains since the Industrial Revolution. Hell, since the bubonic plague. Anything that breaks with tradition creates a stir.'

'Be that as it may,' Mr P. said, 'you're not here to take part in protests, Melvin. I mean, what's been going through your mind? Plunkett's entrusts you with this assignment, and you go and jeopardize it like this? You're hanging out with this crowd of rabble-rousers, trying to block construction?'

'Rabble-rousers' reminded me of when I was about thirteen and he forbade me from going to a bowling alley, where 'unsavory characters' hung out. It was safest to his uncompromising mind to herd any animal vaguely countercultural into the pen marked 'Undesirable'.

'Naw buh look,' Nicole started in, 'They've no ri' –'

But Klang spoke over her. 'That's a point I made, Dick. That's the point I made. It's not really appropriate. It's unprofessional.'

Who the hell was Klang siding with? He seemed to be just an all-around ass-kisser.

'First of all, this was on my free time!' I said. 'I only stayed down at the park one night! Okay, I've been doing my job one hundred per cent. Eight hours a day.'

'Well, I should hope so,' Mrs P. said. She wasn't going to come all this way and endure all this worry without scolding me a bit. 'That's what they pay you to do, isn't it?' She always tempered her assertions with doubt, especially in the company of men.

'Of course, Mom,' I said. 'But what I do after hours is my business. Besides, Klang, you never told me it was inappropriate.'

'Aye, Klang,' Nicole backed me up, 'you came down to the Free State yersel'.' She sat sideways, legs crossed out in the aisle. When she spoke, both my parents continued to lag behind in comprehension. At home, when someone said, 'I seen ya yesterday' or 'I ain't doin' that,' my folks knew what to make of them. Their elocution placed them on a spectrum they understood. Here, with Nicole, these guideposts gone, her dialect disoriented.

'Well, sure,' Klang said. 'In the interest of investigation.'

'Investigation?' Mr P. asked. He'd ordered a pint of Tennents 70 Shilling (probably believing that to be its price), and sipped at it now, timidly. Nicole had noisily hit bottom on another vodka-lemonade and eyed for the waiter's return.

'Klang's been cooped up in London too long,' I said with a laugh. 'He thought I was with Wimpy, the developer. He fancies' – I corrected myself – 'He thinks he's an amateur detective or something.'

'Hey, I could be on a force right now if I wanted,' Klang stated, mainly to us men, myself and Mr P., who were clustered nearest the inside end of the booth.

'What's Wimpy?' Mrs P. wondered aloud, in that way of hers that too proudly proclaimed her forgetfulness, that conceded all hope of comprehending even as she asked.

'The road builders,' Nicole told her from her close proximity, but the older woman's puzzlement remained.

'The construction company,' I said with a sigh. I felt guilty feeling critical of her, but the problem was so glaring to me now – and exhausting, inexcusable. Surely Wimpy had been mentioned in the CNN story and its odd name explained. Wimpy Homes, the UK's biggest builder. Yet it didn't register because she couldn't think straight when distressed. She literally could not process negative information, to the degree that even the factual stuff at the periphery was blocked out. No doubt this had played a part in my reluctance to confide in her about my and Margaret's troubles.

'I'd make a damn fine detective,' Klang was assuring the table. 'Madison PD would be glad to have me. Believe me, I've had offers. I just can't live on that salary.' This came across as a sad excuse he'd been telling himself for too long – it was all used up. 'It's not worth it. The system's corrupt.' He asserted himself in twitchy looks given one by one to each of us, settling on Mr P., from whom he seemed to expect a manly confirmation of his hardened exasperation. Met instead by my father's expressionless, lens-warped eyes, he stumbled on. 'Anyway, I was investigating. Fact is, there're still unanswered questions.'

'Klang, no,' I said, knowing he intended to pull out the decades-old news cutting. I did not want to stop him because demanding details about the patriarch's past was antithetical to the Podgorski tradition; and not because this was a power coup no less grievous than the Maxwell heir, that seventh-generation great-niece or whoever she was, selling off the Pollok parcel despite her fore-bears' wish for open space in perpetuity. I wanted Klang to back off because, since Ben Nevis, I wasn't motivated anymore to have a reckoning with my parents. I'd always thought there was something in them that had to be faced down, but it had turned out to be something in myself. I couldn't change them or the past, a stone unturnable, but I could change myself. Unfortunately, Klang and Nicole didn't see things this way. They'd taken on familial grievances vicariously.

'Aye, Ah've got questions as well,' Nicole said.

'You think you've got questions, missy?' Mr P. said. 'I wanna know what the hell my son's getting into over here. Why he's on the god damn nightly news.'

'Everyone's got questions,' Mrs P. uttered with a playful tip of her Chardonnay, perversely making light.

'Dad, don't worry,' I said. 'I'm gonna go to the police back in Glasgow. I'll talk to them. There're no charges against me. Ruaridh told them I was a double agent, but he's off his rocker. It's a long story.'

'Rurry?' Mr P. said, grinding out the word on his American palette.

'This bloke Ah wuz seein',' Nicole stated, starting in on a fresh drink, the desire for which had been expertly signaled by a rattle of ice when the meals had been brought.

'Ex-boyfriend,' I translated.

Mr P. seemed to receive this description as dismissible information – nothing to do with him.

'I was investigating,' Klang drunkenly interposed – he'd been drinking for hours now; impatience was evident in the way he clutched his new full pint. He'd been short-changed, his glory parade rained on. 'I wondered about this guy. How did a guy with no post-secondary education, a guy with no experience, get hired for this gig? An overseas assignment in market research – a specialized field?' He pulled out exhibit C or D, the one with the photos from the seventies, and laid it on Mr and Mrs P.'s side of the table, between them.

'Come on,' I said, reaching for the documents. Klang elbowed me away, nearly toppling several jars. I could only sit back.

'Oh, I remember this,' Mrs P. said dreamily.

Klang's pack of smokes lay on the table near my elbow, top flipped, looking better and better by the moment.

Mr P. was not so touched. 'You're out of line, Mr Klang,' he firmly asserted, giving the article only a glance. 'This is none of your damn business. Why don't we put this away, I'll buy you a drink –'

'I'm making it my business,' Klang fired. 'I work for this company too. I'm here on the same assignment, and I have a stake in it. I have a right to know what's going on.'

'Mel wants tay know as well,' Nicole said. 'Dohn ye?'

'Oh, aye,' I said sarcastically.

Mr P. looked to his wife, whose haddock-chewing mouth nevertheless pursed in contemplation – the fateful considering of the cornered whether to come clean or dash. Her eyes flickered with helpless panic. Mr P. set down his silverware and wiped his hands. He looked at me, then removed his heavy glasses and rubbed his marble-sized eyes. Finally, he said, 'Mel, listen. You were pretty down in the dumps after Margaret passed. And that was killing us, your mom and me. We hated to see it. You'd always been a go-getter. Active, full of life. All of a sudden, you were directionless. You were hurting, lost. You weren't going out. You weren't talking to anyone.'

'Yeah, but –' I wasn't just *down*, I wanted to say.

'Hang on, son.' He tinkered with his place setting, aligning it to the table's edge. 'I wanted to help you, because . . .'

'Because he could empathize,' Mrs P. eagerly answered for him, as if she'd been waiting for this a long time.

'Yes, because I empathized,' Mr P. agreed. 'I'd been depressed.'

'Well, I was thinking about that,' I said.

'So you got him the job,' Klang said.

'Mr Klang, please.' Mr P. said, bitingly.

'Well, you did. You must have pulled some strings.'

'Is that true?' I asked.

'Your father only wanted to help you,' Mrs P. said. 'He loves you. It's only fair to use your connections. That's what they're for.'

Everyone was quiet. I looked to Mr P., who confirmed, 'I know Bob Carson.' He passed the photocopied article to Klang. 'We go way back. He owed me a favor.'

'What'd'ya have on tha', Klang?' Nicole said, trying to lighten the mood. 'Did he do a hit for him or somethin'? Rub somebody out?' She was joking, knowing I'd taken on this job proudly and wanting to protect me from devastation. Plus, she was half blootered.

'Must be the contract,' Klang said. 'Probably worth a pretty penny.'

'Yep, worth a pretty penny,' said Mr P. with a smirk. He liked people who used these expressions; he liked using them himself; and he loved it, I thought, that his moment of confession had so quickly passed into the colloquial lingo-laden mode he was most comfortable in. But he must have seen the hurt in me and felt he should say more. 'Bob saw how much these third-party research firms were making and the freedom they had, so he branched out on his own. Some people in the company saw him as a defector, taking advantage. But I had a say in who this work went to, and I threw him a bone. It was a big deal. A big study about the company image in the household, how the brands were perceived, all that. It got him on his feet. Things took off from there. He won work with other technology firms – IBM, Texas Instruments. We fell out of touch over the years. Then last year he saw Margaret's obituary in the paper, recognized the Podgorski name, and got in touch. He asked after me, my family, and asked what he could do. When he said he'd won a bid for Burback's ...' He blushed now, embarrassed by the care for me, the thoughtfulness, evident in this reminiscence. He was cut from an old cloth in this way: a man uncomfortable with his affections, shamed by expressing them.

Mrs P. picked up, addressing everyone. 'Mel needed a break. He needed experience, to get his confidence back. And for it to be about coffee – it was like the angels delivered this! We couldn't turn Bob down.'

'Yeah, but Dad, you just *told* me about the position,' I said. 'I still made a resumé. I applied. I interviewed.'

Mrs P. sheepishly drank her wine, Mr P. his beer.

'Those are formalities,' Mr P. said. 'They have to be done.' He pressed his glasses up – shielding his contrite face with his hand.

I remembered how Mrs P. had spread the news of my good fortune even before I'd been offered the job. Like it was a foregone conclusion.

'Holy shit.'

Surprisingly, Klang didn't gloat over the correctness of his intuitions, but instead peevishly took issue with Mr P.'s handling of things. 'All due respect, but that's a shitty way to treat your son. At least be up-front with him, not mislead him into thinking he's earned a job.'

'Aye, buh tha's how they work,' Nicole piped in, her tongue good and loose, rested. Klang in his agitation had lit a cigarette, and Nicole helped herself now too, reaching across me and saying, as she fumbled with the lighter, 'They werenay on the level abou' Margaret's dyin' either. Did Mel noh tell ya?'

'Hey, he didn't even tell me she'd died. He gave me the "divorced" story, remember?' Klang laughed.

'Divorced?' Mrs P. asked.

I waved this question away like a insignificant gnat, muttering, 'Never mind, Mom.'

'Guess it's tit fer tat then, eh,' Nicole said, exhaling, and addressing my folks now. 'Mel didnay tell ya when Margaret was cuttin' hersel', so you didnay tell him when you pulled the strings.' Gratitude came in strange forms. I'd had an unwitting role in extirpating Nicole from Ruaridh's abusive lunacy, I'd helped with her project – she wanted to fight my battles for me.

'Cutting herself?' Mrs P. said. 'Melvin?!'

Finally, I sat up. 'Remember when the autopsy report was mailed to me, and I said I lost it?' I explained that that was because there were marks on Margaret's legs, and that she used to cut herself. Naturally, they were confused. Cut herself? What do you mean? On purpose? Yes, on purpose. To kill herself? No, not to kill herself. Just to hurt herself. But why would she do that? They had all the usual questions, the expected questions, the same ones I'd had. They were shocked, but I had to hustle them beyond that to say that that's why we went to Arizona, because Margaret'd been depressed and lonely, even within the marriage, and hurt by my preoccupation with work and photography. 'The trip was meant to put everything behind and reconnect. But the fighting continued, and she cut herself in Albuquerque. I didn't want them showing, the cuts, at the Grand Canyon, so that's why we'd stopped. I was making her put on pants. If I hadn't done that . . .'

Listening to me, Klang in turns recoiled and winced, shook his head with pity, and sucked air through his teeth in mild horror. Mr P. was hard and still, managing this perturbing information as he knew best, secretly relieved to have the attention off him. Mrs P. uttered dismayed Dear Lords and Dear Gods. From Nicole came repeated, Aye, Ayes, as from someone watching a Hitchcock film the second time.

'See, there's something you don't understand,' I said. 'Mom, Dad, I waited and waited for the right time to bring it up, but it never came. Still, I thought you knew something wasn't right. I mean, it was obvious to me things hadn't been going well from the start, that Margaret and I were off kilter, that I wasn't happy.'

'We didn't know anything about that!' Mrs P. said. 'We can't read your mind!'

'You know,' Mr P. said, clearing his throat in a seeming effort to add clarity and thus veracity, 'you can talk to us about anything.'

'But I couldn't!' I said, riled now, adrenaline spiking. 'That's just it! I couldn't!'

Outrageously, Mr P. suggested this wasn't the appropriate time for this outburst.

'It's never the appropriate time!' I raised my voice, and Nicole put her hand on my arm to settle me. But I had to explain. 'That's the problem. Dad, I wasn't "down in the dumps". I was dying to tell you guys she'd been self-destructive, we couldn't communicate, I regretted marrying. I wanted to tell you all about the fights and why we were stopped on the side of the road. But you clung so strongly to the randomness. Chance. A chance accident. You kept impressing that on me. It didn't make me feel better. That was like putting me in a cage. All I needed to do to move on was come clean and have everything out in the open. But you guys give signals like you're wary of something out there – the truth. Reality. "Don't go there! We don't want to know!"'

'Okay, okay,' Mr P. said, trying to subdue me. It wasn't my agenda to lambast them, only do what I had to do to get where I needed to get – to let them know I was breaking with the Podgorski tradition.

I lit one of Klang's cigarettes. My parents knew I smoked and didn't ride me about it but Mrs P. gave her disapproving look anyway.

'When that deceit is around you, coming from people close to you, you do what you have to do. You want to be loved, not rejected. You want to be a good son. I felt like I was being asked to get with the program, deny the problems, tell everyone it was just unlucky when I was just reaping what I'd sown. And I resented that. If it wasn't for all the secrecy in this family, the behind-the-back stuff,' I said, 'Margaret might be alive.'

'Now hold on, Mel,' Mrs P. said, 'that's not fair. It's not like we wanted the accident to happen.'

'I'm sorry,' I said. 'But that's how it felt.' I turned to Klang, then Nicole, to see just how uncomfortable I'd made them, airing out this laundry in front of them, over a meal, at a holiday destination.

They seemed fine. This was right up Klang's alley – all the gruesome motives and deceptions. Nicole, my ever-vigilant supporter, my ringside trainer, had been through worse.

'I know you didn't want Margaret to die,' I said to the elder Podgorskis. 'Christ, neither did I! But, ironically, that was another part of it. I wasn't just sad that she was gone or feeling sorry for myself. That day when I was over, Mom, I said a prayer at your kneeler. Dad, you saw me through the window.'

'What did you pray for!' Mrs P. asked, shocked, as if I'd never even heard of prayer. Sure, I quit joining her for mass after I'd been confirmed. But I had been confirmed, and all the sacraments before it too.

'I prayed for an end to our problems,' I said.

'Then you got it,' Klang said. 'Your prayers were answered.'

I nodded. Nicole put her hand on my back now.

'I can understand if you're angry,' Mr P. went on, urged by the silent expectancy of the rest of us. 'I'm sorry. Maybe we never taught you how to deal with difficulties. We weren't good role models in that regard.' He stuttered and stumbled, but seemed to be following my lead, even seemed – and this was outrageous – inspired. 'For a long time, I didn't know how to either. I was depressed,' he said, with such aw-shucks pride that all but his wife laughed. 'I was!' he said. 'I was! But I guess, in your formative years, you didn't have an example.'

'Why were you depressed?' Klang asked, just before I could.

'Oh,' Mr P. sighed, 'I had dreams once too. I didn't necessarily want to grow up and formulate adhesives and live in the suburbs. When Mel was young, we went through some tough times. All of a sudden I had a family to support and a kid to raise. I had to work, whether I liked it or not. I'd kind of hemmed myself in. That took some getting used to.'

'Well, what did you want to do, Dad?' I asked. Sad that this was so unfamiliar a level of intimacy; sorry that it should come at such a late date; strange that it should come among strangers; cosmically apropos that it should occur so far from the idyllically named Meadow Prairie Lane, where the familiar silences and cover-ups had been made so customary, and instead, here, in this politically rent, chronically oppressed (some would argue self-repressed), and culturally morphing country which is nonetheless boasted of in brochures and lore as so anciently romantic and pure.

When he was a kid, he'd wanted to be an astronaut, he said. But his eyes went bad at a young age, and that was the end of that. In high school, Cold War patriotism intrigued him, the defense of liberty from the Reds; he hoped to pursue military science – rockets and warheads and missile defense. But then in '67 he had been drafted. I had known this – we weren't *that* secretive a family – but the career repercussions had never been shared. Thanks to his poor vision and flat feet, he never set foot out of the country. He served as a Remington Raider, tapping out reports behind a typewriter in Leavenworth, Kansas. When he got out of there, his own dad was in pretty rough shape with drink – news to me – and he lived with his mom and got her through his illness and eventual death. 'The stubborn old coot,' Mr P. said. 'smoked Lucky Strikes till the day he died.

'Then I did a chemistry degree on the GI bill at Urbana-Champaign. That's where I met Rose. Pretty soon Mel came along.' He put his hand atop Mrs P.'s. 'We needed money, needed a house. I finished the degree, got in at 3M as a lab assistant. Then we bought the Wynton place.'

Somewhere through it all, he'd lost his faith. He been raised Catholic – I knew that – and he'd jumped through the hoops, the matrimonial boot camp, answering all the questions correctly, so that Mother's wish could be fulfilled – getting hitched Catholic, their marriage recognized by the Church and presided over by the Big Man himself. But Mr P. couldn't stomach the pope's stance on birth control, and Vatican II wasn't all it was cracked up to be. Once a believer in fate, his buddies arriving home from Vietnam in flag-draped coffins put an end to that too. If that was their fate, God had a sick sense of purpose, not to mention humor.

He emptied the Tennents. Despite the outpouring, he was still a sober man. Putting the pint down, he seemed to draw the curtain on this rarely visited chamber of the past. He sat back and turned to his wife. A fair amount of integrity was restored to Mr P. in this telling. Mrs P. glowed with a mixture of sad nostalgia at the memories and appreciation for her husband's efforts. Nicole and Klang's swords of suspicion and scorn were lowered. Me – I felt somewhere maybe Margaret was listening and finally had an answer to that question she'd always posed: 'What is with your dad? What's his damage?' At least part of an answer. A beginning.

Another beginning was the shift inside me as the protagonist of my as-yet in-vitro screenplay *The Scientist* made a step forward, out of shadow, into fuller light. The caricature I had relied upon for an understanding of the actual man twinkled out of the abstract into solidity. But though it was a forward-feeling movement, it was also a healthy distancing, creating needed space between the imagined and the real-life man. In fact, second only to hard work, this distinction would prove integral for bringing the script out of stagnation, for bringing the scientist to life. In the months after my return to the US, I'd work on the project earnestly for the first time. Days in the Burback's offices, nights in a Burback's with a laptop.

Until then, we'd talk more, Mr P. and me, first on the 9.20 ScotRail back to Glasgow the next morning, Mr P.'s grudging pace encouraged by the tracks' rhythm. I'd recall for him his sleeping in Sunday mornings and being in bed still when Mom and I got back from church, how confusing that was, what a mixed message. He'd tell me all that had weighed on him, how depression had crept in, Grandpa's passing sinking in, things left unsaid between them lingering, churning. He had never been able to please him. Grandpa had disparaged him his whole life. He was an abusive drunk – again, news to me. He painted a picture of Grandpa – who I knew only from photos, a diminutive sag-jowled man always in a grey work sweatshirt – driving Mr P. out on his paper route back in Elgin pulling from a flask at four in the morning, cussing him to hurry up, calling him 'blind as a bat'. With grief visibly welling, Mr P. told me how he'd wanted to go far in life to spite the man, because he could never please him. Things fell out from under him when blazing success didn't come. He'd worked hard, studied hard, had a family, had a good job, but was far from content. For years he refused counseling, fearful of the stigma. It was weak. It was for the downtrodden and insane. Naturally, his depression affected his marriage so, for Rose's sake, for their sake, when I was perhaps ten, eleven, he gave in. He found it fruitless at first. Rationally, he felt he had nothing to be down about. He was a success by many standards. Eventually, though, he saw how he had continued to fill in the absent cussing and castigation himself, in his head. 'That was an eye-opener. But,' he said, of counseling, 'you're never cured. You just stop going.'

That was the next day, clattering through Perth and the rolling Cairngorms, past the William Wallace monument at Stirling. And talk would go on, less urgently, back in the States. For now, the King's Arms table was cluttered. Plates were picked over, napkins crumpled, pints rimmed with dried foam. The smell of the cigarette ash mingled with fish bones and vinegar rime. Everyone was stuffed and restless. The candidness had been needed but intense, and now, collectively, we were a little oppressed, all this baggage having been opened and dumped around like the aftereffects of our meal. We paid up, filed one by one through the closet-sized restroom, and shuffled out the door.

'Do you call it a loo?' Mrs P. asked out in the fresh air, as relieved to have made it through the uncertainty of a Scottish meal as she was at having survived the openness of the discourse.

'Nah, we call it a toilet,' Nicole said.

'Oh, I thought it was a loo over here.'

'Everyone thinks that,' I said.

It was evening now, frigid and damp, as usual.

A walk was suggested. We were drawn like moths to an orange glow above the rooftops whose origin we discerned once on Castle Road: the skyward-aimed spotlights flanking the sandstone walls of Inverness Castle, bestowing it with a stately, timeless, worthy air even in the dormancy of night.

26 *Exhibition*

Architecture and design were not my specialties, but stepping into the Mackintosh Building, I was immediately struck by a familiarity: its eponymous designer was an obvious precursor to Frank Lloyd Wright. Both used elongated proportions and geometrical odes. Both loved the line. The architect celebrated as an Illinois original seemed greatly diminished. America, by extension, seemed faulty in its bravado and power, another aspect of its greatness revealed as imitation. It was typical. Overlooked Glasgow, overlooked Glaswegians. All of Scotland packaged in a tin of shortbread. But perhaps there was more to it, and I the blind one. Perhaps Wright himself had admitted his influence, confessed to borrowing the low-slung Zen qualities – of Japanese origin anyway. Perhaps this was old hat to the experts, the likenesses parsed and the credit of original genius wrangled over by scholars in obscure trade journals long before I was born. That cities had flourished and fallen and people lived and died and styles come and gone on monumental scales before me, independent of me, outside of me, possessed both a new weight and new buoyancy. It put me in a state of excited contentment.

The Mackintosh Building, though, was not buoyant; it was bogged down, girded by scaffolds and netting emitting sandblasters' shrieks and dust clouds. An easel-mounted display in the lobby gave me the only complete view I would get of the hidden façade, explaining the purpose of the refacing, thanking donors, and showing before and after images: the black and green of soot and moss yielding, in an artist's rendering, to freshly whitened limestone.

Nicole chatted with a few people in the foyer before taking me upstairs. We climbed a creaky wooden flight lined by ennobling tall rails and entered an airy gallery under exposed roof timbers. It was as if a ship's hull had been inverted, a nod to Glasgow's core industry. Outsized double doors bestowed due grandeur on the student workspaces they led to, the doors swinging shut behind us like dividers sealing off the world. From a cubby in a high loft Nicole gathered supplies and her school ID. I looked down with envy on a spacious studio fronted by towering windows. In the center of the floor an empty mattress evoked its absent occupant – a life model. It was Saturday. Naked easels stood like party guests, with their dignified spines and paint-splattered backs, in angles of repose. Clip-drying oils hung on the walls, the same rotund figure repeated in a multitude of perspectives and distances. We descended the loft stairs and Nicole walked among these works that impressively, candidly, captured the subtleties of skin tone and shadow and the studio's volume – as if past a fishmonger's stand. This was her world. The fostering of talent; the recognition of beauty; the praise, via replication, of sublimity.

The darkroom was in the basement – a lighted area with work-tops and a door with a warning sign. The fans were blowing – another student already at work inside. Nicole hadn't loaded a developing tank in the dark before and was terrified of ruining her film, so I went in the closet first. The tanks were Paterson univer-sals like the ones I had at home. My hands popping the canister and threading the reel by feel – like riding a bike. All the GSA's gear was top-notch – electric temp controls on the baths, all the proper beakers and squeegees. It was also strangely devoid of Britishized quirks; exactly the same stuff used in the States. The big plus was the drying cabinet. No clothesline and pins here, and certainly no Jewel-Osco red Party Lite. These were luxuries, and I felt deserving of them.

With the first roll drying, Nicole had a go at the next, practicing first in the hall with her eyes closed, using the dead roll they had for that purpose. I'd sped through my roll so we could get to print-making soon, but now walked her through everything. By the time her spool was agitated and bubble-free and stopped, the first was nearly ready. We slipped out a side door onto Dalhousie Street, picked up a coffee at the tea room and sat on a Sauchiehall Street bench.

'So they didnay say anythin', the polis?' Nicole asked.

'Nah.' I told her how I'd gone that morning to the Pitt Street station, or 'police office', as they call it, only to have them drive me out to the South and East Renfrewshire Division. Quite a load of carry-on. My infraction was a non-issue in the eyes of Strathclyde Police, now that Douglas had resigned. The need to clear rabble from the Free State had all but dried up as Wimpy security now outnumbered the remaining holdouts. The *Herald* had said that morning that after the CarHenge party broke up, tree-felling progressed. Forty had been downed over the weekend. 'A sergeant reprimanded me, said I took the privilege of residency too lightly. He sent me on my way, and told me to "mind order".'

When we hit the darkroom, it was strange to me that the student inside didn't flinch. So many times I'd come into my dark-room to see Greg leap in front of the enlarger where he was exposing, an attempt to shield his paper from light leaks. Here were double sliding doors with a no-man's-land in between. Not a single beam of light came through. 'That's slick,' I said, eyes dilating in the gap with Nicole, the lit world shut out, a red one before us.

I showed Nicole how to make a contact sheet. There was a cut-ting table with a built-in sliding square and markers for increments of 35-mm frames. A pre-cut piece of clean glass was available (at home I'd used a storm window) for flattening the curly negative strips against the paper. There was even a stack of negative holder sheets free for the taking. Timers with glow-in-the-dark hands presided over the motorized bath trays. I felt like a king.

'I can't wait to go home,' I said to Nicole as she pushed the submerged sheet around with the tongs, 'and get my shit in order.' Nicole turned startled eyes to me – reality slamming into her. I would really be going. 'I mean, all my stuff's in disarray,' I said, softening. 'My negatives aren't stored right. I've got all this half-assed gear.'

'Cheap and cheerful's good though, eh?' she said, distantly.

'Och, aye,' I said. This imitation was a kind of avoidance now, a denial and delay, a jokey confirmation of my present presence here. I loved Nicole's language but looked forward to returning to American patter – the yeah, yeahs, and gotta wannas.

We went back through the protective gate, and Nicole looked at the contact sheet with a magnifying glass. 'Aw, brilliant!' she said, leaning over the light table. 'No, noh that. Hmm, noh bad. Dohn remember him.' Delighted laughter.

'Lemme see.'

But she didn't want me to, not in this rough state. Her selectivity was part of her process, and she wanted that kept pure. 'You can see 'em on the big day.' I was only to see a few in getting her oriented to the equipment.

I recommended fiber-based paper, but Nicole wanted a big presentation, and the largest stuff in the supply closet was multi-grade. A little slicker, contrast not as pronounced. She was disappointed at first that her portraits lacked the starkness and intensity of Avedon's, but I assured her this was through no fault of her own. They weren't powerfully lit on a controlled set. They were taken with a smaller, cheaper lens. Her subjects didn't carry the gravity of fame, or wealth – not to say they were void of greatness. They turned out well, after some trial and error – me resurrecting my math, Nicole sussing out the results to aim for, which she smartly did by letting the photos reveal their strengths, their theme, their emotional tone. Once she found a manageable, pleasing size, the negatives were popped in and out of the carrier in fluid succession. Production flowed. She dipped and clipped the unwieldy 17 × 11 sheets and moved on to the next exposure.

In the evening, Carson called. It was early afternoon in Chicago.

'Podgorksi!' he belted. I immediately pictured him in his fishbowl corner office, corpulent and lordly in his executive chair. 'Are you an idiot or a genius?' All my blood came to a standstill then bubbled like gravy in a pan.

Klang was at my flat. He hadn't gone on to London yet since coming down from Inverness. He felt we should stick together and form an action plan regarding Plunkett's and my escapades. For starters, we were to keep mum in case it somehow didn't ignite at headquarters. In the meantime, he'd find an internet café and see what the American news outlets were saying about me, if they were still following the story. Personally, I think he liked the excitement – my turmoil kept his mind off himself. He was a conflicted misanthrope, begrudgingly preferring company.

Now he sat in my armchair like Stalin at Malta – I'm thinking only of the photo – grave and churlish, beside the orange coil fireplace, trying to keep off the Glasgow wind that pinpricked through the drafty windows. Everything seemed closer and sharper, more intense, back in Glasgow, including the constant icy piddle. Klang went manic and cross, knowing who was on the line.

Carson had caught wind – big wind. A full and blustery wind. He was in the information business and made it his business to be informed. 'I saw the news when it came over the wire,' he said, showing his age with this anachronism. 'But don't worry, I know fluff when I see it. I mean, what did they have on you? Trespassing? Obstruction of justice? Do they even have that there? Didn't seem like much. I put Gedes on it just in case.'

Rick Gedes – the branding guru, spin doctor extraordinaire.

'It really *was* nothing, sir,' I said. 'The story's all blown over now. The camp is all but broken up.' It was my prerogative to keep details to a minimum, but Carson had in mind to showcase his pressure-thinking self, his diplomacy and leadership. He wanted to run me through his tactics, let me know that, though he was being soft, it was also in his repertoire to play hardball.

'Hey, but it wasn't nothing at first,' Carson said. 'Hell, we were all set to cut you loose, Podgorski. Gedes had damage-control options ready. Press releases, apologies. I think he went with "alcohol problem", or was it prescription-drug reaction? Anyway, if it had escalated, we were going offensive. Then the damnedest thing happened.'

'The damnedest thing?' I parroted, with a sense that Carson wanted only these cues. He was founder of a prominent and prosperous firm; he was accustomed to tables of toadies at his elbows nodding to yarns of wheelings and dealings, obsequious junior ladder-climbers.

Klang didn't like the sound of what I'd said. He reached for his smokes. I shifted the phone to the ear that was not blood-hot, and sat on the settee.

'Turns out Burback's execs watch CNN,' Carson said.

'Holy shit.'

'Yeah, precisely. But wait now,' Carson changed his tone, dropped the executive bluster. I pictured him on his elbows now, perhaps having shut the office door. 'Your old man's over there right now, right?'

'Yes,' I said. 'How did you know?'

'I'm the one who told him to get his keister over there, Melvin,' he said. There was muffled noise on the line – he was speaking to someone in the room. Then, staggeringly, cryptically, he went on. 'I gave you the benefit of the doubt. You're a good kid. And you've been through hell and back.' Here he was referring to Margaret. 'I know your dad. He's a stand-up guy. Runs a tight ship. I wanted to let him handle it. I trusted him. It wasn't my place to discipline you.'

'Right,' I said, quietly. 'Right.' Klang was on the edge of his seat, trying to figure out what was being said.

'So your old man's had a word with you?' Carson asked. I could see he had it in mind to pull the Band-Aid of ugly truth off me slowly.

'Yes, we've spoken.'

'Well, don't take it hard, son,' Carson said, edging around this business about the favor. (Can you call it nepotism when it's not family?) 'He meant well, and I was glad to help.'

'But I was thinking,' I said. 'Why didn't you stick me in a mail-room or something? It's expensive over here, and if you're not using my data . . .? I don't know – are you using my data?'

'Ha – about that. Look at it this way, there's good news and bad news. Which do you want first?'

'Didn't I already get the bad news?' I said. Klang's eyes narrowed; his shoulders slumped.

'Well,' Carson said, ignoring my comment. 'Glasgow was never meant to be a test group. London was the A-one consideration from the start.' Assigning me to Glasgow, he said, the idea was for me to be somewhere out of the way where I could stay out of trouble and not be overwhelmed, get back on my feet. 'Burback's didn't want a study in Scotland. Ireland, Wales – all those places would be second-tier phase. And a separate RFP.' Request for Proposal – he was buffeting me with all kinds of industry speak and cozy generalities. 'That's understandable, right? London's obviously the place to start if you're looking at the UK. Even after that, there's dozens of places that, you know, on paper, look more viable, population-wise. Income-wise. Demographically. Manchester, Leeds, Liverpool. We touched on it, and if we were gonna get into Scotland, they thought Edinburgh. I agreed – I've been through there on golf jag. It's more cosmopolitan. Wealthier. Shiny. Big tourist destination. Who goes to Glasgow? It's like Philly without the cheesesteaks.'

Poor Carson, he had some compassion in him after all: he had a catch in his throat and breathed heavily with guilty nervousness. 'No, it's not exactly glamorous,' I concurred. I spoke again, giving him air. 'So you could afford to put me on payroll?'

'Strictly speaking, we're not using Burback's contract dollars for your salary. Not to date. Comes out of a general fund. But Melissa will have to shift that around. But sure. My company does well. I've been at it a long time. I have capital. I have investments. You're on short-term contract – what's twenty grand for an old friend?'

'Man,' I groaned. 'And my 27Gs? What are they, bird-cage liner?'

'Come on, that's where the good news comes in, my boy!'

So I was his boy now. Klang sensed this positivity on the line from across the lounge. His eyes widened, and for good reason. What Carson informed me of I'd relate to Klang after hanging up, in a state of treacherous excitement – of surprise, of fear over Klang's jealousy, of eagerness to assure him that his financial expectations would not be disappointed.

Carson had been reading my reports all along, herding them at his desk, keeping them separate. They'd piqued his interest at first, with their grassroots straight-shooting. Verbose, yes, but impassioned. Made an impression. I could sketch a scene, he said. It was like watching a movie. After the second batch, he decided he was impressed. This was how he operated: everything was dealt a manager's prudence and a statistician's chance to level out or prove a fluke. They were unique, he said, that was for sure. If I was one thing, I was thorough. And honest, like my old man. No BS. Called a spade a spade. It was refreshing, getting my batches in. It was mundane work usually, quantifying consumer trends, opinions, habits, tendencies – the stock and trade of market research. But my stuff really got his juices flowing. He said he could just see the types of places he'd popped into in small towns up by St Andrew's, where he'd played the Old Course many years ago.

I thanked him.

I was welcome, he said. But more important was what my forms painted a picture of: a ripe market. 'I mean, talk about ripe!' Carson exclaimed. 'I started thinking – Sanka and tap water? This place is ripe for the picking. This is juicy!' He really was beside himself on the ripeness issue. He felt strongly that a place like Glasgow, based on what I had described, was begging for a Burback's, crying out. He had a strong hunch this was going to be one of those con-fluences of factors where the elements are firing on all cylinders. (Carson's fluency was in retail markets, not metaphors.) Burback's was a relatively adventurous company, not too staid, tons of capital. Liked a challenge. They hadn't gotten to five thousand stores by hedging their bets. Opening in Glasgow would make waves, fly in the face of the notion that four-dollar cappuccinos are only for the upper crust. Furthermore, he said, with *Braveheart* out and all this hype about the place, the timing couldn't be better. Mel Gibson had talked about Glasgow on *The Tonight Show*. It was going to be the next 'it' town, like Seattle and its music scene. 'And, hell, Burback's started in Tacoma – another rainy port town! It'll be like starting in their UK sister city! It's a no-brainer!'

'Braveheart?' I'd asked. It was a film about the Scotsman William Wallace, evidently. It had opened at number one in the States. The twitchy Australian-cum-American hunk played the fearless Highland warrior. 'You're joking,' I said. I couldn't picture it. Most

Scottish men I'd seen were saggy-eyed and pale, heavy smokers. They lurched from pub to pub with round shoulders under leather jackets.

No, he wasn't joking. The point was, Carson had a meeting scheduled with the Burback's people; he and Gedes would be doing a PSP, Progress Summary Presentation. Glasgow would be the focus, my reports the supporting evidence. He had a feeling about this – *the* feeling. He'd been here before with clients.

'Holy shit.'

Furthermore, the research contract terms had been met. They'd be talking dollars and cents and shaking hands, which meant Plunkett's would be talking bonuses.

We celebrated, Klang and I, with drams of the twenty-four-year-old Glenfiddich Klang had bought as a souvenir. He was over the moon, as they say, and tore into it with abandon after a round of fist pumps and skyward exhortations – yeses! and god damns! and whoos! I'd never seen someone so enthused and validated by money. But then I hadn't yet moved and mixed in the corporate world to the extent that I would.

My folks stayed at the Grosvenor Hotel. They took in the sights for a few days; I came along when I could. Actually, I came along when I could tolerate them. Mr P. had bought a travel book and commandeered it into his scrutinizing possession, filling it with mini Post-Its and illuminating passages with his company's neon markers. The management of timetables and maps, and the weighing of priorities must have reordered the world that topsy-turvy emotions and memories had upset.

The day after developing with Nicole, I went over to the hotel to take him and Mom out and around. The room filled with the tang of Old Spice on shower steam – Dad was dressed and wet-haired. While Mom finished her make-up, he sat on the window ledge, wind-shaken elm boughs in the silver air behind him, and read from the book. There was the City Chambers, the Botanic Gardens, Hill House. He read descriptions of each attraction, its hours, its admission price, its location, which meant nothing to him, just a road name which I had to locate for him. We could go here, then there, he'd suggest. Or first there, then here. Which way made sense logistically? How long would it take to get to Hill House? Would they cab or tube or bus? Should they buy a day pass? Then again, they didn't mind walking some. You see things better that way.

'What do you want to do, Rose?'

'I don't know,' she answered. 'What do you think?' She was worried about where we'd eat lunch and thought we might decide that first. I emptied their room's supply of coffee (single-serving stuff in filter pouches) while they hashed this out and mother loaded her purse with baggies of candies and snacks she'd brought from home. Should she bring an umbrella? Would she be too warm in her sweater? They were both out of their element.

Finally, I brought them in a cab to the Cathedral and Necropolis, where Mother took pleasure being under the mammoth arches, among the pews, stained glass, aisles and altars. Dad hardly looked up. Their appreciations were inverse: she shrugged off the building's role in the Reformation; Dad was not impacted by its holy grandeur, only the facts related on plaques and leaflets. The walk up the winding Necropolis trail in the bracing wind seemed to refresh and strengthen their confidence – here were the familiar elements: gravity and wind, grass and the universal permanence of death, more enduring than even the stone used to mark it. Names on headstones were read, as if in surprise at the complete Scottishness of the litany: Campbell, Miller, Jamieson, Jarvie, Whitelaw, MacFarlane. Atop the hill, the abundance of the dead seemed to overcome them. Either that or the grandiloquent, poetical epitaphs threatened them; or the legacy of Knox's religious devotion, symbolized by his over-large tomb, tainted their leisure, as it had done mine on previous visits. The long view was taken in instead, and remarks made on the topography. When the reedy strains of a bagpipe reached us on the wind coming from the direction of the soccer stadium, my folks were delighted. O Scotland! The authenticity!

We went to the shopping districts next. Once we'd ridden Prince's Square's gaudy, futuristic escalators, it seemed to be mission accomplished – they weren't interested in buying anything they'd have to lug home. We sat in the food court for lunch.

'Margaret would have liked this place,' Mom said.

'Glasgow or the mall?' I said.

'Oh, this – these shops and all the people. She loved people. And the gold, I guess.' There was a gold motif on the walls and rails and trim.

'The gold? Why?' I asked, puzzled, even a little offended. Margaret's style wasn't so common and broad.

'She wore a lot of gold.'

'No, she didn't.'

'She didn't? Wasn't it her favorite color or something?'

'Not really. That was red.'

'I guess she had a gold aura then. Oh, well. She'd be proud of you, you know.'

'You think so?'

'Absolutely.'

It was strange thinking of her as gone now – fully gone, not harboring the tale that we were divorced. It had kind of brought her back in my mind. I'd banished her to an oblivion, erased the truth of her. It was like she could come out of hiding. Which is what she liked. She liked to be seen.

'Thanks, Mom.'

Dad said he was sorry things had gotten how they had. He missed Margaret too. They both did. It was painful for them, too, to lose her, and they had wanted to soften the blow. They knew we were having difficulty. He'd been thinking about it, he said, recalling times he just didn't say what he wanted to – not asking us how things were going. In his family, they weren't blunt about things, and he regretted that. Hell, they had had the elephant in the room, Grandpa's drinking. But then if it had been his way, he would have spoken up before Margaret and I had married. He thought I should have a career first.

'Thanks, I guess.'

Another day they went to the museums and I met them for lunch at Whistler's Mother. Enlivened by a display on Scottish inventors, Dad was talkative. He seemed connected to his younger self, his once-dreamed dreams of innovation and discovery. He spoke out on depression, for the first time without shame, without bowing his head, without meekly pushing up his glasses. He recalled his father again. 'I could never please your grandpa,' he said. 'The first thing he said to me when I got my BA was "When are you gonna get your master's?" I was literally in my cap and gown. But now I know that was more about him than me. It wasn't my failure. He just couldn't let it be known that I'd made him proud. I suppose it goes back to his father.'

Most of all, Dad said, he didn't want anything like this to start between us; if he thought it already had, he'd be deeply sorry.

I said, no, it hadn't. Nothing like that. A satisfactory answer for the time being, though later, home in the States and writing *The Scientist*, it would seem a fissure had formed. But then, in my new life on American soil, it would prove satisfactory to explore this – vetting the tension, the disappointment – via fictional filmic depiction.

When we finished lunch, I ordered three coffees. 'You have to try it,' I said. 'It's the best in Glasgow. At least for now.'

'For now?' Mom asked.

'Oh, yeah. I haven't told you. Well, nothing's confirmed yet, but Carson says Glasgow is a very promising market.' I told them all that Carson had planned and all he hoped for.

They were jubilant and relieved, since their intentions of getting me back on my feet by getting me the job had almost backfired – by almost getting me jailed or deported or, who knows?, married again.

I left them to their own devices in the evenings. They went out to try Indian curries and to hear session music and to the panto *Goosey Goosey, Glasgow!*, lured by the omnipresent tube-station posters. I went, most nights, to Nicole's flat, when she wasn't barmaiding at The Corn Exchange, and had tea and Hob Nobs while she prepared for the exhibition. From school she had brought home the matte cutting tools, the angled blades and backing boards and T-squares. She was better than me at this. I didn't know about adding a third to the bottom – a visual trick, not centering the cut-out vertically, but boosting it up with added heft below. Also her hand was steadier. These were the advancements now rather than the quest for discovery in each other, learning to tie knots of intimacy. We kissed when greeting each other and sat close like lovers and snogged when it got late and Sophie and Deb went to bed. But it felt like last call. Eat, drink and be merry for tomorrow . . . only not that grave a finish. Only a departure.

One afternoon, Klang and I joined my parents for tea near my flat. My mother brought up Margaret's cutting. What a phenomenon it was. She had read an article about it some time ago. As a teacher, she was alerted via staff meetings and seminars to abuse and neglect and other dangers to be on the look-out for in students. Self-inflicted cuts had been one of them, though it didn't apply to the age group she taught; it typically came out in high-schoolers. Nevertheless, it was horrible. What did I know about it, she wondered. Had I heard of such a thing when it happened?

Very little, I had to confess. I'd sought information on it after the fact, using that archaic paperbound index to periodicals at the library. It had not been a fruitful hunt. What was its clinical name? How was it categorized? There's no affliction attached to it – not depression strictly, or suicidal tendencies. It's not concretely linked to other conditions, like schizophrenia or other acts of violence. It kind of falls through the cracks. It's regarded as an anomaly, largely. Its history and causes are not known. No studies on the brain chemistry involved have been published – at least not within the journal-subscription range of the DuPage County library system. But there had been the occasional general interest story in places like *Newsweek*. The idea is that self-harm acts as an outward sign of internal pain. It adds coherence to the emotional torment being felt because, crucially, it's in a comprehensible form. With Margaret, for example, she didn't necessarily know what hurt her. It was like Nessie, a beast submerged. She didn't have the tools to identify it. So of course it festered. It had no outlet.

Klang, to my relief, hung back in this conversation, not deigning to interject one of his brazen but uninformed opinions. Ever since the news from Carson, he was involved in contemplation of his own. How he'd spend his dough, I guessed. Binoculars, a finger-print kit, perhaps authentic handcuffs.

'What was her pain?' my dad asked – no differently than he'd inquired about the cost of Underground tickets.

'Well,' I said, 'That's hard to say.' In fact, I had a theory on this, a theory of my own. But the things that flashed in my mind were not only abstract and unfounded, but tangential – comets that veered beyond the realm of my parents' emotional capacities. Could I say? Would it help? Would my dad sympathize or take offense? I felt she was deeply affected by her father's absence, the message sent by his remove. An absent father could be as damaging as a father present and abusive. With a father there, at least a person can look and discern. Without one, Margaret could learn nothing and remained lost, anguished, unresolved – ambitious but never rewarded. No sense of accomplishment ever reached. There could be no gratification. My love didn't sate her thirst for male affection, male praise, male acknowledgment. Maybe she'd sworn, without knowing it, to reject all male gifts because they'd been elusive, yanked away before. It was a con-venient, self-relieving theory, excusing the neglect I had dealt her.

Then there was the feeling of direction that comes from the fact of a father's being. Whatever he's impressed upon you, you could guide yourself by, always looking down at any stage of life and observing if your wheels were on rails of his teachings. In her dancing, was Margaret doing right? Was she on the right road? She never knew. Driving in the Texas storm, I had felt her distrust of me as perpetual and unshakable – a man at the wheel of her life, the partner she's vowed to honor one of the enemy team. But may-be that was too much inference. Who was I to put a summation on this for her?

That left Janis, her mother. Well, she just wasn't qualified or interested in the responsibility. Once divorced, she quickly snatched up the freedom she'd lost by having a family. To her credit, she'd been consistent about it, rather than playing along like she might be a caregiver.

And then on top of it all was the idea of Father with a capital F. A stabilizing stand-in for many. But none of that for Margaret. Another void. No church. No icons. No sin, no salvation. Anything goes. That was a common enough thing in America, but horrific really. Like all the nourishment kept on a high shelf and the child given hard candy. When weakness and debilitation come, what is there for nourishment? The wrappers and tooth-scum. We are devastatingly insufficient to ourselves. Our perceptions are thin and unsustaining. Prayer had gotten me through, though. Hadn't it? I'd said my Our Father's. Even though it was a last resort, I'd said them. Then somehow I found myself no longer at the end of my rope – though the rope was severed. How do you put that into polite conversation? Especially when the precedent isn't there to put on the table your thanks and your grievances, one night in Inverness notwithstanding?

I didn't answer my dad's question. Not over tea in the afternoon with Klang and good news in the air for once.

'I don't know what her pain was, Dad,' I said. 'That's the way she kept it. Which is symptomatic of the condition, I guess. The cutter keeps her cutting to herself. It's a private practice, a secret exchange.'

This answer was accepted with the tacit acknowledgment that it was incomplete; and also with respectful deference to the privacy of our married life; and too with the vaguely jealous suspicion – I was covetous of it – that what Margaret and I had endured had given me a rich, dark knowledge that I'd always carry with me. Like a stone carried in my pocket.

There was the silence of tea-sipping, remarks on the weather, then my father asked Klang what he thought about my turn of fortune.

'It's really something,' Klang said. He had the aspect of an over-achiever bested by a C student, like he'd filled in all the right bubbles on the wrong lines. 'What's good for Plunkett's is good for Burback's,' he said, sportingly. 'And what's good for Burback's is good for me.'

We all knew what he meant.

Nicole's photographs were exhibited in the Hen's Nest, an attic-level space in the Mackintosh Building with a canted ceiling of window panes – squares of old leaded glass, thick and rain-stained. The room was rhombus-shaped, with the interior wall highest and paneled in wood slats, and so named because female students, back in the school's early days, would set up their easels to paint and sketch in the natural light. I could picture them in Victorian dresses down to their ankles and bodices and frills, hair in buns.

Other students' work spread into the hallways and to the main gallery on the second floor below. Still-lifes and self-portraits on unframed stretched canvases or boards looked like windows onto past moments in nearby rooms – as most had been done in the building's studios. There were also collages and sculptures which neither I, nor Klang and my parents, who as guests of mine stuck by me, inspected closely. Nevertheless, compared to these color-rich works, Nicole's black-and-white prints made a statement of content and context rather than of form. Here were people, Scotland's people. Not artist's models or artists themselves in their self-gazing Rembrandt modes, but people in their natural element, caught like flies in time's web.

To my embarrassment and pride, my portrait began the display; at least it was seen first coming from the stairs. This was a surprise Nicole sprung on me. 'Are ya fucked off?' she asked. She wore her blue dress again and was nervous. 'Ah was gonny ask, buh Ah wuz afraid you'd say no. Dohn take it wrong, allri'?'

How could I take it? There I was, the opening bars to a fugue of sadness, longing and hope – for that was the total effect of her work's assemblage. She'd sagely used only the most provocative and evocative shots, arranging them in a succession that took the viewer on a journey not chronological and not a comparison of gender or a commentary on class (though class was an element of British daily life), but across landscapes of human emotion. The depravity and regret suggested by tired eyes; the myopia and self-deception of the too-eagerly beaming; the ironic vigor of the heavy brow and sunken cheek. The coffee drinks in the bottom of each shot served as footnotes, curiously linking props, a commonality. In the land of whiskey and lager, a talisman of sobriety. There were nationalities – evidenced by pale skin and freckles, bindis, and hair blond or ginger or receded on a Slavic, orb-like cranium. There were ages. There were tall and short, clean and unclean, sullen and bright, enthused and indignant. But, ultimately, when you finished through the line and came to the western end of the Hen's Nest, there was the glimmering idea, like a fizzy drink in the mind's mouth, that each person had arisen and opted, by deliberate choice, to engage the day's offering, their purchase an optional, free-will ingestion of stimulant, both a confession of intent and an admission of feebleness, of need for strength and assistance, to do that thing that, for better or for worse, folly and foible be damned, they would do: try.

We'd arrived early, and I viewed the display before the crowds picked up. Klang, my mother and father followed behind me. Nicole awaited my reaction with hope and trepidation, rising on her toes with excess energy.

'Marvelous,' I said, coming to her. 'Just marvelous. Full marks. You should be really pleased.'

'Aw, cheers.' A blush-rose smile bloomed on her face. 'Ah'm dead chuffed.'

We embraced. We kissed. This was the one I would remember. Better than any that night, kisses of drunkenness, or at the airport, kisses in the sad haze of leaving.

We stayed, and stayed together, as an American foursome, me, Klang, Mom and Dad, until the end. Nicole acted as greeter and traffic warden to her avenue of work, as friends, family and colleagues arrived. Sophie and Deb came dressed up, beaus on their arms. We also met Nicole's mother. She had a disapproving air for me to reckon with, but was kind in word. Thoroughly slight, she stood Nicole's height, a bony frame concealed by a raincoat, a bony hand to shake, hair whose thinness revealed patches of scalp, a voice that ears strained to hear. This was not offensive, though it was to sense, as I did, that she had come only out of obligation. She'd already viewed the exhibit when we were introduced, and her mien bore no inner elevation.

Nicole made no elaboration to her mother regarding me, of boyfriend or any some such, which suited me. It was a bit late for all that.

Finally, there were Nicole's art instructors who came through the Hen's Nest to begin the conference with Nicole that was part of the assessment process. The social cluster split up when the room was closed off. Mrs Marston went out for a fag, Sophie and Deb and their men across the street to the campus pub. The four of us hovered around the refreshment table in the main lobby, dunking our tea bags and clutching our cups. We made individual sojourns amongst the paintings and sculptures, sipping, impatiently casual, always returning quickly to the safety of the group. The individualism on display threatened the family dynamic, of which Klang was now a surrogate member. We huddled like a wolf pack.

Eventually, Nicole came down the stairs saying, 'Shall we?' She was ready for a drink, I could tell. At the coat check, a woman stopped her.

'Did ya hear?'

'No, wha'?' Nicole said.

'The carry-on.'

'Eh?'

'Did ya noh hear the shoutin'?'

There'd been a commotion at the front doors, evidently, sometime during the last hour. Ruaridh had come, tried to get in and been ejected. This was not a public showing, and he didn't have a school ID or a guest pass. He'd been de-enrolled in the last week, after a period of probation, for absenteeism and failing to turn in work.

'You know Ruaridh – never lets up. He was passin' these out outside the pub.'

The woman gave Nicole a slip of paper. Nicole said cheers and we looked at it together. It was a handbill for a march, a protest march. SAVE POLLOK PARK. Saturday morning, from George Square to Pollok Free State.

'Oh, gawd,' Nicole sighed.

'At least we missed him,' I said, holding her jacket while she slipped her arms in the sleeves. 'Let's go. Don't worry about him.'

Outside, she and I both stopped and scanned the shadows for the familiar figure, listened for the antagonizing voice.

'Is something the matter?' my mom asked.

'Nah,' Nicole said. 'Juz everythin's doin' mah head in.'

Mom didn't understand. 'A bit stressed,' I said to her.

We set out towards a pub Nicole had in mind. Walking, my mom asked me, 'What did she say back there?'

'Doing her head in. You know, a mental strain.'

'Do you noh say tha'?' Nicole asked. She knew we didn't, we Americans.

'No,' Mom said.

'Wha' do you say?'

Mom thought.

I've had it up to here and *getting on my nerves* and *that's the last straw* and *what a pain in the ass* all came to my mind.

'Nothing probably,' Mom answered, unable to think of an equivalent. I doubt she realized how correct her answer was.

A vocabulary lesson ensued, Nicole indulging us all in the spectacle and novelty of her native tongue.

'Teach them *stroppy*,' I said.

'Stroppy? Tha's juz, you know, in a bad mood.'

'Crabby,' I added. 'Ornery.'

'Stroppy,' Mom said, her fuchsia arm locked, in a union of sympathies, with my dad's.

'Stroppy,' Dad intoned gladly – he loved the strict order of these lexicological equivalences. 'Without his morning coffee, Mel gets very stroppy.'

'Okay, how about *mingin'*?' I asked.

'Mingin',' Dad repeated eagerly.

'But what's it mean? Take a guess.'

'I know,' Klang put in. He was walking ahead of us, in his forward-lurching way, dragging his fingers along the stone wall, releasing clouds of smoke like a locomotive.

'Not you,' I said.

'Mingin',' Mom mused. 'I don't know. Musical?'

Nicole laughed.

'Hip? Stylish?' Dad tried. 'That's a mingin' hat you have on.'

'Yer miles off,' Nicole said with mock disappointment.

I said, 'Means disgusting.'

'Aye, like blood and guts – or dog shite,' Nicole emphasized.

Sussed, daft, grotty, knackered, and *snog*, got us down Kelvin Way along the southern edge of Kelvingrove Park. There the Brewery Tap came into view.

'There ih is,' Nicole said. 'Brilliant pub.'

And so it was. We had an hour to raise glasses to Nicole's exhibit before the band came on.

'I don't see how they could give you anything but an A,' my dad said.

'Really?' Nicole asked. She modestly drank in the praise, which I enjoyed seeing. She had been strict about her project since the beginning – a determination born of the Free State gaffe, it seemed. It was gratifying to see her reap the benefits now. 'Wha' did you like abou' it?' she wanted to know.

'Oh, the clarity. The contrast in the pictures. And people's expressions of course. They were so deep and varied.'

'It was interesting,' Klang noted, 'that people with the bigger cups were generally older, looked sleepier, like they really needed that double latte!' This was quite a shallow observation, but a ready thoroughfare to conversation about the retail market here and Burback's and speculation on how they would make out.

'They'll probably clean up,' my dad said.

Klang agreed. 'Yeah, they'll probably make out like bandits.'

'Like bandits.'

A toast was made to my success – the role I'd played in laying such a fortune on their laps, if that's what it meant. Strange to celebrate one's accomplishments thinking of another's gains. Hard to gauge what exactly I'd achieved. But that was not an immediate concern.

'Here,' Dad said, peeling off a £20 note from a wad. 'Get another round. I've got to use these up.' They were flying home in two days.

Nicole came with me to the bar to carry the drinks – and there, Sophie and Deb and their boyfriends Neil and Iain materialized. The four of them kicked things off with drams of Macallan, and we all got to talking until the band came on and started tuning up. My folks and Klang were holding a choice table by the stage, so we brought everyone over.

The group was called The Fred Quimby Quintet, which Klang recognized as a reference to the animator in the old Tom & Jerry cartoons. And, sure enough, the cursive writing on the bass drum, with the long tail under the Q, rang a bell. An obscure tribute by skinny guys in hip-hugger jeans, shiny shirts and white vinyl shoes. But the music was genius. Magic, as they say here. Vintage funk and R&B covers, Steely Dan and Parliament and improvised jams with Hammond organ and trumpet solos. Nothing could be more antithetical to the pained bleating of a bagpipe. Shishing cymbals and snapping snares, punchy staccato horns, choruses of Get Down, and Get Up. Out the window with droning dirges and mournful violin trills and the plaintive high diddle dees of session music. No toe-tapping, rather *boom boom clack*. As if by an unstoppable force, the tables were shoved aside to widen the dance floor. After a few songs, we were all in a sweat.

Not my folks, though. They watched from the sidelines, then shortly shoved off. Dad gestured to his watch and mouthed something. We waved to them amid the din – smiles were exchanged. They passed outside the window, arm in arm, umbrella-sheltered.

It was a dancing orgy. Nicole and I danced. She and Klang danced. I grooved with Sophie and shimmied with Deb. Neil and Iain, possessive, came in and grinded and twirled their girls. Drinks were readily accessed at the nearby tables; frequent trips to the bar were made, replenishing everyone, money-minding be damned. Klang made an art of twisting and bobbing, dipping and ducking with pint in hand, gulping as if a step itself, following his liquid partner's lead. Soul classics reprised in Tarantino films segued into Barry White's 'Can't Get Enough of Your Love' into Tower of Power into Sly and the Family Stone anthems.

Klang slipped away for cigarettes. Deb and Neil were seen snogging at the table. At one point, I spotted Nicole going out the door and returning with Sophie. 'What's up?' I yelled in Nicole's ear when she returned to the dance floor.

'Soph and Iain had a row! He's fucked off!'

But time heals all wounds. After last call, we found Sophie and Klang snogging in the close of a nearby building. We dragged them out of there and gave them a good razzing, then all tromped into Kelvingrove Park to get home. Nicole and I made a few stops of our own and were told to hurry the fuck up. The six of us belted 'Jungle Boogie' at the top of our lungs, reaching an impressive volume. Voices from the shadows told us to shut our gobs. 'Fuck off!' Neil suggested. We made poor time, all in a line, three staggering couples, until by the footbridge we came upon some lads well pished, one of them barking violently, 'Gi'e uz a fag!' They were older and the real deal and saying, 'Ah'll fuckin cut ya ear ta ear, ya cunts!' They followed us a short ways, but were too drunk to keep up. We picked up the pace, eyes on the street lamp at the fence gate. Adrenaline will sober you up some.

So will a trip to the chippie's. My dad had left me with a few twenties, so it was fish suppers on me from Loreto's on Byres Road. IRN-BRUs too. After all, health professionals advise to stay hydrated.

27 March

A well-attended march is a sluggish affair. There's much anticipation and the endorphin release at the initial steps is near orgasmic. You're eager. You're bursting. After all, you're walking in the centre of the street, legally, with no fear of harm, and that is very novel and empowering. But there's a glacial pace that presses against you, holds you back. You think, This languor doesn't bespeak the urgency of the cause. It wasn't such casualness that brought this disparate clan together on this morning. It's all very leisurely. You feel rather like you're on the deck of an ocean liner. Your inclination is to look off at distances and judge your speed, your course. You get kind of dreamy-eyed and deluded. You think you can be perceived individually by those you pass – people in high buildings, in cars, on side streets. You should carry a countenance, you think, that indicates the ideology being supported. But you must pay attention and keep from stepping on the heels of those in front of you. The very success of the endeavor oppresses the pleasure of your participation. Now you're faintly miffed. So you recall that role encouraged in voters: just a grain in a sandcastle, but essential nonetheless. If *everyone* was apathetic – well, then it's social collapse.

So you walk. You try to converse with your people, but the environment is hostile to it. There are myriad ambulatory energies preventing you from synching with those near you. There are strangers whose motives and histories intrigue you. There's ambient noise. And, topically, like your course among the city streets, only a narrow corridor is prescribed. To converse about other matters seems frivolous, as if you're not committed; to talk about the cause – well, everything's been said already, you all know why you're here, and to dredge it up would be vulgar and naïve. As if talk would do anything.

Still available are the pleasures of a regular walk. The air, the gaining of ground, your body's utility and self-propulsion. You settle in. You surrender to the larger entity. You humble yourself to the role of molecule in a being. A drop of rain in a storm. That's better. Hmm. It flashes in you, somewhere unidentifiable, like a light above and behind your head – maybe this is your greater role. Your ultimate role. Beginning and end. You are a fleck. A certainty blinks, instantaneous, amorphous, dreadfully luminescent.

Then your toe catches on the tar. You trip, yet right yourself by some miracle of the reflexes. Just a stumble. Your people kid you. *Oops. Mel needs a cup of coffee.* Wake up, Mel. *Ha ha.*

The needle has bounced back to start. You want to revive your sense of purpose. Can't you look off at distances and judge your speed, your pace and progress? Shouldn't you wear a countenance? People can discern you individually. No. No, they can't.

The *Herald* said the next day that two thousand people had marched. Two thousand, and we were five: myself, Nicole, Klang, Mr and Mrs P. We assembled at George Square, in City Centre, at 9 a.m. and went seven miles over three hours. Sauchiehall Street was our starting gate, past gobsmacked and nonplussed shoppers, to Bath Street, symbolically parading before Wimpy's building. We crossed the river on Commerce Street and picked up Paisley Road out to Pollok Park and the sliver of mud that was the remaining Free State.

We took instruction and encouragement from people with bullhorns – none of them Ruaridh. We didn't encounter him until reaching the park, where the crowd lingered, uncertain what to do with itself, until chants stirred up. There were news cameras and police, so we had to do something. 'NO EM SEVENTY SEVEN!' we shouted, and 'HANDS OFF POLLOK PARK!' Even though, obviously, hands had been all over it.

The Free State had shrunk remarkably under the advancement of construction. The marchers all fit on the plot of land that remained. Not only that, its character had been reordered, making recognition difficult. The old landmarks, the finger-like copse, the treehouses and banners, were gone. The ground had been scraped and populated with debris: steel lampposts, hexagonal like giants' pencils, laid on the ground awaiting installment; rebar grids were stacked in the dirt, already rust-colored. The earth had been retooled into the slight slopes and gradual curves agreeable to travel.

Where the campfire had been was now a wide, smooth field of packed dirt, a fresh-cut brown. A motorway minus the asphalt. This is an immense thing in proportion to a pedestrian, physically and politically. Three lanes each way, six total, with a median and shoulders both inner and outer. Barren of trees and cars. Something belonged there, that was undeniable. Its incompletion was fleeting. Under guard was not what the land was but what it would become; those who had erected the orange barriers that protected not so much the space itself as its intended outcome would take them down and transform this plot into permanent (or unforeseeably continuous) animation.

Atop the mammoth yellow machines, by the trailers in which crews and foremen lunched and sheltered, we spotted Ruaridh. He stood on the engine compartment of a back hoe, gesturing, lighting a fag, gazing out over the crowd like a despot in a balcony. He had no bullhorn. Who knew what his role was now. Organizer? Agitator? He didn't think of himself as a grain of sand, that's for sure. What would become of him? Would he just wash away? I hoped not. The world needs Ruaridhs. To shake things up and get things done. To exemplify ideals, if nothing else. His family had money; he personally wouldn't become extinct.

'Tell him goodbye for me,' Klang said to Nicole, 'if you run into him sometime.'

'Are ya jokin'?' she asked.

'No, it was nice to meet him. He's an interesting guy.'

'Okee.' She looked to me inquisitively. Did I want to second this?

'Sure, say cheerio from me too,' I said. 'Tell him . . .' What? Best of luck in all your pursuits? No. 'Tell him to keep the faith.'

My parents hadn't met Ruaridh and were curious as to who we were talking about.

'An old flame,' Nicole said, loudly to be heard among the din. Or was that phrase forceful out of readiness? Like it had been on the tip of her tongue? As if contemplated in reconfirmation. An *old* flame, reminding herself. Maybe the ember would reignite. If it did, I wouldn't be there to douse it this time.

On that point – there was one area where trees remained, and it was where Nicole and I had put up in the tent. At least, I believed so. Like I say, the area was somewhat unrecognizable. But if the campfire had been where the diggers were parked now – and I believe it was – then just beyond that we'd stayed up, and she'd heard my story. And there a cluster of a dozen oaks remained. Wimpy and Strathclyde Regional had argued all along that some areas would remain untouched and others replanted. This happened to be one untouched. How that was, or why, was a matter for Nicole's horoscopes and tea leaves.

My folks flew out that night. Nicole came over to the hotel with me, and we put them in a cab. I stuffed their suitcases with IRN-BRU for me to have back at home. They worried that the cans might burst because of the air pressure. I couldn't guarantee they wouldn't. But then they were concerned about lots of things – my apartment, my job, had everything been done, my belongings, funds. Who would pick me up from O'Hare? The questions seemed to be surrogates for their concern that dislodging me from Glasgow would be painful, and so I answered them confidently for their sake. It would be hard, but all I had to do was leave. I'd see them in thirty-six hours, so we didn't fuss with long goodbyes.

Klang shoved off the next day. There were follow-up meetings planned at Plunkett's on the following Tuesday, so he had to get back and get organized. He'd clean up his flat and fly out of Gatwick in a day or two. Nicole had stayed at home the night before, but came into town with me and saw him off at Queen Street station. Then we had a pasta lunch and clambered up and down Argyle Street looking for souvenirs, stopping and listening to the buskers and throwing change in their open cases, and talking. I don't know what we talked about. All my words seemed to vanish.

I heard other people distinctly though. Old women hobbled by, ankles like sausage casings, saying, 'Aye, we used tay get the bus from here on a Saturdee.' We were killing time, Nicole and I, being together. We wanted to be, but I was heavy-hearted and she brave with steeliness. She wouldn't let me buy her anything. 'You've dealt that thin' enuff punishment,' she said, of the credit card.

We talked about writing, I guess – glancing suggestions, confirming that we would send letters.

We were both relieved when she had to go. She had a lecture at school, and an evening shift afterwards.

I understood why she brought Sophie and Deb along to the airport. It made it easier for me too. She was bashful and apologetic getting into the cab with them, and I tried to convey, by greeting her friends warmly, that she didn't need to be. It was early, though, and I was not only heavy-hearted still but tired. It was probably a gruff, strained muttering, 'Hi-ya.'

None of us had eaten breakfast, and we all had egg butties in the concourse. There was something new up to the last – a butty is anything put into a roll and made into a sandwich. There were sausage butties and fish butties and even chip butties, just French fries between bread, usually with loads of HP brown sauce.

'When I get home,' I said, 'I'm going to Greek town and getting the Kotopulo Gemisto.' And I told them all about it. A whole chicken roasted with herbs, and orange potatoes on the side and cucumber sauce that would make your saliva gland explode.

Then the waiting began. Shuffling from kiosk to kiosk. Establishing seats by the gate. Trips to the lav. Buying a paper. A drink of water. Small talk. I said silly things like 'Work hard in school' and 'No more climbing on buildings'. Funny ha ha. Melancholy turned me avuncular. I fought this distancing with touches – just touching her. I couldn't help it, my hands drifted onto her, brushing her arm with my knuckles, touching her hair, pulling away. She understood. I was trying to take something away with me. She put her hand on mine and squeezed. I took deep breaths, opened my eyes as wide as they could go, looked up and swallowed through a clenched throat.

Finally, boarding. Hugs. It was over all too fast, but mercifully fast. My ticket torn, descending the ramp, counting rows, squeezing in my seat. That hyper-observant narrator who preoccupies the mind came alive. Oh, look here, an *in-flight magazine*. Under his possession, all the brilliant utility of words shines, as if all the terminology we have and all the identifying civilization has done has established an order compensatory to the chaos of grief and longing. I'll put my *carry-on* under the seat in front of me. Be mindful not to hog the *armrest*. Oh, good, the *window shade* is up already, how I like it.

I leaned against the Plexiglas and looked out. Even the UK's runways and luggage handlers and chain hotels seem more refined, less brash than American ones, I don't know why. They seem less capitalist in nature, though they surely aren't. The sky was gray, the gray of pavement. The men gliding around and hopping out of their doorless, neon-festooned carts, wore hooded raincoats.

Waterworks might start any time.

They did, at take-off. The first careened off my left cheek as if it were a ski ramp. I turned to wipe it up and found the center seats had been filled without my noticing. A boy of eight or so sat in the center, in a football jersey, his sleeve darkened by a spot.

'Oops,' I sputtered. 'Sorry.'

Sar-ee.

His mother, in the aisle seat, leaned over, 'S'okee.'

The boy was brown-haired and orb-eyed. On the long flight, we'd speak. He and his mother were going to Boston to visit his 'Da', who worked there. They boy had been there loads of times and liked flying. He supported Rangers and also fancied bikes.

But that was later. I'm getting ahead of myself. I'm always getting ahead of myself.

Now, the boy, seeing my tears, asked, 'Are you sad?' His mother gasped lightly and apologized, with the practiced embarrassment of a parent.

I pretend-considered with a thoughtful scrunch of my nose and told him the truth.

Epilogue

Fade from black. Exterior. Glasgow. The four spires of the university at sunset. Fife and harp music plays. Cut to the armadillo-like SECC building, its silver hull gleaming in the sun. Cut to foreshortened shipyards, cranes, piers, docks. Cut to children skipping along a path in Kelvingrove Park, in tartan school uniforms. Cut to an aged gentleman in ruddy health sitting on a stool in a pub, a smiling red-headed woman beside him; they raise pint glasses and clink. Cut to a kilted man huffing into a bagpipe, cradling the wind bag (whatever it's called) in one arm, fingering the recorder-type piece (whatever it's called) in the other. He's got the hat, a tam, and the sash, and the knee socks (whatever they're called) with the knife – is it a *snee*?

I never did find out these things, I think, watching the video in the darkened conference room.

A male voice speaks, in deep, sonorous American tones. *Congratulations to Glasgow on being named the 1995 European City of Culture.* Further twee images rotate, a variety of close and far subjects, interior and exterior, bright and cool, night and day. Every conceivable contrast extracted. But they're all sunny somehow. *It came as a surprise to some. But not us.*

The rhythm of the pictures' changing stops, settling on a shot of Pollok Park, pre-M77 expansion. The open green, the little rivulet visible as a depression in the foreground if you know to look for it. The Maxwell House. A stand of trees. The camera pans slowly into the copse – or rather, into the still photo of the copse. A fife's soaring, diving note brings to mind an eagle's flight.

Here at Burback's, we've known for a long while that Glasgow was a great city with great promise. Full of people who enjoy the simple things in life, like a walk in the woods and a good cup of coffee. And we want it to stay that way. That's why our Quality Analyst Mel travelled all the way from Chicago – my self-timer shot of Klang and me outside the Pollokshields train station, the camera pans to my face – *to protest the loss of Pollok Park, Glasgow's largest green space.*

Images of the PFS, none too graphic or violent, but giving the impression of an encampment, people tenting in the elements, sacrificing, a makeshift effort to defy something large, claim a space. Diggers, some of my shots of the clearing, the stone-laid message in the dirt.

My voice overlaid: *I was there studying the coffee tastes and traditions* . . . Now I appear on-screen, candid, interview-style, hair sculpted in a tidier way than I usually wear it, the backdrop and lights that had seemed so cluttered during the filming unnoticed now, just my bright, clean face, necktie's knot below. My manner is casual and professional and honest, even though my words have been molded by producers and women in smart business skirt suits from the marketing department and reiterated in take after take. Always simplified, boiled down. . . . *when they began cutting down this forest to build a motorway,* I say.

Cut away from me to more shots of trees, generic shots of waterfalls that are not even Scotland, then Highland dales. Grass-munching sheep. Each image is sandwiched between pulses of black screen, fading in an out. An aerial shot of the march from George Square. *I just had to do something about it* . . . An unnatural break, a pause, where I've been spliced. *It really broke my heart.* That one totally scripted, handed to me.

Shots of me in an anorak and wool cap – an energetic sprite from wardrobe had put them on me – shaking hands with some people from the Chicago offices, people who could pass for Scottish, taken down at Grant Park, with its oaks and elms, crucially nothing distinctively American, in the background.

This park is so great, I thought . . . *you can't cut this down* . . . *This is vital, this is us* . . . *We are nature. These trees are living, we need them* . . . *This is more important than development.*

Each sentence has a different tone, the cadence is non-contiguous. The flow is halting, unnatural. This is what they've made of me. They've fashioned a narrative and thus a corporate image, a corporate attitude, out of phrases fed to me and coaxed back out – regurgitated soundbites. An audio engineer's handiwork.

In my seat, I blush, though the room is dark, and everyone else there – Klang, Carson, Rick Gedes, a bunch of people I've just met, some Burback's bigwigs – has their eyes on the screen, for the unveiling of this new media campaign aimed at deflecting a chilly reception to the American franchise renowned for its ubiquity.

The narrator explains about my caring: caring about great coffee, and about the environment. About Burback's opening in the UK. *A Burback's on every corner?* This is textbook: refute the worst part of your reputation, replace the unlikeable parts of your image with something pleasant and memorable. Hammer it into place if you have to, nail that pretty painting right over the crack in the wall. *Well,* I say with flippant knowingness, *not all corners are created equal.* Now a shot of me from ladder height, looking down, at the edge of the tree line, again Grant Park, the image bent digitally to look like it's shot with a fisheye lens and thus making the treeline look like the 'corner' mentioned in the voiceover. I'm holding a paper cup of Burback's (it was in fact empty), the logo turned toward the camera by production supervisors, my fingers arranged in a handsome even cluster, not covering the recognizable emblem. *Neither is coffee.*

How did they do that to my voice, I wonder. So rich and sonorous, deeper than it sounds in my own head. Manly, authoritative. The wonder of digital tools, filtering out spectrums, leaving the desired impression.

Cut to a black screen and the logo: the diamond with the band flanking it, like a cigar band or wrestler's trophy belt, and the word Burback's in their immediately recognized lettering, the single coffee bean in the top quadrant, the silhouette of steaming mug in the bottom. My voice again. My voice only. *Burback's,* I say. *Sauchiehall Street, Glasgow,* I say. *Now open.*

Acknowledgements

Special thanks to Willy Maley and Judy Moir, whose special attentions and support made this work possible.

Thanks to Mom and Dad, Lynne Gilmour, Philip Kloehn, Suzanne Marner, Claire Smith, residents of Horselethill House (The Horse) 1994–1995, Rachel Seiffert and all at GU and Strathclyde 1998–1999, James Doerfler, David and Janis Babcock, Mike Eldred, everyone from the House of Pain and the Brillo Pad, 'Coach' Jacob Nguyen.